In Bitter Chill

SARAH WARD

FABER & FABER

First published in 2015
by Faber & Faber Ltd
Bloomsbury House
74-77 Great Russell Street
London WC1B 3DA
This paperback edition published in 2015

Typeset by Faber and Faber Ltd
Printed and bound by CPI Group (UK) Ltd, Croydon CR0 4YY

A CIP record for this book
Is available from the British Library

ISBN 978-0-571-32100-1

2 4 6 8 10 9 7 5 3 1

For Mum

'An intelligent and fast-paced debut, *In Bitter Chill* is a tale of loss and long-hidden secrets that makes for uncomfortable reading. Chilling and thrilling in equal measure, it showcases Ward's undoubted prowess as a writer ... Ward truly excels by producing a clever and twisty tale, effortlessly interweaving two time frames while gripping the reader until the very end.' *Stylist*, ****

'Gives the Scandi authors a run for their money.' Yrsa Sigurðardóttir

'Deserves to be one of the standout debuts of 2015. A tense, page-turning mystery that grips readers from the first. I'm looking forward to more from Sarah Ward.' William Ryan

'An elegant and thoughtful novel ... This is a fine debut, and Sarah Ward is a writer to watch.' Chris Ewan

'A debut that hits the ground running, showing that the author has the measure of the exigencies of the police procedural and (more importantly) the conflicted psychology of her characters ... While it is true to say that Sarah Ward does nothing radical with the apparatus of the crime novel, she proves to be highly adept at characterisation – notably of the unh... Bu... ...asses with fly...ing colours the test of r... ...e and vividly chara...te... ...kely to be

guessed even by die-hard aficionados of the crime fiction genre. On the evidence of *In Bitter Chill*, it's clear that Sarah Ward has a bright future in the crime genre.'
Barry Forshaw, *Crime Time*

'A twisted, skilful and entirely intriguing mystery.' Quentin Bates

'Relentless, compelling, and meticulously suspenseful. Fans of Ian Rankin and Elizabeth George will rejoice at this atmospheric and authentic debut, expertly told, where modern-day police struggle to untangle disturbing secrets of the past. Terrific.' Hank Phillippi Ryan

'A very assured first novel, with compellingly good story-telling and a deep humanity.' Alison Joseph

'This remarkable debut is an intricate and thoroughly intriguing crime thriller. A masterclass in plotting and character, it is realistically set and compellingly told. I struggled to put it down.' Zoë Sharp

'A beautifully written and perfectly poised debut; old secrets, fractured families and a detective duo to root for, make this a bona fide must read.' Eva Dolan

'A beautifully woven mystery which, like the peak district in winter, chilled this reader to the bone.' Steven Dunne

'A fine debut, with well-conceived characters and an engaging story.' Paul Johnston

'A splendid crime novel – beautifully written, very cleverly plotted, with a surprising twist and a detective team I'd love to meet again!' Ragnar Jonasson

'It's always baffled me that more crime authors don't use family history as a theme in their stories. So hats off to Sarah Ward whose debut novel, *In Bitter Chill*, pulls in all those birth, marriage and death certificates, local records, genealogical charts and dark family secrets into a police procedural. And it's all the more powerful for doing so.' Crime Fiction Lover

'One of the standout debuts that I've read so far this year.' *Liz Loves Books*

'A top-class, page-turning debut.' *Woman & Home*

'The title suggests that this debut novel ought to be yet another example of Nordic Noir and, although it is set in rural Derbyshire, it does have a Scandinavian sensibility exerting its grip through strength of characterisation.' Jake Kerridge, *Sunday Express* magazine

'A promising debut.' Laura Wilson, *Guardian*

'A tense, well-told story of loss and family secrets.' *Daily Mail*

'*In Bitter Chill* features a compelling, complex plot, loaded with emotive issues, fascinating psychological insights, a pervasive sense of unease and gripping police procedural. Ward's cast of outstanding characters, from the police officers and the victims to a local community with a shared history, are powerfully portrayed.' *Lancashire Evening Post*

'Enthralling, intelligent, and profoundly moving, *In Bitter Chill* effectively combines a vivid picture of a now lost era when parents thought it was safe to let their children roam free in the countryside with a harder-edged age in which the risk of abduction and abuse is ever present.' Andy Lawrence, *Eurodrama*

'Easy reading for a hot summer's day.' *Shiny New Books*

'This is an extremely well-written, accomplished debut, which, in spite of its chilly title, is a perfect summer read. Get that deckchair out now and enjoy!' *Mrs Peabody Investigates*

'I'm conscious that one has to be wary of comparing one writer with another, but the other comparison that did cross my mind when reading this book was with Ann Cleeves. Ann has a gift for combining her well-plotted mysteries with sound evocation of character and place, a gift that amazingly was long underestimated before the massive success of *Vera* and *Shetland* caused her to receive her well-deserved international acclaim. I don't expect Sarah to have to wait as long for widespread recognition. She is, like Ann, someone whose work demonstrates an understanding of human frailty, but also a good deal of compassion, a combination that is very appealing to many readers.' Martin Edwards

Sarah Ward is an online book reviewer whose blog, *Crimepieces* (www.crimepieces.com), reviews the best of current crime fiction published around the world. She has also reviewed for Euro Crime and CrimeSquad. She is a judge for the Petrona Award for Scandinavian translated crime novels. She lives in Derbyshire.

Follow Sarah on Twitter @sarahrward1

Prologue

Blade clanked on flint. Again. Causing the man to recoil. He turned, looking for reassurance from the woman whose stone-coloured eyes gave as little relief as the hard ground he was trying to part. Small fissures lay in a criss-cross pattern over the unforgiving soil, made by ineffectual glances from the blade. The woman nodded for him to continue. He shrugged off his tweed jacket, the smell of his own acrid sweat mingling with the lanolin to create a nauseating aroma of toil and, much worse, of life. Stepping back, he felt his heel sink into softer, more yielding ground covered by a smattering of twigs and decomposing leaves. He moved back further, the ground still soft. Panic had dulled his senses; he had wasted important minutes trying to break ground that his ancestors knew to leave well alone.

Their burden lay to one side, the winding sheet beginning to part, and the man could see golden threads of hair spilling out onto the drab ground. The woman followed his gaze but did nothing, her eyes challenging him to stop their task. He imagined the small body beneath its makeshift shroud. In another, parallel world, the tiny heart would still be beating and his wouldn't have frozen at the moment he realised that it was all over.

He shifted position and began again. The organic matter crackled and groaned but parted to the touch of the blade.

The pit widened and, when it was finished, the man looked down and remembered the wicker cradle that he had recently placed his newborn daughter into so carefully. A nudge on his shoulder moved him out of the way. The woman laid her load into the makeshift tomb and, with her shoe, began kicking over the leaves and twigs and other fruits of that ancient forest. Angry, he picked up his spade again and used it to sweep his toil back over the body. His white shirt slapped against his chest and damp oozed into his shoes, turning the pale fawn leather a brackish brown. When he was finished, he looked down and the ground swam before his eyes. The cold earth had accepted its new charge and even now he doubted he could locate the exact position of the damp grave. His body twitched with the impulse to start digging again.

He felt a chill ripple over him as the woman touched him on the arm. The eternal pull of her presence was now turning into a fear that he could not succumb to. The bile rising in his throat must be ignored and conquered. It was she who, once more, would need to help him out of the crisis that threatened to overwhelm them both. He allowed her to lead him back through the wood: he, stumbling slightly, his heavy limbs trying to root him to the ground; she, guiding the way with her gloved hands. As the trees parted, they came to the entrance and light began to trickle through the overhanging branches. Gradually he could make out the shape of the white car sitting in the car park. There, inside, the other girl waited for him.

'Stop!' The command, unfamiliar on his lips, halted them both. She turned around, her mouth a line of displeasure.

'I need to do this. Alone.'

She let him go and he walked slowly towards the car.

Chapter 1

Detective Inspector Francis Sadler watched the heavy clouds gather through the window and cursed the role that central heating had played in dislocating him from the elements. In his childhood home, his frugal father had banned switching on the radiators until the first day of December. It meant that, as a boy, he had become used to connecting the weather outside with the sensations of his body. His memories of getting dressed wrapped in his still warm duvet, the icy crispness of the air mixing with the comfort of the breaking dawn, could never be entirely banished. Now, looking down at his dark trousers and pressed shirt, no need to wear a jacket in this overheated office, he wondered if he could ever feel that physical connection again.

The door opened, letting in a swift blast of cooler air.

'Is it the Wilton Hotel that's haunted?'

Sadler looked up and frowned at Detective Sergeant Damian Palmer. He wondered, once again, if he'd employed someone in his own image. It was what you were warned against on those interminable police training courses. But all the boxes that had to be ticked and the forms to be completed failed to eliminate the pull of subjectivity. When you were choosing a member of your team, what you wanted was someone a little bit like yourself. You might recognise your own flaws, but you were rarely prepared to condemn them.

3

And Palmer, with his cropped hair and stocky build, might be physically worlds apart from his own rangy restlessness, but at the heart of them both was the need for success.

His silence was making his sergeant nervous. Sadler wondered about this. Perhaps this was where they differed. Because it was a long time since Sadler had felt fear or even the tingling of nerves. Maybe it was the difference in their ages. Fifteen years was a long time, especially in this job. But the day would come, Sadler had no doubt, when Palmer would be inspiring his own brand of fear in his subordinates.

'Sorry. I've just had a call. The body of a woman's been found there – at the Wilton Hotel, I mean. Discovered by the chambermaid or whatever they call them now. Maid, cleaning staff, room valet.'

Sadler swallowed his espresso.

'A murder?'

'The forensic team's there now. There's something they want you to look at.'

'And did the forensic team give any clue why they might require our presence?' Sadler threw the small paper cup across the room towards the grey metal bin. It missed. 'Or are they hoping that we build up a sense of anticipation as we travel down to the scene?'

'It was a bit like that.' Palmer slid his eyes towards the bin. 'Shall I get you another to drink in the car?'

Sadler felt the caffeine hit his empty stomach and a warmth spread through him. It didn't extend to his mood. Ignoring Palmer, he grabbed his overcoat and led the way out of the station, noting the quiet around him. The weather was clearly putting the town's regular drunks and other miscreants off their

4

stride. The desk sergeant was flicking through a copy of *The Sun*. They hurried to Palmer's car as the stinging wind whipped across the police compound. Sadler glanced at the clouds moving quickly across the sky, mimicking the speeded-up images you sometimes saw on television. No need for artificial trickery in the Derbyshire Peak District though. That spine of rolling hills and gritstone edges that traversed the middle of England ended in Derbyshire, in a landscape of heart-stopping beauty. When you could see it, that was. Because winter mornings in Bampton were, more often than not, shrouded in mist and dusk fell in the mid-afternoon when the shops were still trying to attract reluctant customers. Don't like the weather? Wait five minutes and it will have changed was the maxim here, although Sadler, who had endured the unrelenting cold of the last three winters, was tempted to disagree.

Palmer drove to the hotel with his foot hard on the accelerator as they battled through the wind, the car buffeted by large gusts that caused Sadler to reach for the grab rail above the passenger door. His father's watch clanked against the window and Sadler turned his wrist to protect the precious timepiece.

'Did they really not tell you why they wanted us there?'

Palmer, concentrating on his driving, shook his head and kept his eyes on the road. 'Other than to inform us that the scene had been secured, they wouldn't tell me anything over the phone. Connie's already there, but her phone's engaged.'

'Why didn't she call and tell us what to expect? I don't come into work in the morning to play "guess my latest victim".'

Palmer shrugged, presumably happy to let a detective constable take some of the flak, and Sadler felt his anger subside. The diminutive DC Connie Childs had arrived at Bampton

CID five years earlier with an attitude that more than compensated for her tiny frame. She was local to Derbyshire, which was a bonus when dealing with some of Bampton's residents. Sadler had seen Palmer's Hampshire accent wind up some of the suspects they'd interviewed. Which could be useful on occasions. But equally effective were Connie's local knowledge and recognisable Derbyshire accent. The downside was that both Connie and Palmer recognised their respective strengths, or perhaps weaknesses, and jostled for position within the team. The fact that Palmer was Connie's superior only added to the air of competition that was evident when they were together in his presence. And Sadler occasionally wondered if he didn't need a more easy-going detective on his team to mitigate the egos of both Connie and Palmer. But then a laid-back attitude wasn't what you wanted in a policeman. And certainly not a detective on a murder investigation.

He glanced at Palmer, who was wearing his usual uniform of pale blue shirt with the sleeves rolled up and dark trousers. No jumper. Christ. He must be freezing. Even the expensive-looking coat draped over the back seat wouldn't protect him from the elements.

They reached the centre of town and the wind dropped suddenly, as if they had reached the eye of the storm. Bampton had started off, like many others in England, as a place of trade. Tourists were often surprised to find that the picturesque Peak town also supported working businesses, a continual gripe with locals trying to find parking spaces during the summer. A cattle market had been in existence since 1309, but Bampton's pinnacle had been during the nineteenth century when a canal had been built to facilitate the movement of goods in and out of the

6

town. The canal had carried coal from the mine thirty miles south and limestone from the nearby quarries. The fact that it had now become a tourist stop had only added to Bampton's image of itself. An air of self-satisfaction was the legacy of its affluent Victorian heritage.

At the main square, Palmer switched off the engine and in the silence they watched as light snow began to fall, the now fragile breeze teasing the flakes up and around the gloomy afternoon, not allowing it to settle. Sadler could see the wind sweeping snow off the hills to the north of the town and people were hurrying through the streets trying to reach their destinations before the weather worsened.

'It's depressing. Winter here, I mean. You should have mentioned it as a disclaimer when you interviewed me for the job. Something along the lines of "working hazards – coping with Derbyshire in the winter".'

Sadler smiled as he looked out of the window. 'You know what it's like when tourists arrive in the summer. You won't be driving like that behind a car full of sightseers.'

Through the frosting glass, Sadler watched a man in a suit standing outside the Wilton Hotel looking anxiously around him, oblivious to the weather. Sadler could see no evidence of any police cars. They must have put them round the back of the hotel, suggesting a lack of urgency. But if it was a natural death, why were they calling in CID? In his experience, people often died in hotel rooms, in the same way that they frequently died in their beds elsewhere.

Palmer was looking up at the facade of the building. 'It's a nice hotel.'

'It was once. It was called the Needham Arms and you could

7

go and have a pint or a cup of coffee with your walking boots on. There was a quiz night on a Monday, too.'

Palmer was smiling. Sadler hoped it wasn't at him.

'What happened?'

'The family sold up.'

Sadler knew this, not because he kept pace with the town's gossip, but because there had been more concrete accusations of embezzlement levelled against one of the three daughters. Nothing proved but enough to hasten the family's departure to pastures new.

'Who owns it now?'

'The Wilton brothers, based in London.'

Sadler felt the niggle of irritation. The two entrepreneurs had stripped the building of its centuries-old name and had rebranded it after themselves, in Sadler's estimation an act of gross self-regard. His architect father would have been more appalled by what they had done to the interior, stripping the Grade II listed building bare, as far as planning had let them, and reopening it as an upmarket boutique hotel. The quiz night had found other premises.

'And it's not haunted.' He opened the car door and looked back at Palmer. 'Although God knows what that's got to do with anything.' He could see the man in the suit making a beeline for him.

'DI Sadler? I'm George Poole, the manager here. Perhaps I could have a word with you in private first.'

Sadler looked past the man to the lobby of the hotel. Connie Childs was standing just inside the doorway and was talking on her mobile.

'Not now. I'll talk to you later.' Sadler made his way up

the front steps, feeling for ice underfoot.

Connie, seeing him approach, put her hand over her mobile and said, 'Sir, a word?'

This time Sadler did stop.

'It's the body of an elderly woman. Suicide, I think. An empty packet of diazepam was found on the bedside table. Ten milligram. And a vodka bottle. Only a quarter full. If she took them together, it's no wonder she never woke up.'

'Worth me taking a look? I presume there's a reason that three of us are standing here on a freezing afternoon.'

Connie nodded towards the stairs leading to the bedrooms. 'She left something by the bedside. You ought to see that at least.'

Sadler turned and started up the stairs. Along the galleried landing, the hive of activity was centred on a room to the far right. Over the banister, he could see a cluster of guests gathered in a doorway below, gawping up at him. He took the overalls proffered by a member of the forensics team, slipped them on and entered the room. It was bathed in a claustrophobic gloom and was icy cold – someone had turned off the radiators. The small room was dominated by a huge king-size bed with the woman lying on the left-hand side. She was on her back with her mouth slightly open. Pale and very thin, Sadler guessed she was in her late sixties. She wasn't dressed for bed, wearing instead a light woollen dress that reached below her knees. Flesh-coloured nylon tights covered her spindly legs, but she had nothing on her feet. Sadler could see a pair of blue court shoes laid neatly in the corner of the room, but no evidence of an overnight bag.

The bedside table was now clear and only the fingerprint powder remained, with indentations where the pills and vodka had lain. The police photographer was taking pictures of a large book on the chest of drawers near the window and Sadler moved closer.

'Can I take a look?'

The man stepped back and Sadler leaned over. Careful not to alter the position of the book he flicked through the pages, the latex gloves making his fingers clumsy. It was a photograph album, each page covered with thin, sticky transparent film. Instead of photos, inserted into the album were newspaper cuttings, yellowed and spotted with age. Sadler flicked through the pages, noting the content of the articles.

'Where was the book left open?'

The photographer flipped to a page near the back of the album and pointed at the headline.

*

Connie had disappeared from the reception area, but Palmer, who was still trying to placate the hotel manager, indicated with his head that she was out on the front steps. The snow was falling hard now and Connie had put on a soft beret style hat that was covered in a sprinkling of white. Sadler braced himself against the weather as he went out to join her. Connie turned round and he noticed that she was smoking a cigarette. She saw him looking.

'I've just started again. Cut out the drink and started on the cigarettes.'

'It doesn't have to be one or the other.' Sadler smiled to soften the words, but he saw a flash of annoyance in her eyes.

'Did you see the album?' Connie drew deeply on her cigarette.

'Yes.'

'Mean anything to you?'

Sadler shrugged. 'I know the case, of course. I was a boy then, but I can remember it on the news.'

'Who investigated it here?' Connie was peering around the empty square. The police cordon had just been put up and this, combined with the weather, had put off all but the most serious gawkers.

'No idea. Way before my time. Superintendent Llewellyn might know. Although it could be before his time too. I'll give him a call. I need to update him. Was there a name on the packet of pills?'

Connie stamped her half-smoked cigarette out on the ground. 'Yvonne Jenkins.'

'Yvonne Jenkins, mother of Sophie Jenkins.'

'Why do you think that she chose to commit suicide now? After all these years. Why wait this long?'

'I don't know. Maybe it was fear of facing old age alone. Maybe she just gave up. It doesn't really matter as far as we're concerned. We just need to satisfy ourselves that it was suicide.'

'What about the old case? I mean, sometimes these things are reopened, aren't they?'

Sadler looked out across the whitening square. 'I don't think it was ever closed.'

Chapter 2

'Hold on, Soph. You're walking too fast.'

Rachel stopped suddenly in the street and yanked up her long white socks for the third time. The elastic had gone, too many washes in her mother's new twin tub that had taken so long to save up for. All those books of Green Shield stamps and Rachel's job to lick them into place, the gluey, musty taste souring her tongue as she carefully laid the strips on the coarse pages. The old wooden washboard had been shoved into the garden shed and the new machine now stood by the kitchen door, banging Rachel's hips as she made her way out into the garden.

But the effect on her socks had been disappointing. Pinged elastic had stretched the tops to twice the size of the ankles and they never reappeared in her drawer white any more but instead with a hue of drab grey or pale inky blue. So she pulled them up constantly and there they would stay for about a minute before they started to creep down her shins again. She knew it was about a minute because she had started to count using the method that Miss Thomson had taught them in school. One thousand, two thousand. If you counted like that and spoke at a normal speed it was the same as a second.

She carried on walking as Sophie, impatient as always, led

the way. Forty-one thousand, forty-two thousand. Slither, slither, down they went. She reached sixty thousand and there they were, flapping around her ankles. Huge, pale orbs that looked ridiculous against her white legs.

Sophie was looking around in irritation and this time stopped, with a sigh, and glanced down at Rachel's legs.

'Hurry up,' she said. 'This is the fifth time we've stopped this morning.'

'I can't help it. They won't stay up.'

Rachel gave her socks what she hoped was a final yank but she could feel them beginning to slip again as they approached the summit of the hill. Rachel had been doing this walk with her friend for the last five weeks, ever since Miss Thomson had singled out Sophie as someone whose mother still took her to school. They were at an age, Miss Thomson had said, when they should now be walking by themselves. Sophie had blushed beetroot red and Rachel that evening heard her mum receive a call from Sophie's mother.

'You're going to walk to school with Sophie Jenkins every day.'

Rachel had screwed up her mouth. 'But . . .'

Rachel's mum held up her hand. 'Don't argue, Rachel. You can start tomorrow. Sophie will be waiting for you. But you need to ring the doorbell.'

Now, together, they puffed as they reached the hill's summit. At the top of the road stood the landmark that told them they were nearly at the school. A red letterbox, its squat shape stamped with the letters GR, the name, according to Rachel's mum, of the old king of England. George something-or-other.

As they reached the letterbox, a white car drew up at the

kerb and Rachel and Sophie watched as a woman reached over and started to wind down the window.

'Can you post this for me?'

The woman held out a white oblong envelope. It looked to Rachel like a birthday card. Both she and Sophie dived for it but it was Sophie who got there first and snatched it out of the woman's hands. She tapped it into the letterbox and turned around to the car window to receive her thanks. The woman smiled at them both.

'Thanks for your help, girls. Are you going to St Paul's? I can give you a lift there.'

Rachel and Sophie glanced at each other. 'It's only round the corner,' said Rachel and looked in the direction to show they knew where they were going.

'I know, I'm going there too.' The woman was still smiling at them. Was she a teacher? Rachel hadn't seen her before, but she didn't know all the teachers in the baby school. She leaned forward to peer into the back of the car. She couldn't see anyone hiding there.

'Jump in the back.' Still Rachel hesitated, but Sophie had opened the door and was clambering in.

'Sophie, do you think . . .'

'Come on, Rachel. It's only round the corner.' Sophie was crawling across the seat and waving at Rachel to follow. Taking a quick look around her, Rachel could see no one who could snitch on them to her mother that they were taking lifts from strangers. Hitching up her socks once more, she followed Sophie into the back seat and pulled the door shut.

Chapter 3

'Got any kids yourself?'

Rachel looked up, the sudden movement causing the stiff green notebook balancing on her lap to wobble. She laid a protective hand on it.

'I'm afraid not. And it's looking unlikely. I'm reaching my "best before" date.'

Eileen Clarke smirked at her. 'Nothing to be sorry about, love. Mine have caused me nothing but grief. It's one of the reasons I've decided to trace my family history. The past can't possibly be worse than the present.'

Rachel said nothing and looked at the rough sketch of the family tree she had begun to flesh out as her client had chatted about her grandparents. Luckily, Clarke was the woman's married name. Although Irish in origin, it was one of the most popular names in England and a nightmare to sift through. Too many variations – Clark without an e, Clarke with an e, Clerke with two es. But fortunately, before her wedding in 1966, she had been Eileen Weeks. Weeks, from the old English *Wikke*, meaning battle. Not an uncommon surname but far, far less popular than Clarke. And fortunately her mother's maiden name had been the even more unusual Calthrop. A nice, solid Derbyshire name that would mean local records and the possibility of some distant relations still living in the area.

The woman chatted on and Rachel, aware that she had let

her thoughts drift off, snapped back to the present and forced herself to focus on the woman opposite.

'. . . changed her name, she had, not to deceive she kept telling her family but to make life easier when she came to England. There was still a lot of prejudice here against foreigners then and in any case the rumour was she had been adopted by an aunt who then pretended she was her real mother.'

Rachel looked confused at her notes. A name change? She had missed something.

'Who changed their name? I need to add it to my notes.'

Eileen Clarke adopted a martyred expression. 'That was my husband, Bill's, mother. I don't want you to look into him. I was just using it as an example of what happens in families sometimes. You know, done not to deceive but to make things . . .' Eileen made quotation marks with her fingers, 'easier.'

Rachel stared at her and gritted her teeth. Her job had made her an expert in the labyrinthine lives that some people made for themselves. Now a woman who would clearly be an expert in any subject they were discussing was telling her what was what. She shut her notebook with a snap and passed over a contract for the woman to look at. Eileen signed it without reading any of the disclaimers that Rachel had already outlined for her verbally. No guarantees. The records she wouldn't have access to. Rachel hoped that Eileen's blasé attitude wouldn't be extending to the payment of her bills, although at least she had a cheque for the woman's deposit in her purse.

She picked up her shoulder bag and stood, her legs numb where she had been resting her notebook. Eileen Clarke also rose and walked with her to the front door.

'Are you . . . ?' The woman stopped, confused, and Rachel,

aware of what would be coming next, waited. Eileen thought better of it. 'It doesn't matter.'

Rachel stepped out into the sharp winter cold and heard the door close behind her as she retrieved the car keys from the depths of her handbag. She could feel the woman watching her from the window, the unasked question still circulating in the air. Ignoring her, Rachel slid her hand under the waistband of her skirt. Plenty of room so no need to skip lunch. She could even justify pasta. Turning on the car's engine, she drove towards Sorelle, an Italian restaurant.

Within five minutes she was sitting in a queue of traffic. She buzzed open the car window and leaned out to see what the delay was. It was a big mistake. Freezing air shot into her car and she fumbled to close the window, her eyes stinging from the cold. From what she could see, it looked like a diversion had been set up around the main Bampton square and cars were being forced to take a sharp left to avoid the centre. Fortunately, the diversion would take her towards her home, but it meant she would have to make do with a sandwich in front of her laptop. She could pick up her research and get something meaningful done for the rest of the day. The traffic inched forward and, as she made the diverted left turn, Rachel could see a small cluster of people congregated outside the Wilton Hotel.

Back in her house she switched on the kettle and brewed some tea. Taking the pot over to the dining room table, she opened her notebook and began to make the outline of what would eventually become Eileen Clarke's family tree. Births, marriages and deaths. The bare bones of life but recorded for posterity and left in perpetuity for the chronically curious.

People like her. As the miniature lives slowly expanded on the screen, Rachel felt the satisfaction seeping through her as the chart became less a computer file and more a human organism, a mass of individual lives linked by shared DNA.

After an hour, the barely touched pot of tea had gone cold and Rachel's eyes were feeling the strain. A knock on the door made her jump; she looked out of the window at the late afternoon sky and tried to make the shadow she could see outside her front door into a recognisable shape. Putting on the chain, she opened the door and saw her diminutive neighbour Jenny shuffling her feet, her brown duffle coat and red scarf reminding Rachel of a robin.

'I can't stop, I was just wondering if you had heard the news? About the woman's body.'

For a moment, the pale gloom of the fading afternoon took on a more sinister hue. Rachel felt herself go cold, the dull weight of nausea causing her to steady herself against the door frame. Her neighbour didn't notice her reaction.

'A woman's body's been found, at the Wilton Hotel. It's just been on the local news.'

Rachel shook her head. 'I don't know anything about it. Why did you ask?'

'I saw you coming up the hill in your car. I thought you might have seen what was going on. You all right?' Behind her tortoiseshell glasses, Jenny looked concerned.

'I hate hearing about death, that's all. Do they know who it is?'

'Nothing on the news. I wondered if you knew. I can't stop, I'm on the way to the school to pick up the kids.'

'I'll come out with you. I need some fresh air.'

Grabbing her handbag, Rachel followed her neighbour halfway up the street towards the school. She could hear shrieks in the distance as the children came out of classes into the cold air.

'I'm a bit late. I'll need to run,' said Jenny.

'You go on. I'm going to take the car instead.'

Watching her neighbour run splayfooted towards the school, Rachel unlocked her car and sat for a moment in the driver's seat. Various parents were trying to find a parking space and she watched one mother as she double parked near a zebra crossing and sounded her horn. Switching on her engine, Rachel did a U-turn in the street and negotiated her car down the slippery hill, past her cottage where the pale living-room light gave little warmth or comfort through the window. The road was still treacherous and the gritting vehicle had clearly been delayed by the diversion. The need to leave her house had been overwhelming when she had heard about the discovery of the woman's body, the four walls of her small sitting room oppressive. But she had nowhere to go.

At the bottom of the hill, she made a decision and took a left turn that would lead her out of the town and towards the village of Clowton. It looked like the gritter had made it to the main road, although drivers were taking it slowly as they passed each other. Frustrated at the speed, Rachel took the next left, a shorter route to the village when the weather was good, but as soon as she entered the narrow lane she realised that it had been a mistake. Her car started to slither at each turn and she could see out of the corner of her eye a steep ditch that abutted the high hedgerow on her left.

She clenched the steering wheel and kept her eyes firmly

fixed on the Church of St John the Baptist, her destination in the distance. The spire had a gold locust at the top and, recently cleaned, it gleamed in the pale low winter sun. At the village, Rachel pulled onto the first verge she came to and left the car behind as she walked down the steep path to the church. It had been nonsensical, of course, to come here. Her boots crunched along the snow that had settled into a thick layer, not yet icy, but the temperature was dropping fast. Reaching the graves, she stepped onto spongy submerged grass and made her way to the far right corner.

There, a bunch of headstones were clustered together that bore the last name Jones. Jones: the Welsh surname so common throughout the British Isles that it was another nightmare for family historians like her.

But it was her last name, and that of her mother who had reverted to her maiden name after the death of her husband and, unusually for that time, had passed it on to her child. Rachel wished she had brought some flowers to put on her mother's grave. The snowdrops that she had planted in the autumn were beginning to unfurl but were not yet in full bloom.

Next to her mother's grave was that of her grandfather, Hughie Jones, whose stone had a half-finished look, probably because that's what it was. Missing a half. The bottom portion of the drab grey limestone was blank awaiting the addition of Rachel's grandmother Nancy, who was soldiering on well into her eighties and wreaking havoc in her private nursing home. But with her mother and grandfather there were two generations of Joneses buried in that churchyard and possibly, if she didn't marry or move away, in due course there would be a third. Her great-grandmother was also there, Mair Price, mother of Nancy. No half-finished stone for her. A great-grandfather had been banished long ago and remained only a name on a marriage certificate.

Rachel wiped the worst of the snowfall from the headstones with a gloved hand and, blotting the damp from her gloves onto her coat, took out a notebook from her bag. Flicking to the familiar page, she started to recite the litany of names.

Chapter 4

'It's not much. Haven't you got anything more for me?'

Sadler fiddled with his papers. 'I've told you all there is so far. I thought you'd be interested in even the scant details we have.'

'Oh, I'm interested all right. It's just you haven't got much for me to comment on, have you?'

Sadler dropped his eyes to Superintendent Llewellyn's desk. A family photo was set to one side. It was an outdated practice in these modern times, thought Sadler, displaying your family to every visitor to your office. At the centre of the studio shot stood the Superintendent, his carefully brushed ginger hair, freckled complexion and broad shoulders giving off an air of solidity and integrity. Next to him, his wife and two children seemed oddly lacking in personality. Sadler had heard that Llewellyn's wife was ambitious and eyeing up a soon-to-be-vacant chief superintendent post. In the photo she merely looked tired.

Sadler swung his eyes back to Llewellyn behind the desk. If it had been any other case, would he have gone straight to his boss without first digging a little more? Yes, was the honest answer, although perhaps he would have made a few quick phone calls first before he presented himself for inspection in front of his keen-eyed boss.

'Bill's carrying out a post-mortem tomorrow. He tried to

squeeze it in today but unexplained deaths no longer jump the queue, apparently. There's a rota they have to stick to. She's been scheduled in for tomorrow. He did say that it looked like a textbook suicide, except for the absence of a note.'

The book of news clippings hadn't been mentioned, although Sadler had spotted the doctor flicking through the pages, humming quietly to himself.

The Superintendent was sitting behind his desk but, unusually, he had taken off his jacket and, in his short-sleeved shirt, seemed to be sweating slightly. He rubbed his ruddy face with large freckled hands and looked at Sadler.

'What a mess.'

Sadler, irritated, shook his head. 'It's not a mess. It was neatly done some time between eight and ten p.m. yesterday evening. We know she checked in at eight and Bill is pretty sure that she wasn't alive after ten o'clock last night. She wasn't dressed for bed; she had no night things with her, which suggests that she had never intended to make it through the night. It seems that she turned off the hotel radiators, although we're not sure why. In my experience, they're usually turned up high in hotels so maybe she didn't want to feel too comfortable.'

Llewellyn grimaced. Well, he had wanted more details, thought Sadler.

'The time she chose also meant that it would have been a clear twelve hours before the body would be discovered. As it happens, the maid didn't even get round to opening the door of the room until about one p.m.,' Sadler continued.

'It was the anniversary of the girls' kidnapping yesterday,' said Llewellyn, dropping his eyes to the calendar on his desk.

'The twentieth of January. That could be a reason for the timing. Any idea why she chose the hotel?'

'Connie's on the way to the woman's house at the moment. But my guess would be that she didn't want to end her life in her own property. Suicides in hotels aren't uncommon.'

'Is she still in Arkwright Lane?'

Sadler nodded and Llewellyn once more rubbed his face.

'Still in the same house, then. After all these years.'

'She never moved?' asked Sadler.

'Well she was hardly going to at first, was she? After the girl went missing. Five, ten years. How long are you supposed to wait? With the lack of anything else, we were all hoping that one day the girl would just reappear.'

'And she didn't.'

Llewellyn smiled bitterly. 'Sometimes I forget how old I am. But no, you're right. Sophie Jenkins did not reappear and at some point I suspect we all just assumed that was it.'

'But you think that Yvonne Jenkins stayed put, hoping that one day her daughter would return.'

'Good God, Francis.' Llewellyn's ruddy complexion had gone purple. 'How the hell would I know? Maybe she did expect her forty-four-year-old daughter to come waltzing back into her bungalow. Or maybe she couldn't face the move. It gets harder as you get older, believe me.' Llewellyn's puce face gradually began to pale into a normal hue.

'You were involved in the initial investigation?'

Llewellyn leaned back in his chair. 'Of sorts. Young PC. First major case. All I did was door-to-doors for about four weeks. I lost a stone in weight, I remember. I was about to get married and Carol was delighted by the new trim me. Funnily

enough, the weight then stayed off for years. It's only now going back on again.' Llewellyn rubbed a hand over his stomach.

'What would you like me to do?'

Sadler tried to sound neutral, but the discouraging tone of
his voice had clearly conveyed itself to Llewellyn. He saw two
red patches appear in his boss's cheeks but he said nothing,
merely spread his hands and looked at them.

'I'm going to think about it.'

'It was suicide.'

Llewellyn looked up at him and slowly nodded.

*

Connie used the keys that she had retrieved from the dead
woman's handbag to open the front door of the bungalow in
Arkwright Lane. It was a solid-looking building. Bungalows,
which had gone strangely out of fashion, held an enduring ap-
peal for Connie as her grandmother had lived in one in the
same village as her parents. As a teenager after school she'd
spent many an afternoon watching telly with her nan when
really she should have been doing her homework. Bungalows
conjured up images of warmth and the smell of food. This
one, though, had a sterile feel to the outside, from the too-tidy
garden to the blank windows unadorned by any vases or other
bric-a-brac.

The front door opened onto a small hallway, an umbrella
stand propped up in the corner and a row of coat pegs fastened
to the left hand side of the wall. Connie recognised the coat
rail as similar to one owned by her family when she was growing up. A cheap wire frame with white orbs attached to each

peg that Connie could remember her mother buying in Woolworth's. There was a single raincoat hanging on the stand, a shade of drab beige.

'Are you supposed to be here?'

Connie whirled round to see a white-haired pensioner with a walking stick clenched across her body like a Samurai warrior.

'Police.' Connie went to get her identification, but the woman had already relaxed.

'I thought you were. I was just checking. It's just been on the news about Yvonne.' The old woman stared around her. 'I haven't seen inside here for a while.'

'I doubt it's changed much.' Connie was discomforted by the woman's stare. Her small black eyes held on to Connie's gaze with a fixed intensity.

'Do you believe in inherited memory?'

'I'm sorry?' Connie wondered if there was a relative anxiously pacing the streets looking for this woman.

'Don't look at me as though I'm daft. It's the concept that places leave a trace or memory that is inherited through your DNA. You know, so a person can remember a place that they've never visited but where their ancestors lived, for example.'

'And your ancestors lived here?'

The elderly woman rolled her eyes. 'It can occur in houses too. Inherited memory, I mean. When this bungalow was built, it was over an old pit from the Black Death.'

'A plague pit?' Connie was determined to see this conversation out. 'The only place in Derbyshire hit by the plague . . .'

'Was Eyam,' finished the old woman. 'I didn't say the plague, did I, though? I said the Black Death. In the fourteenth century. It spread from Derby up through to Bampton and by the time it rolled past, half the town had died. And they buried them in a pit.'

'What, underneath this bungalow?'

'Around here. No one knows exactly but in this street somewhere. And some think that Arkwright Lane remembers those bodies well enough.'

Connie shook her head and saw the woman frown.

'You don't believe me. Well, fair enough. But this house brought nothing but grief for Yvonne.'

'You knew her, then? What was she like?'

The woman turned to go, clearly tired of the conversation. But over her shoulder she said, 'Frozen. She was frozen.'

Connie shut the front door to ensure no other eccentric neighbours could disturb her. She inspected the cheerless living room. There was a mustard-coloured carpet on the floor, worn, but very clean. Perhaps, thought Connie, the woman had hoovered it before leaving the house for the last time. The Wilton Hotel had been a strange destination for this woman living in a spartan bungalow. The hotel was the height of modern chic. Why hadn't Yvonne Jenkins chosen somewhere more comfortable or anonymous?

Connie pushed open the doors of the other rooms that radiated off the hall. All were old-fashioned, clean and devoid of any personality. Even in the kitchen, the dishcloth was hanging over the tap, a practice that Connie hadn't seen for years. She touched the stained material. It was bone dry. She checked all the rooms, but if she was hoping for something untouched since the 1970s, she was disappointed. All traces of Yvonne Jenkins's daughter had been erased, at least from sight. With a sigh, Connie put down her bag and looked at the trapdoor to the loft above her.

Chapter 5

When she had finished, Rachel became aware of the stillness surrounding her. Nearing four o'clock on a wintry afternoon, the evening twilight was approaching fast. Rachel looked down at her damp notebook. The ink of the names was beginning to smudge and she wiped some of the sheen off the page with her sleeve. Shutting the notebook, she tucked it into her jacket and trudged back to the car. A lone man was making his way towards her, a stocky figure in a large dark overcoat. A scarf was wound around his head like a mediaeval shroud. She looked towards her car, wondering if she could make it there before he reached her. Perhaps her anxiety conveyed itself to him and he called to her across the thin air.

'I was checking your car wasn't stuck. If it's not now, it soon will be.'

She recognised the voice. He was the vicar, new to the village, and he clearly didn't know her. 'I'm moving it now.'

She ducked to avoid an overhanging branch that was bouncing with its new load of compact snow. It hit the top of her head as she went past, sending a shower of ice into the cold air. Rachel looked up at the branch still hanging suspended above her – glossy green leaves, grey sky and white snow creating a kaleidoscope of colours and a heady aroma. He had reached her now.

'Are you all right?'

She grasped the branch, feeling the spikes pierce her gloves and dig into her skin. 'What's this?'

He looked up. 'It's a yew tree. Why?'

Rachel let go of the branch, sending it soaring up above her and kept her fists clenched, feeling the blood begin to pool in her palm. She shook her head at him and carried on walking to the car.

'Are you sure you're OK?'

She waved an arm at him and climbed inside, switching on the engine to create some warmth. It was just as well that she had left the car on the road. The snow now covered the tarmac completely, but she should be able to exit the village at the other end, without having to turn the car round. She drove slowly and the car skidded to a halt at the T-junction. As Rachel turned onto the main road, she noted that someone, perhaps a local farmer, had been out to clear the worst of the snow. Breathing a sigh of relief she turned on her radio and listened as the announcer forecast more heavy snow for the weekend. As the pips of the four o'clock news sounded, she turned the volume up. The announcer's headline caused her to slam her foot on the brakes and then curse as, despite the grit, the car's two front wheels locked into an inexorable slide. Within seconds she had plunged off the road.

The ditch was shallow, but the wheels spun as she tried to reverse back onto where she thought the whitened road was. She opened the car's boot but remembered that she had taken out the shovel to clear her back garden at the weekend. She needed help.

The tow truck took forty minutes to arrive, which gave her plenty of time to think. She found shelter under a small copse of trees and, crouching down, concealed herself from view of the road. A few cars slowed down, obviously concerned for the welfare of the car's occupant, but Rachel refused to reveal herself. She was waiting for the authority of officialdom and would take no help from a passing stranger. Especially not one driving a car.

When the welcome lights of the red truck arrived, the driver looked surprised as Rachel slid out of the bushes. He had a thick Derbyshire accent, that strange mixture of clipped Northern and lilting Midland twang. The car was salvageable, with only a slight dent in the offside front bumper, but it took the pair of them fifteen minutes to retrieve it from the ditch.

'You're shaking, love. I'll stick it on the back of my truck and drive you home.'

Rachel felt violently sick. 'I'm fine to drive myself. It's just the cold making me shiver.'

'You sure?' The driver again looked at her curiously. 'Tell you what, I'll drive behind you until we get into Bampton.'

This Rachel was willing to accept and she started the engine. At Bampton centre, the pick-up truck tooted and sped off. Rachel, instead of heading towards her house, drove towards the Wilton Hotel. The main square was still closed to traffic, but the side streets were clear. After parking her car, Rachel walked up to the police cordon that had been erected in front of the hotel and waited.

Chapter 6

Sadler accompanied Llewellyn into the hotel room and the sea of police personnel parted to accommodate them, each continuing with their task but conscious that Llewellyn had moved out of his lair to the place of death. Llewellyn did attend crime scenes, of course. His rank didn't shield him from the realities of working as a policeman, but Sadler couldn't remember him ever attending something as mundane as a suicide. He hung back, letting his boss lead the way into the room.

The woman was still lying on the bed but now looked more dead than she had done a couple of hours earlier. It was one of the first things that Sadler had noticed as he had become more acquainted with death over the course of his career. There were degrees of being dead, despite what priests and other experts in the field might tell you. There was a time, just after the essence of the person had departed, when the cooling corpse would resemble someone sleeping, assuming the death hadn't been too violent. Even at the more gruesome fatality scenes, there was a sense that, only recently, the body had housed a living and breathing person. But death set in quickly, robbing bit by bit all the attributes that were so essential to living. And now, here, Yvonne Jenkins looked more dead than she had done two hours ago.

The team around them looked a little embarrassed. The

body ought to have been removed by now, but Sadler had telephoned ahead and informed them that the Super wanted a look. Two men from the hospital mortuary were standing to one side, arms folded, clearly waiting to be allowed to do their job. But Llewellyn gave Yvonne Jenkins only a cursory glance before nodding his head. Instead, his large hands, encased in latex gloves, were flicking through the photograph album that was still on the table.

'What do you think?' asked Sadler.

Llewellyn snorted. 'It's a selection of the most lurid headlines of the time. The disappearance was reported throughout the press, of course, for weeks on end. This seems to be a pick of the worst, so to speak. Bloody animals. Nothing's changed as far as they're concerned.'

Llewellyn shut the album and looked back over to the woman on the bed. Reduced to grey permed hair and a thin body lying rod straight as white-clad experts moved about her.

'Has she changed much?' Sadler asked, unable to get any sense of the woman she had once been.

'She's virtually unrecognisable. She was attractive once. Trim, with short ash-blonde hair, cut in a feathered style. Her husband had left her and the child and wanted nothing to do with them. So she was bringing up Sophie alone. But she still looked after herself and made an effort. Then, after Sophie went missing, she had to cope with everything without anyone to support her.'

Llewellyn continued to look at the body as Sadler's phone rang. He took the call quietly and then switched it to silent.

'The PM's been rescheduled for six tonight.'

'That's quick. I thought you said there was a queue.'

'Bill remembers the case. Said he would give it priority and sod procedure.'

Llewellyn's pale freckled face reddened. Voice thick, he said. 'It's fine to go. I've seen all I need to.'

In silence they walked back down the stairs and out into the Bampton cold. A lone woman was standing by the yellow and black police tape in a grey quilted jacket. She was looking up at the first-floor windows, ignoring the bustle going in and out of the front doors. Sadler saw Llewellyn looking at the woman. He moved towards the tape, his eyes squinting against the glare of the snow on the ground.

'Rachel?' he asked.

She stared at them both, her eyes cautious. She was tall and solid looking, but with an attractive face. Her dark hair was cut into a soft bob that suited her wide features but made her instantly recognisable from the photo of 1978 that had been plastered all over the media. Dark rings that had a look of permanence about them shadowed her eyes. Sadler, who was a poor sleeper, wondered if Rachel had the same problem.

'Mrs Jenkins is dead?'

Llewellyn walked forward and touched her sleeve. 'She is. I'm sorry you heard about it before we had a chance to contact you. I should have thought of it sooner. I'm sorry.'

He'd said sorry twice in the same breath, which must be a first, thought Sadler. He noticed that the woman responded to the kindness shown by moving closer to Llewellyn.

'Was she killed?'

Sadler frowned, his detective's instincts alert. Why was that her first question?

Llewellyn was shaking his head. 'We don't know. Why don't

you go home, Rachel? It'll be better when we have some news. Proper news, I mean. Go home, and don't turn on the television.'

*

In the attic, Connie had discovered two large wooden tea chests covered with blankets. Uncovering the first had revealed that here were the mementoes of the missing Sophie Jenkins, the first items being a pair of black leather shoes, the kind she herself had worn as a child. There was a stack of other stuff also in the chest, but in the pale yellow light it looked like a jumble of miscellaneous children's items. She needed to get the chests down to have a better look but didn't have the strength to do it herself. Presumably Yvonne Jenkins had got someone to lift these up into the attic.

Connie clambered back down the loft ladder and, leaving the opening ajar, she radioed for some uniforms to give her a hand. Until the post-mortem confirmed that Yvonne Jenkins had died by her own hand, the bungalow could be treated as a secondary crime scene. Which meant she could legitimately have a look through those packing cases before they were handed over to the woman's next of kin. She switched on the gas fire in the lounge to take the chill off the room and knelt on the floor beside it.

The old neighbour had been right. If a place reflected the personality of its occupant then the woman had summed it up accurately. Frozen. Here, the impression was of a life encased in ice. And that had nothing to do with the temperature outside. Life had obviously stopped here in 1978 and there was little evidence of the next three decades. There were no photographs, no evidence of any hobbies. How had Yvonne Jenkins spent her days? Perhaps watching that flat-screen television in the corner, the only item that she could see that must have been purchased in the last few years.

Connie's phone was buzzing in her bag. Sadler's name came up on the display. He seemed to be walking as he spoke into his mobile, his voice just slightly out of breath.

'Got anything for me?'

'Not much here, I'm afraid. I'm waiting for some backup to help me get some crates down from the attic.'

A guilty tone had entered her voice, though realistically her inability to move the boxes was nothing to do with the fact that she was a woman. It needed two people to shift them. But she needn't have bothered, Sadler wasn't interested.

'That's fine. I'll want to have a look through that stuff myself. Hang on there until the uniforms arrive; tell them to take the crates down to the station.'

'You want to see them yourself – you mean it wasn't suicide?'

'The PM's tonight so we might get a preliminary cause of death later, but we'll have to wait for toxicology tests anyway. I want to see the contents of those boxes because Llewellyn's asked me to take charge of this. We're going to be relooking at the disappearance of eight-year-old Sophie Jenkins, abducted in January 1978.'

Chapter 7

The ravenous hunger that had consumed Rachel since she was a child had, this evening, deserted her. Her stomach felt like it had a fist curled up inside, waiting to unfold and take her from within. The house was now icy cold. She tried to make the small terraced cottage as cosy as possible on winter evenings by lighting the fire in the living room to give an extra warmth to the cold stone. But this evening only the threat of hypothermia had led her to flick the switch of the central heating, which was now slowly catching against the cold.

She willed herself to stay calm. All that had happened was that Sophie's mother was dead. This was no surprise, for surely Mrs Jenkins must now be in her sixties and while it wasn't that old these days, it wasn't exactly young either. Her own mother had died at the age of sixty-one, the bladder cancer slowly sapping her strength until she had faded into nothingness. But why was Mrs Jenkins dead in the Wilton Hotel? This was the mystery that was threatening to implode her calm facade. She had heard that Mrs Jenkins still lived in the house in Arkwright Lane. Number twenty-three. Rachel could still remember the two white iron numbers, set at a jaunty angle on the front of the bungalow that she had called at every morning on her way to school.

She picked up the phone and dialled the familiar number. 'Nan? It's Rachel. I was just checking to see if you're all right.'

'I'm playing patience. Can I call you back?'

'Nan! You play patience by yourself. You can interrupt your own game for five minutes.'

Nancy sighed, and must have placed the pack of cards onto her table, for Rachel could sense the shift in focus to herself.

'What's wrong, dear?'

The direct question made Rachel recoil. 'I had a shock today, that's all. Yvonne Jenkins is dead. Remember? Sophie's mum.'

There was a silence at the other end of the phone and for a moment Rachel thought she had lost the connection.

'Mrs Jenkins. She's dead? What of?'

'I don't know.' For some reason, the thought of discussing with her grandmother the possible causes of Yvonne Jenkins's death seemed monstrous.

But Nancy was back in the past. 'She was a lovely woman, but nervy. Wouldn't let Sophie out on the street to play. And it was more common then. It couldn't have happened to a worse person – to lose a child, I mean. She never got over it.'

Rachel had to ask the question. 'But would Mum have got over it if it was me who had never come back? She might have been the same.'

There was a silence at the other end of the phone. 'Come on, Rachel. You did come back, didn't you? Don't go over this again.'

Again? They'd never been over it the first time. That was the problem. Rachel's mother had moved out of Arkwright Lane and gone to Clowton in August 1978, seven months or so after the kidnapping. A new start, she had called it. Rachel had moved school, made new friends and the past had never been spoken of. The psychologist she had been sent to hadn't wanted to talk about the case. He'd just wanted to hear about Rachel's reactions to it. He'd tried to discuss her burgeoning weight. Rolls of fat were gathering around her waist and he'd gently suggested to her mother that they might think about going to Weight Watchers together. So off they had trotted and it was her mother who'd lost two stone, although Rachel had managed to shift the worst of it. Two years of counselling and all she'd got out of it was a slightly slimmer silhouette and a lifelong aversion to full-length mirrors.

After promising to visit her nan that Sunday as usual, Rachel hung up and retrieved her laptop from the table where she had left it in the early afternoon before her fragile world had started to unfurl. The BBC had nothing about the death, not even on the local pages, but the websites of some of the more salacious daily newspapers had started to pick up on the story. The first that Rachel clicked on resulted in her coming face-to-face with her eight-year-old self. The picture had become familiar over the years, although not as famous as that of Sophie, for whom there was no adult equivalent. It had been taken in the autumn of 1977 at St Paul's primary school's summer fete and showed her with that ubiquitous pageboy haircut of the era, smiling brightly into the camera. Her mother had been standing beside her, she remembered, but over the years it was the picture of Rachel only that had made it into the newspapers. She had won a big prize on the tombola and a local journalist, searching for a photo to use in that week's events page, had snapped away, unaware that the resulting image would be reproduced for years to come to illustrate the danger facing young girls who got into the cars of strangers.

Someone had given the press a picture of Sophie dressed up for a party in a light purple sprigged dress with pristine white socks and black patent Mary-Jane shoes. She was smiling into the camera, her blonde hair parted into immaculate bunches. She'd owned a similar dress, Rachel remembered now; hers was a fern green, but with the same broderie anglaise border. At the bottom was a picture of Rachel taken a few years ago when some aspiring hack had decided to do a bit of digging into the old case. She squinted at the picture; she had been thinner then, probably a stone lighter, she reckoned.

After the shock of the photos, the text of the accompanying piece was reassuringly anodyne. No fresh news, just the announcement of the death of Mrs Jenkins. The headline of the piece read 'Grieving mother's suicide after thirty years'. Suicide? Rachel frowned. There had been nothing on the news about suicide. At least that explained what she was doing in the Wilton Hotel. But why would she commit suicide after all this time? If she had killed herself in 1978 that would have been understandable. But not now. She could remember Mrs Jenkins as a slightly nervous perfectionist who had been inclined to mollycoddle Sophie. The devastation at her daughter's disappearance would surely have lasted a lifetime. But the timing was strange. Although she must have killed herself on the anniversary of their kidnapping, why wait all this time? Something wasn't right.

Chapter 8

In Sadler's room, Connie and Palmer sat side by side. The office was pristine as usual, with little evidence of the detritus that usually accompanied investigations – files, photographs, reports. Connie slid her eyes sideways to Palmer. They were natural competitors for Sadler's favours. When she had first arrived at Bampton, Connie had taken one look at Palmer and recognised a rival. He must have done the same because he had, from the start, referred to her by her first name and it had stuck. Everyone called her Connie, from the Super to the late night cleaner.

The main drawback for Connie was that he was astute. While she relied on intuition and instinct, he could spot the flaw in a theory and an untruth in a suspect's testimony while she was still digesting the information. And although he treated her with respect and rarely pulled rank, she suspected that he wouldn't hesitate to do so if it would earn Sadler's approval. They were alike in their ambition. The difference, though, was that this was her home. Where she'd been brought up. For Palmer, the move was simply to be closer to his fiancée, Joanne. And Connie was yet to be convinced how much emotional investment he had in Derbyshire.

Today, however, he wasn't his usual self. His right knee was bouncing up and down in agitation or stress, perhaps both.

'What's the matter?' she asked, glancing down at the jigging knee.

'The matter? The matter is I'm getting married next month. Have you forgotten?'

It had slipped her mind. She knew it was sometime this year but had assumed it was a couple of months away, at least. Who the hell got married in winter? Perhaps his fiancée was pregnant. She tried a sympathetic look.

'You got a lot to do? Tell Sadler, I'm sure he'll cut you some slack if that's the problem. This is an old case – nothing's going to happen quickly, is it?'

He glanced down at her, knee momentarily stalled. 'Well, yes, but that's hardly the point. We're having the reception at the Wilton. Joanne will have a fit when she hears about that dead woman.'

'It was suicide. People kill themselves all the time. I don't need to tell you that.'

'She'll have a fit anyway. Nothing is right for her at the moment.'

What was it with people, wondered Connie. A sixty-five-year-old woman commits suicide and now everyone was jumpy – Llewellyn, Sadler and now Palmer.

'Tell Joanne that a woman killed herself in one of the bedrooms nowhere near the bridal suite. And make sure you don't point out which room it was when you arrive at the hotel. Even if she asks.'

'Easy enough for you to say.'

Stung, Connie turned to him. 'And what's all this about you asking Sadler if the place was haunted?'

Before Palmer could reply, the door to the office opened and Sadler walked in. He looked tired, his skin a pale grey.

'OK, as I mentioned to you on the phone, Connie,

Llewellyn's asked me to look again at the investigation into the disappearance of Sophie Jenkins in 1978.'

Connie opened her mouth to speak, but Sadler cut across her.

'I know what you're going to say and you're right. The matter should really be handed over to a cold-case team. However, given that things are quiet here at the moment, we're getting first crack at it. The case is still officially open, although no personnel have been assigned since DC Brierly's retirement in 2010.'

'Brierly?' said Connie. 'Good God, that was the first leaving do I went to when I joined CID. And no one else has looked at the case since?'

Sadler leaned back in his chair. 'It's only been a few years. But you're right; it is an oversight. Someone should have been assigned to keep a watching brief at least. But the fact that this was overlooked means that Llewellyn has the opportunity to appoint someone more senior than he would otherwise have done.'

'Because of the events of today?' asked Palmer. 'I mean, presumably now the press know the identity of Yvonne Jenkins they'll be here in a flash.'

Sadler didn't look happy. 'The press are almost certainly going to be a distraction. But Yvonne Jenkins's death gives us as good a reason as any to look at the case. There's no fresh evidence that we can assess, but, on the other hand, until we have an official verdict from the coroner, we have the opportunity to pry in a manner that will become less appropriate when it's officially ruled suicide.'

Connie looked down at her notepad, dispirited. Sadler clearly couldn't wait for the official verdict. He didn't want this case. 'Where are all the files?'

'I assume they're in the archive, but there are a couple of things that I want to make clear to you before we start.'

Sadler was fiddling with his shirt cuffs. 'First, the police in 1978 weren't idiots. The detectives might have worn flares and tweed jackets, but they were professionals like us. They collected evidence, recorded it and made an assessment. Of course, we've read about incompetent investigations from that time, but Llewellyn tells me the CID then was OK. Straight. And I respect his judgement.'

It sounded defensive and Connie could keep quiet no longer. 'The press were fairly critical about certain aspects of the investigation. The fact, for example, that no one bothered to seal off the crime scene until—'

Sadler made a dismissive gesture with his hands. 'I'm not saying there weren't mistakes, but let's not try to project twenty-first-century protocol onto 1978 policing. All I'm saying is that, in Llewellyn's opinion, the original investigation wasn't fatally compromised in any way.'

Connie shrugged. 'They must have missed something. The girl was never found.'

She could feel Sadler looking at her and she willed herself not to flush.

'The point I'm making is that we don't have the resources to reassess every piece of evidence in what I suspect are boxes and boxes of files. It'll be just the three of us and I'm sure this case will drop down the list of priorities should something come up in the meantime.'

'But I've asked the uniforms to bring over the chests that I found in Mrs Jenkins's attic,' Connie protested.

'That's fine. As I said to you on the phone, I'm interested to see what's in them too. Take a look when you can – get someone to itemise what's in them, at least.'

'So what are we going to concentrate on?' asked Palmer. 'If you don't want us to start from scratch.'

'We're going to take a strategic review of the case. What advances can modern policing bring to the investigation?'

'What about forensics – DNA and so forth? They wouldn't have had that in 1978.' Connie could feel her irritation rising. What were they going to be working with?

'No, but forensic tests are expensive and time consuming. We'll only use them when we know where our focus is. I can't use a scattergun approach to what we decide to test. We have limited resources. What we're going to do is bring fresh eyes to this very complicated case.' Sadler looked down at his tidy desk. 'It was huge in 1978. Don't underestimate what strains the original team were under.'

'And what are we trying to achieve?' Connie asked. 'Do we really think we might be able to find out what happened to the girl after all this time?'

'Superintendent Llewellyn is of the opinion that it is still possible to bring this case to a conclusion. I have to tell you that I'm not so sure we can. But we're going to try. I promised him that.'

'So,' said Connie, 'is someone going to give us an overview of the case if we can't read the police files? Or are we relying on press reports?'

'I didn't say the files are completely out of bounds, Connie. We should, at least, find out where they are being held. But I suspect, given that it was the 1970s, that the paperwork will be overwhelming. Nothing will have been computerised. There's just the three of us and it will seriously slow us down if we start poring through the old case reports. I want us to take a top-down approach. Assess what happened from a broad perspective first and, if some discrepancy comes up, great. We go back to the original files and try and work out what happened. But they don't form the basis of our investigation.'

'What about the team that worked on the case? They're all retired, or dead. We've got no one here who can give us a feel for that original investigation.'

'That's not quite true. There's one member of that original team left.' He looked at his watch. 'We've got an appointment with him in five minutes.'

*

Connie was surprised when Llewellyn stood up for them as they entered his office. This wasn't the usual way of things. What generally happened was that they would knock and be called in and Llewellyn would carry on with what he was doing for the requisite few minutes, which showed to all concerned the hierarchy of things. Not for so long that you thought he was a complete tosser, but long enough to make it clear who was in charge. Today, Llewellyn stood to attention when they entered his room, the first sign that this case was going to be different from others she had worked on. He motioned them to sit in the three chairs in front of his desk but remained standing himself. He didn't look exactly ill at ease; more, Connie thought, agonised.

'It's been a while since this case was headline news, but over the last thirty years it's occasionally been resurrected by bored journalists and those with a salacious bent. This is about to change. According to our press officer, the online sites have already picked up the news and tomorrow I expect it to be all over the papers.' Llewellyn glared at them. 'I don't want any of you reading those articles. Got it?'

Connie and Palmer nodded, although she noted that Sadler didn't move.

'The media liaison officer will be keeping an eye on the press. What I'm going to do is tell you the official version and that's your starting point. No conjecture, no gossip. We did all that and it got us bloody nowhere. So we start again. And this time we do it the clever way. Strategically.' Llewellyn glanced at Sadler and seemed irritated at his disconnection. 'Strategically, that's the word I want, isn't it, Sadler?'

Sadler roused himself. 'Yes, I think it is.'

Connie glanced curiously at her boss. Never mind the time that had elapsed; they were still talking about a missing eight-year-old. What was the matter with him?

Llewellyn gave Sadler a suspicious glance and carried on. 'The facts as far as we were able to get were these. On the morning of January the twentieth 1978, a Friday, two Bampton schoolgirls from the same class, Rachel Jones and Sophie Jenkins, took their usual walk to school. Rachel would call for Sophie at her bungalow and then together they would walk up the hill to St Paul's.'

'The school's still there,' said Palmer. 'It's not far from my house.'

Llewellyn ignored him. 'At the top of the road, a woman stopped the car and got the two girls to post a letter for her. From now on we're relying on the evidence of Rachel Jones, who, as we know, was later found alive. This is problem number one. We have to rely on the testimony of a girl who by all accounts was understandably traumatised by events.'

'Did anyone else see the car draw up?' asked Connie.

Llewellyn shook his head. 'You are going to see this problem time and time again. One witness. I'll come back to Rachel. For the moment, let's stay in 1978. The girls realised that there was something wrong immediately: the woman driving the car made a right turn at the top of the road. The school is in the opposite direction and it was clear that the woman never intended to drop them there.'

'Did the girls try to get out?' Palmer was becoming interested in the story.

'Rachel says she did, although she thinks Sophie was just banging the window. She remembers being unable to open the doors. This was before the days of central locking, so we presume the doors must have been modified to allow access from outside but left the person unable to open the door once inside the car. Perhaps an early form of a child lock, although they certainly weren't commonly used in cars then.'

'Didn't anyone notice two girls hammering on the windows?' Connie began to jot down some notes. 'The road must have been packed with people taking their kids to school.'

'No one spotted anything. We think that the woman must have turned into a side road almost immediately to avoid detection. And don't forget there was no CCTV in those days. Rachel couldn't remember anything about the details of the journey. Just the frustration and rising panic of not being able to attract attention.'

'Then what?' asked Palmer. 'The famous woods scene?'

Connie watched Llewellyn wince. Palmer muttered, 'Sorry.'

'I told you, you're to forget everything you read. The famous woods scene in essence boils down to this. At some point, the car was driven into Truscott Woods where Rachel escaped. What happened to the girls in the intervening period, we have no idea. As you know, Rachel was found at around midday wandering along the main Bampton Road, about a hundred metres from the fields, in a dazed state.'

'And there were no signs of abuse?' said Connie. 'I mean stuff that never got into the papers?'

'None, thank God. No sexual or other physical abuse. It gave us hope for Sophie.'

'But she was never found,' said Sadler. 'No trace whatsoever.'

'No and the working theory became that Sophie may well have been the intended target and that Rachel was simply in the wrong place at the wrong time.'

Connie couldn't understand how it was possible for a girl to be missing for so long. Palmer, as if suddenly aware that he had contributed little to the conversation, roused himself.

'What about Rachel?' he asked. 'Do we interview her again? She may have remembered something over the intervening years.'

Llewellyn finally sat down in his chair. 'I saw her at the Wilton Hotel yesterday afternoon. She was standing behind the police tape and I spoke to her briefly. I'm not sure if she remembered me. She seemed stunned by the news.'

'She asked if Yvonne Jenkins had been killed.' Sadler's tone was neutral, but Connie's ears pricked up at the statement. She looked towards Llewellyn.

'Yvonne's death would have had a big impact on her. Let's not read too much into this for the moment. Unless, of course, the PM turns up something.'

At the use of the victim's Christian name, Connie's head snapped up.

Llewellyn saw the movement and frowned. 'You went to her bungalow. What was it like?'

'Very sterile. She can't have had a very fulfilling life. And I met a strange neighbour. Told me the bungalow had been built over an old plague pit. Something about inherited memory.'

Llewellyn was stony faced. 'You're going to come across this a lot. Everyone's got an opinion. Everyone remembers the case. You're going to need to see past it to get to the bottom of what happened.'

Palmer wasn't to be put off by the distraction. His question about Rachel Jones's reaction hadn't been answered. 'And Rachel Jones? When do you think we should go and see her?'

Llewellyn looked at him coldly. 'She'll need to be re-interviewed, of course. But make sure you've all acquainted yourself with the case first. I don't want us going in with stupid questions. She's suffered enough over the years.'

Llewellyn looked at the three of them. 'I know what you're thinking – the old fool is reopening a case because it's haunted him all these years. Like in the TV shows. Well, you're right and you're wrong. I've seen my fair share of stuff since and some of it much worse than this investigation. But we don't know what happened on that January day and we had no repeat of the incident. No further child abductions, no paedophiles. Whatever happened was out of the ordinary and I think enough time has passed to give it one more shot.'

Connie watched Sadler out of the corner of her eye. He

definitely wasn't convinced. 'What are we hoping to achieve in the ideal scenario?' she asked. 'Discovery of Sophie's whereabouts or we find out what happened that day?'

Llewellyn looked down at his large hands and flexed them as if he were about to play the piano. He was shaking his head. 'The two are unfortunately inseparable. Discover what happened and we will find Sophie's body.'

'You think she's definitely dead?' said Connie.

Llewellyn opened a drawer and took out a file. They were dismissed. 'I'm sure of it.'

Chapter 9

'Muuuuuuum!'

Sophie's wails were increasing in pitch and Rachel swallowed the bile rising in her throat as she struggled to find a way out of their situation. She'd already tried the car door. She flicked up the button at the window, which should have meant that the door was now open, and she'd braced, ready to hurl herself out of the door and make a grab for Sophie to pull her through too. But the door had refused to budge and the windows weren't winding down either. It didn't make sense and this, along with the noise from Sophie, made her head feel like it was about to explode. She looked across at Sophie, who was banging hard on the glass, her face pressed up against the door.

The woman was sitting in front of Sophie, her large sunglasses covering most of her face. Her mouth was set in a thin line and she hadn't spoken to either of them since they'd got into the car.

'Are you going to kill us?' It was the only question Rachel could think of to ask, even though it set Sophie wailing even louder.

'Don't be stupid.' Now the woman looked round briefly at Rachel and lines knitted across her brow. She could feel this woman's anger.

'Can't you shut your friend up?'

Rachel slid along the seat and laid an arm round Sophie's thin shoulders. 'It's all right,' she whispered. Sophie was now purple in the face and would take no comfort from anyone. Rachel stroked her friend's hair and wiped a tear away from her own face with her sleeve.

Suddenly the car halted and Rachel lifted her head to see where they were, but through the watery film in her eyes all she could make out was a sea of dark green snake-like fingers tapping against the car window. Where were they? The wind was whipping up and behind them she could see a slick of black glistening in the pale sunlight.

The woman turned round to them. 'Are you going to be good girls?'

Sophie's scream caused Rachel's eardrums to vibrate. She looked in alarm at the woman, who was reaching into her huge handbag.

'Right. That's it.'

*

Rachel woke up and found herself on the back seat of a car. It was cold and the windows were misted up. Her head was fuzzy, like she'd felt in the winter when she'd had a cold and her mum had fed her with hot milk and digestive biscuits laid out on the plate that she always had when she was sick. She pulled herself up, her hands sticky against the cold black vinyl of the car seat. The woman who was sitting in the front seat had gone and so had Sophie.

A wave of sickness assailed her and she sank back down

onto the seat. She listened but could hear nothing outside the car. Where was Sophie and why had she been left here? She looked down at her feet and saw that one of her shoes had come off. She put her hand down onto the floor and found it. She stared and stared, trying to focus on the shiny leather. She looked at her foot with her sock around her ankle and in one sweep pulled it off. She scrunched it up in her hand and used it to wipe the side window of the car. She could see only green fields. Where was she now? This wasn't where they had first stopped. She shuffled across the seat to the other side of the car, Sophie's side, and used the same sock to wipe that window. She could see trees. Lots of them. She had been here before, she was sure. With her mother, the week she looked after Nana Nancy's dog.

She could see people – maybe two, or perhaps three. The window was blurring everything, making the images look like the bottom of a kaleidoscope. She used her bare hands this time, making an arc across the window. There were two people there. One tall and the other shorter. Where was Sophie? 'Sophie!' she shouted, but no one could hear her. Her tongue was stuck to the roof of her mouth. But perhaps she had been heard, for one of the tall figures had broken away from the other and was walking back towards the car. Towards her.

Rachel's head was swimming. A man opened the car door. She couldn't understand what he wanted. She couldn't understand the words. They were coming out of his mouth but by the time they entered her mind they disappeared. Nothing would stick and so nothing made sense.

But now he was gone and she was left in the car again. She looked out of the window and saw a man and woman standing together. The man and the woman. There was no one else around. No other cars. No one to help. A wave of sickness came over her.

She leaned against the car door and it swung open. The man mustn't have closed it properly. She lurched sideways, half her body hanging out of the car. *Freedom*, she thought. Her brain could assimilate that. *Freedom*.

Chapter 10

A cold bitter January evening in Bampton, thought Sadler, as he drove home, noticing that the icy roads had already claimed a few victims. Abandoned cars were perched on verges, discarded by their owners as they waited for the longed-for thaw. Most of Bampton were keeping to their warm homes, only venturing out on foot to the local pub or restaurant.

Inside his canal-side cottage, Sadler drew his curtains against the January gloom, watching for a moment as a fresh wave of sleet tapped against the frosting windowpane. He couldn't bring himself to cook anything, although his stomach was beginning to groan in protest at the enforced starvation.

It was a mistake to reopen the case. Llewellyn didn't, in his experience, make many mistakes. He had honed the art of being respected by the rank and file along with an ability to appease those at the top of the hierarchy, most importantly the chief constable. Sadler had seen flashes of his famous Celtic temper, but it had rarely been directed at him. Usually some hapless bureaucrat, as Llewellyn hated anything that paid lip service to the latest government directives but slowed down policing. But here Llewellyn wasn't thinking strategically. That, Sadler could identify with. They would be investigating a case with a thirty-six-year-old cold trail. And with only one unreliable witness. It was going to be a nightmare to add anything meaningful to the original investigation, and as to finding out what had really happened – forget it.

Sadler felt a pang at his lacklustre response to the case. Palmer and Connie were not only experienced detectives, they were ambitious and competent. They deserved a stronger sense of purpose from their commanding officer and he would have to give them this. Palmer had seemed distracted in the meeting with Llewellyn. But Sadler suspected that it was wishful thinking that Palmer's doubts matched his own. His mind was probably elsewhere. His wedding was coming up next month. Perhaps this was why he had sensed a lack of enthusiasm from his detective sergeant. Connie Childs, on the other hand, once she got her teeth into the case would need close management. He had spotted the spark of interest in her expression. And given that she was too young to remember the case as well as he, the investigation would have the benefit of being a historic curiosity.

In 1978, Sadler had just started secondary school. He had been eleven and his local authority had been one that had still embraced the grammar school tradition. It had been taken for granted by his parents that he would pass the eleven-plus exam, and he could remember now sitting in that classroom with his fellow schoolmates trying to answer the questions that had been a mixture of fun and a challenge. And then off to Bampton High, a grammar school where, because he was good at sports, especially cricket, he had enjoyed himself. The case of the missing schoolgirl he could remember from the news. The papers had plastered the photo of the missing Sophie Jenkins across their front pages. The image of both girls had become a symbol for the late 1970s, before the days of rolling news coverage and Internet media.

Sadler could remember his dad sitting down to the six o'clock news and neither he nor his sister had been allowed to talk while the headlines were being read. It hadn't seemed strange at the time, but now Sadler could hardly believe that his busy architect father had finished work in time to see the six o'clock news.

The news of a girl missing in Bampton had shocked the whole community, obviously, but at eleven, Sadler had been at the age between boyhood and those turbulent teenage years and had paid little attention to what was going on. Even his parents hadn't felt the need to reiterate that he mustn't get into cars with total strangers. Sadler couldn't remember them mentioning the incident at all to him. But surely his sister would have been more affected? She had been older than both girls, but at thirteen would still have been vulnerable to any potential predators.

Sadler looked at the clock on his wall. It was quarter to eight, not too late to call. Camilla, as usual, answered the phone on the first ring. Sadler had long suspected that she carried the phone around the house with her and this had been confirmed on his last visit when he had spotted her stuffing the phone into her bra as she wandered from room to room.

'Hello? Camilla speaking.'

'For God's sake, Camilla. You're not supposed to answer a phone giving out your name straight away. I could be anyone.'

'Francis, it's you. Don't be such a fusspot. I've got a perfectly good burglar alarm that I switch on at night should nefarious forces come knocking.'

She could always make him laugh and Sadler felt the tension leave his shoulders as his sister carried on unheeding.

'I was thinking about you today when I saw on the news about that woman who died. Are you involved at all? I looked out for you on the television.'

'I was at the hotel for while – but I try and dodge the cameras if I see them.'

'Poor woman. I can't imagine what I'd do if I lost any of mine. Not that they'd be getting into a car with a stranger. Man or woman.'

'Do you warn them against women too?'

'Of course I bloody do. And those parents should have done so too. It was after Myra Hindley, wasn't it? What the hell were they doing getting into a car in the first place?'

'Actually, Cam, that's what I was calling about. I'm struggling to remember the attitudes of the time. What was and wasn't acceptable. Can you remember our parents saying anything to you about what you should and shouldn't be doing? I don't remember them talking to me about it at all.'

'They wouldn't have bothered. You were still into your train sets and cricket bats then. It was before you discovered girls, then there was no stopping you.'

'Thanks, Cam. If I wanted—'

'Keep your hair on, Francis. I was stating a fact. You were oblivious to it all.'

'And you?'

His sister sighed down the line. 'You remember Mum and Dad. Dad was as grumpy as you are. No, don't interrupt – it's true. We weren't allowed to talk to him for about two hours after he came home from work. And Mum compensated for his coldness by joining every society going. So she was never in. I don't think either would have said a word to me if it hadn't been literally on our doorstep. But it was a bit hard to ignore something like that taking place nearby.'

'So they did say something?'

'They?' laughed Camilla. 'Dad didn't say a word. He would have been mortified, discussing anything like that. It was Mum who took me to one side and told me that if anyone approached me, especially a woman, I had to tell her straight away.'

'And were you scared. By the warning, I mean?'

'Do you remember me at thirteen, Francis? I was about five foot six and eleven stone. I wasn't going to be hoiked off the street by anyone. But I remember Mum implying that there were ways of tricking you.'

'Tricking?'

'Yes. I'm sure that's the word she used. That it was easy to trick people and that was what you had to watch out for.'

'And did anyone try to trick you?'

'God no, Francis. I was a hefty thirteen-year-old, interested in Abba and Wings and mooning over Prince Andrew. Those were the days. Have you seen him recently?'

'Who?'

'Prince Andrew, idiot. I can't believe I used to fancy him.'

This was always the way with Camilla. You started at one point and then you ended up somewhere completely different. Francis could feel himself beginning to smile.

'I have to go. If you remember anything else about those days you will call me, won't you? In any case, I'll ring you again soon.'

'Preferably before next Christmas,' she said cheerfully and cut him off.

She must drive her husband mad, thought Sadler. Her relentless cheerfulness didn't come from either of their parents. She was right. His father had been a serious, easily irritated man who had weighed up his words with care. Their mother was more light-hearted but had spent most of her evenings flitting between Labour Party gatherings and the Woman's Institute, an organisation that behind the jam making and home-baked cakes provided a network of camaraderie and support for rural women.

His sister hadn't told him much that he didn't already know, but it had been useful to get a contemporary view of the events. The trouble was that she had been a child when the kidnapping had occurred. Llewellyn had made it clear he didn't want the team relying on newspaper coverage, but neither did he want them combing through old police files. Sadler needed a person who could provide a contemporary version of events and he had just hit on one possibility. He dialled another number.

'You free, Clive?'

'Do you know what, I was just thinking about you!'

Another one, thought Sadler. *I seem to be on everyone's mind this evening.*

'Fancy a drink? There's something I'd like to ask you.'

'Sure. Is it too much of a cliché to say "your place or mine"?'

Clive Mottram lived in the adjoining cottage. A solicitor with one of the local firms, after the early death of his wife, he'd downsized and moved into the small end terrace. Sadler had nothing to do with him professionally – the man dealt mainly with matrimonial cases, a specialism which kept him at work till all hours, although this may have also been to stave off the loneliness of an empty house. For the first three years, they had been on nodding acquaintance only, but one evening Clive had invited Sadler into his cottage for a drink. Sadler had enjoyed himself and every six months they repeated the evening, chatting about inconsequential matters.

Sadler opened a bottle of French wine and, as he let in Clive Mottram, he noticed that he was still wearing his work suit underneath his coat.

'I hope I haven't dragged you away from anything important.'

The solicitor grimaced as he shrugged himself out of his winter coat. 'Don't worry, we've just had Christmas. This is the busiest time of the year for us, although most come to nothing, thank God. Most people seem to trot down to the solicitor before they've even decided whether or not they want to leave their spouse. I let them know the process, they get cold feet, mainly at the cost, and I thankfully don't see them again.'

Sadler poured them both a glass of wine and sat opposite his guest. Clive had settled into the leather chair and seemed glad to have someone to talk to.

'I saw on the news that the woman who died was Yvonne Jenkins, Sophie's mum. You're not reopening the case, are you?' He caught sight of Sadler's face. 'You *are* reopening it. Jeesh. You'll have your work cut out for you after all this time.'

Sadler took a sip of the wine. 'We're giving the case one of its periodical reviews. But I agree with you about the difficulties we face. It's one of the reasons I called. Without wishing to make any bold assumptions about your age, I need to speak to someone who was an adult at the time and can remember some of the details of the case. I thought you might be able to help me.'

Clive looked thoughtfully at his glass. 'I do remember it actually. I was in my twenties and had just joined my father's practice. I'd had these grand ideas about how I was going to change the world with my legal career, but one of the first things I remember noticing was that more couples were splitting up. People talk about the swinging sixties, but when I was growing up no one's parents got divorced. It was the seventies when society, primarily women I have to say, took a good look around them and if they weren't happy with what they saw, decided to make some changes.'

'So you specialised in matrimonial law. Yvonne Jenkins was divorced.'

'I handled the case. Don't look at me like that, Francis. How many solicitors' practices were in Bampton then? There were two of us. Me and Daniel Weiss. And Daniel's practice was far more traditional. Little old ladies doing their wills.'

'It's still going, isn't it?'

'We both are, thank God, although there's far more competition these days. But we're both fixtures, Daniel Weiss and me. Danny's son Richard has more or less taken over the business and I have a two partners working for me. So it's not all doom and gloom. Anyway, Yvonne Jenkins came to me and asked me to handle her divorce and I agreed. Do you still want to talk or am I now connected to the case?'

Sadler did some rapid thinking. How many independent witnesses was he likely to find? 'Sophie's parents were eliminated as suspects early on. Were you interviewed by the police in relation to this?'

'No one came near me. It wouldn't have done any good anyway as I was still negotiating some of the financial arrangements for Sophie. They would have been protected by client confidentiality, even though the girl had gone missing. For a long time we really thought Sophie would return alive so we kept the case files in the basement.'

'And now?' Sadler looked across at his neighbour and thought about how little he knew about the people living around him. 'Are you still protected by client confidentiality?'

'It's been over thirty years. The passage of time gives me more freedom to talk about the case and, to be honest, I always wondered what really happened.'

Sadler poured them both another glass of wine.

'It all started routinely enough. A nervous Yvonne Jenkins walked into the practice one day and asked to see a solicitor.'

'Did she have your name specifically?'

'God, Francis, I don't remember that much. All I remember is she saw me without an appointment. In those days I had time to see people who came off the streets. Now you have to wait a week, sometimes two, just to get an appointment with me.'

'Not as bad as a dentist yet.'

'We're getting there. Anyway, so Yvonne Jenkins sat down in my office and told me that the previous evening, her husband had announced he was leaving her for another woman.'

'Just like that.'

Clive sipped at his wine. 'It's funny, really, but now I come to think of it, it was much more like that in those days. Grand gestures and sudden schisms. Now, it's about attrition, complicated lives, second and third marriages.'

'Was she shocked? Yvonne Jenkins?'

'Yes, I think she was. Her sense of outrage was exacerbated by the fact that this woman – the woman he was leaving her for

– had a ready-made family, two small boys, and Peter Jenkins had apparently been perfectly willing to swap his own family for another. There was never going to be any drawn-out custody battle because Peter Jenkins simply no longer wished to see his daughter.'

'Thank God those days are over at least.'

Clive snorted into his wine. 'It's less common now, admittedly, but once upon a time that sort of thing was the norm. You simply left your children behind.'

'But you said you were sorting out the financial arrangements.'

'Just to confirm that Yvonne Jenkins would have sole custody and that Peter Jenkins would be providing maintenance.'

And it had all been checked out, according to Llewellyn. Peter Jenkins had been one of the earliest people interviewed and he had had a perfect alibi. A lecturer at the local tech, he had been seen in the college building at eight thirty a.m. around the time that Sophie and Rachel had been abducted. For the rest of the morning, he had been lecturing to his students. And Yvonne Jenkins had never learned to drive and couldn't have been the woman, even in disguise from her own child.

'So you met Yvonne Jenkins and agreed to represent her in her divorce. What were your initial thoughts of her?'

'She was very attractive. Short dyed blonde hair, good figure. I remember thinking that this divorce wouldn't be an absolute disaster for her. That she would soon find someone else.'

'Did you think that there was someone else at the time?'

'Actually, no. She seemed genuinely upset by the situation, but determined to sort out her own financial and domestic position.'

'And how long was this before Sophie was abducted?'

'Eight months. As I said, we were finalising the custody arrangements when Sophie went missing. I had, in effect, finished with her as a client.'

'What about the rest of your firm? She presumably made a will?'

'I don't think so, no. I would almost certainly have advised her to make a will at the time of her divorce, but if she did make one it wasn't with me – perhaps she went to Daniel Weiss. I never saw her again after her daughter was abducted. I can remember the files lay open for a while, because we didn't know what to do with them. There was no longer any need to make any financial arrangements for Sophie and he had already signed over the house to Yvonne Jenkins as part of the financial settlement.'

'The whole house?'

'Yes, I know it was quite unusual. What usually happened was that the woman kept the house to bring up the children in, and then when they reached eighteen it would be sold and the proceeds divided up.'

'But that hadn't been the arrangement?'

'No. It was my first glimpse of the person behind the mask that Yvonne Jenkins presented to the world. She was adamant that she wanted to keep the house, I think it was a bungalow, and that it was Peter Jenkins's duty to give it to her.'

'Presumably he thought differently?'

'Initially yes, but I think he wanted to marry his new partner and losing half the house was to be the quid pro quo.'

'And Sophie. It was definitely his decision to cut all ties with her?'

'According to Mrs Jenkins, yes. And he certainly never made any alternative requests through his solicitor.'

Sadler thought back to Connie's description of the bungalow. She had stayed in the same house all this time. But even before Sophie had been abducted, her mother had not wanted to leave. Perhaps this seemingly minor detail was a crack widening into something large, something everyone else had missed. Sadler shook his head and brought his thoughts around to the present and back to Clive Mottram sitting across the room from him.

'OK, so I've had your professional opinion. Now tell me about the events in January. You knew Yvonne Jenkins professionally. What were your thoughts when you heard about the missing girls?'

'Well, the first interesting thing I remember hearing was that there had been no news about the abduction until after Rachel Jones had been discovered. The two girls were supposed to turn up for school and when neither of them arrived it had just been assumed by the school that they were both off sick.'

'No one called home?'

'I don't think that anyone was unduly worried about two friends being off sick. Things were much more relaxed then.'

'And then Rachel Jones was found in a distressed state about a quarter of a mile away from the school.' Sadler poured the rest of the bottle into their glasses.

'It was about midday. Rachel Jones was found, as you say, stumbling around in a dazed state off the Bampton Road. I think that there was something about her missing her shoes and socks, but I can't really remember now.'

'I'll need to check the file – it might be important. And she could remember nothing about her abduction?'

Clive Mottram looked at Sadler with keen eyes. 'We're on your territory now, Francis. I remember the papers saying that she had been chloroformed, or something similar. She could remember getting into a car with a female driver, with Sophie, and the next thing she remembered was being in Truscott Woods. And no Sophie.'

Chapter 11

The house now felt pleasantly warm. Rachel sat cross-legged on the floor with her back to the hot radiator and looked at her notebook. The writing had become slightly blurred after the sleet of the afternoon and the pages had small ridges in them from the damp. She had files of all the material anyway, in case of accident, and they were sitting in her desk drawer, but she preferred to work from the notebook. There was a reassuring solidity about handwriting, something tangible that computer files couldn't give her.

She had often returned to these notebooks over the course of her career. She found other people's family history absorbing but, early on, she'd constructed her own chart, fascinated by the maternal line that was often ignored by traditional history. Her grandmother Nancy had initially been dismissive about her work.

'What do you want to be getting involved in all that for?' she'd grumbled, but as Rachel went further and further back into the past, to the farming family in rural Wales, Nancy's interest had grown and she even asked questions about long-forgotten ancestors.

'You're just like my mother,' she kept repeating. 'Only interested in the women of the family.' But when Rachel had questioned her further about this, Nancy refused to say anything else. Suddenly tired, Rachel gently shut the notebook and placed it on top of the radiator so that the pages could dry out completely.

The doorbell of her cottage buzzed and, surprised, Rachel got up to answer it, glancing at the clock. As soon as she opened her door, she realised her mistake. Journalists hadn't really changed in the last thirty-odd years. The old ones had usually been men and usually very persistent. Now they were both sexes but still with that keen-eyed hunger. This one was a thin-faced woman with a long nose. Immaculately dressed, with a cherry-red trench coat that Rachel coveted immediately.

'Can I have a word, Ms Jones?'

Rachel went to shut the door and the woman made the mistake of putting her foot out. An old trick. And one the woman must have regretted when she saw the look of fury in Rachel's eyes. She hurriedly withdrew her suede-clad foot and Rachel slammed the door shut and leaned back against it. Through the closed door she could hear the woman shouting at her. A sum of money was mentioned, more than she had earned last year.

'Did you know they're reopening your case? How do you feel about that, Ms Jones?'

Rachel felt her heart pause. Had she heard that correctly? Shaking, she walked over to the phone and pulled out the card Superintendent Llewellyn had given to her yesterday outside the hotel. With trembling hands she dialled the number.

'Llewellyn here.' She remembered the younger him now. When he had spoken to her on the steps of the Wilton Hotel, her shock at the news of Mrs Jenkins's death hadn't stopped her noticing his familiarity with her but she had been too stunned to comment on it. Now she could marry up the name on the card with her memory of the young policeman in the interview room with his shock of ginger hair carefully brushed to one side. He had been kind, she remembered that. And now he was a superintendent, high up in the echelons of the police force.

'It's Rachel. Rachel Jones. They're here already.'

'Who? Who's there?' The voice was sharp, concerned.

'The press. A journalist's just knocked on my door. Trying to get in.' She sounded calm to her own ears and it cost her an effort.

There was a sigh down the line. 'I'm sorry, Rachel. It doesn't take them long to pick up on a story.'

'But they said that you're reopening the case. Is that true? Are you?'

There was a silence down the line. 'I'm getting a team together to look over the case again. It's been a while since there was a review. Look, Rachel . . .'

'But I don't want it reopened. I don't want people looking at me all over again. I—'

'It's time the case was looked at again, especially in the light of Yvonne Jenkins's death. It's important to do these things, however painful. I'm sorry.'

He sounded firm but also genuinely sorry.

'Will they want to speak to me?'

'They're going to have to, Rachel. I can send—'

'I don't want a policewoman. I'd prefer a man.'

Again, silence.

'And what should I do about all those journalists outside the door?'

'Draw all the curtains and put lights on in a couple of rooms so they can't work out where you are in the house. Don't answer the telephone or mobile unless you recognise the number. Add my mobile to your contacts so I can get hold of you. And sit tight for tonight. I'll send a patrol car past your house a few times to check all is OK. And I'll be back in touch tomorrow morning. And Rachel . . .'

'Yes?' She couldn't conceal the tremor any longer.

'Try and get some sleep.'

Chapter 12

As usual, Connie woke at five and listened to the birds chatter as they anticipated the cheerless dawn. She switched on her bedside lamp and contemplated her newly painted ceiling. The first thing she had done once her probationary period at Bampton had been concluded was to look for another flat to replace the dank bolt hole taken in haste when she arrived in the town from nearby Matlock. Unfortunately, despite the recession, house prices were still high, people attracted to the market town with its views of the Derbyshire Peaks. The landscape was stunning whatever the weather, from the slate grey hues of the wintry hills overhung with heavy black clouds to the verdant green of a summer's day. It was a landscape to catch your breath and wonder. So to buy anything had been out of reach of her limited budget. However, instead of rushing to find a replacement for her scruffy apartment, she had taken her time over three months and had eventually found this place.

What had surprised her was that it overlooked the town's canal. In her old flat, she had hated the fact that the stagnant water ran across the bottom of the garden. She refused to venture near it, but it preyed on her mind, its deep still waters rocking unseen at night. She had nearly not viewed her present flat. Once she saw from the agent's particulars that it overlooked the canal she'd passed it over. But a month later she was on her way to investigate a burglary in the area and had realised that the 'To Let' sign was the same apartment she'd rejected. It hadn't been an auspicious start. The burglary had taken place in the same block, although the owner cheerfully admitted to having left a window open on the ground floor. After taking the man's statement she'd wandered up the stairs of the old wharf building and been surprised by the charm of the views. Here the canal was open, with a small life force moving the water along. The only possible blot on an otherwise perfect arrangement was that she had heard that Sadler's cottage lay about five hundred metres along the same stretch of canal. Fortunately, they had different access roads and Connie was yet to stumble across him outside work.

In Sadler, Connie sensed a tacit approval of her attempts to climb the ranks of the force. He had, after all, supported her application to move from uniform into CID, although the interview had been gruelling enough. Perhaps that was where her instinctive reserve towards her boss came from. When she had sat in front of the interview panel, Sadler had asked her the one question that she had been dreading. 'Why do you want to become a detective?' Of course she'd had a few stock answers ready but one look at his cool blue eyes had frozen the platitudes on her lips. So she'd taken a deep breath and gone for it.

'Derbyshire CID, from what I can see, is full of southern university graduates looking for a nice place to bring up their children. I'd like someone whose family has worked in this place for generations to make their mark.'

She later realised her mistake. Sadler, too, was a local, although the hard edge of the north Derbyshire vowels could only just be heard. But he'd given her the job despite, or perhaps because of, her answer. Her problem was that she had never been able to work out which one it was. He was also physically attractive. Not like Palmer's compact physicality. Sadler was tall and remote. But she'd seen other women at the station looking at him. She had too much sense to explore what his attractiveness might mean to her, relationships between colleagues were generally discouraged, but, within her, she was drawn to his distant energy.

She'd been warned by Llewellyn not to look at any press coverage of the old case. And if that's what they had been instructed to do then Sadler would be watching his team to ensure that they abided by the rules. Which was all very well if you'd worked on the investigation first time round but how exactly was she to find out any information? Sadler had scheduled a meeting for that morning but she could hardly turn up and expect to sit and not speak. She bet that at this very moment Palmer was also awake and brushing up on the case, despite his impending nuptials, and she had no intention of being left behind.

She sent him a text. *Are you awake?*

The phone beeped a reply. *Sod off Connie. It's 5 a.m.*

Still in bed, she opened up her laptop and started to search under the names of Yvonne and Sophie Jenkins. It was pointless. She had 257,389 results, most of which when she clicked on them were the same reports rehashed in different ways. She opened a few of the links, skim read the contents and then shut them down again. She tried next the name of Rachel Jones and Bampton. Same result, although the first hit was the website for a Rachel Jones, a family historian based in Bampton. It probably wasn't the same person. Jones was a common surname, although it couldn't be helpful having a name like that with this case going on.

Connie opened up the site and clicked the 'About' tab. There was a photo at the top of the page showing an attractive plump woman in her early forties with a short brown bob that she had tucked behind her ears. She was smiling at the camera and holding a cup of tea in her hands. The tea was presumably to reassure potential customers. She was easily identifiable as an updated version of the schoolgirl whose picture had dominated the news in 1978.

A quick look around the site revealed that, for a fee, Rachel could prepare a family tree for you. Unusually for an Internet site, the fee structure that she charged was on the website – starting with a basic family tree and then an hourly rate. Connie, who had no interest in her ancestors, wondered who would use a genealogist. People with unusual family histories, perhaps, or with an interesting surname.

Next to the 'About' tab was another named 'My Ancestry'. Connie clicked on the button and was taken to an extensive family tree. She looked for the oldest name – someone born in 1780. Connie quickly scanned the chart and then, noticing something, looked again. There wasn't a single man's name on the tree. That was a strange omission. Even Connie's limited knowledge recognised that men were the usual focus of family research. But the chart in front of her held not a single male ancestor. Connie flicked back to the photo and looked again at the photograph. An ordinary woman in her early forties with an extraordinary past and, looking at her family history chart, a skewed slant on the world. Well, that was all right by her. Not everybody was obsessed with the male line. She wasn't, for a start. That was something in Rachel's favour.

Four hours later, the three of them were in Sadler's small office and Connie felt the familiar thrill of satisfaction. The case might be a dead duck as far as Sadler was concerned but at least they had an interesting investigation to work on together.

'So, Connie,' said Sadler. 'Where did you start last night?'

'This morning,' muttered Palmer.

Connie flushed and she looked to see if he was smirking at her. He had his eyes down and looked subdued.

'I did a search on the Internet to see if I could find anything beyond the press stories. And I came across Rachel Jones's website. She apparently works as a family historian. You know – family trees and all that. She researches people's history for them. A genealogist. Her website was very well done. Very professional.'

Sadler picked up his pen. 'That's what she's doing now? She was quite professional looking when I saw her outside the hotel, despite the cold and obvious shock she'd had.'

'What's interesting is that she's still recognisable as the schoolgirl who disappeared in 1978. She's even got a similar hairstyle. And she's made no effort to hide her identity, same name and everything.'

'She didn't have anything to be ashamed of, though, did she?' pointed out Palmer, his hectoring tone out of place in the small office.

'Any significance that she's a family historian in your opinion?' Sadler asked her.

'Almost certainly not. And that was as far as I got. There's probably plenty online rehashing the old news. Most of it a load of rubbish. I avoided those sites.' She shot a sideways glance at Palmer, who, instead of meeting it with a conspiratorial gaze of his own, kept his eyes to the floor.

'And you, Palmer?' said Sadler.

Palmer rubbed his hand over his forehead. 'Nothing, sir. You said not to look at anything in advance so I didn't bother.' He shot Connie a reproachful glance. She looked at him in surprise. Unlike him to miss a trick like that. Now she looked at him more closely she could see he looked a bit pale. It must be all the wedding plans. She'd seen him furtively looking at his mobile while he was sitting at his desk, tapping a text message, presumably to his fiancée, Joanne. It was unlike him not to be totally focused on an investigation. It was both an opportunity and an irritant for her. A chance to shine in Sadler's eyes, maybe. But she could feel a niggle of abandonment in Palmer's lack of focus. She would have to corner him later and have it out with him.

Sadler turned in his seat towards them both. 'If two girls were abducted today and one later turned up alive and apparently unhurt, who would be the first suspect?'

'The father,' said Connie. 'Or other close relative – uncle, cousin, friend.'

'Of which girl?' asked Palmer.

Sadler was looking at him with approval, noticed Connie. *So he's still with us despite his truculence*, she thought quickly.

'I would say possibly of the girl who was unharmed – Rachel Jones. It's our first major stumbling block. Why did she survive? This suggests an element of malevolence towards Sophie Jenkins, or possibly protection of Rachel Jones.'

'Exactly,' said Sadler. 'This is going to be our first line of enquiry. Why did one girl come back? Let's leave that there for the moment, but I want you to keep it in mind all through this investigation.'

'She escaped,' pointed out Connie.

'Agreed, she managed to get out of the car. But according to Rachel, Sophie was already missing from the vehicle.'

Palmer was frowning. 'Going back to the male relatives, Rachel Jones's father was dead. He died before she was born. Sophie's father was estranged from the family.'

'Yes, but as far as I can tell no one even looked at any other male relatives in Rachel's life. There must have been uncles, grandfathers and so on.'

I wouldn't count on it, thought Connie, thinking of the family tree. 'I thought we weren't going to reopen old lines of enquiry. We were going to assume that the initial investigation had proceeded correctly.'

Sadler was looking at her with his cold blue eyes but he smiled at her. 'I may have made a mistake saying that up front. What I wanted to say was that the team in 1978 weren't thick. But they may have been fallible. And they missed that. So that's our first line of enquiry.'

The office fell silent. Connie could see that there was something on Sadler's mind. She took a deep breath.

'I'm wondering what all this has got to do with Yvonne Jenkins's suicide.' She had hit the spot, she could tell, and it wasn't the first time she had instinctively known what was troubling Sadler. 'I think we should also try and find out why Yvonne killed herself now. At this precise moment in time.'

Sadler looked irritated that she had articulated what he was thinking. He clearly had reservations about the investigation that, for the moment, he was keeping to himself. 'You think there's a specific reason why she chose to commit suicide in the Wilton Hotel this week? A trigger more than the events of more than thirty years ago?'

Connie nodded and looked at Palmer. He shrugged and looked at the floor. She looked back to Sadler for help. 'When are we interviewing Rachel Jones? She might be able to give us some pointers.'

Palmer coughed. 'According to Rachel's statement, although she was confused at the time she was found, she was adamant that her abductor had been a woman. She also gave quite a good description of the woman. Female, mid-to-late twenties. Long dark hair and sunglasses.'

'Sunglasses in January. In Derbyshire,' said Connie. 'That would have got my suspicions going straight away.'

Now Palmer smirked and Connie was surprised at how glad she was that he was back to his old self. She definitely needed to speak to him later.

'That's the other aspect of this case that is particularly puzzling. If Rachel is right, and the detectives working the original investigation believed her, then we need to start looking at motives as to why a woman would kidnap two young girls. I want your minds kept open on this one. No mindless assumptions about childless women and men dressed in drag. These aren't usually the perpetrators of child abductions. There's something else that went on here and we need to find it out.'

Sadler nodded at Connie. 'I think this is one for you.'

She looked at her boss in surprise. 'Why me in particular?'

'Because I need your instinct on this. You're a woman and

in this instance it's going to give you an advantage. Think of scenarios why a woman might abduct not one child but two, and start eliminating those that sound either ridiculous or unfeasible. But consider them anyway. Something must have been missed at the time and we may be able to find it now.'

Connie made a face. 'Do you think we're assuming too much by the fact that Rachel wasn't sexually assaulted? We've extrapolated this to conclude that there was no sexual motive whatsoever. For all we know, there may have been a sexual intent directed at Sophie but not Rachel.'

Palmer wrinkled his nose. 'That doesn't sound right.'

There was a knock on the door and Connie swivelled round in her seat. Llewellyn was standing in the doorway, his tall frame filling the space. 'I had a call from Rachel Jones late last night. The press are pestering her already. She's asked for some police presence, which I'm going to give her. Station a car outside her house for today, which should help for a start. And maybe tomorrow. After that, I'm not sure. I'm going have to juggle some resources to do that much.'

'We were just discussing when to re-interview Rachel in relation to the 1978 case.'

'Ahh'. Llewellyn looked at his feet. 'She's not happy about being spoken to again but I think I managed to persuade her of the necessity of doing so. But she specifically requested that it wasn't a woman.'

Connie looked at him in surprise, swallowing her outrage. That was a new one on her. If they specified, it was usually that they wanted a woman. Llewellyn looked down at her.

'She never came across as particularly traumatised as a child. She just seemed to pick up and carry on as though the incident never happened. Now I'm beginning to wonder if we didn't underestimate the ordeal she went through.'

He looked at Sadler. 'Anyway, she asked for a man and I'd prefer, Sadler, if it was you.'

Chapter 13

Rachel wondered if they had sent the best-looking detective in Bampton on purpose. He wasn't young, maybe five years older than her, but he was still attractive, although there was a wariness in his face. Don't come too close, his expression shouted, which was fine by her. He was also very tall, filling her small living room, and she was relieved when he sat down in her armchair. She felt less claustrophobic with him like that. At least Llewellyn hadn't sent a woman. However surprised he'd been by her request, he had listened to her. She remembered the young PC called Wendy who had been assigned to her in 1978. She'd insisted on treating Rachel like a five-year-old. She was eight at the time of her kidnapping and already used to looking after herself. Not like Sophie, who wanted to be mummied all the time. Wendy had gone down on her knees and tried to interest her in dolls and teddies, which had heightened Rachel's sense of the unreality of the situation.

The detective refused tea and sat watching her. Llewellyn had been kind on the phone. She could still recall his kindness from before and it hadn't disappeared in the intervening years. He had sent this policeman to her.

'We're going to assign a patrol car outside your house for the time being. It won't be there all the time; we can't afford the resources, I'm afraid. But it'll pass by your house on a regular basis and it'll park itself for a while across the road from you. As your front door opens straight onto the street, there isn't a huge amount we can do. They can even peer in through your windows if they're standing on the pavement.'

'Am I not entitled to any privacy at all?'

'Inside your house, of course. And if the press start being a nuisance we can try and get an order, restraining them from coming closer than a specific distance from your property. But if all they've done is knock on your door so far, then there's not much we can do.'

'They've left me alone all these years and now – after Mrs Jenkins chooses to take her own life – I'm being pestered again.'

She saw a look of distaste cross his face. It had probably been the wrong choice of words. But the woman had had a choice. More than she and Sophie had back then.

'In my experience, the press move quickly when it comes to news. When Yvonne Jenkins's suicide is confirmed, you'll most likely be left alone.'

'You're sure it's suicide?'

She noticed the detective looking at her shelf of books. 'We need to wait for toxicology tests to come back but, yes, we're fairly certain it was suicide.'

'But why now?' Rachel's voice had risen a fraction and again she saw that look of distaste.

'There's been a lot of research into suicides. The reasons are rarely cut and dried. It may be that Mrs Jenkins simply decided to end her own life one day.'

'And the Wilton Hotel?'

He looked at her now. 'Suicides often choose a neutral space to kill themselves. It distances them from their actions. That's probably all there is to it.'

Rachel stood up and crossed to the window. Through the sheer curtains she could see the huddle of reporters. It looked like Sadler was right. There were fewer of them than there had been that morning. Or perhaps it was simply lunchtime.

'She never got in touch with me, you know,' said Rachel, still staring out of the window.

'What, after the abduction?'

Rachel swung round to face him.

'Never. The last time I saw her was the morning that I knocked on Sophie's house to pick her up for the walk to school. She never bothered to come round after that.'

Sadler was staring at her. 'Not even to get your version of events?'

'Nothing. It really upset my mother. And after about eight months we moved out to Clowton.'

Still he stared. 'Rachel, she'd lost her daughter. The most shocking and unthinkable act that any mother should have to face. No chance to say goodbye; no idea where Sophie had disappeared to. And there was never any resolution. Her mind must have been turning over possible scenarios.'

Rachel could feel her head begin to pound.

'And however traumatic your experience, and that of your mother, she at least got you back. Did *your* mother visit Yvonne Jenkins?'

Rachel shook her head. 'I don't think so.'

'And don't you think that's strange. That the mother who'd had her child returned to her didn't go and see the woman who'd lost hers.'

His eyes were still on her. Beyond the compassion she could read something else. He was assessing her. She'd read him wrong at first glance, she realised now.

'I do need to ask you, Rachel, if anything has come back to you over the intervening years. About what happened in 1978.'

She was relieved to get off the subject of her mother. 'Nothing. I remember nothing beyond getting into the car and the woman making the wrong turn at the top of the road. Sophie was crying and I was banging on the windows, but no one could see us. She was driving fast, the woman, and she said nothing to us. Just kept her eyes on the road and kept driving. I remember thinking, I'm going to climb over and turn the wheel so she crashes the car. But there was no time even to do that.'

'You ended up in Truscott Woods.'

'Exactly, but I don't remember getting there. I remember banging on the windows and then the next thing someone looking after me after I had been found on the road. I don't even remember the car stopping. It's all a complete blank.'

'You don't remember seeing something, another car for example, waiting for you at the woods. Or perhaps another place.'

Rachel looked across at him. 'I remember nothing. Sometimes I think I can remember figures standing together in a group, but I'm never sure if that is my imagination. What I definitely do remember is being in a person's car, with a dog blanket around my shoulders, and someone was telling me that my mum was on her way. And feeling really, really sick. A sickness that I've never felt before. The doctors thought it might have been the chloroform.' She looked down. 'The rest you know.'

'And nothing has ever come back?'

'I told you no. Nothing. Can you imagine how that feels? I've lain awake night after night trying to remember, but nothing comes back.'

Chapter 14

Connie sidled up to Palmer and watched in amusement as he gave a small start when he noticed how close she was to him.

'Jesus, Connie. You gave me a shock.'

'You all right, Palmer? You looked a bit ill in the meeting.'

Now she was close up, Connie could see Palmer's skin was veiled in a thin sheen of sweat. Palmer looked away but stepped closer to her. 'Between you and me, Joanne's being a complete nightmare. I'm getting married next month and I'm not sure I can stand it any more.'

How Palmer and Joanne had ever got together was a complete mystery to Connie. The only thing they seemed to have in common was groomed good looks, but perhaps that was enough. Joanne worked as a physiotherapist in one of the doctor's surgeries in Bampton and, on the rare social events that she had turned up to, had shown little interest in the workings of the detective team. However, when Joanne had spotted her and Palmer one evening huddled together discussing the possible suspects in a recent hit-and-run accident, things had nearly turned nasty. A headache had been invented and a reluctant Palmer had been dragged off home with a martyred air. And now they were getting married. Connie stepped back. 'Is it because of the body in the Wilton Hotel? Look—'

'It's not just that. It's everything. Nothing I do is right. I'm seriously thinking I made a mistake ever agreeing to get married. We were happy as we were.'

'Seriously?'

He looked at her in agony. 'Are all women like this before they get married?'

'No idea. Don't ask me. I've got nowhere near the altar. Have you tried to have it out with her?'

'She spends all her time with her mother. I can't get near enough to have a proper chat.'

Connie considered. 'Maybe talk to Sadler,' she suggested finally.

Palmer gave her an affronted look and walked off.

She walked over to her desk and waited for the computer to boot up. The room was empty and she frowned, looking around. There should be more people than this coming in and out of the large open-plan office. When the archaic computer finally cranked to life she opened the Internet browser. A quick trawl online revealed what she already had suspected. That women were rarely the perpetrators of child abductions. Myra Hindley was the famous one of course, but there were people who thought that she was just an accomplice of Ian Brady, and if their paths had never crossed in that Hattersley housing estate, Hindley might have led a different life. Connie wasn't so sure about this, but the tragic events to the west of Derbyshire over forty years ago were a distraction she didn't need at the moment.

There were also plenty of news reports about the role Rose West had played in abducting the girls selected by her husband. She had allegedly been in the car with him when he'd picked up his victims, her presence reassuring the wary, which in Connie's eyes was a heinous crime. Both had been accomplices of men though, so perhaps a man had been behind the 1978 kidnapping. The woman with the sunglasses in January an accessory to a more devilish personality. She wouldn't get far looking at the Internet. Sadler was interviewing Rachel now – she needed help from another direction. Psychologists bored Connie. They would give her some waffle about women dominated by men and she'd be no nearer finding a solution. Connie preferred tangible facts to wishy-washy imaginings.

She went hunting for the tea chests that she'd found in Yvonne Jenkins's attic. They'd been shoved into the corner of an empty office, a breach of procedure that cheered her up. It seemed that recently everything in this station was about adhering to correct policy and scrutinising your methods of working as part of the drive for standardisation. It made for dreary detective work. But, as Sadler had rightly pointed out, in 1978 with their more primitive policing the team had still done a half-decent job. They hadn't solved the case, admittedly, but still, Connie envied the freedom the team must have had compared to today.

There were two large chests, with no lids, made of pale plywood with metal rims, going slightly rusty. Both were covered with tartan blankets which had been pushed around the contents. She felt for the one that she had rummaged through in the attic, with the child's shoes on top. But the contents were disappointing. A collection of children's clothes from the 1970s, including dresses that Sophie must have grown out of by the time she'd been kidnapped. Yvonne Jenkins had obviously kept some items for sentimental reasons.

The second chest initially looked as hopeless, filled at the top with soft toys and a doll with hard brittle limbs. But at the bottom were two photo frames, made from moulded wood with gilt edging. The photos inside showed a family of three people. Yvonne Jenkins, as Llewellyn had indicated, had been a very attractive woman, although her large eyes had stared confused at the camera in both shots. Then there was little Sophie Jenkins. In the first portrait she looked, to Connie's inexperienced eyes, about two years old. She had been a chubby child, with her pale hair parted into two neat bunches. By the second photo, she had lost most of the baby fat and was a serious child, about school age, although Connie was now struggling to guess her exact age. But in any case, she was more interested in the man standing in both photographs, wearing the same beige suit. In the earliest photo, he looked resigned. In the second, angry. This, presumably, was Peter Jenkins.

She was about to put everything back when she noticed something screwed up in the corner. She reached into the chest and groped for it. What emerged was a grubby child's sock, its shabbiness a startling contrast to the pristine neatness of the rest of the chest's contents. It had been scrunched up and thrown into the corner of the box. Connie stuck her head into the chest to double-check she hadn't missed its pair but the chest was completely empty. Slowly, Connie unfurled the sock. It would probably have been knee high on an eight-year-old child. She could remember wearing similar styles made out of knobbly white material with small flowers snaking down one side. Connie weighed it up in her hand and wondered.

Chapter 15

Outside Rachel Jones's cottage, Sadler's mobile phone vibrated in his jacket pocket. He looked at the number. Christina. Plus five missed calls. She wasn't going to be happy.

Christina was married to a Greek businessman who had decidedly traditional views on marriage. This meant that he dallied with the occasional lover while she was remunerated handsomely for her role as homemaker and mother. Christina, whose paternal grandmother had taught her a few things about how this arrangement worked in practice, had met Sadler at a party about six years ago and they had become lovers. He thought about ignoring the call but she seemed to have a sixth sense when it came to being given the brush off.

'I'm in the middle of something.'

'Morning to you too,' said the voice and Sadler reluctantly smiled. 'Are we still on for later?' Christina's deep, slightly masculine voice had been one of the first attractions for Sadler. Now that she was cross with him, it had lost that rich depth.

'Yes, six o'clock,' he said looking at his watch. 'There's no reason I should be delayed.'

'Well, ring me if you are. I'm not sitting in that pub for half an hour like last time. If you're going to be late, call me.'

'Of course, Christina. Bye.' He cut the connection and wondered. He'd heard the sounds of breakfast being eaten in the background. How much did her family know about their meetings?

Sadler looked at the group of reporters huddled together and went across to the patrol car that had recently drawn up outside the house. Inside were two uniformed officers he hadn't seen before. They were both listening intently to the police radio. Sadler rapped on the window.

'Sorry about this. You just need to keep an eye on the reporters. If you see them peering in the windows, warn them off. The woman inside needs to be able to go about her business.'

'Of course.' The officer in the passenger seat nodded at the car radio. 'Something's going on over the other side of town. Any idea what that's all about?'

Sadler frowned and listened to the disembodied voices coming across the airwaves. There was an urgency about the responses which the two professionals in the car had picked up on.

'What was the initial call?' he asked.

'A hysterical woman dialled 999 saying she had found a body. The dispatcher couldn't even get a location from her to begin with as the woman was in such a state.'

'And now?'

'They're heading towards Truscott Fields, behind the woods.'

Sadler's heart gave a lurch and yet his brain was struggling to make a connection. Body meant recent. Not the old bones they would be looking for. He reached for his phone that had been vibrating in his pocket during the interview with Rachel Jones and accessed his call log. Four of the five missed calls were from Palmer, the other from Connie.

'And have they found someone?'

'Body of a woman, apparently. First response is saying it looks like she was strangled. And recently.'

Sadler looked back at Rachel's house. 'I need to get down there. Can you stay here and keep an eye on things? Although, once the news gets out my guess is you'll be watching an empty street.'

*

Truscott Woods was an ancient site, the remnants of a great forest that had once cut a swathe over the lower parts of the Derbyshire Peaks. The area that remained was about a square mile in size, and Sadler could remember his father being fascinated by the patch of woodland with its ancient history. He'd tried to instil the same awe in his young son and Sadler, anxious to please his usually unemotional parent, had accompanied him deep into the forest, along the overgrown pathways, to get a sense of what had once been.

But if he'd been given a choice, Sadler would have joined the thousands of visitors who ventured no further than thirty metres or so from the wood's entrance in the car park off the Bampton Road. The outer pathways were well maintained by the council and regularly used by dog walkers and families at the weekend to lark about amongst the trees. But as you went deeper into the woods the paths, although still well kept, became boggy and the trees denser. The sense of claustrophobia was enhanced by the profusion in this area of birch trees, their thin silvery trunks masking the sturdy branches leaning towards each other to form a canopy. Next to the wood's entrance stood Truscott Fields, common land enshrined in a charter dating back to 1415. Nothing was allowed to be done to change the nature of this piece of land. Over the years, groups of parents had petitioned the local authority for a play area to be erected near the car park but to no avail. An ancient edict was a law to be obeyed, however much time had changed, and no leeway was to be given, even to accommodate the voting public.

Few who came on a summer's day to wander along the paths or to exercise their dogs knew the dark history of the place. As thirty miles to the west the regeneration of Hattersley was sweeping away traces of the material lives of Myra Hindley and Ian Brady, in Truscott Woods emphasis was given to its ancient existence and mediaeval importance. The discovery of a shivering girl in 1978 had been eradicated from the wood's history although the case had made Bampton infamous throughout the country. However, Truscott Woods was about to stake a claim for notoriety in the twenty-first century, judging by the hive of activity in the distance. Pulling up at the car park, Sadler glanced into the entrance of the woods. Perhaps, somewhere in that dense woodland, the body of Sophie Jenkins lay undisturbed.

Connie padded over to meet him in floral wellingtons, her face scrunched up against the cold. He'd spotted the boots in the back of the car but this was the first time she'd worn them. The crude red poppies dabbed gaudily on a white background seemed out of place in the bleak scrub of this setting. She was bursting to tell him something and pulled against his arm in a proprietorial manner.

'You're not going to believe this,' she hissed, pulling him away from the entrance to Truscott Fields where he could see the familiar white tent erected. 'The SOCOs are working there now. It's going to be another couple of hours at least before we can get anywhere near it.'

'Did you get to see anything?'

Connie leaned closer to him. 'I arrived not long after the patrol car called it in. Either the death is very recent, I mean as in today, or the cold weather helped preservation. Because the victim isn't in that bad a state, considering that she has been exposed to the elements.'

'Any sign of cause of death?'

'There's a kind of cord around her neck. A piece of thin rope, it looked like to me. Still left *in situ*.'

'ID?'

'It looks like her handbag had been slung over the fence from the field into the woods. It was easy to find. The killer obviously made an attempt to get rid of it. Probably couldn't take the risk of being seen leaving with it.'

'And any ID inside? Come on, Connie, answer the question.' Sadler was looking at the white tent, where he noticed the pathologist Bill Shields heaving his body under the tape.

'Credit cards in the name of Mrs Penny Lander. Didn't mean anything to me. But the old boy in the patrol car says a Mrs Lander in St Paul's primary school used to teach his daughter before she retired.'

'St Pauls?' asked Sadler. 'Wasn't that where . . .'

'Yes, where Sophie and Rachel were pupils in 1978. We think we're on the right track as there's a car in the car park registered to a Mr James Lander. The blue BMW over there.'

Sadler looked at where Connie was pointing. A dirty dark blue BMW was parked at an angle in the car park. It looked like it had been put there in a hurry, taking up two spaces.

'Hadn't anyone noticed it sitting there?' asked Sadler.

'We're checking now, but we don't think there have been any reports of a missing car.' She looked up at him. 'You think there's a connection to our case?'

Sadler thought back to Rachel Jones, whom he'd left sitting disconsolately on the sofa. First Yvonne Jenkins and now Penny Lander.

'Do you believe in coincidence, Connie?'

She didn't even pause to think. 'In this job? Never.'

Chapter 16

20 January 1978

Rachel looked through fuzzy eyes to a blur at the end of the track. She could see objects hurtling past and her soft, woolly brain tried to identify the name for them. Cars. It was cars that were rushing past at the top of the track. She frowned slightly. Cars sounded bad to her. Her mum didn't have one, so they had to ride on the bus wherever they went. No, the thought of cars gave her a bad feeling in her chest. But cars contained people, didn't they? And people usually could help. And that was what she needed right now. Help.

She stumbled up the track, even though she could hear a shout behind her. And a car starting. They were after her. She'd lost both her shoes now and one of her socks which was slowing her down, the imbalance made her want to plunge headlong into the soft ground. She pulled off the other sock and started to run. But she had always been a terrible runner and today was no exception. A pain was now starting in her fuzzy head. It was getting bigger and bigger and she could feel a huge pressure behind her nose. She concentrated on the opening at the top of the track and not the sound behind her. Those blurry cars held the key to her rescue.

The roar entered her ears as the car came up behind her. Rachel felt her stomach lurch but her legs propelled her on. She was nearly there and, as she arrived at the road, she waved her arms in the cold air. She sensed the car behind her slow and turned, in consternation, at the dulling sound. But another car, speeding around the corner, saw her and braked. A man in a blue suit got out.

He ran over to her. 'Are you all right, love?'

Rachel turned and briefly caught a glimpse of a woman's sunglasses before the white car that had been following her sped away. She pointed at the retreating vehicle, but the man was crouching down beside her.

'Is everything OK?'

Rachel felt the cold enter her and stared at her numbed feet. She lifted her head and looked into his concerned eyes.

'Where's Sophie?'

Chapter 17

Following a nod from the pathologist, Connie followed Sadler under the crime scene tape and towards the white tent. When she had told Sadler about Penny Lander's connection with the two schoolgirls she had seen something in his eyes that she hadn't seen before – a spark of interest. At the entrance to the tent, he turned to her.

'You don't need to follow me in, Connie.'

'It's not a problem, sir.' She thrust a mint into her mouth as soon as his back was turned.

Inside the tent, Sadler crouched down and examined the body. The woman was about Yvonne Jenkins's age but there the resemblance ended. She was dressed in a round-necked fern green sweatshirt and brown cords and had hiking books on her feet. Her face was turned away from them and Connie moved slightly to catch a glimpse of the woman's features. She wished she hadn't.

'Can you confirm cause of death?' Sadler stood up and looked at Bill Shields.

The pathologist was packing up his bag and seemed tired. 'It looks like strangulation – there's a rope-like ligature still around the neck. But I need to have a good look back at the mortuary. There's something a bit strange I want to check.'

Connie watched Sadler make a face of distaste as he looked

at the body. 'Strange? Anything relevant to the investigation when you say strange?'

The pathologist shut his bag with a snap.

'It might be nothing. Let me have a good look when I'm out of this tent. She's been dead about two days. She was most likely killed here and her body left where she fell, judging by the ground around the victim. It looks like leaves and branches were used as a form of covering for the body. Then, of course, the snow came. Today's thaw seems to have caused the make-shift grave to move, exposing the body so she was visible to anyone passing this way.'

'How quickly can you do the PM, Bill? I know you made an exception for Yvonne Jenkins and now I'm going to ask you to do so with this one.'

Bill Shields frowned at Sadler. 'You think they're con-nected?'

Sadler shrugged. 'Maybe.'

They stared at each other for a moment.

'I'll talk to you again tomorrow,' said Sadler. 'I don't think there's any point us being present when you do the PM. Give Connie a call if anything interesting comes up.'

Connie watched the pathologist massage his back. 'You normally send someone along, Francis. This one not to your taste?'

Sadler shook his head. 'Resources. I need the team out in the field. You know how it is.'

Bill Shields looked sympathetic and glanced at Connie. 'I'll miss our cup of tea.'

Connie flushed. Since their first meeting, when she had turned up late for an autopsy, she and the pathologist had got into the habit of having a cup of tea together in his office after he had finished with the body. An informal affair, Connie had struck up a useful relationship with the doctor and knew that she was his preferred detective at autopsies. She could feel Sadler's eyes on her back.

She smiled at Bill. 'Perhaps I'll pop in after work. See how you got on.'

She turned and walked out of the tent, Sadler following her. If she had expected him to comment on the conversation she was going to be disappointed. He had listened to her exchange with Bill with watchful curiosity but was, for the moment, going to be keeping his thoughts to himself. Once more Connie wondered what passions lay behind the calm mask that Sadler wore. He was looking towards the car park.

'If Bill is right and she fell where she was killed, what made her come into the field? There's a footpath into the woods from the car park and one straight across this field. What would she have been doing by the fence?'

Connie followed Sadler's gaze. The woman's body was about eight metres from the footpath running down the scrubby field.

'Perhaps she saw something?' said Connie. 'Or someone.'

Sadler nodded. 'The car was left in a hurry. That suggests some urgency. We need to get an estimated time when the car was driven here. Go to the house, Connie, and speak to the car's registered owner, James Lander. It'll be interesting to hear what he has to say for himself.'

*

The BMW was registered to an address in Stephenson Crescent to the west of Bampton. It was one of the newer parts of the town; good-quality 1960s housing built using the same limestone that had been used for Bampton's older residences. It looked slightly incongruous in the carefully landscaped cul-de-sacs that had been all the rage in the post-war period but the houses were sought after by families who needed a garden and a respectable Bampton address.

As Connie drew up to the large detached house, there seemed to be no evidence of occupancy. The grass in the front garden was slightly overgrown, that late-winter messiness that has diligent gardeners itching for the first dry day of spring. Connie walked up to the front door, made of solid oak by the look of it, and after searching for a bell, rapped hard with the brass knocker. She could hear the report echo through the house, the reverberation of an empty space. Definitely no signs of occupancy. She moved to the front window and peered into the gloom. She could see a large living room, stretching the full length of the house with patio doors the other end, leading, she presumed, to the back garden. The curtains were half-drawn, pulled in a way that suggested haste. On the coffee table she could see a cup full of liquid sitting next to a magazine. Not good. She rummaged in her bag for her phone and called for backup. There was no way she was going to heave her small frame through that sturdy front door.

She turned and surveyed Stephenson Crescent. The houses that ringed it were of a similar design but with enough individuality to ensure that the street couldn't be described in any sales particulars as an 'estate'. She was looking for the proverbial twitching of a lace curtain but of course times had moved on.

TV programmes such as *Crimewatch* had given concerned citizens permission to take an active interest in what was going on in their neighbourhood and most people were now willing to interrogate strangers hanging around empty properties. A man at the house directly opposite had opened his door and was standing at the entrance with his arms folded. Connie, stifling a twitch of annoyance, smiled and walked down the path and across the road towards him. He watched as she approached. Up close, he was younger than his V-necked pullover and grey trousers suggested, probably early forties. She pulled out her warrant card and watched his expression change from suspicion to open curiosity.

'I'm looking for a Mr James Lander. I believe that he lives at number twelve.'

'James? He died last year of a heart attack. It happened in the front garden one Sunday. I saw him fall over and by the time I had reached him he was gone. Nothing could be done.'

Something in his tone made Connie frown.

'I'm a doctor, a paediatrician at St Crispin's. I tried to help with CPR for about ten minutes but nothing doing. He was gone. It was a massive coronary according to the post-mortem.'

'And his wife?'

The man frowned. 'Penny? I presume she's gone away, the car's not there. She has a daughter in Kent. I assume she's visiting there.'

'When did you last see the car, Doctor . . . ?' Connie got out her notebook.

'Stephen Graham, look has anything happened? We've all been a bit worried about Penny since James died. All of us neighbours in the street, I mean. We all look out for each other and keep an eye on each other's houses.'

Connie looked behind her as the patrol car turned up and two hefty-looking constables emerged, one hitching up his trousers. She turned back to Doctor Graham.

'Worried in what way?'

'It's just that she shut herself off from us. We're a pretty sociable street; we often go to each other's parties and so on. Penny retired from the school she was teaching at just after James's death and we never really saw her. She seemed to retreat inside the house. Has anything happened?'

Connie shut her notebook. 'We've found a blue BMW registered to the address and we're making our normal enquiries. Is that the car Mrs Lander normally drove?'

The doctor seemed incapable of speech as his eyes went to the two policemen, one of whom was carrying a small, one-person ram that would be used to force open the door. He managed a nod with his mouth slightly open. Seeing she had lost his attention, Connie left him standing in the doorway and hurried across the road. One of the policemen grinned at her.

'Just happened to have it in the boot. There was a drugs raid last night and I haven't got round to signing it back in yet. We were round the corner on the way back to the station. Don't tell the boss.'

The battering ram was the modern type. As soon as the cylinder hit the solid wood, a piston fired, giving added momentum, and the right side of the door caved in. The policeman used a gloved hand to manoeuvre the lock and soon Connie was inside the living room, staring at a half-eaten sandwich and what looked like a cup of tea. She looked around the room, which had the air of a well-kept family home. Three large photos sat on a sideboard, one a graduation picture of a girl with long fair hair and the other two family shots. Connie pulled out her iPhone and took a snap of each of the photographs.

She could hear the policemen searching the rest of the house and finally the one with the smirk stuck his head round the door.

'There's no one here. Do you want us to stay?'

Connie looked at the remains of someone's last supper and shook her head. 'I'll make the call. Thanks, guys.'

Chapter 18

Some years ago, a psychologist friend of Rachel's had tried to make a link between her choice of career and the 1978 kidnapping.

'You're transferring your inability to discover what happened that day in 1978 onto your profession,' she'd told her. 'You're determined to discover the undiscoverable, know the unknowable.'

Rachel had as little time for psychoanalysis today as she'd had in 1978. The attempts to pick at the past when some things just couldn't be brought to light. The therapy sessions that followed her abduction had brought her little respite and no answers. Perhaps part of the problem was her. She hadn't really wanted to remember. The minute she had stepped into that car, a seismic change had occurred and she hadn't wanted to go back. Survival had meant forgetting. Even if that meant leaving Sophie in the past.

But her aversion to therapy didn't mean she wasn't interested in unpicking others' secrets. Although there were some truths that were for ever locked in the mists of time, other mysteries could be unravelled through persistence and diligence And the people who chose to search out their ancestors were a source of fascination.

Pam Millett was one such example. She sat opposite Rachel, her face heavily made up, beneath a photograph of her family.

The picture must have been taken in the early 1980s judging by the style of the clothes and gelled hair.

'He always went on about the war, did my granddad. It was a joke in the family, "Don't mention the war," we used to say, as it would set Granddad off. And the thing was, my grandmother hated the subject. She lost two brothers in the First World War so it was a painful subject, but Granddad, good God, you couldn't get him off the topic.'

So far, so predictable, thought Rachel. Pam Millett wanted to find out a bit more about the origins of her grandparents and there wasn't anything strange in that. And yet Rachel had gone to school with Pam's son Graham. He'd dyed his hair using peroxide at the age of fourteen, probably just after the photograph over the mantelpiece had been taken. Shaved his head at fifteen and had a drug habit by seventeen. Remarkably, he was still alive, confounding everyone's expectations, but when Rachel had asked after him, Pam had confided that she had not seen him for years. 'I assume he's still living in London.'

Graham Millett had been named after his paternal great-grandfather, who'd fought in 1917 in Arras with what had then been called the Sherwood Foresters. The Nottingham and Derbyshire Regiment. He was hardly a credit to his great-grandfather, yet his mother could see no irony in spending a significant amount of money on tracing back her roots while the next generation casually abused their bodies to the point of extinction.

'It's not about the sins of the present, is it? It's the achievements of the past I want to celebrate. And their sins if necessary.' She winked at Rachel. 'You got any servicemen in your family?'

Rachel liked Pam's irrepressible style. 'I've hardly any men in my family, full stop.'

Pam had stopped smiling and was eyeing Rachel up and down. 'I heard about the suicide of Sophie's mum. I'm sorry to hear of it.'

Rachel rustled in her handbag for car keys. 'I'm sorry too, but I hadn't heard from her for years. My only memories of her are as a child.'

'I work in Sainsbury's three times a week and she sometimes used to come in. I recognised her, of course, but I never let on.'

Rachel stopped fumbling in her bag and looked at her client. 'What was she like? Later on, I mean.'

Pam picked at a thread on her trousers. 'It's funny but I would have said that she was doing all right. She was a bit old-fashioned. I mean, I don't think she'd updated her hairstyle since the seventies, but she was friendly enough.'

'You were surprised she committed suicide, then?'

'I would've been if I hadn't seen her that last time.'

Rachel stared at Pam. 'Why? When was the last time?'

'It must have been last week. I saw her at the till and she looked dishevelled and dusty. Like she had been down in a cellar. And distraught. I was really shocked and I would've said something, but the queue behind her was a nightmare, so I just let it go. And a few days later she was dead.'

'Dusty? Mrs Jenkins was dusty?'

Pam was now defensive. 'I don't know. It was the impression I got. I'm sorry I mentioned it.'

*

Rachel left the house and sat in her car for a moment. Dusty? She turned on the ignition and drove up the hill to her cottage, checking to see how many reporters she'd have to push her way past. The street was empty. The journalists who'd huddled against the Bampton cold on the pavement opposite her front door as she left the house that morning had disappeared. Unable to believe that she'd got off so lightly, she parked the car and walked round to the back of the house, fully expecting to see them waiting at the gate at the bottom of her small garden, having decided to change position. But there was no one there either. Only the lone patrol car was sitting by the side of the road, the man in the passenger seat reading a tabloid.

She crossed over to the car. 'Everything OK, Miss Jones?' asked the driver.

'Fine. But was it anything I did? They all seem to have disappeared.'

'Something more juicy on the other side of town. A body's been found up by Truscott Fields.'

Rachel felt her world spin and the policeman must have noticed too – and remembered who he was talking to.

'Not a girl, love. A woman. And a recent death,' he said hastily. 'Nothing to concern yourself with. Just be thankful they're not pestering you any more.'

Incapable of speech, Rachel backed away and looked at her small cottage. She couldn't bear to go back in there. But her notebook was still in the house. She could go nowhere without it.

The policeman was looking at her with a concerned expression while his passenger had put down his newspaper with what Rachel thought was annoyance.

'If they're gone then there's no need to keep an eye on the house any more.'

'Sorry, miss,' said the policeman at the wheel. 'We stand down when the DI tells us to.'

Rachel turned and walked to her house, feeling the eyes of the two policemen on her.

Back in her living room, she sat at her desk and reached over to the radiator for her notebook. She opened it and with shaking hands began once more to copy out her maternal family tree, an act that never failed to soothe her. She had plenty of computer programs that would have done the trick but something in the act of writing by hand anchored her to both the present and the past. She started on the left-hand side of an A3 sheet of paper and inside a small box wrote her date of birth. She then wrote an 'm.' and put a long underline against it. No husband. And none in the offing, which was OK as in genealogy terms this maternal line would be coming to an end with her.

She thought about adding a 'd.' and leaving another line but decided that it was a horrible mixture of wild optimism and morbidity. When she died at some point no one would be likely to be filling in the date themselves. But at the bottom of the box she added 'occ.', wrote 'family historian' and smiled. Then, drawing a connecting line, she added another box and put in her mother's details. Birth, marriage and death. Mary Jones who briefly became Mary Saxton but had changed her name back to Jones before Rachel was born. Occupation – dental nurse. It had been an unremarkable life made remarkable by that one life-changing event in 1978. Next, her grandmother Nancy Jones, still alive and fighting. Here Rachel felt her usual pang of regret that her sweet grandfather Hughie wouldn't be making it onto the tree. The affable Hughie who had thrown her into the air as a child, giving her that strange exhilaration of flying that she'd so loved.

Nancy had a more interesting past, mainly because of her work as a land girl in the Second World War. She'd worked on the great Needham estate, picking cabbages, but there'd been plenty of time for dancing and chatting, if Nancy's stories were anything to go by. And Nancy had learned to smoke during those years too, a habit that, despite the family's exhortations, she'd refused to give up. Even in the nursing home, a smoking room that had been little used before Nancy's arrival was the place you were most likely to find her these days. Cigarette in one hand and, in the other, a pack of playing cards. According to one of the carers, even the most fervent anti-smokers of the residential home were willing to make an exception for a hand of rummy with Nancy.

Another line and there was her great-grandmother Mair, who'd died when Rachel was four. Spoken about with acerbity by Nancy, as the mother who didn't like men and would be willing to see off anyone who wasn't good enough for her daughter. Rachel's own mother had been less willing to discuss her headstrong grandmother and when pressed by a teenage Rachel had simply said, 'she was good in a crisis' and left it at that.

Chapter 19

By the time Sadler got to Stephenson Crescent, Connie was standing next to her car smoking a cigarette. The forensic team had obviously arrived and turfed her out and she had an air of a chess player considering her next move. Sadler pulled his car alongside her and slid down the window.

'Bored, Connie?'

She took a final drag on her cigarette. 'Not at all. I've been told to wait outside. You know how it is.'

'I hear that there's no Mr Lander.'

Connie reached inside her car window and stubbed out the cigarette in the ashtray.

'It seems like she never got round to changing over the ownership of the car. Hardly crime of the year.'

'I've spoken to the head teacher of St Paul's, Penny Lander's school. They've got an inset day today, whatever that means. It seems that there are no children at the school at the moment, so today is a good day to interview her. Do you want to come?'

'There's a daughter, apparently, who lives in Kent. We need to contact her as next of kin.'

'I'll get Palmer onto it. Hop in with me and I'll phone him on the way to the school.'

Connie glanced at her car. She shouted at the police constable guarding the entrance to the house, 'I'm leaving this here. Make sure that forensics know it's mine.'

Sadler winced as she got in and slammed the door of his car. 'They've got decent locks these days. It doesn't need shutting by brute force.'

Out of the corner of his eye he saw Connie smirk.

St Paul's school was about a quarter of a mile away. They could have walked it if they'd wanted to. Possibly Penny Lander had occasionally done so. According to the head teacher, there were still two entrances to the school, as there had been in 1978. The first was a pedestrian path, past the church that had given the school its name, and through the adjoining church-yard. The second was the more commonly used main entrance off Tideland Road. Rachel Jones and Sophie Jenkins had been heading towards the churchyard entrance when they had been abducted in 1978. Pupils had regularly used it at that time, but over the intervening years parents had begun to take their children to school by car.

He parked in the staff car park and they entered the school building, passing by the secretary's office, which was empty. A few teachers were in the classrooms, obviously making prepar-ations for the following day. As they passed one teacher in the corridor, she turned around and asked, 'DI Sadler? I'm Sally Arden, the head here.'

Sally Arden was tiny, about five feet tall wearing very high heels which were presumably to give her an air of authority. She was at least ten years younger than him, and although her bust-ling personality gave her an air of confidence, Sadler wondered how superficial this would prove to be. Something about her struck him as false; an essence of sham, of a mantle assumed by her that wasn't anchored in her personality. She took them both into her office and shut the door.

'Would you like some tea?'

He looked at Connie and she shook her head.

'No, thanks. You're probably wondering about the reason we've come to see you. I mentioned over the phone that it was about a teacher who used to work here at the school. Her name was Penny Lander, although I'm not sure if you'll remember her. Were you head teacher when she worked here?'

'Only just. I took up the post at Easter last year and Penny retired that summer. So I only had a term with her. She had a very good reputation here. Not particularly old-fashioned, given her age, if you see what I mean. She'd kept up to date with advances in teaching methods and standards. She didn't particularly mind the bureaucracy. I was sad to see her go.'

'Why did she retire?' asked Connie.

'She'd reached sixty, which was the age she'd decided to leave teaching. I was surprised. Her husband had died earlier in the year and the plans they'd made, travel and so on, were suddenly redundant. She gave me the impression of being at a loose end. But, to be honest, teaching is hard at any age. Running round after kids when you're over sixty isn't fun at all.'

Sally Arden looked at Sadler expectantly. She had a chirpy personality that he didn't like. He noticed Connie was frowning too. He suspected that Sally Arden wouldn't be to Connie's taste either.

'We're here,' Sadler told her, 'because a body has been found near Truscott Woods that we have reason to believe is Penny Lander.'

He watched the woman's face fall and a flush spread up her neck. For a moment he felt sorry for her, although Connie's expression implied satisfaction.

'Did she kill herself?' she asked.

'We're awaiting the results of the post-mortem so at the moment we're treating the death as suspicious.'

'Are you aware of anything or anyone who may have wished Mrs Lander harm,' asked Connie, watching Sally Arden closely.

'No. Nothing at all.'

Some of the woman's chirpiness had disappeared but the smile remained.

'What about another teacher? Who's the longest serving member of staff you have here?'

'Jane Thomson. Miss. She insists on the "miss". Unfortunately, she *is* of the old-fashioned school. She'll be retiring next year and it's probably about time. I'll get her for you.'

And she rose quickly and left the room.

Sadler had got to know the minor tics in Connie's personality. He didn't look at her now, not least because he knew at present she wouldn't be forthcoming. She would store it up for later and then give it all guns blazing. He preferred her like that. It was her reticence that always caused him pangs of anxiety. With Connie, her silence was usually a sign of deep thinking. She would only share when she had reached her conclusions, and that was never good in a team, especially one working on a murder investigation.

The door of the room reopened and Sally Arden re-entered, followed by a much older woman whom she introduced as Jane Thomson. The head teacher had obviously revealed the news of Penny Lander's death to her colleague, a tactical mistake, and Sadler had to quell the spurt of irritation that was his first impulse. Imparting the news of a victim's death was the first line in a murder enquiry. He cursed himself for not insisting that she keep the news quiet; it was a beginner's mistake and he wasn't an amateur. He saw Connie shoot him a sideways look.

Jane Thomson was tall and thin, her grey hair cut into an old-fashioned bob with a severe fringe. This was a woman who carried an air of competency but was a textbook example of how authority wasn't enough in the teaching profession any longer. To the students who attended this admittedly middle-class school, she would look like a mix of Mary Poppins and Nanny McPhee. Without invitation she dropped onto the sofa against the side wall.

'I can't believe it. Penny, dead. I never would have thought it.' She seemed visibly shocked by the news.

Sadler looked up at Sally Arden and, taking the hint, she left. Jane Thomson sat on the sofa, dry-eyed but with a tissue in her hands.

Connie leaned forward in her chair. 'Miss Thomson. Were you teaching here when Rachel Jones and Sophie Jenkins went missing?'

Whatever the woman had been expecting, it wasn't this. Her head jerked up and she looked from one to the other.

'What's that got to do with anything? Just because Yvonne Jenkins committed suicide last week doesn't mean Penny would have followed suit. That was years ago. We've all lived with the guilt since then.'

'Guilt?' asked Sadler.

Jane Thomson looked out of the window. 'I was Rachel and Sophie's form teacher. It wasn't like now where there is in effect a procedure for every eventuality. It wears you down. But then things were a bit freer. If a child didn't turn up for school, the parents were supposed to ring up and tell us. But not all remembered and although we were then supposed to chase, we didn't always remember to do that either, and we certainly wouldn't have had time before the lunch break. It was the same that day. I took the register. Both girls were absent and I marked them as so. And I never thought of them again until the school secretary came into my classroom that afternoon and called me out. I couldn't believe it when I heard what had happened.'

'Had you cautioned your pupils about the dangers of getting into a car with strangers?' asked Connie.

Jane Thomson looked angry. 'Of course we did. We even had a policewoman come into the school to talk to the children.'

'So you were surprised that Sophie and Rachel would have got into the car.'

'Yes, I was. Especially Sophie, who was a very sensible child. Very obedient.'

Perhaps it was Sophie's obedience that got her into trouble, thought Sadler.

'And Rachel?' asked Connie.

'She too would have known not to get into a car,' admitted Jane Thomson, pursing her lips.

'Although the fact it was a woman might have confused them,' said Sadler.

'A stranger is a stranger.'

Sadler could see the dogmatic personality that would make this woman so hard to manage. He changed tack. 'Can you remember at all Penny Lander's reaction to the kidnapping? Any comments she might have made at the time, for example.'

Jane Thomson looked at the tissue in her hands. 'She didn't

say anything at school. I remember there was a discussion about whether to send all the pupils home, but it would have been a logistical nightmare, not least because not everyone had a phone in those days. We were asked to keep the classes going, which was very hard, particularly for me, as I couldn't help looking at the empty desks.'

'Can you remember exactly how and what you were told?'

Jane Thomson frowned. 'We were all – all the teachers, I mean – called individually from the classroom by Miss Coles, who was the head teacher then. The class was left on its own for the few minutes that it took to give us the news – that Rachel Jones had been found at Truscott Woods claiming she had been kidnapped.'

'Claiming?' asked Connie. 'Who said that?'

'Perhaps they didn't use the word *claim*.' Jane Thomson looked down at the handkerchief in her hands.

Sadler could see Connie assessing the teacher. 'Back to Penny Lander. So you had no time during the afternoon to discuss the kidnapping with her? What about after the children had left?'

'Not then either. Some of the parents had already got wind of what had happened so we spent the time after lessons reassuring them and making sure the children got off safely. Some of them picked up on what was happening and were frightened to walk home, so we did have to call parents then.'

'So you didn't speak at all about the incident, until when?'

'Penny rang me that evening. We rarely called each other outside school hours, but we did have each other's numbers in case something came up. We just talked about what had happened. We hadn't been told much by the police then.'

'But you spoke of guilt,' Connie persisted. 'You've explained why you might have felt guilty because you didn't follow up on their absence. But why would Penny Lander feel responsible? She wasn't their teacher.'

Jane Thomson looked again out of the window. 'I don't know why but she did feel responsible. We all did. It was different in those days. As a school we felt we were a whole unit. We felt collective responsibility towards what happened to those girls.'

Sadler willed himself not to look at Connie but she was shifting slightly in her seat, always a clue to her repressed excitement. And it was justified too. Collective responsibility wouldn't account for Penny Lander's guilt and her death so close to Yvonne Jenkins's suicide was a coincidence too far. But Jane Thomson looked like a woman who would hold on to her secrets. He only had one more chance.

'Miss Thomson. We are treating the death of Penny Lander as both unexplained and suspicious. Is there anyone that you can think of who might have wished Penny Lander harm?'

The look of shock and astonishment told him that, for the moment, Jane Thomson would be of no further help to them.

Chapter 20

Sadler and Connie sat in the Aroma cafe on Bampton High Street sipping the strong coffee that made it famous amongst the locals. If you walked off the street into the cafe, you would never expect the riches that the place provided, but it held its own against the designer franchise across the road. There were booths with hard red plastic benches, the type made to be easily wiped down. It was clean, but garish, and for different reasons both Sadler and Connie looked out of place. It was popular with students and Connie guessed that Sadler was one of the oldest people there, with the exception of the woman behind the till. Connie stood out because of her well-cut clothes and carefully applied make-up. The cafe was run by Greek Cypriots who had ended up in Bampton after the crisis of 1974. The coffee was strong, rich and cheap. Eleni, who ran the till, watched over proceedings with a practised eye and payment was upfront for a large cup of black coffee, with a free top-up if you wanted it. Just the once, though. Milk and sugar were the optional extras.

Connie knew that Sadler liked his coffee black and strong. She'd hesitated to suggest the cafe. She imagined he would want something more upmarket, but the readiness with which he agreed suggested he knew the place already. Intriguingly, he also seemed to know Eleni behind the till.

'It's been quite a week, hasn't it? We started off with a suicide. And now we have a murder, or at least one that looks that way.'

For a moment, remembering the body in the field, Connie felt the coffee in her mouth turn sour. 'Will we get more resources now? We both think there's a link between Yvonne Jenkins's death and Penny Lander's. Will you be able to make a case to Llewellyn?'

Sadler looked across at the woman at the counter. 'Of course we'll get more resources; this is a current murder case. The problem is that if the two deaths are connected, then the answer will still lie in the past. And we don't have enough to go on. I feel like I'm scrabbling around in the dark.'

'If Penny Lander was murdered two days ago, that was still after Yvonne Jenkins killed herself. Which means that whatever a connection might be, Mrs Jenkins was already dead and can't have been the person directly responsible.'

Sadler took a sip of his coffee. 'It would certainly have been neat if Yvonne Jenkins had committed the crime, although I doubt that we would be finished with the case. Llewellyn would want to know why Yvonne killed a teacher in her daughter's old school. And, to be honest, so would I.'

'So we're looking for the murderer of Penny Lander, given Bill's preliminary assessment of cause of death. And what about Yvonne Jenkins? Do you think something prompted her act of suicide?'

Sadler looked at her with his pale blue eyes, which never failed to put a dart of fear through her.

'Suicide is always a difficult act to quantify. Things are rarely clear-cut. But there's a lot to think about. We have a girl who is kidnapped and then released, apparently unharmed.

We have another girl, kidnapped and presumably killed.'

'Why are you talking about them separately? They were kidnapped together.'

'Because I'm starting to think, Connie, that the mistake in the investigation may have been the fact that the case was never separated. We have two different types of victim here. Rachel Jones was the victim of an unexplained kidnapping. Sophie Jenkins was kidnapped and either killed or permanently removed from her home. I suspect the reason for that is the key to the whole case.'

'But it could have been an accident. Sophie accidentally killed, for example, and then the abductors panicked and released Rachel Jones.'

Sadler shook his head. 'It doesn't sound right. Why not kill Rachel and then there are no witnesses at all. Something else went on in that woods and that's where we are going to start.'

'So who was the intended victim, Sophie or Rachel?'

Sadler made a face and Connie leaned back against the hard bench in frustration. They would be splitting the 1978 case into two investigations and now they had Penny Lander to add to the mix.

'What about Rachel Jones?' asked Connie. 'Are you sure she remembers nothing at all.'

'She sounded pretty convincing and I believe her, to a certain extent.'

Connie looked up at the qualification. 'You think she's holding something back though?'

Sadler smiled at her. 'I'm certain of it.'

'Will it be important?'

'It's difficult to say. But she's not telling us everything. The interesting question is whether she's deliberately holding out on us or whether she knows something but is currently unable to tell us anything.'

'I could go back and have a look at the police interviews with her at the time, if you think it'd help.'

'I don't think so. I don't think interviewing children amounted to much then. Everything was taken at face value.'

'Do you think it's significant that neither of them had their fathers living with them? A link that might explain why the two of them were taken together?'

Sadler picked up a spoon and began to stir his coffee. 'Go on.'

'I don't know. It's just an idea. It's just that it was quite un-usual for those days – one-parent families. They weren't the norm they are now. I mean, I had two parents; didn't you?'

He looked at her and she suspected that she had pushed him too far. He gave little information about his background. She had heard he had a girlfriend and that he'd grown up in Bampton. But that was it. Finally, he answered.

'I did have two parents and you're right, very few of my friends came from one-parent families, although I think that did change later.' The spoon that he had been using to stir the coffee clanked onto the table. 'I've been thinking a lot about family recently. Something about this case, I suppose. My father, who was a presence throughout my childhood but who I never really knew.'

'Me too.' He was staring at her as she spoke. That was the problem with Sadler. He always looked right into your eyes. Hadn't she read somewhere that it was a form of aggression? 'I mean, I've been thinking about my family too. My mother. It's funny you've been thinking of the fathers but it's brought my mother back to me. Not that she's dead or anything.' Connie stopped. It wasn't really the time for confidences.

'Go on.'

She could feel a colour rising in her cheeks. 'My mother was an alcoholic when I was growing up. One of these educated ones that you read about in the papers now. She was a pharmacist, had her own little shop in Matlock. She ran it until she retired. But every day, the minute the shop shut at five, she started drinking. Wine and gin were her tipples.'

'Did no one notice?'

'Notice? Everyone knew. That's the funny thing about it. Everyone knew and did nothing. That's what you and I need to remember about the past. That secrets could be everywhere and no one would mention a thing.'

'I'm closing up!' Both Sadler and Connie started at the loud voice and Sadler looked at his watch.

'We'd better go.'

As they left the cafe, Connie was intrigued by the cheery goodbye the woman behind the till shouted after them. It appeared to be directed at Sadler. He smiled back but ignored Connie's enquiring look. He seemed keen to get back to the office, where the investigation team into Penny Lander's death needing assembling and tasks had to be assigned. The promised more important case that Llewellyn had warned them of when they had picked up the 1978 kidnapping had now materialised but, to Connie's relief, Sadler wanted her for the moment to keep digging into 1978. She would join the team in the incident room later that evening for an update. Palmer, she presumed, would be given the initial choice tasks but, given the obvious connection between the cases, she wasn't exactly wasted pursuing the old investigation.

Connie's problem was that most of the people who might have been in a position to help her were dead: Rachel's mother Mary, Yvonne Jenkins and now Penny Lander. Jane Thomson had told them everything that she was planning to. So, as far as Connie could see, the women in the old case, dead or alive, were not going to give up their secrets easily. That just left the men. Sophie's father, Peter Jenkins, and Rachel's, a Paul Saxton. Saxton had apparently died before Rachel was born, which should be easy enough to check. Peter Jenkins might be more difficult to track down, but he'd been interviewed in the original investigation so at least there was a starting point.

But now that she was temporarily removed from Sadler's watchful presence, she intended to have a quick peek at the files from the initial investigation. Even if it was a quick size-up of the mountainous pile of paperwork, she would at least feel connected to that initial investigation. Which meant a trip to the constabulary's records centre.

It took about fifteen minutes to reach the small industrial estate on the outskirts of Bampton where the files were housed. Once inside the vast warehouse, the place seemed deserted. If the building hadn't been so modern, Connie would have been tempted to look out for ghosts, such was the feeling of complete isolation with only the hum of the air-conditioning unit, set to high even in this cold weather. Connie counted three people in total as she walked to the relevant rack, two of whom were wearing headphones.

The rack holding the records for the 1978 case was about half full of stuff, somewhere between thirty and forty boxes, she estimated. She opened the lid of the first few cardboard cartons, most of which contained files full of case notes. The different colours suggested a system of some sorts, but, without any explanation of the colour coding, the files seemed random to Connie. One carton was labelled 'Interviews' and Connie heaved this box on to the trolley she had been provided with. A cursory look through the other cartons revealed more files until to her surprise a lid she lifted revealed a void inside. Empty? Connie lifted off the lid fully, tipped the box towards her and peered inside. There was a plastic evidence bag lying across the bottom, slightly cloudy with age. Inside was something white with a slight ribbed pattern. Connie touched the item through the plastic and saw with surprise that it was a girl's sock.

Chapter 21

Nancy was in the smoking room and the nurse who pointed Rachel to her grandmother's whereabouts whispered that Nancy was trying to cut down. This came as no surprise to Rachel, who'd noticed that Nancy's lungs were finally beginning to show the strain. Although for a woman who wouldn't see eighty-five again it might even be expected. The doctor who came to the Maytree nursing home had a soft spot for Nancy, recognising perhaps, in the still dyed brown hair and powdered face, a former beauty. Nancy's cutting down of cigarettes amounted to missing out her two o'clock smoke, but with tea due at four, she was obviously having a quick one in front of a game of clock patience.

Rachel sat down and batted away the puffs of smoke with irritation. 'You'll kill yourself with that habit.'

Nancy smirked, enjoying the long-running joke between them. 'I'm two minutes off finishing this,' she said, nodding at the game, and Rachel sat back in her chair watching her grandmother neatly place the cards into piles.

Finally finished, Nancy crossed her hands over her stomach and regarded her. 'So what's new?'

Rachel snorted, and picking up a magazine from a side table started wafting it over her face. A shadow of concern passed over Nancy.

'What's the matter?'

With her grandmother staring at her, Rachel could feel her eyes beginning to fill. 'They've found the body of a woman at Truscott Fields.'

'A woman . . .'

'Yes. Nothing to do with my case, apparently, but I haven't been able to find out anything about it on the news. It just says a body.'

'And just after Yvonne Jenkins killed herself.' Nancy looked down at the cards and carefully gathered them into a single pile. 'Do you think they're connected? The two cases, I mean.'

Rachel felt her eyes begin to sting with the smoke. 'I don't know. I'm not sure. I don't even know who it is. I tried to ring Superintendent Llewellyn but he was out. They came to interview me, though. About Mrs Jenkins's death.'

'She lasted longer than your mother.' Nancy's tone was neutral but Rachel could detect a sliver of flint in the words.

'I doubt she was happy, though. I think Mum was.'

Nancy nodded and inspected her long painted nails. 'Like my own mum, she was. A realist. Took whatever life threw at her and got on with it.'

'I'm like that too.' Rachel could hear the plaintive note in her voice but was unable to stop it.

Nancy had lit another cigarette and was regarding her. 'You're a bit like them both, I suppose. But those two – thick as thieves they were. Just don't get too much like them. It's not too late.'

'What do you mean, "too late"?'

'She could never stand men could my mother. They were a pain in the arse as far as she was concerned and better off out of the way.'

'She never remarried after . . .'

Nancy was snorting. 'Buried him when I was twelve and it was good riddance as far as she was concerned.'

Rachel reached out to touch Nancy. 'But you weren't like that. You and Granddad. It was a love match.'

Nancy's expression had softened. 'But your mum went the way of her nan. I told her she should remarry. If not for her sake, then for yours. But she wasn't having any of it. The look she gave me when I suggested it. You're not like that, a man-hater, are you?'

'Nan!' Rachel was shocked. 'Mum didn't hate men. She just . . .' Rachel came to a standstill.

Nancy was looking at her through the smoke. She reached over and patted Rachel's arm. 'It's been a while since you brought a man with you on your visits. Don't leave it too late, love. Look how happy Hughie and me were. I'll never forget that barn dance.'

The story. Every family has one: an incident that's revisited time and time again, passed down through generations, so that the past becomes familiar. And Nancy's story was the barn dance. Rachel opened her mouth to interrupt, but Nancy was off, closing her eyes to better evoke the memories.

'Mum had patched a dress for the do, her favourite dove grey number with little covered buttons running down the centre, bought from Marmets in Cardiff. It'd gone under the arms, but a bit of grey thread and the lining of my old school hat soon repaired the hole.'

'Make do and mend.' Rachel jumped at the voice behind her. It was Vivian, she with the glamorous 1950s name and the home-dyed ginger hair. She wheeled the tea trolley around five times a day and eked out the intervening hours by chatting to the residents. She made no move to go now.

Nancy carried on, unheeding. 'We were sick of the winter. The war was never-ending although we were all excited that America was finally going to fight with us. It looked like, now, we might win it. We could still hear the German planes overhead on their way to the Manchester Ship Canal but they weren't as bad as the year before.'

'I was born nine months to the day after the last bomb fell on Matlock,' said Vivian. They both ignored her.

'I was on the dance floor, such as it was, with Hughie swinging me round and round. Mum gave me hell afterwards. She said my skirt showed more thigh than she thought proper.'

Rachel knew the story inside out. Her great-grandmother Mair had sewn in some silk panels, offcuts from the parachute material produced at the mill where she worked, and it had added volume to the skirt. As Nancy danced it lifted slightly, showing off her bare legs and causing outrage. Or perhaps not. Nancy liked to embroider a story and surely, in the general scheme of things, the fear of invasion and the loss of young men to the war, Mair would have turned a blind eye to a flash of leg.

'We'd talked of nothing else all over Christmas. Waiting for the barn dance being organised by the Needhams. The vicar had been cross, saying we should concentrate on Christmas first. But we were so excited. Mrs Needham had organised a raffle and the first prize was a leg of lamb. But no one wanted that. We all wanted second, which was a pair of silk stockings.'

'I bet you looked lovely, stockings or not,' cut in Vivian. 'Do you want a cuppa, love, too?' she asked Rachel as she handed Nancy her milky tea. Rachel shook her head.

'I wasn't bad,' admitted Nancy, 'even though I say it myself. It was the start of me and Hughie courting properly.'

'And Mair liked Hughie,' said Rachel. 'You've always said that she had a soft spot for him.'

Nancy narrowed her eyes, taking a final draw on the cigarette. 'It didn't start off well, through. She threw a fit that evening; I can remember it like yesterday. One minute I was dancing and the next, she was dragging me off home. Hughie was left standing there like a lemon.'

Rachel frowned. She'd heard this part too, although for the first time it held a jarring note. Mair had grown up on a farm. She must have known about the birds and the bees. Surely Nancy flashing her leg wouldn't have been enough to send even the uppity Mair into such a rage.

'What? She came onto the dance floor and just grabbed you. Are you sure something hadn't happened?'

'Nothing! I was frogmarched out of there like I'd been caught with my knickers down.'

Rachel could hear Vivian snorting with laughter behind her.

'And it was right in front of the Needhams and all their friends too. There they were feeding their kids nasty cake that someone had managed to concoct using powdered egg. And they're all watching me as I'm being dragged outside by Mum, who didn't even look at them or say goodbye. When she had it on her, there was nothing you could do.' Nancy shook her head as if to rid herself of the unwanted humiliation. 'But it was the start of me and Hughie. He was always perfectly polite to Mum but would take no nonsense from her. And that's what you need. Find someone like your granddad and don't become a man-hater like my mum.'

Rachel, swallowing her incredulity, took her Nan's hand in her own. 'This whole business with Mrs Jenkins has been stressing me out. It's just so strange and it's made me think again about 1978 and what happened then.'

She looked at Nancy, wondering if she would be prepared to discuss those days again, but she had picked up the pack of cards and was arranging them once more in a circle.

'These things are best forgotten.'

Chapter 22

'Sadler! I've got something.'

Even though the mobile reception was poor, Connie could hear Sadler moving papers around on his desk. It was a continual ritual for him. He would leave his office as neat as a pin and come back to an assortment of files and reports left in a heap on his desk by a variety of station personnel. He never said anything, as far as she was aware, but nothing would get done until the tidying had been completed. So, now, she had only half his attention.

'I'm having a good look at the files at the moment. When Rachel Jones was found in Truscott Woods she didn't have any shoes and socks on. The police, I think, suspected some sexual connotation and tried to keep it quiet, but it was in all the newspaper reports at the time. It leaked out and the press got hold of it.'

'I vaguely remember.' Sadler sounded distracted. 'I thought we'd ruled out a sexual motive.'

'That's not what I'm trying to say. The thing is the shoes and one of the socks were subsequently found on the track leading from the woods that Rachel had run up to reach the Bampton Road. But the other sock was never found, so police presumably thought it had been left in the kidnapper's car.'

She had his full attention. 'And?'

'When I went up in the attic the afternoon that Yvonne

Jenkins was found in the hotel, there were two tea chests there. Inside one, I found a child's sock crumpled.'

'From what I understand, Yvonne Jenkins had an obsessive personality. It's no surprise she kept items of her missing child's clothes.'

'But it matches the one that was found on Rachel Jones.' Connie lifted up the evidence bag and dangled it in front of her mobile as if willing Sadler to see it. 'I've retrieved the original sock from the evidence box in 1978 – don't say anything, you did say I could go and have a look if I wanted – and it matches the one I found in Yvonne Jenkins's attic.'

Sadler had started shuffling papers again. 'You sure about this?'

'They look identical. They have a row of flowers running down each side. I'm going to send it to the lab to be analysed to make sure they're a match. You OK with that?'

'I think we have to check. And if they are proved to be a pair – you're suggesting that Yvonne Jenkins must have played a role in the kidnapping of 1978?'

No, thought Connie. *No, no, no.*

'I think one "no" would suffice, Con. I do understand the meaning of the word.'

Damn, she had said it out loud.

'It's not right. That sock being there. Something really strange has gone on. Everything in that tea chest was neatly folded and that sock had been shoved down the side. As an afterthought or an addition.'

'It doesn't rule out her involvement in the kidnapping, though, does it? The rest of the clothes belong to her daughter. This sock, if it's a match, will belong to Rachel, so why should it be given the same care as Sophie's clothes?'

'Yes, but why is it in the same chest in the first place?'

Connie could hear a chair creak. The morning tidy was clearly over. 'Let's mull it over. Call me if you have anything else. Do you know where Palmer is? He's not on leave yet, is he?'

'Not till next week. But I've no idea where he is. Sorry.'

Connie cut the connection and eyed the mouldy carton that she had removed from the file storage. She had chosen a different one from the evidence box where she had discovered Rachel's sock. The number of boxes inside the storage facility had felt like a setback, but what she wanted really was a feel of the participants in the 1978 investigation. Who they'd investigated and why. Opening the box, a whiff of stagnant decay assailed her nostrils and she jerked her head back, causing her neck to crick alarmingly. The buff beige folders had been assembled carefully, written in small handwriting which looked like a relic from another era, full of loops and swirls. She mentally noted the colour of the files. Perhaps beige was for interviewees. She picked up the first one that came to hand, entitled 'Interview with Peter Jenkins'. Leaning back, Connie rested against one of the kitchen units and started to read.

Peter Jenkins didn't appear to have left his home for a grand sexual passion or for an adventurous middle age. Another motive must have compelled him to start afresh with a new woman. His job as a lecturer at Bampton technical college had brought him into contact with a secretary called Margaret, a divorcee with two young children. Reading between the lines, he obviously had a 'type' because Margaret sounded like a clone of Yvonne Jenkins – slim and well dressed. He had left his wife to set up home with Margaret and, at the time of the interview, both of her children were calling him dad. He claimed to have had no contact with his daughter since the day he had left the family home the previous year, a fact that he seemed to offer without justification. Connie could just remember when divorce had been a source of shame and fathers had just disappeared. Thank God times had changed now, she thought.

Connie flicked through the file. On the day of the girls' kidnapping, Peter Jenkins had apparently been lecturing in front of a class for most of the morning. A number of students had been interviewed, had backed up his alibi and he had been immediately removed as a suspect from the enquiry. The car he had driven to work was the family's pea green Austin Allegro. And Rachel in her statement had been adamant that the car had either been white or a very pale colour.

Margaret, Peter Jenkins's soon-to-be wife, had also been investigated, and although she couldn't find a witness to confirm that she had been in the house all morning, the fact that she couldn't drive, nor did she have access to a car other than his, meant that she too had been eliminated.

Connie put the file down with a frown. Sadler was right, really. The coppers then had done a pretty good job. She wouldn't have done anything differently. They'd interviewed two obvious suspects, checked their alibis and then eliminated them from the enquiry. It was funny that both Yvonne and Margaret Jenkins were from a generation of women who never learned to drive, but again this was the 1970s and entirely plausible. And then there was the question of motive. Why would either of them want to kidnap Sophie when presumably

Peter Jenkins could have had access through legal custody if he had so wanted?

Connie riffled through the box of interviews but could find nothing to indicate whether they'd attempted to confirm the death of Rachel Jones's father sometime in 1970. There was certainly no file under the name of Paul Saxton. Perhaps Mary Jones had readily produced a death certificate and it had been left at that? It should be easy enough to check on the work computer when she got back to the office.

*

The phone on Sadler's desk rang and Scott, the pathologist's young assistant, came on the line.

'DI Sadler? Doctor Shields has just finished the post-mortem. He asked if you would call in to see him.'

Sadler put down the report he had been reading. 'Anything urgent?'

Scott's voice dropped a fraction. 'You know how it is. Everything's urgent. But yes, I think you should come sooner rather than later.'

'I thought Connie was the detective of choice these days. What have I done to deserve the honour?'

There was a pause. 'I don't think it is what *you've* done but rather what someone else did.'

'Right. I'm on my way down.'

Sadler passed Palmer on the way out of the station and his visage was one of pure misery. Sadler thought about asking him what the problem was, but considering that his wedding was taking place soon, it was probably marriage related. And that was something he knew nothing about and didn't particularly want to get involved in.

Snow was starting to fall again in Bampton and, combined with gusty winds, descended in swirls in front of the car windscreen as Sadler drove to the hospital, far more carefully than Palmer would have done. As he pulled into St Crispin's and parked outside the prefabricated building where Bill Shields carried out his post-mortems, he placed his police pass carefully so that the hospital's parking attendants could see it. After he was buzzed in, Bill waved him into his office and leaned over to switch on the kettle. Sadler was surprised at how long it had been since he had sat inside that small room. For years they had taken tea and discussed the results of the pathologist's work, but since Connie had joined the team he hadn't once set foot inside the building. Connie and the pathologist had, in layman's terms, 'hit it off', although what the genial but slightly grumpy doctor had found in common with the spiky and very grumpy Connie Childs eluded Sadler.

When he had been handed a large mug of steaming tea the pathologist started.

'Toxicology results are back from the lab on Yvonne Jenkins. Nothing other than the large amount of diazepam and vodka that she used for the overdose. Not that I was expecting anything else but I thought you'd want to know. I've reported the results to the coroner and I expect him to release the body for burial fairly soon.'

'So it looks like suicide?'

'She died of an excess of diazepam in her body which, combined with the alcohol, proved fatal. She went to sleep and never woke up. It's not a drug I like particularly. Nasty reputation. People die accidentally, but in this case it looks like it was deliberate.'

Sadler drank his tea and winced. 'Jesus, Bill, I'd forgotten you like it strong.'

The pathologist grinned. 'It's not just coffee that you can make strong, Sadler. This tea's just like my mother used to make. Coats your innards orange.'

'Well, you would know.' Sadler put his cup to one side. 'So you've got me all the way down here and now you're being coy. What did you find out about Penny Lander?'

'Penny Lander. Well, that turned out to be an interesting PM. The body, as you know, wasn't in a bad state. The covering of leaves and snow to some extent mitigated exposure to the elements. As I said to you *in situ*, there was clear evidence of a ligature around the victim's neck. A thin but strong rope. My best guess is a guy-rope. Any of the camping shops around here would sell them for tents. It's gone off to the lab for analysis.'

'So she was strangled?'

'The rope caused compression of the carotid arteries which resulted in a lack of blood to the brain.'

'And this was the cause of death?'

'Exactly. However, I haven't got you down here to tell you that. What I saw at the scene, and was confirmed during my examination, was evidence of manual strangulation as well.'

'You mean . . .'

'There were finger marks around the victim's neck, consistent with what I'd expect from throttling.'

Sadler massaged his temples. 'So Penny Lander was throttled first?'

'Which caused a compression of her airways – I can see

from the damage to the larynx. She would have suffered what we call "air hunger", a frightening sensation of lack of breath.'

'The damage to the larynx wasn't because of the rope?'

'Well, of course the rope caused damage too, but this was on top of the initial injuries caused by the hands of the attacker.'

'So Penny Lander was overpowered through manual strangulation and then the rope was used to kill her. You sure it was that way round?'

Bill Shields shot him a look. 'I'm sure. Do you want me to go over—'

Sadler raised his hands. 'Sorry.'

The pathologist looked mollified. Connie clearly could handle Bill better than he could.

'So that's why I called you down here. I've got evidence of two types of strangulation: manual and ligature. The first to overpower the victim and the second to kill.'

The pathologist took a sip of his tea.

'I think I'm basically looking at my first case where the victim was strangled twice.'

Chapter 23

'Rachel, are you all right?'

Her neighbour Jenny had opened the front door of her cottage when she had spotted Rachel making her way to the car. Not a bad ID, considering it was pitch black with only the orangey glow of a single street lamp.

Rachel halted for a moment. 'I can't stop, I'm on my way to the library. I'm giving a talk to the local history society. I'll catch up with you tomorrow maybe.'

'Yes, but I heard on the news about . . .'

Rachel waved a hand as she got into the car and slammed the door. A body found in Truscott Woods would inevitably be associated with her despite the intervening years, especially coming so soon after Yvonne Jenkins's death.

As she drove towards the library, she prayed that the scant preparation she had given her speech that evening wouldn't be noticed. She was usually more diligent when speaking in public. She needed the twin reassurances of preparation and knowledge. But tonight she would need to rely on her experience. Because her turmoil had left her no mental energy to do anything else.

There was a difference between local history and genealogy of course. Local history was the history of Bampton and the nearby Derbyshire towns. Some of the people attending these meetings had no interest in their own personal histories but were fascinated by the landscape and buildings that surrounded them. Those tracing their family histories, on the other hand, weren't always interested in the physical environment but the complex relationships that emerged from developing a family tree. But there was a crossover, and when Rachel gave a talk to the society she usually managed to find a topic of interest for local historians.

Richard Weiss, whose paternal family had arrived in Britain from the Kiev pogroms in 1905, ran the group. His great-grandfather Avram, who had originally settled in Bristol, finding employment amongst the docks, had looked to move his family up the social scale and had relocated to Bampton, where he worked at the town's tiny wharf. Despite the canal's demise, the family had stayed and Avram's son Benjamin – Richard Weiss's grandfather – used the advantages offered by the now-defunct grammar school to become a respected solicitor in Bampton. One of Benjamin's sons, Daniel, had taken over the family practice, while another had become an actor in London. In turn, the reins had passed to Daniel's son Richard and, although there were other partners, he was the only member of the Weiss family still working in the legal profession.

One day, bored with his fill of domestic disputes and cantankerous heirs, Richard had turned his eyes on his own family and begun to trace his lineage. Fascinated by the Bampton connection, he had set up a local history society which now ran to about eighty members and met on a monthly basis in Bampton library. About half that number would probably turn up tonight.

Rachel had first met Richard about five years earlier. It was strange that their paths hadn't crossed earlier, given the parochiality of Bampton. It was Sydney Markham, the senior librarian, who'd first introduced them. Rachel had been suspicious of her motives, sensing a potential matchmaking attempt. But Richard, with his easy manner and relaxed view of the world, had pre-empted any discomfort by confiding in her that he had recently finished with his girlfriend – which he said was just as well, given the amount of work he had on at the office – and they had fallen into a relaxed friendship which, although unthreatening had, if she was totally honest with herself, an undercurrent of something else. She certainly found him attractive but couldn't decipher his feelings towards her beyond his open kindness.

Rachel could hear her phone ringing in her bag. She hoped it wasn't the library cancelling the talk. With one hand on the wheel, she retrieved the phone from her bag and saw she'd missed a call from Superintendent Llewellyn. With a talk to make in front of people, she needed her composure intact. She'd call him afterwards.

At the library Sydney was waiting for her at the front entrance. This was the first sign of anything unusual. Rachel often saw her when she visited during the day, but she had never seen her before at a history group meeting. Sydney immediately pre-empted any questions.

'I've come here to support you. God knows, with what you've been through, people should be leaving you alone, but it's the question-and-answer session I'm worried about.'

'There aren't any journalists here, are there?' asked Rachel. 'It's not advertised on my website.'

'No, and I didn't get round to putting it on the library's site either,' Sydney admitted. 'It's our usual regulars I'm worried about. Most are sensitive but there's always one. Or in this case three. They'll couch it in terms of "here to support you", of course. But really they're nosy beggars and will want to ask you about the murder today.'

Rachel stared at Sydney and felt her mouth go dry. 'The murder at Truscott Fields? Just because it's the same location people are going to try and link it with my kidnapping? I've just about had enough of this.'

Sydney was now staring back at her. 'It's not just the location, Rachel. Haven't you heard who it is? Remember Mrs Lander at St Paul's? I don't think she was ever your teacher. But she taught both my boys and a bloomin' good teacher she was too.'

'Mrs Lander is dead?' Rachel felt her legs begin to shake. She made for the nearest chair in the corridor. Sydney sat down next to her, clutching her arm in sympathy.

'They say she was strangled. But that's just gossip from Mrs Atkins who came in and whose son is a dispatcher at the police station. It's not made it into the papers yet.'

No wonder those journalists had headed away from the house with such speed, thought Rachel. But now it was a dead cert that they'd be back.

Rachel looked at the librarian. 'But why Mrs Lander? Why is she dead?'

Sydney patted her arm. 'Don't you worry. It's nothing to do with you. I just wanted to warn you about some of the busy-bodies in this group. Richard will give you moral support. Here he is now.'

Rachel looked up and watched Richard Weiss walk towards her. He was a large man, tall and barrel-chested, scruffily dressed in a brown woollen pullover and faded once-navy-blue trousers. She heard he hardly dressed any more smartly in the office, but he was a popular solicitor in the town. He looked like he'd had a haircut for the occasion. His fair hair was cropped shorter than usual and he was self-consciously rubbing the back of his head as if getting used to the new length. As he approached her, she felt a pang of relief at his presence, his kind brown eyes reassuring her.

He smiled down at her. 'All OK? Don't worry yourself about any troublemakers. I know all their secrets.'

'I'm not sure if I can do this.'

He frowned. 'I'll call it off if you like. It's not a problem. People will understand.'

Rachel dug into her handbag and looked at her phone. It must have been why Llewellyn was trying to reach her. Should she call him now? In the distance she could hear the chatter of the assembled group. They'd be a more attentive audience now.

'No, it's OK. I'll do it.' Rachel got up and followed Richard down the passageway and into the room, which fell silent as she approached the front. Richard was already introducing her before the panic could begin to rise.

'Here's someone who needs no introduction, our resident genealogist and Bampton expert, Rachel Jones.'

Taking her prompt cards out of her bag, Rachel began to speak. She soon became aware that the silence wasn't hostile. A sea of sympathetic faces stared up at her, and even the usual troublemakers seemed to have pulled in sufficiently to protect one of Bampton's own. Her talk was on the trades of women in Bampton in the nineteenth century. A variation on one she'd given to a different group the previous year. Many families had been involved with a trade in the town and the mix of shopping and scandal made for an interesting talk.

During the question-and-answer session, a woman put up her hand. Red-faced and grey-haired, Rachel recognised her as one of the busybodies that Sydney so feared. Maureen something or other. She braced herself for the question.

'My great-nan was a cobbler, in Bampton's High Street, according to the 1881 census. Were there many woman doing that at the time?'

The silence that stretched out into the room caused a few heads to rise. Richard had noticed it too. Rachel, feeling sick, eventually managed a few words.

'It was unusual, yes, but not unheard of. Often widows took over the shops from their dead husbands. I can give you some more information afterwards, if you like.'

As the group broke up, a few came to lay an encouraging hand on Rachel. Richard hung around while she was chatting to the people who had stayed behind, a reassuring presence. While Rachel was packing up her things after the last person had left, he stood idly by, hands in his pockets, looking at one of the library's bookshelves. With everything stuffed into her brown satchel, Rachel called over, 'Fancy a drink?'

She often did this with men. Anticipated what they were going to say and said it herself before they had a chance to. It was probably a control thing and something her mother would have heartily approved of. 'Take control of the situation' was her mantra and Rachel had learned early on that it worked. If she spoke and acted first, then she could set the boundaries of the relationship. You could stop people getting too close that way. But what had it cost her mother? Nancy had been right this morning. There had been a few men friends around in her mother's life as she had been growing up but none had stayed around long.

Richard Weiss looked surprised but pleased. 'Do you want to stay in Bampton or go for a drive?'

Richard's intelligent warmth was what she wanted at this moment and it was a relief that she wouldn't be alone this evening. And she wanted more than one drink, which meant staying in Bampton so she could leave the car behind if necessary.

'How about the Rose and Crown?' she suggested.

'The Rose and Crown, formerly known as the Wheatsheaf,' said Richard, smiling at her.

Rachel grinned back. 'You're as bad as me.'

They walked out of the library and slowly towards the pub. The January Bampton night was once more threatening snow. The sky hung heavily over the town and the clouds were being blown by the winds quickly across the sky. The moon dipped in and out of view, very nearly a full disc, illuminating the street when the clouds cleared. The Rose and Crown was very hot, the air streaming out every time the doors were opened. There was a quiz going on in the main room and they nearly turned around and walked out. But there was a back room to the pub, where only two men sat in the corner, reading newspapers. Richard went to the bar and came back with a bottle of red wine under one arm and large bottle of water. He hadn't even asked her what she wanted to drink.

'It was a good talk tonight, Rachel,' he said, filling each glass halfway. 'It can't have been easy.'

'I'd hardly done any preparation beforehand so it could've

gone either way. But Sydney did well to forewarn me about Mrs Lander. There are other ways I could have heard about it. At least it was Sydney.' She frowned, remembering her neighbour, Jenny. Had she wanted to tell her about the identity of the body?

'Funny about the name changes of pubs like the one we're sitting in,' he said swilling his wine around the glass. 'What's the difference between calling the same building the Prince Regent, for example, and then the Church Inn.'

Rachel shrugged. 'Names are changed for all sorts of reasons. Sometimes on commercial grounds, sometimes to reflect the trend of the time. Sometimes by the brewery.'

'I suppose for the same reason people change their own names.'

Rachel looked at Richard, wondering where this was going.

'My family changed their name, you know. My great-grandfather arrived in Bristol as Avram Weitzenbaum. Only a minor difference, you might think. But Avram knew the importance of small things and the story is that he wanted to change it immediately. Jews were reasonably common in Bristol, given that it was a busy working port, but there was plenty of prejudice. Anyway, his wife felt it important to hang on to her identity and her name was part of that. Then two weeks spent tramping the Bristol dock warehouses and seeing the contempt on people's faces as he tried to give his name meant he was forced to put his foot down. Apparently it was the first time he ever stood up to his wife. From then on, they were named Weiss.'

'It doesn't sound that much less Jewish. It would still have identified your religion.'

'These people were pig ignorant. It wasn't the fact that my great-grandfather was Jewish. In fact, a couple of the prominent slave-trading families in Bristol were Jews. The problem was that he had an Eastern European name that they couldn't pronounce. As I said, pig ignorant.'

Rachel could sense that he was angry underneath the calm exterior. This was a man that she'd previously written off as charming but ultimately harmless who now seemed to be something else. She could sense a passion under his calm exterior and an anger that seemed more righteous than threatening. It was a powerful cocktail and, for the first time, Rachel felt the pull of desire.

'When I heard about the teacher found at Truscott Woods I thought you might cancel. It never occurred to me that you wouldn't have known the woman's identity. I'd have rung you and told you myself, if I'd known, rather than you hear about it from that old gossip Sydney. I'm really sorry about that.'

Rachel took a gulp of her wine. 'I couldn't believe it when Sydney told me. Mrs Lander. God, what a mess.'

'She was your teacher?'

'No, that's just it. She was a teacher at our school but we were never in her class. So I can't think of any connection between us. As far as I can see there are two, actually make it three, random events that some people are determined to connect somehow. The kidnapping of Sophie and me in 1978, the suicide of Yvonne Jenkins and now the murder of Mrs Lander today.'

'It's definitely murder?'

Rachel sniffed. 'Well, according to Sydney.'

To her surprise he roared with laughter. 'Well, that's settled then.'

She found herself smiling too. 'I have taken her version as gospel.'

He lifted up the bottle and poured her another glass of wine. 'Look. If the police think there's a connection between this teacher's body and that awful event in your past, I can guarantee that you'll be one of the first officially to know.'

'That's what I'm worried about, Richard.'

She saw him smile at the use of his name. The thought of this man's approval all at once seemed important to her. Could she open up to him? She felt the overwhelming urge to confide in him and take some of the comfort he offered.

'I remember nothing about the kidnapping. I remember getting into the car with Sophie, us finding that we were both locked in. And after that nothing. How much more can they hope to get out of me?'

Rachel could feel the panic rising from within. Richard remained calm, sipping his wine.

'What happened tonight? When Maureen Roberts asked the question about her great-grandmother who was a cobbler, you went white as a sheet.'

'Oh, God. You noticed that? I don't know. Something about the question really got to me. I didn't have time to think about it. They were waiting for an answer.'

'But it was something. To do with the kidnapping?'

'I think so. I just keep feeling something that's just out of my reach. It happens sometimes just before I'm about to go to sleep. Something comes into my head and I'm trying to grasp it.'

'You never tried hypnotherapy or something like that?'

'God, no. My mother wasn't going to have anything of that and I'm not going down that route now either.'

'How did you cope, then? Don't say you came through the experience without any trauma, as I wouldn't believe you. Something like that happens and it affects you physically and mentally.'

Rachel was silent. He was forcing her to think about something that she had locked away in her mind. She could envisage a great wall of metal drawers and within one of them, if she was willing to open it, were some of the answers she was looking for.

'I made lists.'

'Lists? What sort of lists does a child make?'

'All sorts of things. Books I'd read, favourite TV programmes, animals I'd seen that day. Then, when I was older, I did my family history. It also felt comforting. Personal on one hand but also objective. Creating a list that only ended when you ran out of sources.'

'You've mentioned before that you concentrate on the maternal side of your family. The female line.'

'It wasn't always the case. My supervisor at university suggested it and it seemed like a good idea. I could link genealogy, which was my main interest, with wider social mores. You know, how the matrilineal line has always been considered less important in Western society. Unlike in others – Judaism, for example.'

'You know about that?'

'Sure. I wrote a little bit about it in my dissertation. How the maternal line is the proof of Jewishness for Orthodox Jews.'

Richard made a snorting noise at the back of his throat.

'You don't agree?'

'No, I don't. Clearly I'm not an Orthodox Jew, but to be

honest I steer well clear of the subject of Jewish identity. It's one of those issues you could tie yourself up into knots with.'

'But you do consider yourself Jewish?'

'Of course.' He seemed unwilling to say more on the subject. 'So you started to compile lists and then you moved on to genealogy. And did it help?'

'Yes, and it still does.'

'And you've never thought about psychotherapy? Are you scared of something?'

She put her glass down and looked at him. 'Wouldn't you bloody well be?'

He reached over and put his hand over hers. She was unable to meet his eyes, although she desperately wanted to see his expression. She had rejected comfort over and over again in the years since 1978. Now, despite having taken the initiative in suggesting they go to the pub, she could feel the weight of her past threaten to drag her under again. And here was someone who was prepared to accept her as she was. Someone who knew about her past and yet didn't censure her for it. For her lack of ability to remember. Or for her reticence in opening up.

As she felt his eyes on her, she made a decision.

Chapter 24

Connie, exhausted from the day, decided to skip dinner and go straight to bed. It was a once-a-month habit, when the accumulated stresses of the job got too overwhelming and she needed to catch up on her much-needed sleep. She left her clothes in a heap by the side of her bed and climbed under the sheets naked. Within two minutes she was asleep. Dreamless, or so she thought, until a loud ringing pierced her consciousness. Her mobile. She reached over and picked it up, noting the time as she answered it. Eleven minutes past nine: not late, but not exactly early either. *Someone had better be dead*, she thought.

'It's Sadler. Thought you would want to know the results of the PM. Strangling has definitely been confirmed.'

Bloody hell, thought Connie. *He's woken me from my beauty sleep for this.* She swung her legs over the edge of her bed and planted her feet on the floor. She noticed that the nail varnish on her toenails had chipped off, leaving an unattractive ragged strip across each nail. And she'd run out of remover too. Just as well it was the middle of winter; no one would notice under her socks.

'It's nothing new, is it? We suspected strangling anyway.'

Something in her voice must have given her annoyance away as the line went silent. Connie waited, too tired to try and fill the empty silence.

When he spoke again, Sadler's voice seemed tired too, 'Bill

says that she was strangled twice. First to disable or disarm her and then a different type of strangulation to kill her.'

Strangled twice? Connie's stomach lurched. She should have eaten something after all.

'So the cord around the neck . . .'

'According to Bill, that was the method used to kill her. A tightening on the carotid arteries that would have blocked the blood flow to the brain and resulted in death.'

'And the other strangulation?'

'Manually. With their hands. And the person must have been stronger than Penny Lander. Manual strangulation is rarely effective on someone of equal size.'

'And why not use the rope straight away? Wouldn't that have been more effective?' Connie stood up and walked over to the window looking over the canal.

'I don't know. The manual strangulation suggests an element of chance. In other words, an opportunistic crime. But the finishing off with rope – Bill thinks it might have been a guy rope – suggests premeditation. I'm also wondering if it gives us an insight into the events of 1978.'

'What do you mean?'

'I don't know. Maybe I'm taking this too far. But perhaps, if we're linking the two cases, then we're looking for someone who likes to overpower their victims before they kill them.'

Connie was silent, mulling over his words.

'Did I wake you?'

'Not at all.' She flopped back down on the bed.

'We can discuss this further in the morning. It's given us something to think about.'

Connie found it impossible to get to sleep after Sadler's call and lay awake in the darkness trying to make sense of it all. She finally gave up on sleep at four o'clock in the morning. The night was inky black as she opened the front door of the building and groped her way to the car. The council had made the decision to have a strategic switching off of street lamps in the middle of the night to save precious money that was needed for resources elsewhere. Which was fine until she one night pitched headlong into the canal as a result of this cost-cutting exercise.

The station was silent. Whatever trouble that had materialised on a Tuesday evening had been dealt with and the desk sergeant barely looked up at her as she passed.

'Anyone who can dig out some BMD certificates for me around here?'

The look he gave her clearly suggested that she should be able to do her own donkey work.

'Field's around somewhere. He can probably help. He's had a quiet shift so far.'

She tracked down the young constable at a desk, playing solitaire on the computer. She sat down beside him as he carried on with his game without a glance at her. She clearly was gaining a fearsome reputation at the station.

'Can you do me a favour?'

She had his attention, but only just.

'I need to see some certificates – birth, marriage and death. Can you print them off for me?'

'It's not rocket science, you know.'

'I'm sorry to remove you from your card game. If I'd known you were busy I'd have stayed in bed an extra hour to let you finish.'

He shut down the game and logged into the computer. 'Go on. Shoot.'

It took about half an hour and she left the room holding the bare bones of the life of Paul Saxton, Rachel's father. Born 25 August 1945; died 4 August 1970, three months before Rachel Jones was born. He had both entered and left this world at the old Bampton cottage hospital. Connie knew it by reputation, as the site was now covered in executive apartments and nothing remained of the original buildings.

The cause of death was listed as pneumonia. Connie frowned as she looked at the certificate. It was usually old people who died of this. How did a young man of twenty-five end up dead of pneumonia in the middle of summer?

The marriage certificate was also dated 1970, the first of May. Connie did some rapid sums in her head. Mary Jones must have been three months pregnant by then. In 1970 pregnancy was clearly still a reason to marry and, even though Paul Saxton had died before the baby was born, it would still have given Rachel precious legitimacy. It would also explain why Mary Jones hadn't changed her name. There had barely been any time between the marriage and the death of her husband.

Connie wafted the certificates in front of her to cool down her tired head and thought. It all seemed OK. Could she eliminate Paul Saxton from the equation?

*

Sadler frowned as he walked past Connie, who seemed to be staring into space.

'You OK?' He looked at his watch. 'Couldn't sleep either? It sounded like you had an early night.'

He saw her jump and then flush. 'Sorry. I was miles away thinking about something.'

'I can't stop for long. I've got an early meeting with Llewellyn. You look like you've been here a while. Anything I should know?'

She turned round fully in her chair and looked at him. 'No. I don't think so. This case is really strange. Llewellyn was right, you know. The team in 1978 did do their job properly. I can't find anything wrong. And yet there is something. There's something we're not seeing. A person we're missing. I'm sure of it.'

Sadler sat down. 'I've really not got long, but tell me.'

Connie spread out some of the notes across the desk. 'Everything here adds up. There are no discrepancies, nothing jars. But I just don't trust it.'

'The team missed something – a person?'

'I *think* so. I would say a person. A Mr X.'

'Mr X?'

'Yes. Or Ms X. An unknown man or woman who the original team never found. Someone whose name we don't yet know.'

'*Nomen nescio*,' said Sadler.

Connie looked confused.

'It's a legal term. For someone we don't know the name of. It's often abbreviated to NN.'

'NN? OK, if you prefer. This *nomen* ... what was the second bit?'

'*Nescio*.'

'OK, this *NN* is the person who is involved in the case but we don't know about.'

'And how did you reach that conclusion? Intuition?'

She looked him directly in the eyes. 'Yes.'

'Fair enough, but it's going to be solid police work that will lead you to NN. Look, I have to see Llewellyn. You realise we're almost certainly going to be dropping this. Don't let it occupy your thoughts too much. Park it away. But you may well be coming back to NN again.'

He left her sitting there, her small body hunched over the desk. At Llewellyn's office, the superintendent's secretary was taking off her coat and smiled as he approached.

'You can go straight in. Do you want coffee?'

He thought of the jar of instant sitting on the side of her desk, smiled as he shook his head. Llewellyn was sitting at his desk writing something on his computer, his large hands spread across the keyboard as he typed with his two index fingers. From what Sadler could see, he was tracking changes to a document.

'I'm not fully reopening the 1978 enquiry any longer. I don't have the resources. You know what I'm about to say. However far you've got with the 1978 case, you'll have to see if it's relevant to the investigation that you're now conducting into Penny Lander's murder.'

'And Yvonne Jenkins?'

'The details have been sent to the Coroner's Office, but looking at the evidence I would say a verdict of suicide was a dead cert. And I have to say, Sadler, that I'm happy with that.' Llewellyn caught himself and winced. 'Not happy, but you know what I mean. Satisfied. I'm fairly clear that Yvonne Jenkins committed suicide.'

'And you're happy to leave it at that?' asked Sadler.

Now Llewellyn did take his eyes off the computer. 'You know my feelings on this. You know that I want to know why Yvonne Jenkins chose now, after all these years, to do away with herself. And only two days before a teacher in Rachel Jones's old school is found murdered.'

'There could be a connection.'

Llewellyn lifted his hands off the keyboard and gave Sadler his full attention. 'Go on.'

'It's a possibility. Perhaps the suicide of Yvonne Jenkins triggered something that led to the death of Penny Lander.'

'Like what?'

He was being perverse, thought Sadler. Exactly how far was the team supposed to have got in so short a space of time?

'I don't know . . .'

'Let me give you a bit of advice, Francis. Don't let this case get to you. Forget what I told you about 1978 when you look at the murder of Penny Lander. I need your objectivity on this one. No hunches.'

Sadler thought back to his young detective constable bent over her desk.

'You can rely on my complete objectivity.'

Chapter 25

The incident room began to fill with personnel. There was that low level of urgency that pervades a space just after a violent crime. In theory, the team were working against the clock: gathering evidence and witness statements and establishing a chronology of events, all of which would provide the bedrock of the investigation. The Crown Prosecution Service required it and the public entrusted the police to do a thorough investigation. But still Connie felt curiously detached from the intense activity that was taking place. Her mind was still stuck in 1978 and the discovery of a shivering girl, wearing no shoes and socks, with a missing friend.

Sadler was in his office, on the telephone, but pointed her towards Palmer, who was drinking a cup of coffee and staring into space.

'All OK?'

Palmer put down his cup and shrugged. 'The usual.'

'You can always call it off, you know.'

'Oh, that's really helpful, Con. Call off the wedding. Do you know how long we've been planning this event?'

'Months.'

'Yes, that's right. Months. Eighteen of them, in fact. And I'm now supposed to call it off.'

Connie could feel herself getting angry. 'I was only trying to help. Do what you like. Has Sadler assigned me any tasks yet?'

Palmer took a deep breath. 'He wants you to look into Penny Lander's personal history. Her back story, as it were. I've been doing the employment angle. Seeing if there are any discrepancies in her employment history, why she chose that school to teach at and so on. You're to dig into her personal life.'

'She's got a daughter, hasn't she?'

'In Kent. Apparently she's on her way up here now.'

'She's been informed that it's murder?'

'I don't know. The local uniforms broke the news to her. I've got the details here.'

'For God's sake, Palmer, perk up.' Connie snatched the file out of his hand and walked out of the office. What was the point of getting married if you felt so bad about it?

Connie plonked herself down at the desk and flicked through the file. The unfortunate PC who had been given the job of breaking the news had let Bampton station know that Penny's daughter, Justine, had been shocked but sufficiently composed to answer some preliminary questions before she set out on her journey. According to Justine, her mother was born in 1953 in Somerset and had moved to Derbyshire aged eighteen to attend teacher training college in Bampton in 1971. The reasons for her move north were unclear. Of course, everyone went away to university these days. But then?

'Anybody know if it was usual to go to university in another town in 1971?' asked Connie across the room.

Two detectives leaning over a computer looked up and then at each other. Palmer was ignoring her.

'My dad was from Nottingham and he went to Leicester Uni,' said one of them.

But not across the country, thought Connie to herself. She turned her attention back to the file. According to Palmer's research, Penny Lander's first teaching job had been at Greenacres primary school, long since closed down. In 1975, she had moved to St Paul's, where she had remained for the rest of her teaching career, which included a year's break in 1977 following the birth of Justine. According to her daughter, she had liked her job except for the fact that every September she had caught a chest infection that on a couple of occasions turned to bronchitis. She had taught almost continuously the junior classes as she preferred the older pupils. That, in summary, had been a teaching career spanning forty years. Nothing remarkable about it whatsoever.

Connie turned to Palmer, about to say something disparaging about the scope of her task, but noticed he'd disappeared. She stuck her pen in her mouth and thought.

In 1978, she would have just returned to St Paul's after the birth of Justine. According to Jane Thomson, she'd never taught the two girls but had, like her, heard of the kidnapping from the headmistress. Penny Lander's personal life had suggested little to get excited over. According to the interview with Justine, her mother had married as soon as she graduated in 1972. Justine came along in 1977 and her father, James, had died last year of a heart attack. According to Justine, her mother had taken the death stoically but, as attested to by Sally Arden, had been bewildered as to what to do with herself.

Somewhere amongst the bare bones of this life there was something hidden deep down. It was the only explanation for Penny Lander lying dead in Bampton mortuary, less than a week after Yvonne Jenkins had killed herself. There had to be a link somewhere. No friends of Mrs Jenkins had come forward and she wouldn't have the time to go looking for people who, if Llewellyn's assessment of the dead woman was right, didn't even exist. Which meant, given that she was now assigned to the Penny Lander murder investigation, finding out about Penny's circle of friends.

She flicked through the file again. According to her daughter, Penny belonged to a book group and had occasionally attended a local history society. It was here that Connie needed to start. The local history group was at least official; it met at the local library once a month and, given that it had a healthy membership of around eighty, should at least provide some insight into Mrs Lander's personality.

Connie drove to Bampton library and stopped outside to admire the Victorian Gothic building. Tall pointed windows were filled with small panes of glass that needed a clean. Perhaps the council's budget didn't stretch to a regular window cleaner. Despite its gloomy lines and decrepit state it had a comforting solidity about it. This made Connie feel better and she greeted the bouncy librarian with some of her own cheeriness.

The librarian was a large woman wearing a long shiny stretchy skirt and an oversized jumper with horizontal stripes that did nothing to hide her prominent cleavage. She looked Connie up and down and, feeling intimidated, Connie reached inside her bag and showed her police identification.

'I'm Sydney Markham, the head librarian here. Is it to do with Rachel Jones?' she asked, and Connie stared at her.

'Rachel Jones? Well, no,' she said, recovering. 'Why do you ask about Rachel Jones?'

Sydney's voice was slightly breathless. 'She was here last

night giving a talk to the local history society. And very interesting it was as well. A history of women's occupations in Bampton.'

'Last night? Was this a scheduled visit?'

'Oh yes. Been in the diary for months. Rachel comes here about once or twice a year to help with the genealogy side of things. But she's also a mine of information about the general history of Bampton, the former uses of buildings, what streets certain families used to live on. That sort of thing. So she usually talks about something to do with that.'

'Anything out of the ordinary happen?' asked Connie.

'Only that she had no idea that the murdered woman was Penny Lander when she turned up. I had to tell her. I can assure you it was a complete shock. She looked like she was rooted to the ground when I told her.'

'You think she was genuinely surprised.'

'Surprised? She looked absolutely gobsmacked. I felt really sorry for her that she then had to go up and give a talk in front of all those people.'

'And was she OK?'

'She was brilliant. A really interesting talk and everyone asked really nice questions, to keep the conversation going without referring to Mrs Lander.'

'But she was a member of the group, wasn't she? I mean, didn't she attend your meetings?'

'I *think* she might have been a member. I don't really know. There will be a list somewhere. You need to speak to the group's president, Richard Weiss. We just host the meetings, and I'm not always working the nights they're held. Of course, there are quite a few people who join for access to the records, or just out of curiosity, but don't come to the sessions. She might have been one of those if she was a member.'

'You knew her?'

'She taught both my kids. They adored her, especially William, the youngest, who had a stutter when he was little. She was wonderful; she'd just sit and wait until he got it out. They didn't offer speech therapists in those days, you just had to hope your child got a decent teacher, and fortunately we struck gold with Penny.'

'And you don't know why she might have joined the local history society? I mean, she wasn't from here originally.'

'Now you come to mention it, she wasn't, was she? But that's nothing strange. Plenty of people join to find out the history of their house or street. Or just out of interest. You don't have to be Bampton born and bred to be a member. You really do need to talk to Richard Weiss. He has the memory of an elephant and nothing much gets past him.'

'You got his address?' Connie saw the expression on the librarian's face. 'This is official, I'm afraid.'

*

Connie hadn't had many expectations in relation to Richard Weiss, but she was nevertheless surprised by his outright hostility when he answered the door.

'I'm not sure why you're asking me. I met Penny Lander twice, maximum. There must be friends who knew her better than me.'

'It's possible,' replied Connie, feeling her hackles rise, 'but as I haven't been able to find anyone yet, you're my first port of call.'

He was a good-looking man. He had pale blonde hair that was closely cropped at the sides and parted at the top. He had on mustard corduroy trousers and a dark burgundy knitted jumper. His slight pot belly failed to detract from his charm. In fact, his bulk was part of his attraction. When she called at his house, he could hardly leave her out in the cold but had invited her only into the hallway of his tall Victorian terrace. Connie could hear someone pottering around in the kitchen; his wife, presumably.

'Can you tell me anything about her? Why she joined the society, for instance.'

Richard sighed and drew his hand through his hair. 'I don't think she ever said. I don't think she was particularly into the far past of Bampton. There are Iron Age settlements up Wickham Hill. The two lectures she actually came along to were to do with Bampton's more recent history.'

Connie looked at him. 'You sure?'

'Positive, because I took a look this morning at my register. It's nothing fancy. I pass a notebook around at every meeting and I ask people to sign their names. It just helps me keep an eye on attendance. When I heard that she'd died, I was curious enough to take a look at what she'd been interested in. Penny Lander came to two meetings last year. The first was a talk, by myself actually, on illegitimacy and adoption before 1976. That was when children were first able to trace their birth parents.'

'Illegitimacy and adoption,' repeated Connie. 'Do the two usually go together?'

Richard leaned back against the wall. 'Oh yes.'

'Did she ask any questions?'

'Not that I can remember.'

'OK. And the second lecture?'

A shadow crossed the man's face. 'A history of Bampton cottage hospital. Given by our resident genealogist Rachel Jones. The hospital was shut down in 1993 but, given that so many of Bampton's residents passed through it, I thought it would make an interesting subject. I approached Rachel because I knew she would know about patient records, admin, that sort of thing and she gave a very informative talk.'

'And were there any questions?'

He shook his head. 'I don't remember.'

The both turned round as the kitchen door opened and Rachel Jones stood on the threshold with a cup in her hand, a mirror of the photograph that she'd posted on her website.

'She did ask a question. She wanted to know about legacy arrangements for the more recent records.'

'Legacy arrangements?' asked Connie, containing her discomposure at Rachel Jones's appearance. She looked perfectly calm. 'You mean wills?'

'No, she meant legacy in terms of who was now looking after the records now the hospital had shut. Not the stuff in the public records but doctors' notes and so on.'

'And how did you answer?'

'I didn't really know but my guess was that any current patient records would have been transferred to the new hospital – St Crispin's.'

'Any idea why she asked the question?'

Rachel shrugged. 'No idea. It seemed a bit odd to come to a history society and ask about more recent things, but I didn't give it much thought, to be honest.'

'Was she happy with the answer?'

Rachel leaned her hip against the door jamb. Connie wondered what she was doing here.

'I think she was more interested in the older stuff. She didn't mention a decade but I got the impression she wanted to know about records that wouldn't be considered current.'

'And what happened to them?'

'A lot of it has been archived at the records office in Bampton. So I suggested she try there. But more recent, say the 1960s, I've no idea if those records are available to the public. Given that people will be still alive, I doubt it is in the public domain.'

'So, was she happy with the answer?'

'It's difficult to say. I think so. I went up to her afterwards and checked if there was anything I could help her with. But she didn't want to talk to me really. She wanted to keep her distance, I think. It's not always like that. Sometimes people are happy to talk on a one-to-one basis but shy away from asking questions from the floor. It seemed to be the opposite with Mrs Lander. She gave nothing away when I questioned her.'

'You remember her from school, then?'

Rachel looked at her feet and Connie noticed she was wearing thick winter socks, the type you would wear with walking boots.

'I remember her. Not well, but I do remember her from St Paul's.'

'And she said nothing to you about your kidnapping.'

Rachel's eyes stayed to her floor. She shook her head.

'There was nothing to say, was there?'

Finally, she looked up at Connie and said faintly, 'How did she die? Mrs Lander? What happened?'

Chapter 26

Rachel was late for her ten o'clock appointment. As her new client lived in the High Oaks area of Bampton, it was easier to walk than take her car and look for a parking space. High Oaks was the town's most affluent area: tall Victorian detached houses that came with a hefty price tag. The fact that Richard lived only a few streets away had never struck Rachel before, but now, as she puffed along the icy pavement trying to pretend she was doing a power walk rather than a clumsy half-run to avoid being late, she realised how little she knew about the Weiss family. If Richard could afford his tall graceful terrace then he must be fairly well off. His father, Daniel, had retired, so perhaps he had passed some of his savings on to his son.

The morning hadn't turned out as she had expected. The detective had been a surprise for a start. There had been no shuffling of feet and avoiding eye contact that she remembered from 1978. Ever since that afternoon, she'd had a poor view of female coppers. Most were either ineffectual or, worse, worthy. They stood over you making clucking noises with no real understanding of what it was like to feel the fear of captivity. Connie, as she had introduced herself, appeared competent. She was tiny. A thin, childlike body dressed head to toe in black clothes. But her eyes held something that Rachel could identify with. Wariness and caution. She decided to file DC Connie Childs at the back of her mind. She might be useful in the future if she needed an ally. Which was the second surprise of the morning.

So Mrs Lander had been strangled. It was a horrible way to die and she remembered the series of panic attacks that she had suffered when she first went to university. She'd made friends quickly enough, but in her first term she'd felt overwhelmed by the new world around her. Sometimes she'd wake in the middle of the night fighting for breath until slowly the panic subsided and she was able to breathe normally. A friend studying medicine had suggested blowing into a paper bag, which had worked. But she could remember the feeling of total absence of anything. Breathing not only kept your heart and lungs moving, it gave you the essence of life. Without it, your body became a vacuum where nothing was allowed to exist.

It must have been a horrible death for Mrs Lander, her breath slowly being squeezed out of her body and the realisation that there was nothing she could do about it. But now, as the cold air stung her lungs, she had to admit to herself that when Connie told her how Mrs Lander had died, it had had no reverberations deep within her psyche. Whatever had happened in 1978, it hadn't involved seeing Sophie being strangled. Rachel was positive that something so violent would have remained with her. And there was nothing. For the moment it seemed that the killing of Mrs Lander might have nothing to do with her kidnap.

Arriving at her client's house, she could see a shadow hovering in the window. Clearly, her lateness wasn't going to go unnoticed. The front door was opened as she puffed up the path and a clearly anxious Mrs Franklin ushered her into a large neat living room. It hadn't been furnished on a grand enough scale for the house. Two small sofas sat primly at right angles to each other, with a teak coffee table laden with a china tea set too small for the vast sitting room. After adding hot water to the pot and pouring out two dainty cups of a pale brew, Cathy Franklin sat down and looked at Rachel expectantly.

Rachel took a sip of the scalding tea. 'You said over the phone that you've done a fair bit of research yourself.'

It was a bad start as the woman immediately was on the defensive. 'It's not difficult, you know. I managed to get birth, marriage and death certificates for all of my great-grandparents and their whereabouts from the census returns right back to 1841.'

Rachel, aware that she had started awkwardly, rushed to make amends. 'You've done well. People usually have an initial dig around but reach a hiccup well before you did. Is that why you called me in?'

Rachel had chosen a word that resonated with her client. She was beaming at her.

'That's it! A hiccup. What a great turn of phrase, and of course you're absolutely right. I've got a problem and I don't know where to go next. It's to do with my great-grandmother. There was a rumour that she was the illegitimate child of Henry Needham, you know up in the big house. In my family, for years, my grandmother would tell the story that my great-grandmother was born after her mother, who was governess to Henry Needham's children, got pregnant by him.'

'Did he marry her off to one of his staff? That's the usual story.'

Cathy looked at her in dismay. 'You've heard of this before?'

'Afraid so, yes,' said Rachel, aware that she was going to put her foot in it with everything she said that morning. Her client had a crestfallen look of someone who had suddenly found that her family heirlooms were mere mass-produced paste imitations. 'Lord of the manor gets the housemaid pregnant and then hushes it up by marrying her to the footman or something.'

Cathy sighed and looked at her hands. Her fingernails were painted a deep crimson colour and Rachel, aware of her own chipped nails, vowed to buy a nail file on the way home. 'The family story is something like that. My great-grandmother was born in 1878 and her mother's name is on the certificate and the father is named as Hugh Walker. In the 1881 census, it just says his occupation is servant. But the thing is the family legend is that he wasn't really her father.' Cathy Franklin paused and looked at Rachel. 'How do I prove that?'

Rachel decided on honesty. 'Sometimes these family rumours turned out to be true and other times it was just wishful thinking. I can have a search around the Needham estate, if you like, the stuff that's in the public domain. The papers I think are spread out amongst different records offices. I could take a look.'

'Anything would help. I've begun to doubt my own family history, which is never a good idea when you are tracing your roots.'

Rachel snorted. 'A healthy dose of scepticism is essential in this line of work. I'll see what I can do.'

Cathy was looking at her through narrowed eyes. 'I heard about Penny Lander's death. I'm sorry you've had more trouble.'

Rachel stood up to leave. 'I'm not sure anyone's linking it

to what happened in 1978. Except the press, that is. She wasn't even my teacher. I'm not sure what it's got to do with me.'

'It's the daughter I feel sorry for. Justine, I think her name is. She's a friend of my youngest son. She moved away and now she's got to come back up here and sort out her mother's stuff.'

'Isn't there any other family?' Rachel was desperate to leave and inched towards the door.

'Only Bridget Lander. Penny's sister-in-law. She lives on Baslow Crescent. I suppose she'll be able to help.'

Rachel couldn't think what to say. 'You can usually rely on family,' she finally managed, which got a sympathetic smile from her new client.

As she walked back to Richard's house to pick up her car, adopting a slower pace, her phone beeped and alerted her to a message. It was from Richard, and Rachel could feel her heart thump as she opened the text. *Gone to work. Thanks for a wonderful evening. Are you all right?* Rachel smiled. It was just like Richard to refuse to use abbreviations. At the pedestrian crossing, waiting for the lights to change, she typed back *Yes* and pressed the 'Send' button. Feeling she ought to say more, she then typed *And yes, it was wonderful.* Which it had been. A pleasant and unexpected surprise. Although they had both been deliberately casual that morning, she'd been surprised at how happy she felt. The text was the first indication that he was still thinking about her.

Her car was sitting outside Richard's house, alone in the street now that other residents had gone to work. It started reluctantly, the damp must have seeped into the engine. She should really go back to her house but the thought of the reporters and the bored policemen still keeping watch in their white Volvo was too much. For a moment she sat absolutely still while her mind whirled around. Finally, she set off towards her destination.

*

Arkwright Lane had changed very little. The semi-detached house that had been her home from her birth to the age of nine looked both familiar and unknowable. It was someone else's house and they had completely taken possession of it, erasing all traces of earlier occupants. It was well kept, and the large black and yellow trampoline that she could glimpse in the back garden suggested that young children lived there. In Rachel's day there had been a turquoise blue metal swing set with a wooden seat and thick rope that had burned her hands when she hung on too tightly. The base of the swing had been messily cemented to the grass, leaving overflowing ridges that always snagged on the push lawnmower her mother had lugged around each summer.

Rachel climbed out of the car and looked around her. The street was more familiar; even the no cycling sign at the front of a passageway looked the same as it had in 1978. Today was refuse collection day and wheelie bins in three different colours stood on the pavement. Theirs had been the old-fashioned metal type, with a large number 5 painted on by her mother. The street was quiet, no one walking on the pavement or looking out of the windows. It was the fatal flaw of suburban streets. People, by and large, minded their own business. A lack of people had once seemed a sign of safety but now Rachel could see how easy it was to abduct a child from such a quiet street.

She set off up the hill on foot and the houses changed from semis to bungalows, their gardens neater but with an old-fashioned air about the tidy borders. One older woman was doing her gardening even in this bitter cold, on her knees with a thick man's coat flapping in the wind. She was tidying up some litter that had blown down the street. She looked up as Rachel passed.

Sophie's old house was exactly the same as it had been in 1978. The front garden was neatly laid out, but devoid of all character. The two windows at the front were clean, no smudges reflecting off the glass in the low winter sun. But there was still a neglected air about the property. Rachel could see no plants or ornaments in the windows and could have sworn that the same curtains from the 1970s were hanging there. On the day of the kidnap she'd walked up to the front door and waited while Mrs Jenkins fussed round Sophie, who'd taken the ministrations with a martyred but satisfied air. Then they had set off together up the hill.

On impulse, she walked up the path to the front door and rang the bell. The chimes echoed through the house, a merry discordant note. The woman from two houses along had straightened up and was staring at her.

'She's gone. The woman who lived there. Gone.'

Gone, thought Rachel. Yes, that was a good euphemism for what had happened to Yvonne Jenkins. She had gone.

'I'm family,' Rachel shouted back. And funnily enough it didn't sound like a complete lie.

She walked around the back, opening the worn, wrought-iron gate and came to the back door. She tried the handle and to her surprise the door swung open easily. Either the police had failed to secure the scene or perhaps Yvonne Jenkins had decided to make it easy for someone to enter the house. She stepped inside and flinched as the musty air hit her. The heating had been left on, presumably to stop the pipes freezing, but instead of providing warmth, there was a yeasty smell in the house that reminded Rachel of fermenting beer.

The back door opened onto the kitchen, which Rachel quickly walked through. She had no memories of that room at all. The hallway was more familiar, the carpet the same as in 1978, clean and very drab, Sophie's bedroom had been off the small corridor to the left of the bungalow. Whatever Rachel had expected, it wasn't this barely furnished room. A single bed stood to one side, bare mattressed and with no evidence of bedclothes elsewhere. The only other piece of furniture was a small wardrobe, presumably Sophie's. This was in the days before children's furniture. Rachel's wardrobe had been a huge mahogany piece inherited from her great-grandmother. During games of hide and seek it had been possible to hide three or four friends inside it.

Rachel opened Sophie's wardrobe. Like the bed, it was bare. Not even spare hangers could be seen. The other bedroom must have belonged to Yvonne Jenkins. It at least bore the signs of recent occupation, with a hairbrush sitting on top of a chest of drawers waiting for its owner to pick it up again. Again Rachel felt drawn to the wardrobe in this room and opened it. Rows of skirts, blouses and trousers neatly hung off the rail. Rachel turned the label of a blouse and saw that it had been purchased from a respectable local boutique. So Yvonne Jenkins had still dressed smartly, even up to her death.

She peered through the net curtains. The old woman was

disappearing into her house, most likely defeated by the cold and damp. Rachel heard a click – and turned her head towards the front door. Someone was standing outside, tall and muffled against the inclement weather. Her heart lurched and, angry at herself, she thought about rapping on the window to catch the shadow's attention. Like Rachel before her, the caller rang the doorbell and this time the chimes echoed around her. *Go away*, prayed Rachel, feeling a pressure behind her nose. Nausea building up from within. The figure moved, not down the pathway but following Rachel's steps around to the back of the house. She faintly heard the gate swing and it was this small noise that brought her from her reverie.

She looked around the spartan room. She had left the back door unlocked, only closing it behind her to prevent the warmth of the house escaping into the cold air. Whoever it was would surely try the door. Perhaps it was a journalist sniffing around and therefore she should go and confront them as she had that other reporter outside her house. But there was something chilling about the tall shadow that she had seen through the net curtains. If they were looking for something, surely they would search everywhere? And Rachel would not hide. Not ever. She would be not be found cowering under the bed. She steeled herself, pulled back the net curtain, opened the window and climbed out.

Chapter 27

Palmer was sitting across from Sadler, fiddling with his jacket and refusing to look him in the eye. The PM report had arrived and Sadler needed someone to bounce ideas off. Usually his sergeant was ideal, in contrast to Connie who, although keen to impress when Palmer was around, worked less well in situations that could be described as a 'meeting'. But today Palmer seemed out of sorts, his mouth pinched and dark shadows under his eyes, noticeable despite the light tan that must have come from a sunbed session. Sadler ploughed ahead.

'Double strangulation has been confirmed. Ever come across that before?'

'Never. And it's creepy, the whole idea of it. Strangled twice. You could make a horror film with that title.'

'It's certainly a first for me too.' Sadler was scanning the rest of the report. He stood by what he had said to Connie over the phone. The method of the killing was an insight to the killer's mind, which felt the need to first overpower and then extinguish the victim.

'What about other cases? Llewellyn was sure that there had been no repeat incidents of kidnapped children, but I wonder if we've missed any cases where a victim is first overpowered and then killed.'

Palmer had stopped fiddling with his jacket and was giving Sadler his full attention. 'I'm not sure. I can go back and look on the computer, if you like. It's a good point, but I'm still not convinced about the link to 1978. A grown woman in 1978 should be fairly elderly by now. Rachel didn't know the precise age of the woman who had kidnapped them but her description to police suggested a woman in her twenties or thirties, no younger. A woman in her early thirties in 1978 would be in her late sixties now.'

His downbeat tone was worthy of Connie and at last Sadler felt compelled to say something. 'You all right?'

Palmer's eyes dropped to the floor. 'I'm fine. Just a lot on my mind at the moment.'

Sadler couldn't think of anything helpful to say. He looked up at the clock and noticed it was an hour until the scheduled press conference. A pre-briefing would take place half an hour before that with the press officer. Which gave him only thirty minutes to start shaping the scant information that they had discovered so far into something more coherent.

*

On her way to interview Penny Lander's few friends, Connie thought back to her interview with Richard Weiss. Rachel Jones and he were obviously an item. She'd looked right at home standing there in the kitchen in woolly hiking socks and what were clearly his pyjama bottoms and T-shirt. Given that Rachel Jones was supposed to dislike women police officers, she'd been as cool as a cucumber answering her questions. Neither had she seemed particularly perturbed about the news that Penny Lander had been strangled. Rachel had been surprised. Connie would have sworn that. But shocked? No. Not shocked.

Connie arrived at a house on a suburban street not far from the High Oaks area but a world apart in terms of the architecture. A small housing estate had been given planning permission in the 1980s and a conservative local house builder had erected three cul-de-sacs of solid mock-Tudor detached houses with postage-stamp-sized gardens. Admittedly, most of the houses had weathered well over the last twenty years. People attracted to this type of development maintained their properties. It reminded Connie of an inferior version of Penny Lander's street.

The door was answered by a woman in her sixties wearing an outfit not dissimilar to that of Richard Weiss, mustard coloured corduroy trousers and a matching V-necked sweater. Her mannish attire was mirrored by the inside of the house that looked like it belonged to an elderly bachelor, although Connie spotted some knitting on the coffee table. Dorothy Cable was the organiser of the book club that Penny Lander attended, which met on the first Tuesday of every month.

'It was my idea to set it up. I didn't advertise it or anything. I just asked a couple of friends, and they asked a couple of theirs, and between us we got together a group of ten.'

'And how did Penny join the group?'

'She was known to a couple of us, I think. She'd taught a few of our kids, mine included.'

Connie rapidly revised her assessment of Dorothy Cable. 'Was this a long time ago?'

'She knew mine in the 1970s. I've two boys and Penny taught both of them. They both liked her.'

'Do you remember the kidnapping of Sophie Jenkins and Rachel Jones?'

'We're not likely to forget any of that around here. David, my eldest, was in the same year as the two girls but a different class. He was a sensitive boy. He still is, in fact. He had nightmares about the whole thing after the girls were taken. The headmistress at the time had to call a parents' meeting because apparently a lot of the kids were suffering from some kind of trauma – anxiety, stress. You name it, although we didn't particularly in those days. I think it came under the catch-all of "shock".'

'The headmistress was a Miss Coles?' asked Connie, checking her notes.

'Yes, the old-fashioned type she was, too. Ran that school like clockwork and recruited both Penny Lander and another teacher who still works there, Jane Thomson. The pair of them were of that traditional mould. Most of the pupils, when they left St Paul's for secondary school, went to Bishop's. Apparently teachers there could tell when a child came from St Paul's because their reading and writing skills were well in advance of children from the other schools.'

'Do you know what became of Miss Coles?'

'She died about ten years ago, I think, well into her nineties. She was on the verge of retiring when the girls were taken, if I remember, and she stayed on for an extra year because she thought it unfair for a new head to have to take on a school that had just experienced that kind of tragedy.'

Connie looked around the bare room, noting the absence of photos of the sons that Dorothy Cable had mentioned. 'Is there anything you can tell me that might shed light on why Mrs Lander was killed?'

'We just discuss books.' Dorothy folded her arms. 'I was

quite adamant about that. I've heard all about these book clubs where all they do is chat about what has been on TV the previous evening. Gossip is for before and after the meeting. Not during discussions. We don't verge on the personal.'

'And what about a particular friend? Was there anyone in the group that Penny was particularly close to?'

Dorothy Cable looked at Connie curiously. 'Have you spoken to Bridget Lander? She was Penny's sister-in-law. Bridget was the sister of James, Penny's husband. I don't think they were particularly close but they were both in the book club and I know they both got a surprise when they turned up for the first meeting and saw each other.'

'Neither knew that the other was coming?'

'Exactly, but I wouldn't read too much into it. I've a sister the other side of Bampton and I wouldn't know what she was up to one week to the next.'

'But you don't think they were close?'

'I don't think they were that friendly, but she would have known as much about Penny Lander as anyone I can think of. She only lives two streets away. Why don't you pay her a visit?'

*

After the press conference, Sadler followed Llewellyn into his office and shut the door. Llewellyn stretched his long legs out underneath his desk. 'That went well.'

'Did it? I don't think we told them anything they didn't already know.'

'Exactly.'

Llewellyn was grinning at him, his red hair and broad face

momentarily reminding Sadler of a picture of the Cheshire cat in one of his childhood books. The phone rang on Llewellyn's desk and as he took the call, Sadler watched the smile fade and a look of concern cross his features. He put his hand over the receiver.

'Sadler, Penny Lander's daughter's just arrived in reception. You go and see her, will you? I'd rather you did this.'

Sadler walked down to the station's reception area and Justine Lander stood up to meet him. She was about Sadler's height and, by today's standards, her solid long limbs and sturdy frame would be considered overweight. But she was beautiful, her pre-Raphaelite face framed by long fair hair that fell loose to her shoulders. Her grey eyes were shaded underneath with smudges of purple-brown. Her hand was cool in his clasp and she withdrew it quickly. He steered her towards an interview room and got a PC to fetch them both a drink.

'The news must have come as a shock.'

She stared at her hands and spread them out in front of her, her long white fingers unadorned by rings. 'I can't believe it. I've lost both my parents in the space of a year. And there I was thinking that they would both live to enjoy a healthy old age.'

'They were healthy, then?'

'Oh yes. Dad played golf; Mum took herself for walks around the Bampton countryside. They both looked after themselves.'

'But your dad died last year of . . .'

'A heart attack. He keeled over outside one morning.'

'How did your mum take it?'

'She was shocked. Like me, she never expected it. But she carried on. Finished her job until retirement and got on with life. We were always a family to get on with things.'

She said it with a slight undertone of bitterness. Sadler tried to guess her age. *Late thirties*, he thought. When had Connie said that her mother took maternity leave?

'And you live in Kent?'

'I went to university in Kent and liked it down there. I still work at the university in Canterbury, in the undergraduate admissions department.'

She'd had a longer drive than he first realised. No wonder she looked exhausted.

'Are you staying at your mother's house? You can go there to freshen up, if you want, before we have this conversation.'

She shook her head. 'I'd really rather get it over with. I presume you want me to identify Mum's body. Then I'll drive to the house.'

Sadler looked at Justine's pale face. 'We won't be requiring a visual identification.' Sadler picked his words with care. 'In circumstances such as this we rely on forensic evidence.'

She looked at him in horror. 'God, what did they do to her?'

'No, it's not that,' he said quickly. 'But when a body has been exposed to the elements for a while, we prefer to rely on medical records and so forth.'

Justine shrugged her shoulders and looked down, a gesture of defeat.

'When were you last in touch with your mother?'

'About two or three weeks ago. I've looked in my diary to see if I could pinpoint the exact date, but I've not been able to. It was mid-week and I called her after work. After my work, I mean.'

'And she seemed normal.'

184

'Completely normal. We chatted about a couple of things and then said our goodbyes.'

'Were you close?'

'We were, actually. The problem was that Mum was useless on the phone. Everything came out in monosyllables so sometimes I used to steel myself before I made the call. We were all right when we were together. It was just over the phone that communication was really difficult.'

'You didn't think of moving nearer to each other?'

'It was in the back of both our minds, I think, but we were letting things settle down after Dad died. I didn't really want to move back up to Bampton and Mum liked it up here. Even though it wasn't where she was from.'

'She was brought up in Somerset?'

'Yes, but her parents died before I was born, so we never visited the place. We're not proving to be a very long-lived family I fear.'

Sadler changed tack. 'Was she interested in family history?'

If she thought the question strange, she gave no sign of it. 'I don't think so. We used to go and visit my grandparents on my dad's side when I was small but they both died before I was a teenager. She was an only child and I don't think she was that interested in the family. Why do you ask?'

'She attended meetings of the Bampton History Society.'

'Oh, that.' Justine was dismissive. 'She was a well read person, my mum, and interested in history. I've heard some of her former pupils say that she used to do some cracking history lessons. I'm sure that's all it was.'

It sounded plausible enough, in Sadler's opinion.

'Any enemies? Feuds and so on? Did she mention anything

that could have given you cause for concern? However trivial.'

But Justine Lander was shaking her head. 'I honestly can't think of anything. She led a blameless life, my mother. I swear there was nothing that ever threatened us as a family and when I spoke to her on the phone she seemed her normal self. Are you sure that this wasn't a tragic mistake?'

*

As Bridget Lander only lived two streets away from the organiser of the book club, Connie left her car outside Dorothy Cable's house and walked there. It was a big mistake. The sheeting wind blew straight into her face and the cold air pierced her lungs, causing her chest to constrict with pain as she breathed. At the bottom of the first street, she debated going back for the car but, feeling that she was already over halfway there, she put her head down and carried on. The street was a mirror image of Dorothy Cable's road and Connie had a sense of déjà vu as she walked up the path to Bridget Lander's house.

A woman was getting out of the car in the drive, a box of icing sugar in one hand and a mobile phone in the other. She glanced at Connie.

'I had to rush down the shops. Mid-recipe I realised I'd forgotten this.'

She was striking. Tall, probably just under six feet, rake thin with long limbs. She was pale-skinned and on her face a smattering of brown marks suggested that, at one time, she'd spent too long in the sun. Her hair held hints of the brunette she must have once have been. The rest was a wiry mop of grey that had been hacked into an unbecoming layered crop. One glance at the woman told Connie that Dorothy had warned Bridget she was coming. Not only was she expected but Bridget's face suggested the visit wasn't particularly welcome.

She opened the front door and led Connie into what was obviously a cook's kitchen. It was all about function over appearance. The cooker, which Connie would have slung out to the nearest tip, was chipped and stained from years of use and next to it was a large chef's chopping board, scored with grooves, presumably made by one of the sturdy knives hanging from a rack bolted to the wall. It was a room that Bridget Lander was obviously comfortable in and Connie, who was usually entertained in people's living rooms, recognised it as a place of refuge. They sat on either side of a small and well-worn table. There was a smell of baking in the air and Connie's stomach emitted an ominous rumble in response, which they both ignored.

'I'm expecting Justine, my niece, sometime today. I offered to go to the house with her but she wanted to be by herself. There won't be anything distressing there, will there?'

'I was the first officer on the scene. There's nothing distressing at all. It seems likely that Penny drove herself to Truscott Fields, where she was killed. We don't think anything happened in the house.'

Bridget turned her face to the oven and squinted to see through the glass. 'I've always liked Justine. She's a down-to-earth person; she reminds me a bit of my mother, her grandmother. She's always calm, doesn't panic.'

'And Penny?'

'Penny was harder to get to know. I didn't *not* like her; it's just that we were never really close. She taught, of course, and in those days it was harder to have a family and a full-time job. I don't think it left you much time for anything else. When she wasn't working she liked to potter around the house. We didn't go for coffee or any of the things you do nowadays.'

'Was theirs a happy marriage?' It was an innocuous question but Connie saw a flash of anger in the woman's eyes.

'What's that got to do with it? James is hardly a suspect, is he?'

'It was just a question.' Connie held the woman's gaze.

'As far as I'm aware the marriage was a happy one.' There was a note of finality in the comment.

'You were close to your brother?'

Bridget looked down at the table, her chin quivering. 'We were very close. He was the elder by nine months. Irish twins, I've heard it called.'

'Just the two of you?'

'Yes.'

Connie looked at the oven. She had no siblings and wondered what it would be like to be so close to someone you had shared your childhood with. She turned back to Bridget, who was struggling to compose herself.

'Have you any idea why someone would have wanted to kill Penny?'

The woman looked stricken. 'Penny kept herself to herself. I can't think of anything more ridiculous than someone deciding to kill her. All the years I knew her, she liked to keep herself in the background. She was a watcher, not a participator. The idea of someone killing her is ridiculous.'

Connie glanced around the kitchen. 'Do you have any kids?'

Bridget Lander flushed. 'I've never married. I spent my career working as a nurse. In the old Bampton hospital. When they shut it down, I decided to retire. I was too old for new things. So no children. But I am close to my niece. She used to come to me after school while we waited for Penny to finish work. I'd bake biscuits and bread for her then, too.' She exclaimed as she looked at the oven, got up and opened the door, and pulled out a loaf of bread.

Connie idly watched her. She wasn't sure if she had ever tasted homemade bread. 'Did Penny ever mention the case of the two girls who were kidnapped in 1978? They were called Rachel Jones and Sophie Jenkins.'

Bridget was easing a palette knife around the loaf. 'She mentioned it at the time. I think she was one of the first people to find out at the school. But that was years ago.'

'She had no idea what had happened?'

'I think she was as mystified as everyone else.'

'And she hadn't mentioned the case recently. After the suicide of Yvonne Jenkins, Sophie's mother, for example?'

Bridget Lander shook her head. 'Nothing.'

'And as far as you are aware, she never kept in touch with Rachel Jones, the kidnapped girl who was later found alive?'

'Kept in touch? I don't remember her knowing the girl in the first place. She was a teacher at the same school but she didn't know either child very well.'

'She wasn't trying to trace her family history, was she?'

'Her family history? What makes you say that?'

'It's just that Rachel Jones is now working as a genealogist in Bampton. I wondered if they'd had any contact.'

Bridget Lander stared in silence. She towered over Connie's

small frame and Connie, as she so often did in these situations, had to stifle the instinct to make herself even smaller.

Finally, she said, 'I can't see any reason why Penny would be interested in the services of a genealogist.'

Chapter 28

'Rachel. I thought it was you. I'd recognise your back any-where.'

Rachel jumped when a hand was placed on her shoulder and she craned her neck round, cricking it in the sudden move-ment. She was still jumpy after the exit from Sophie's house earlier that week but now felt ashamed. It could easily have been the police or a legitimate caller who'd arrived at the bun-galow while she was inside. What must they have thought if they'd seen her clambering out of the window?

This morning she had felt the urge for comfort food and Sorelle seemed just the place. As she had walked towards Bampton town centre, the pavements were still slippery but no longer treacherous. Instead the chill wind had increased a notch, blowing icy gusts into her face. The warmth of the res-taurant was a welcome relief, although only a few of the tables were taken. People were presumably keeping to the comfort of their homes and staying out of the cold. She took a table in the corner, ordered a plate of pasta and sat down with her back facing the door. Clearly, this wasn't incognito enough to fool someone like Sydney.

The librarian sat down opposite her without asking, pulled across a chair from another table and dumped her shopping down.

'It's market day today, not that you would know it. It's like a morgue out there. And all the stalls had was a choice between oranges or cabbages.'

'No wonder you came in here,' said Rachel, shoving a forkful of spaghetti into her mouth. 'We all need a bit of Mediterranean in our lives.'

'The Med,' snorted Sydney. 'Fred who runs this place went to Bampton Grammar, same as me, although I do remember him having a foreign grandma – I think she was Irish.'

Rachel laughed and started to choke. Sydney, enjoying her audience, carried on. 'If you want proper Med you need to go to Cafe Aroma on the high street. It's run by Greeks, or is it Cypriots? I can never remember. Anyway, they are your authentic package.'

'I rarely fancy it. It's always full of students. And the decor is so 1980s: red, white and black.'

'I know. William spends all his time in there. I tell him he can get a decent cup of coffee from the cappuccino machine at home. But you know what it's like. Teenagers prefer to spend their money feeding themselves away from the decent stuff they can get in their own houses.'

Sydney waved at a waiter and ordered without looking at the menu. She was obviously a regular and, looking at her ample curves, Rachel wondered what her own body would look like in ten years' time if she carried on eating as she did. She took a sip of her glass of white wine and luxuriated in the indulgence of lunchtime drinking.

'How's work?'

Rachel shrugged. 'OK, I suppose.'

'I've been looking at your website today. Don't look at me like that. I felt guilty I hadn't advertised your talk the other day.

So I've updated all the links on the library's site. And I had a good nosy around your site while I was at it.'

Rachel made a face and carried on eating.

'I like your family tree. No men on it. Love it.' Sydney laughed raucously and took a gulp of her wine.

It put Rachel on the defensive. 'I've done both sides, you know. It's just that it was my research topic at university. You know, the disparity between male and female lines.' Rachel thought back to the conversation with her grandmother. 'Which isn't to say I'm not interested in the men in my family – or men in general, in fact.'

Sydney smirked across the table at her. 'Well, I did see you leave with Richard after your talk.'

Rachel put down her fork and picked up the wine glass. 'It was just a quick drink.'

'Have the police been in touch with you again?'

Rachel shrugged. Should she mention having seen DC Childs at Richard's house? It would lead to a line of questioning from Sydney that she wasn't sure she could cope with. Coffee arrived and Rachel stared down at hers, the strong aroma making her nauseous. She pushed it away.

'They're keeping me updated as much as they can, I think. But it's bringing things back to the surface. I have this image of glossy green and black. I know it sounds daft but that's what I see when I think back to the time. I remember getting in the car and then it's like looking down a kaleidoscope. Fragment colours come back to me. Green and black.'

'From the woods, maybe?'

'I'm not sure. Maybe. But when I was in the churchyard last week, when the snow arrived here, I saw a yew tree and I got the same sensation as now. I feel sick to the pit of my stomach.'

'I'm not surprised that it's all coming back again. First Sophie's mum dies and then Mrs Lander is killed. They're saying she was strangled.'

'I know. The police have, at least, told me that.' Rachel looked at Sydney, whose sympathetic eyes were assessing her. 'Can I tell you something? In confidence, I mean. I don't want anyone to know, not even the police.'

'Sure. Is it something you've remembered?'

'Nothing like that. You know you said you'd been looking at my website? Was it the first time you'd looked at it?'

'I think I flicked through it last year sometime. It'd been a while, as I told you.'

'Well, I noticed this week that my site had a huge jump in stats about three weeks ago. I'd gone on to check. What with everything happening, it's not really surprising that more people are clicking on my site. Journalists and so forth. But what's really strange is that the surge happened *before* Mrs Jenkins killed herself.'

'Before?' Sydney's voice rose a fraction and she turned around to check no one had heard.

'Yes, that's what's so strange.' Rachel's voice had dropped to a whisper. 'The week before Mrs Jenkins died, the hits to my website quadrupled in number. But what's really strange is the page they were looking at.'

'Which was . . .'

'My family tree.'

Chapter 29

Sadler's phone vibrated on his desk. Christina. He couldn't hold the conversation off any longer and he answered the call. 'How are you?'

She didn't return the greeting. 'Are you in work?'

'Yes, but at my desk.'

'I've been trying to get through to you.' There was a reproachful tone in her voice that had become more and more common in the last few weeks.

'Yes, I saw. I've been busy.' It was lame, and it sounded so to his ears, but there it was. Lack of will to make it better.

'Is this it?'

Sadler didn't pretend not to understand her. 'Christina. I have a case on, and I need to concentrate on that. I hope . . .'

The line had gone dead. Once, she would never have done that. She'd been one to stand up and make her point. Say what she was happy about and what needed addressing. The silent line was one more confirmation of how things had changed. But was it the end? It was a question that demanded an answer and he hadn't given her an honest one. Not for the first time a relationship had petered out with little or no effort on his part. And yet he was fond of Christina and, if pushed, he would have said that he felt love. But there had never been a discussion about her leaving her husband. No talk of long-term commitment. Surely, in the end, that wasn't what real love was.

His mind strayed to Justine Lander. She must be at her parents' house by now, sorting through things. Connie was out interviewing Penny's friends. And Palmer? Well, Palmer, whom he could see through his office window, looked busy but was undoubtedly winding down in anticipation of his forthcoming nuptials. Sadler opened the office door and walked over to him.

'Found anything?'

Palmer waved a sheaf of papers helplessly. 'Nothing at all. These are Penny Lander's phone records. She didn't make or receive a single call or text message on the day she died.'

'But the half-finished sandwich suggested she'd been interrupted by someone.'

Palmer shook his head. 'Not by telephone, she hadn't. And I've looked again at the interviews with neighbours. No one remembers seeing a visitor arriving at the house. And in that cul-de-sac I doubt a strange car would go unnoticed.'

'What about her computer?'

'I'll follow it up. I suppose it's possible an e-mail might have come in.'

Sadler thought it unlikely. Penny Lander didn't sound like the type to eat a sandwich in front of the computer. And her laptop had been found in the small upstairs office, not on the coffee table where the remains of the meal were. Sadler's mobile rang once more; Christina must be having second thoughts. He let the phone go to voicemail and didn't bother to check the message as he walked out to his car. He missed having Connie with him and would have welcomed her presence. Whether she liked it or not, Connie was a catalyst for change and that was what this case, or cases, desperately needed.

The drive to Truscott Fields was short. The police station

was in the same location as in 1978 and it had taken officers a few minutes to respond to the 999 call received after the discovery of Rachel Jones. Sadler, usually happy to walk, couldn't face the bite of the winter wind and so drove the short distance to the woods. It took him six minutes exactly.

The car park was deserted. Presumably the cold was deterring people from taking their dogs for a walk. The place where Penny Lander's car had been left for two days was still visible. Deep indentations scored the ground, which also showed evidence of the forensic team having done their work.

Sadler walked over to the edge of Truscott Fields where her body had been found. Again there was evidence of the work of the Scientific Support Unit but little else. Sadler was convinced that the woman had come here to meet someone, although the mystery of the half-finished food was yet to be explained. Without any phone records it was impossible to identify the time she had arrived at the fields. Sadler doubted that she had been killed in broad daylight but she would only have driven here in the dark if she was meeting someone she trusted. Sadler suspected that the killing had taken place at night, as the killer would have needed time to bury the body under leaves and branches. It had been a fullish moon on the day she was killed, perhaps providing enough light by which to cover up a body.

The adjacent woods looked dank and uninviting. Sadler could smell rotting foliage from yesterday's rain and the leaves underfoot had crisped to ice. He forced himself to cross the empty car park towards the narrow entrance. The first part of the walk took him along a gravel path where litterbins and dog-waste receptacles encouraged visitors to clear up during their visit. After a hundred metres this came to an end and two narrower paths, forming a Y, angled off. Sadler took the left one for no reason other than it would take him away from the road that led to the car park entrance and further into the woods. The path was one person wide, well maintained but eerily silent. He had noticed that there were no maps at the entrance. The woods were being kept as a wilderness of sorts. It was probably beautiful in the summer.

Sadler, feeling the cold seep into his leather shoes, came to a halt and looked around him. Sophie's body could be anywhere in these woods. No wonder the initial investigating team had been so disheartened. Unless the body, assuming Sophie was dead, was personally revealed by someone who knew where it was, Sadler doubted that it would ever be found. She would be one of those eternally missing. To be discovered, perhaps in a hundred or so years from now, or possibly never at all.

*

Connie left Bridget Lander's house and battled the wind back to her car. According to everyone she had spoken to, Penny Lander had led a blameless life and there was absolutely no reason for her to have been killed. As far as Connie could see she had exhausted the only leads that she had. Admittedly, it was interesting that she'd attended two meetings of the same society where Rachel Jones occasionally lectured. Interesting, but hardly earth shattering. And yet. Police work was based on anomalies. Something that didn't fit. A crack in the smooth surface of truth that could be prised open.

It wasn't a dead end. Experience told Connie that those two local history meetings were important. She checked her watch. It was coming up to two o'clock. She should really eat something but food at lunchtime always left her feeling tired and sluggish.

She drove to the college situated on the main Bampton Road. It was known as Bampton Tech in 1978, teaching mainly vocational subjects. Peter Jenkins, Sophie's father, had lectured there in actuarial studies. Connie had looked up what an actuary did that morning. A specialist in statistical risk. Was that significant? There had been an element of considered risk – in snatching two young girls off the street in broad daylight and it made him, in Connie's eyes, a person of interest.

He still lectured at the college one day a week. She'd telephoned the college from her office that morning and was told that Peter Jenkins now worked as an actuary from home and came in once a week to lecture two classes, at eleven and three. He'd be there that afternoon.

It was two thirty by the time she'd found a parking space and then a newsagent's to change her five-pound note. She rushed back and found a traffic warden beginning to write her a ticket.

'Hey, I went to get some change,' she shook a fist full of coins at him which he ignored and carried on writing on his pad.

'Look! I'm going to pay. I just need to go to the machine.'

He looked up at her now. 'You're too late. I've started writing.'

'Bollocks!' she exploded. 'Don't give me that bullshit.'

She dropped the coins in her pocket and pulled out her police ID. 'I know for a fact you can tear that up.'

He glanced at the ID and then carried on writing. 'Then

you also know that the police don't get any preferential treatment from us. Hard luck.'

Connie swallowed the fury rising in her chest and walked off.

'Oi! That doesn't mean you don't still need to buy a ticket.'

She ignored him and walked towards the building's entrance. Sadler would sign off the payment for the parking ticket. He had done it once before. He wasn't bothered about that type of thing. He might have his ratty side, but minor petty infringements he seemed perfectly willing to ignore.

The college was pretty much what Connie had been expecting. The Victorian facade hid a utilitarian interior, designed to withstand the daily trampling of hundreds of young students. The woman at the reception desk seemed impressed by Connie's badge and directed her towards a room at the far end of the building. When she got there, it was empty and Connie sat for a few minutes, catching up with the news on her iPhone. Penny Lander's murder wasn't headline material any longer on the Internet sites. Fortunately a popular politician had been spotted having an intimate dinner with a woman who wasn't his wife and the papers were having a field day with the story.

Eventually, she heard footsteps coming down the corridor and a small man entered, wearing what she considered to be a 'flasher's' mac, a flared raincoat, slightly too large for him in an indeterminate sludgy brown colour. It was belted tightly around his waist. He looked surprised to see her but as soon as she reached into her handbag for her card he spotted her profession.

'I wondered if you lot would be paying me a visit.' He put

his leather case onto the desk and flicked up the clasps.

'You know why I'm here, then, Mr Jenkins?' Connie stood up and walked over to the desk.

'I saw the news about Yvonne's death. I wondered if you'd be getting in touch.'

Yvonne Jenkins's next of kin had proved to be a distant cousin who was organising the funeral arrangements. And yet her death would still have impacted on her ex-husband's life. You gave up some responsibilities on divorce, but not all, and Connie wondered whether this neat little man had any regrets over his failed marriage.

'I've not come to see you about your former wife's death. We're treating it as suicide, but we are alarmed by its proximity to the later murder of Penny Lander. I'd just like to ask you a few questions about that.'

The man stopped shuffling his papers. 'The teacher who worked at St Paul's? What would I know about that? It was over thirty years ago. I never knew the woman.'

'You didn't see her at parents' evenings?'

'I never went. Yvonne used to do all that. I was too busy with work.'

Too busy carrying on with your soon-to-be new wife, thought Connie. 'You never kept in touch with Sophie after your divorce? It must have been hard to leave your child behind.'

He looked at her now. Willing her to judge him. 'You have no idea what it was like then. I've never felt so much abject misery as I did in those early years of my marriage. Every day, when I came home from the college, I'd put my key in the lock of that door and feel sick to the bottom of my stomach. I couldn't stand it. I was looking for any way out and then I met Margaret and it didn't take me long to see where happiness lay.'

'You're still together?'

He looked angry now. 'We've been married for over thirty years. Longer than most. That first marriage seems like a nightmare. Sometimes I dream about those days, the claustrophobia and the misery, and I have to force myself to wake up. Can you imagine that? I deliberately wake myself up so I don't have to keep dreaming about the misery.'

'And Sophie? Was she part of the misery too?'

Peter Jenkins sat down at his desk. Connie reckoned she had about five minutes maximum until students would start to trickle in but it looked like he still had something to tell her. He appeared even smaller sitting at his desk and she wondered how he dealt with rowdy students, but then perhaps the disruptive ones didn't take actuarial courses. He seemed to be struggling to form a sentence, his small mouth working.

'I met Yvonne at school. It was the early sixties and we were in the same class. We started going out when I was in the sixth form and Yvonne had left school to go to secretarial college. Our families knew each other and it was natural that we get engaged and then married.'

'And marriage wasn't all it was cracked up to be?' suggested Connie. 'It's a common problem.' She thought of Palmer and his white face that week. He was about to find this out the hard way. But Peter Jenkins was shaking his head.

'It wasn't that. I think we were happy those first few years. We were both working, we had some money coming in and we both enjoyed our jobs.'

'So what changed? Did you meet someone else?'

His head shot up and Peter Jenkins glared at her angrily. Connie saw with a start that his eyes were red and bloodshot.

'Despite what you and everyone else might think of me, I was for a long time a loving husband and father. What changed was Yvonne when Sophie was born. She suffered from post-natal depression. That's all you read about these days in the papers. This person's depressed after she's had a baby. You have no idea, no idea whatsoever, how utterly destructive it can be.'

'She was severely depressed?'

'It was a nightmare. Yvonne couldn't sleep. She would roam around the house with Sophie in her arms. I was absolutely terrified that she would drop her. She didn't cook, she didn't wash. She went through a stage where she would just knit. I can see her now, her elbows out at right angles, as those needles clackety-clacked. God I feel sick even thinking about it.'

'Didn't she get any help? I mean, I know we're talking about over forty years ago, but a doctor would have been able to see she was depressed.'

'I took her to a doctor. I had to force her into a car and he took a look at her. He wanted her to take Valium but she wouldn't because she was still breastfeeding. She adored that baby. Whatever problems she might have had, she never took it out on Sophie.'

Yvonne Jenkins had died from an overdose of diazepam – unbranded Valium. Perhaps Yvonne had been sending a message to her ex-husband when she had taken that final overdose.

'Was she ever suicidal?' asked Connie, aware that time was ticking away.

'I wouldn't have said so. She had no energy, no life for

months on end. But I don't think she ever seriously thought of killing herself. And as I said, she adored Sophie.'

'And in the end it all got too much for you?' Connie tried to imagine this self-effacing man reaching the end of the line in his marriage and bailing to leave his daughter with a depressed mother. But there had been nothing on file about this. Perhaps in the unenlightened seventies depression had been the illness that could not be spoken about. But once more he was shaking his head.

'I didn't leave until Sophie was six. After about nine months, maybe a year after Sophie was born, Yvonne gradually began to improve. She lost the weight she had put on and started to go out, meet other mothers and so on. And our marriage began to improve. It had never been our intention that Yvonne go back to work and she began to make a life for herself as a wife and mother. I genuinely thought that our marriage would survive all of the problems.'

'So what happened?'

They both turned as a student walked into the room and, ignoring them both, slung a bag on one of the tables while texting on his iPhone.

Peter Jenkins dropped his voice to a whisper. 'What happened was that Yvonne got pregnant again.'

Chapter 30

Sadler walked over to Connie's desk, looking at the jumble of papers, pens, pencils and reports. He had a problem with the latter. He didn't like official files left scattered around the office. It smacked of inefficiency and haste, neither of which was a characteristic he would apply to Connie's determined approach to her job. He picked up one of the papers. Inside were certificates pinned together, in the name of Paul Saxton, Rachel Jones's father. Sadler scanned the details. Paul Saxton had been clearly dead by the time the girls were kidnapped and Sadler wasn't so fanciful to think that the certificates were faked.

Palmer was tidying his desk in readiness for his annual leave. He was completing each movement in slow time, as if his limbs ached with the heaviness of his actions. He noticed Sadler frowning at him and, shutting a drawer, came over to Connie's desk.

'What've you got there?'

'It looks like Connie did some digging into Rachel Jones's past before we were pulled from the case. She's lined up Rachel's father's BMD certificates.'

Sadler switched on a desk light and examined them. 'The marriage and death certificates have the same address as the birth certificate, which suggests that Paul Saxton remained in the family home after his marriage. A bit unusual, I suppose, but hardly earth shattering.'

'What's the piece of paper pinned to the back?'

'It looks like a copy of a page from an electoral register.'

Sadler skimmed over the details. Registered at the address in 1969 were Paul Saxton, aged twenty-four, Roger Saxton, aged twenty-one, and Tom and Shirley Saxton, aged fifty-six and fifty-four respectively. Mary Jones had presumably moved into her new husband's house after their marriage, possibly while they saved up for a home of their own. Connie had also photocopied a recent copy of the electoral register. Roger Saxton was still living there.

Sadler looked at the clock. The house was a fifteen-minute walk away. Would Connie be angry at him pinching her work?

'I'm going to pay Roger Saxton a visit. If Connie calls, tell her that's where I'm headed.' Sadler glanced over at his sergeant's desk. 'When does your leave start?'

Palmer looked down. 'Tomorrow.'

*

Connie pushed open the door to Cafe Aroma and ordered a large coffee. The place had quietened down now that lessons had started at the college and the few students left were trying to do some work. She took her coffee to one of the far tables and sat down facing the window looking on to the high street. Shoppers were walking past with far fewer plastic carrier bags than she would have expected a couple of years ago. Three years of recession had taken its toll on the shops. The place she had often bought clothes in had shut down and the unit still lay empty, its blank windows giving it a desolate air.

When she was twenty-three, Connie had got pregnant by

her then boyfriend Stuart and had an abortion. She was two years into her police career, he was studying for his sergeant's exams and a baby figured in neither of their plans. It had never been discussed. She simply told him that she was pregnant and he'd taken it as read that she would know what to do about it. The operation had passed by in a blur and two days later she had been back at work. She never thought about that time. Her life had experienced other traumas, other more pressing worries, and she'd filed the incident to the back of her mind. Stuart remained a figure of her past. He was apparently married and probably had his own children by now.

In 1972, she supposed it had not been so easy to procure an abortion. She wondered when the procedure had been legalised. She took out her phone and looked it up: 1967. So five years later, Yvonne Jenkins had taken advantage of the relaxation of the rules and had an abortion when she had become pregnant with her second child. Connie wondered what she had felt about that. Whatever the devastation of postnatal depression, surely the fact that she had doted on Sophie had counted for something? The thought of going through that period again must have been too awful for Yvonne Jenkins to contemplate. Peter Jenkins was adamant that he'd been the father of the new baby.

The dynamics of that long-finished relationship fascinated Connie. From Peter Jenkins's reddened eyes, she guessed that the termination had affected him deeply, but something in the manner he had told the story suggested to Connie that part of the impetus had come from him. She replayed his words and tried to grasp at what had given her that impression. His tone? The challenge in his eyes, perhaps?

So there had been no new child but the marriage had failed nevertheless. This didn't surprise Connie. Her relationship hadn't survived the termination either. It was women who carried around the vestiges of their decision, however buried the consequences might be. What a life for Yvonne Jenkins. Two dead children, depression and a husband who started a new life elsewhere. And yet Llewellyn remembered her as a smart, well-dressed woman. She had tried. But life had just ground her down.

The cafe had now cleared and Connie was left as a lone customer. The woman at the till had the machine's lid up and was poking around inside. She saw Connie looking around and said without smiling, 'Give us an hour and we'll be full again.'

Connie took a sip of her coffee. 'It looks like you do a roaring trade most days.'

The woman started to insert a new receipt roll into the till. 'Can't complain. You a friend of Francis?'

'Sadler? Yeah, though not sure "friend" really covers it. He's my boss.'

'Your boss? You a copper, then?' The woman had stopped what she was doing and stared openly at Connie.

'That's right. Don't I look like one?'

The woman shrugged. 'I wouldn't have had you down as a copper, I have to say. I had you pegged as Francis's new squeeze.'

Connie felt the colour creep up her neck. 'I think the boss has a girlfriend already.'

The woman bent her head back to the task and mumbled, 'Try telling that to Christina.'

*

The house that had been the Saxton family home for four decades was on a 1930s former council estate. Few of the homes were now under the control of the local authority and most owners had attempted to rid their property of the utilitarian look so common to houses built on an estate. The most obvious giveaway was the sludge brown pebble-dashing that some, like the Saxtons, had neither the means nor inclination to paint. Sadler looked for a bell, then a knocker, and finding neither, rapped loudly on the door.

Roger Saxton was massive. Grotesquely overweight, he had to push his body back against the wall to open the door. He wheezed with the exertion of moving around his massive bulk as Sadler stood on the doorstep and tried to explain himself.

'Paul's been dead over forty years. What you after him for now?'

'It's not a case of being after anybody. I just want to confirm the details of his life. Could I come in for a moment?'

Reluctantly, Roger Saxton let Sadler into the hall and led the way towards the living room. It was sparsely furnished but immaculately tidy, a surprise to Sadler, who had assumed that a man who was possibly disabled would have been put at a severe physical disadvantage by his bulk. Sadler handed over Connie's papers and sat in an armchair. Roger Saxton remained standing as he scrutinised the papers.

'What's all this, then? Checking up on us?'

'I just wanted to confirm that the information contained within the papers is correct. In relation to your brother Paul Saxton in particular.'

Roger levered himself into an armchair, his fat spilling over each side.

'It's been years since anyone asked me about Paul. He died when I was a young man.'

'Of pneumonia?'

Roger shrugged, sending a ripple of fat across his body. 'So they said. He was never that strong. He had bad asthma that was difficult to control.'

'But he did die?'

A wheezy laugh came from the huge flesh. 'He definitely died. I saw the body myself. What's this all about?'

'I'm trying to pull some loose ends together. Were you questioned by the investigation team looking into the kidnapping of Rachel Jones and Sophie Jenkins?'

'Them? They came round here asking questions. I was away working in Dundee. They interviewed my mum, but she couldn't tell them anything. We hadn't seen sight nor sound of Mary Jones since the day our Paul died.'

'They didn't travel to Dundee to interview you?'

'Eh? What would they want to interview me for? I was nowhere near the place they were kidnapped.'

'You were the uncle of one of the kidnapped children.'

'Uncle? I had nothing to do with the child. I never set eyes on her. Paul died while Mary was pregnant and that was the last I saw of her. Never set eyes on the baby.'

Sadler frowned and kept his eyes on the indignant man in front of him. 'You had a falling out?'

Thin lips in the large face pursed. 'Falling out? Nothing quite so grand I can assure you, although I never liked the woman.'

'Who? Mary Jones? Why didn't you like her?'

'Proper madam, she was. She had our Paul under her thumb.

He'd known her since school and was willing to do anything for her. She waltzed into our lives and straight back out of them as soon as Paul was dead.'

'What do you mean by "willing to do anything for her"?'

'Just that. Anything she asked he was prepared to do. Marry her, pretend her child was his. Nothing was too much when it came to the determined Mary.'

'You mean the child wasn't his?' Sadler felt a warmth sweeping through him.

'Hardly. One minute they were going out, next minute she was pregnant. Then in a blink she'd had the baby. The dates didn't add up. My mother had it worked out straight away. She wasn't daft. There was no way that baby was his.'

'So you all knew that Rachel Jones wasn't the daughter of your brother?'

'She wasn't Rachel Jones then, though, was she? She hadn't been born. Mary was pregnant with a baby that we knew couldn't have been our Paul's.'

Sadler could feel his parched throat clam up. He could do with a drink of water, but how long would it take this man to fetch it? 'Do you think he was aware that the child wasn't his?'

'He might have been. It wouldn't have made any difference. He adored Mary. His child or not, he would have married her anyway.'

'And you're telling me that no one informed the investigation team of this fact when they interviewed your parents?'

'Just Mum. Dad died in 1974. They interviewed my mother and she never told them anything.'

'But why not?'

'Family business. Nothing to do with anyone else.'

Sadler sighed and looked at his feet. What can an investigation team do in the face of a 'family' that closes in on itself when troubles arrive? 'And so you never saw Mary Jones after the death of your brother.'

The man looked at him slyly. 'Ah well. I didn't say that. I said that we hadn't seen her up to when the kids disappeared.'

'But you saw her . . .'

'After. She came round. Proud Mary. I was back from Dundee by then and was here when she turned up. Wanted to know if anyone had asked about her and Paul.'

'Didn't your mother keep in touch with her grandchild?'

'I tell you, that baby was nothing to do with us. Mary left us as soon as Paul died. She was about seven months gone. We never saw her again until just after the kidnapping.'

'And she wanted to know if you had anything to do with it?'

Roger Saxton looked at him aghast. 'Me! She never thought that. That wasn't the reason she came round. She wanted to know if the police had been asking about Paul. That's what the little madam was worried about. Whether her big secret would be coming out.'

'That another man was the father of her child.'

'Exactly. And I told her then what I'm telling you now. We told no one what had happened. It was nothing to do with anyone else. Her secret was safe.'

'Is that what you said to her?'

'Oh yes. She didn't like it, of course. But that's what it was, wasn't it? A secret.'

Chapter 31

Rachel left Sydney to pay the bill after thrusting some notes at her. She waved off Sydney's concern and left the bistro feeling slightly sick. She'd had two small glasses of wine and she wondered, as she climbed back in the car, whether it would make her over the limit. But over lunch an idea had been forming in her mind. To go back to Sophie's house and find out what the visitor had been looking for. Because, perhaps, it was finally time to stop running and face the fear head on. It was either that or wait for whoever it was to continue on the road that might, eventually, lead them to her.

Her initial fright had subsided, but when she arrived at the house her courage failed her. She stared at the blank-faced bungalow with her car keys in her hand and tried to talk herself into going inside. A door to her left opened and an old woman stood looking at her.

'You're the girl that got taken.'

It was said as a statement, not a question, and Rachel shook her head. 'That was my friend, Sophie.'

The woman came out onto the path. 'I know. You're the other one. The one that came back. The one that was returned.'

'Returned?' Rachel walked towards the woman. 'What do you mean by returned?'

She thought the woman might shrink back from her

213

approach but she held her ground. 'You were returned. By those who would do you harm.'

Rachel was angry now. 'This is my life you're speculating about. How do you know that I was *returned*, as you say? It might have been an accident that I survived.'

'Violence does, in truth, recoil upon the violent, and the schemer falls into the pit which he digs for another.'

Rachel gaped at the woman. What the hell was this about? 'Is that from the Bible?'

The woman turned her back on her and said over her shoulder, 'Sherlock Holmes.'

Rachel stared after her for a moment and then turned towards the hill stretching away from the crescent. She could remember puffing up the incline as a child. She had always been slightly overweight and now, a size fourteen, she could really do with losing a stone. Perhaps walking off the lunch might help as she clearly could not or would not enter that bungalow again. It was the first time that she'd done the walk since the kidnapping. From the day of her abduction to the move to their new house in Clowton, Rachel had been walked to school by her mum. She realised now it must have made her mother late for work every day.

She'd been breathless doing that walk every day in 1978 and nothing had changed. As she neared the brow of the hill, she realised with a shock that the postbox was still there, shiny and with the familiar GR letters adorning the front. She felt a spurt of anger, the first that she had felt in a long time, if ever, at the thought of the woman who had tempted them into the car like a witch in a fairy tale. The ironic thing was that, if she'd been on her own, she would never have got into that car. She wasn't stupid and her mother had instilled in her the basic awareness that had been less common then but was now the basis of all parenting. You never got into a stranger's car. Surely Sophie had been told that too, but perhaps Mrs Jenkins had emphasised the gender of any driver too much. Perhaps danger had been associated with men. Because Sophie had blithely climbed into that car without a care in the world.

At the top of the road, Rachel debated turning left and then left again into the churchyard of St Paul's and walking down to the back school entrance. But there was something compelling about the movements of that 1978 January day and her body was being propelled in another direction. She hurried back down the road, slid into her car and started the engine. She slowly drove to the top of the street, stopped at the letterbox and thought. She could remember that the woman immediately turned right, which had alerted them straight away that they'd made a big mistake. She could remember looking aghast at Sophie, whose face had been slow to show any recognition of the trouble that they were in. And then, like a balloon whose stopper has suddenly been removed, she had let out a piercing cry.

She could swear that the woman then made an immediate left, off the main road and down a side street. Rachel could remember looking out of the window and there being nothing or no one who would be able to help her. The woman had driven quickly but with determination, not calling attention to herself. She could remember trying to open the doors but a child lock must have been fitted and nothing happened. Then she remembered pulling up at an entrance. Not Truscott Woods, another place.

There was a place missing from her recollections. Between the top of the road and the woods. But she wasn't going to remember it sitting in her twenty-first-century car. She would have to skip the missing part and go straight to Truscott Woods.

It wasn't the first time she'd been back since that fateful day. Two weeks after the kidnapping she'd been brought there by Wendy, the shiny-faced policewoman, driving an inconspicuous unmarked car. Rachel sat in the back holding hands with her mother, who looked angry. Her mother was told to stay in the car and it was the policewoman who gently led Rachel to the spot and asked her all those questions. But she couldn't remember anything. According to the evidence on the soft ground, she had run up the lane towards the main road but she had no memory of doing that. The policewoman had looked disappointed and, scared of letting people down, Rachel looked towards her mother for reassurance. But she was sitting in the back of the car looking in towards the dense, dark trees.

Now Rachel looked back at her own car, parked neatly between the rows of others. It was milder today and the dog walkers and regular exercisers that used the wood's parkland were taking advantage of the weak wintry sun to get some relief from the indoors. She could hear one dog owner just inside the wood, calling 'Benjy' sharply and then more desperately. An errant dog. The voice gave her courage and she stepped through the opening and straight into the path of a man. She looked up to apologise and her mouth opened in shock.

'What the hell are you doing here?'

Richard Weiss's face was scarlet with embarrassment. 'Rachel. I never thought that you'd—'

'Be here?' she finished for him. 'Well, I am. And I have a right to be here like anyone else. Except you're supposed to be in work. And don't tell me you fancied a lunchtime stroll.'

What on earth had brought him here? Two nights earlier she had spent the night with him and savoured the comfort he had offered. Now she remembered that she barely knew the man standing in front of her. 'Did you come to have a gawp? Well, you wouldn't be the first. Half of St Paul's school came down in 1978. It was one of the reasons I moved. It had become a day's outing for the students.'

'Rachel, I know you're angry—'

'Yes, you're right. I am.' Angry didn't even begin to describe her terror that he might not be with her out of affection. Or the growing love that she felt towards him. As a teenager she'd been an outsider in high school. She'd made a few friends but had allowed none of them to come close to her. Her notoriety had both attracted and repelled her fellow students and she had learned to live with it. It was only university that had given her a fresh start. A clean slate where friendships had been made based on nothing more sinister than enjoyment of each other's company. But suspicion still gripped her. Was Richard, who also liked to dig out the past, only with her because of the mystery of her abduction?

'Please give me a chance to explain. I met my dad this morning when he came into the office.'

'Your dad? What the hell's he got to do with it?'

'Nothing, he's got nothing to do with anything. It's just that—'

'*What?*' Rachel was shouting now and a dog walker emerging from the woods gave them a wide berth.

'I mentioned to him that I'd had a drink with you the other night. Nothing else.'

'And?'

'And nothing. Rachel what's the matter with you?'

'Me? You told your dad that we'd had a drink the other night and then you end up in these woods?'

Richard rubbed his face with his hands. 'Look. My dad mentioned that he knew your mother once.'

'He knew Mum? I never knew that.' Rachel could feel the anger draining out of her to be replaced by the more familiar tug of grief. 'Why did that make you come to the woods?'

He was looking away from her now. 'He asked after you. Asked what sort of person you'd become after the kidnapping. It was strange because I've only ever known you as an adult. I've consciously tried to avoid thinking about you as a child. It's the adult you I'm interested in.' He was trying to smile at her. 'So I came down here. Just to see what it must have been like all those years ago.'

'And was it helpful?'

Her bitterness made him wince. 'Not particularly.' He looked unhappy.

'Are you sure that's the only reason that you came down here?'

He looked her in the eyes. 'Of course.'

*

'I've remembered something.'

They were in a different pub this time. The Green Man, a popular place with Bampton's workers who fancied a quick drink at lunchtime. One man in particular looked like he'd had a few too many. Tall, ruddy-faced, the large glass of red wine he was holding was clearly the latest in a line going back many years. Richard spotted her looking at the man.

'Charles needs to start taking it easy if he wants to get home in one piece today. The road up to Needham Hall is a sheet of ice.'

'That's Charles Needham? Good God, he's aged. He was so handsome when he was younger.'

'You knew him then?'

'My mum knew him. He was in the same year at school. He had a thing for her for a while, I think. He'd pop in now and then when we moved to Clowton. But, my God, I would have hardly recognised him.'

'Keep your voice down, Rachel. He's looking over here.'

Rachel deliberately turned in her seat and stared at the florid man. He blinked slightly at her and then narrowed his eyes.

'I don't think he recognises me,' she said, picking up her glass and taking a large gulp. It wasn't settling properly in her stomach though. The slight acidity was sticking in her gullet and causing a searing pain in her throat. It made her want to drink more not less of it. She turned her attention back to Richard.

He was looking at her with a neutral expression. Despite his reserved manner he appeared sensitive to her moods. It was a potent combination for her. She could feel his concern radiating off him, which pulled her towards him. Yet he held back. Letting her take the initiative. With him, she didn't feel threatened. If he'd come on any stronger Rachel doubted that she would be sitting here, drawing comfort from him. She was prepared to accept his explanation for being in the woods. For now.

'You've remembered something from before. When you were kidnapped?'

She nodded her head, not sure how much to say. 'It's fragments, really, like in a dream. But I can't seem to make it into a reality. Something is trying to break through. There's a man. He's really big. Big hands and arms. That's all I can feel. And there's a woman standing behind him, saying something.'

'The woman who kidnapped you?'

'I'm certain it's her. She's saying something to him. Telling him to hurry up.'

A silence fell between them. 'Rachel, I—'

'I wasn't assaulted, if that's what you're thinking. The police could prove that. And I'm sure that this isn't what I'm remembering. I know I keep saying big hands, but I don't mean that in a horrible way. In fact I don't really know what way I do mean it. But that's what I'm beginning to remember. A big man stooping over me.'

'Any adult male would have seemed big to you when you were eight years old. I have a niece who's that age. She seems tiny compared to me.'

'But you *are* tall. That's what I mean. It was someone your height or taller. I'm sure of it.' Rachel shook her head, trying simultaneously to clear her thoughts and pull from the depths of her memory something else.

'There's another thing. These colours. I'm sure we didn't go to Truscott Woods straight away. When I think back to that time very quickly, you know, think of something else and then quickly flick my mind to that time, I get these colours in my head. Like dark green and glossy black. It's difficult to describe. But that's what I get. This ferny green colour and a glossy black.'

'Do you think you've seen the colours painted somewhere?'

'I don't know. Yes, I think so. But I just can't clarify the image.'

'Have you told the police?' Richard took a sip of his wine and looked at her with a concerned expression. He really was a lovely man, thought Rachel. But was he what she needed right now in the middle of the resurgence of old memories?

'It's all just happened. I mentioned it to Sydney today though. Do you think I should tell them?'

He shrugged and looked into his glass of wine. 'I'm not sure. They may be looking for something more concrete than that. Do you think he was someone you knew?'

'I don't think so. I didn't really have that many adult men in my life at that time. My dad was dead and my mother never really looked for anyone else. So I'm not sure who he could be if I knew him.'

'Don't you think that's strange? About her not getting anyone else. She was quite young when your dad died. Did she never have any boyfriends?'

'You're Rachel Jones.'

Charles Needham had walked across the room to their table and was now looming over her. He seemed in control of his movements but Rachel had no doubt that he was very drunk. She fixed a smile to her face and nodded.

'I am. And you're Charles. I remember you from when I was little. You used to come and visit us in Clowton.'

Charles Needham looked nonplussed. 'You remember me? I don't suppose I've changed that much but then again neither have you. I'd recognise you anywhere. And you look like your nan.'

'Nancy? We don't look anything like each other.' Rachel thought of her slim, glamorous grandmother. He was on the wrong track with that one.

'Not Nancy – Mair. The Welsh one.'

Rachel frowned at him. 'Mair? She was my great-grandmother – Mair Price. Do I really look like her?'

Charles Needham rocked on his heels. 'Mair Price. I'm not likely to forget her in a hurry. There's a woman you didn't want to get on the wrong side of.'

Rachel smiled genuinely this time. She'd heard that Mair had been a tartar. Well, good for her.

'Have you heard anything more about the murder up at Truscott Woods? I wondered if the police were keeping you in-formed.'

The smile left Rachel's face. 'Nothing. And I don't think it's anything to do with me.'

'I don't think so either,' said Charles robustly. 'Bugger all to do with you, in fact.'

'What makes you say that?' She looked over at Richard who was clearly furious with the interruption.

'The woman came to see me the week before she died. Bark-ing mad, she was. Asking me all about my parents.'

'Mrs Lander, you mean? You saw her the week she died?'

'Could hardly help it, could I? Walked up to my front door, banged on it and asked what role my parents had with the old Bampton hospital.'

'What did she mean?'

Charles Needham rocked on his heels. 'No idea. She wasn't making much sense to me.'

'And had they been involved in the hospital?'

'How the hell should I know? My mother had her finger in every pie going, so if she was on some hospital committee I wouldn't be surprised. But what the hell it had to do with me, I don't know.'

'Were you born there?'

A furtive look came into the man's face. 'None of your business, you nosy bitch.'

'Now, you look here...' Richard had risen and Charles stepped back in surprise, blinking at the man who matched him for height and bulk.

'Come on, Charles, you've got a pint waiting for you here,' shouted one of his friends from the bar.

Hitching up his trousers, Charles Needham walked back to join the group.

'What the hell was that all about?' Rachel felt sick, as she often did when things turned nasty. Richard had sat down and looked angry.

'I think we should go. I need to get back to the office.'

Rachel stood and picked up her coat. As she shrugged it on she glanced over to the bar where Charles Needham was talking to his friends, gesticulating expansively as he told his story. Something or other about a dog who had gone down a foxhole. And all the time, his eyes were on her.

Chapter 32

Bampton's main church stood on the top of the hill overlooking the town. As neither of Sadler's parents was religious, it wasn't a place he was familiar with, although he had attended a handful of weddings and christenings there over the years. This was his first funeral in the building. The church's spacious interior, a throwback to the days when people regularly attended church, made a mockery of the handful of people who had turned up to attend Yvonne Jenkins's funeral.

Why have a church service at all? thought Sadler. Who had made the decision when surely a plain graveside ceremony would have been sufficient? Perhaps it was the officious-looking priest whose monotone intonation was making the interminable service seem even longer. Connie was sitting next to him, shivering. Her gaze was fixed on two women who occupied the second pew from the front. Both were tall and dressed in black.

The service ended and a small, stooping woman was the first to follow the priest as he led the congregation out of the church and into the attached graveyard. The church had been cold but was nothing compared to the biting wind that met them as they left the porch. The crowns of the yew trees that ringed the perimeter of the churchyard bent in an arc towards them, their pungent aroma scenting even this wintry day.

'Jesus,' he heard Connie mutter. One of the mourners turned to them with a frown.

Sadler was discomfited. He had assumed that after the funeral, the cortège would be heading towards the large cemetery on the outskirts of Bampton and had parked his car to ensure that he could get away quickly. He hadn't anticipated attending the burial as well.

He pulled on her sleeve. 'We don't need to go to the grave, do we? Let's get back.'

She looked freezing but shook her head. 'I want to watch those two.' She nodded at the women who were making their way towards the newly dug grave.

'Who's the old woman who sat at the front?' he asked.

'A neighbour. She's mad as a hatter. Don't get into a conversation with her.' Connie's eyes were still on the other women.

'And those two? The women you're staring at.'

Connie glanced at him out of the side of her eyes and smirked. 'The one on the left, the manly looking one, is Dorothy Cable. She's the organiser of Penny Lander's book club. She never mentioned that she knew Yvonne Jenkins, though.'

'And the other?'

'Bridget Lander. Penny's sister-in-law.'

They had reached the grave. Bridget, sensing their scrutiny, was now, in turn, watching them. Her gaze was neutral but direct. She kept her eyes on them as the coffin was lowered into the grave.

After a final prayer, the mourners began to drift off. Sadler was desperate to get into the warmth of the car but took the lead from Connie, who remained watching the two women. Bridget Lander came across to them.

'I always hate funerals. You get to my age and their frequency increases considerably.'

'Did you know Yvonne Jenkins?' Connie was clearly in no mood for niceties.

'Not as such. We saw her around town, of course. And everyone knew who she was. But I didn't know her personally.'

'Then why are you here?' Connie's tone remained polite but determined.

Bridget directed her answer to Sadler. 'She died at around the same time as Penny. We're not going to be able to bury her for a while yet. It seemed important that we marked their deaths somehow.'

'You think the two deaths are connected?' asked Connie. The woman ignored her.

'Did either Penny or your brother know Yvonne Jenkins?' Sadler was merely curious but her reaction was a surprise.

'My brother? What's he got to do with it.' Sadler sensed that she was angry and he couldn't understand why. Underneath her pale skin, a few red blotches appeared, working their way up her neck.

'It was just a question.'

His mild tone mollified her slightly. She stepped away from them.

'Not that I'm aware of.'

She walked away from them, her rigid body giving little away.

'She didn't like it when you mentioned her brother,' Connie noted.

'No.' He pulled out his phone from his pocket and switched it back on, waiting to see who'd been trying to contact him while he was at the funeral. 'What are you going to do now?'

'Me? I'll go back to the station and see what's happening there. What about you?'

'I need to talk to Rachel about what Roger Saxton told me.'

'You think it'll be a surprise?'

'I'm not sure. She's a difficult person to read.' He turned to her. 'It was good work on your part, matching up all those certificates. I hope you didn't mind me following it up.'

She gave him a look and turned away. 'I'll be off, then.' And then smiled.

He was forgiven. After checking for messages, Sadler scrolled down his phone and retrieved the number Rachel Jones gave to him at their first meeting.

'Could we get together for a quick update? Nothing formal. Perhaps we could meet in a cafe?'

The connection was bad and her reply muffled. At first Sadler thought that he had misheard her. 'Sorry. Can you repeat that?'

Her voice was clearer this time. 'How do you feel about meeting at Truscott Fields?'

Sadler felt a jolt of shock. 'You want to go back to Truscott Fields?'

She sounded defensive. 'I was there this week but I met someone I know and didn't spend as much time there as I'd intended. I'd like to go back. The only thing is I'm in Bampton without the car. It'll take me about twenty minutes on foot. Shall I meet you in the car park – we can go for a walk.'

Sadler was momentarily stunned. Here was a woman whom Llewellyn was asking to be treated with kid gloves and she was suggesting that a meeting with a police officer took place at the scene of not only her kidnapping but that of a recent, possibly connected, murder. Sadler thought that it was about time that he revised his opinion of Rachel Jones.

'Fine. Twenty minutes it is.'

*

Connie walked down Bampton High Street and glanced at a shop window which had a display of pans and other kitchen equipment artfully arranged. The funeral had left her exhausted and she had plenty to think about. But window shopping relied on nothing more than unseeing eyes, safe in the knowledge that she couldn't afford much anyway. Her new flat had a modern kitchen. Not gleaming chrome or anything flash, but modern enough for Connie's assortment of plates and saucepans that she'd collected over the years to be woefully out of place. She needed to treat herself to some new stuff on her next payday, although the price of the 'iodised aluminium' saucepan set in the window made her wince. She became aware of steps behind her; sounds which she suddenly knew were keeping in time with hers and stopping when she did. She carried on walking briskly and then stopped suddenly in front of a building society. A man with curly black hair careered into her. She looked up at him.

'Who the fuck are you?'

He looked both shocked and disapproving at Connie's language.

'You following me?' she demanded, and now the man's face flushed a red hue. He was a blusher like her. Good. But his powers of recovery seemed to be better.

'DC Childs? I'm Nick Oates from the *Daily Mirror*. I just wanted to ask you a few questions about the case that you're currently working on. The murder of Penny Lander. Can you give me an update on your progress?'

She turned away from him and started walking quickly down the street. 'You know the score. There's another press conference scheduled for tomorrow. You'll get an update then.'

'But you're not telling us anything that we don't already know. You know how it is – we're one step in front of you. Can't you give me something else?'

Now she stopped and faced him. 'Yes, I do know how it is and you do too. I can't give you anything because my boss would have me served up on a platter if I did. You know what the score is. We've even had a directive from the Home Office. All the way from London up to us in Derbyshire. Stop those flirtatious drinks with journalists and keep your mouths shut about current investigations. So you can stop following me down the street for a start. I'm not going to be able to tell you anything.'

He carried on walking next to her. 'Do you think I'm flirting with you, then?'

Connie sighed and stopped in her tracks. 'Look . . .'

'Do you know that Penny Lander had said she was scared of someone in the weeks leading up to her death?'

'Where did you hear that?'

'She told the next-door neighbour. Number fourteen. Alan Barnett was cutting his hedge and he saw Penny Lander come out of the house and jump out of her skin when she saw him. They'd lived next door to each other for years and she said something along the lines of "my nerves are on edge".'

'Is that it? My own nerves are constantly on edge, it doesn't mean that I'm scared of anyone.'

'If you'd let me finish. Are all policewomen like you?'

'Detective. I'm a—'

'Anyway. She went back into the house muttering something along the lines of "it's not you I'm scared of".'

Connie did some rapid thinking. Barnett should have told this to the uniforms who'd questioned the neighbours following Penny Lander's death. Either it'd been missed or this clever journo had wheedled it out of a man who'd been intending to keep quiet about things. 'That it?'

'How much do you want? Were you aware of her being scared of someone?'

'Jesus. She was strangled twice. I'd be scared of someone if I thought that fate was coming my way. You've got nothing for me.'

'Strangled twice? What do you mean?'

Shit. He was in the right profession. Furious with herself, she pulled her handbag closer to her and made to walk off. The journalist reached out and laid a hand on her sleeve.

'Look, can you give me anything? You know what it's like. Anything would be better than nothing. What do you mean when you say she was strangled twice? How's that possible?'

Connie thought about all the people she had interviewed and how little she had discovered. They were concentrating on the murder of Penny Lander when what she really wanted to do was dig right down into the past. But there was little time and precious public funds needed to be accounted for down to the last penny. She looked at the man. He was about her age. Good looking, if a bit drippy. Probably well educated and now dumbing down while working on the tabloid. 'What did you say your name was again?'

He looked surprised. 'Nick. Nick Oates. Look, I know—'

'Never mind about that. Is there somewhere we can talk? Maybe you can help me but you tell no one about this, OK?'

'There's no point giving me information if I can't use it.' She could hear it now. That public-school accent she came across now and then. Sadler didn't have it. She knew his background was far, far wealthier than hers. But he had a neutral accent to match his measured way of speaking. Perhaps he had worked at it. But this man standing in front of her, Nick, with his scruffy jumper and clipped vowels, might have been wearing his old school tie because he was so clearly from a different class to her.

'What I tell you, you can use to *infer*,' she laid stress on the word, 'the direction of the investigation. You'll get no hard facts from me. I like my job and I intend to keep it. But I can't do everything and I'm interested in the past. In the old case.'

'So you are linking the two.' He was excited now and his curly hair flopped about as he shook his head. 'You think the two cases are connected.'

'Three,' she corrected him. 'Look, is there somewhere we can go that's private but not compromising, if you see what I mean?'

He looked across the road. 'What about the cinema?'

*

Sadler waited at the entrance to Truscott Fields, glancing occasionally in the rear-view mirror to catch a glimpse of Rachel Jones. She finally came into view, her tall, stocky figure loping down the path towards his car. What must she be thinking? As a young girl, she'd run barefoot in the opposite direction, towards the road. But her gait was confident in the mirror. Sadler opened the car door and got out to meet her approach. Rachel's dark hair was hidden under a hat and she was stylishly dressed with jeans tucked into long boots teamed with a black felt jacket.

'It's not changed at all.'

'Here?' Sadler looked around him. 'No, I suppose you're right. It's always looked the same to me. I came once or twice as a boy.'

'Before or after the kidnapping?'

'Almost certainly before. I don't remember coming here after the event. It's funny,' Sadler turned and started walking towards the woods and she followed him '. . . but I was talking to my sister about the kidnapping recently. We all have our different memories of that time and, if you put them all together, you would get about five different scenarios, any of which may or may not be correct.'

They had reached the entrance of the woods and Sadler made a 'shall we or shan't we' gesture. With an incline of her head, Rachel assented and they entered. They walked in silence as the path, at first welcoming and commodious, narrowed and thickets of long spikes shot up from the ground making walking treacherous. When it got so that they could only walk in single file, Sadler stopped.

'Rachel, I need to ask you something about your father.'

'My father?' She turned and stared at him in surprise. 'He died before I was born.'

'Did your mother ever talk about him?'

Rachel seemed lost for words. 'What's all this about? Of course she talked about him. Not much and especially after the kidnapping hardly at all. But she did talk about him sometimes.'

'What did she say about him?'

'That he was young when they met and she got pregnant just before they were married. And then before I was born he died.' She stared at him, angry. 'You're not trying to pin this on him, are you? He's definitely dead. I've got a copy of the death certificate. He died in 1970 of pneumonia.'

Sadler laid a placating hand on her arm. He saw her flinch. 'I'm trying to tie up some loose ends.'

'Well, there's nothing loose about my father's life. He was born, got married and died. In genealogical terms it's the bare bones of our life.' She started to walk away, still angry, further into the woods. 'None of my family were responsible for my kidnapping.'

He followed her, trying to keep up with her brisk pace. 'I have to ask these questions, Rachel.' She stopped suddenly, forcing Sadler to do the same.

'I can prove my father's death. I'll show you at the house.'

Sadler nodded, and some of Rachel's aggression fell away. She looked around them. The thick canopy of trees and encompassing silence was oppressive. Some distance away, Sadler could hear the rustling of an animal making its way through the undergrowth.

'Do you think she's buried here?' asked Rachel. 'This is the furthest in I've ever been. I've never fancied coming this far in on my own, but I wanted to see how I felt.'

'And how do you feel?'

'Nothing. I feel nothing.'

She turned to face him. 'Do you think she's buried here?'

Sadler looked at the dense, impenetrable woodland.

'Probably.'

*

Bampton's picture house was kept open by volunteers. By rights it should have shut long ago, with the cinemagoers heading to Chesterfield or Sheffield to one of the large out-of-town places there. But the attractive building had a posse of devoted admirers who volunteered time and money to help keep the historic cinema open. The single matinee showing was an animated film involving a sly cat. Connie, who hated the animals, thought whoever had drawn the images probably shared her feelings. All the deviousness and stealth that marked the feline species were shown in their crafty glory. Connie had expected some suspicious glances when they had entered the cinema but the bored teenage girl, chewing gum and texting, hadn't even looked up at them. It was a stroke of genius by Nick Oates to suggest the cinema, although God knows what she would say if anyone challenged her about going there while she was on duty. But he had even thought of that.

'If anyone asks, just say that I came to you offering to give you some information regarding Penny Lander's murder and I insisted that the cinema was the only confidential place to go.'

It wouldn't stop her getting the sack if anyone found out about it though, thought Connie. They were sitting towards the back, near a noisy group of teenagers who were more interested in groping and hitting each other than paying attention to the adults behind them.

'We're linking the three cases. The 1978 abduction, the suicide of Yvonne Jenkins and the murder of Penny Lander. Whether or not Sadler tells you that formally in the press conference I don't know, but I'm telling you anyway. Firstly, it's nothing you couldn't pick up if you listened to the uniforms chatting in the pub on Friday night and, secondly, you need to know because the help I need is on 1978, not the murder last week. But it's all connected.'

She sensed him nod in the dark. He leaned over and said in her ear. 'I've looked at everything I could find on that case. There's not much in the public domain that hasn't already been sifted over.'

'No, but we've got a few discrepancies that no one can explain. First of all, Rachel Jones's father, who died before she was born. There's something strange there.'

'Strange? What do you mean strange? You think he's not really dead?'

'He's definitely dead, but I think someone should have a good look at the dates and so on. Just check up on that angle.' Connie debated whether to tell him about Sadler's interview with Roger Saxton but decided to leave it. Better he discover it himself. It shouldn't take long for him to work out all was not right.

'You know something, though?'

'You need to be careful,' she said, sidestepping the question. 'I think Rachel doesn't know anything about it. But something's not right about the whole set-up. You might want to look into it.'

'OK, I've got it. Go on.'

Connie paused as she watched a fight scene between the hated cat brandishing a sword and an enemy of indeterminate species. Dog? Mouse?

'We've also got a problem with what happened between the time of the abduction and when Rachel was found up by Truscott Woods. Where did they go and what happened in between?'

'But that's impossible. If I find that out, I in effect solve the case. Where am I supposed to look?'

'I didn't say it was going to be easy. But you must be able to find something. Look around other events; find out what was going on at the time. Where could you have taken two girls for about three hours without anyone noticing?'

He grunted besides her. 'Anything else?'

Connie thought, as she leaned towards him and caught the smell from his body. Citrus soap and the tang of his own scent. 'Tell anyone that you've met me and I'll sort you out myself.'

Chapter 33

20 January 1978

Rachel was sitting in a room. The heat was so great that she could feel trickles of sweat running down her back. It reminded her of something, a cloying smell and moisture on skin that her brain was telling her that she must forget. She was wearing a dressing gown that was too long for her, a pale lemony colour with buttons down the front. It looked a bit like her one at home, except hers was purple and was getting too small for her. All of her clothes had disappeared. A lady took her into a room and asked her to undress and put them all in a bag. She could hear them whispering outside while she took off her sock. She heard the words 'wait' and 'Mum'. She was glad to get the damp clothes off her, but she could still feel water and cold in this stuffy room.

The door opened and her mum came in. She sat and waited as her mother rushed towards her and she was engulfed by even more warmth and a sickly smell, *Je Reviens* perfume from the round glass bottle on the dressing-room table. Behind her mum's back, a tall policeman stood watching them. He had bright red hair brushed to one side but with a bit sticking up at the back. Rachel noticed his large hands, all knuckle and bone, and she looked away quickly. Behind that large police-man there was someone else hovering. A woman policeman and this thought turned her stomach. She looked to her mother for reassurance and something in her face gave her that at least.

Her mum turned around to the tall policeman and Rachel heard him cough.

'Rachel, do you know where Sophie is?'

She looked down at her feet, her pale toes a sickly pinky-brown colour, and she clenched them tightly.

'No,' she replied. But it seemed that this wasn't enough. The silence in the room grew and grew. But she couldn't say anything else. The man coughed again.

'Can you remember what happened to her?' Rachel had an image of sweat trickling down her back and looking at her pale brown toes she turned her head to one side and threw up on the bench.

Chapter 34

Rachel drove towards her house, her movements made clumsy by the agitation she could feel rising within her. Sadler was following her in his car, a watchful presence keeping a respectful distance behind her. She used her mobile phone to cancel her five o'clock appointment, telling her client that something urgent had come up, which in one sense was true. It had been an exhausting day and her dissipating weariness was fighting with that familiar instinct for survival.

She found a parking spot near her house and watched as Sadler sped up the hill to look for a free space. There was a single journalist still stationed outside her home. The sharp-faced woman in the cherry red trench coat, talking to someone on her phone.

Rachel crossed to her house and opened the front door, flicking on the heating as she crossed the living room. She automatically checked her organised desk, looking for signs of disorder and, satisfied that everything was as it should be, opened her large notebook. The one with its pages still wrinkled from the damp churchyard visit. The time before everything had started again. She flicked to the section that held her father's information. The weaker strain, in her eyes, since that family had dumped her mother the minute her father had died. For completeness, Rachel had compiled the tree but her heart hadn't been in it then, and even now her lassitude made concentrating on the names difficult.

She pulled open her filing cabinet and pulled out the folder containing her father's certificates. Birth, marriage and death. She crossed to her dining-room table and laid them out side by side.

Sadler knocked on the door a couple of minutes later and she let him in. She led him over to the table and pointed at the documents.

'See: nothing strange here.'

He pulled out a chair and sat down. Rachel was once again struck by how attractive he was. His blond hair showed no signs of the baldness that usually characterised a man of his age. She wondered if he had a girlfriend.

'You're a professional like me, Rachel. Tell me, do you come across cases where what is told within a family is completely incorrect. A family story, for example, that isn't right?'

Rachel pulled out a chair, sat down opposite him and jammed her hands underneath her legs. 'Of course. There are always stories within families that prove not to be true.'

'And it's just like policing. We hear stories: sometimes they're correct and often they're not. But there's also something else I noticed when I first joined the police. Some people have an excessive love of something that's written down. I meet policemen who, for example, see something official and decide it must be true. Do you see what I mean?'

Rachel pulled her father's birth certificate towards her. 'I suppose so, but it's something I try to avoid. I have to take an open approach when I'm looking through records. People's names can be spelt incorrectly; dates are wrong and so on. Is that what you mean?'

'I suppose what I'm trying to say is something can be talked about within a family and you can have the paperwork to back it up, and it still might not be true.'

She looked at him now. 'Are you talking about me?'

'How much do you know about your father?'

'Not much. I told you, Mum didn't really talk about him.'

'Doesn't this strike you as strange? Weren't you entitled to have information about your father?'

Rachel found she couldn't meet his eyes. 'But lots of things weren't talked about then. What are you trying to say? I've just looked at that death certificate again. There's nothing wrong with it and, believe me, I would know.'

'It's not the death certificate I'm worried about.'

'Then what?' Rachel pulled all the certificates towards her and scanned her eyes across them. 'What's the problem?'

'We don't believe that Paul Saxton was your natural father.'

She started to laugh. 'I can categorically tell you that Paul Saxton was my father.'

'How? How can you categorically tell me that?'

She picked up the hard-backed notebook and waved it at him. 'My whole life is in here. This notebook. Research that I've done over the years. And my mother helped me. Where do you think I got those certificates from? Not from the Family Records although, believe me, they're there on the registers. My mother gave them to me. She wouldn't have lied to me about something that was my life and my job. This was important to me and Mum always put me first.'

Sadler let the silence open out in the room. 'I'm sorry, Rachel. But I believe Paul Saxton wasn't your father.'

She was angry now. 'Why? Why do you think that?'

He was looking at her with calm eyes and Rachel couldn't drag her gaze away.

'Paul Saxton's brother, Roger, confirmed to us that the dates don't fit. He believes that your mother was already pregnant when Paul married her.'

'I know she was already pregnant. I told you that. So they had sex before they were married. So what?'

'According to Roger Saxton, the dates don't fit at all. Your mother was already pregnant when she got together with Paul.'

The bile rose in her throat. 'I don't believe you. Why would my mother tell me that a dead man was my father? Why would she make it up?'

'Why do *you* think? You knew your mother better than anyone.'

She looked at the floor and let the silence open out into the room. 'Because you think that my natural father was still alive.'

'It has got to be a possibility, hasn't it? The original investigation team missed it. They took your mother's word that she had nothing to do with Paul Saxton's family and they were never investigated.'

'And you think my natural father had something to do with our kidnapping?' She thought about her web page and its skewed number of hits.

'Look,' she continued, 'there's something you need to know. Someone's been looking at the family tree on my website. I don't know who. I can't tell from the stats counter that I use. But I've had an unusual amount of hits. About a month ago. Before all this started.'

Sadler stood up and walked over to the front window, his

hands in his pockets, and looked out. She could hear his phone buzzing but he ignored it.

'Is there anything about your father on the site?'

'That's the thing. It's my maternal line that I've put on my website. Nothing to do with my father at all. It starts with me, then Mary Jones, my mother. Then Nancy, my grandmother, and her mother, Mair Price. And so on.'

'My colleague, Connie Childs, has a theory that there's someone missing from this case. A *nomen nescio*. Sorry, that means—'

'I know what it means.' He turned his head sharply and she could see that she'd surprised him. 'We use the term in genealogy. When we don't know the name of someone we put in, for example, NN Jones.'

'I don't think we're looking for an NN Jones. In the background is an NN who was your natural father.'

'And you believe my mother colluded in this deceit?' She stood up now, challenging him to speak to her directly. He turned round fully to face her.

'I think she was the architect of it.'

Chapter 35

Connie tried Sadler's phone but it went to voicemail and she decided against leaving a message. What was she supposed to tell him? That she'd just had an illicit meeting with a journalist from a tabloid paper and, without permission, had asked him to help with the investigation? Sadler was unpredictable at the best of times. She wondered where he was. What had that woman in the cafe said – ask Christina?

She headed back to the station, where most of the team were beginning to drift off home. Only Palmer sat at his desk, idly flicking through Internet sites.

'Anything interesting?'

'What? Sorry, I'm now officially on annual leave. As of five this evening. I was just having a look at the sports pages before heading home.'

'You need to get off. It's the big day next Saturday.'

He winced. 'Don't remind me.'

She looked at him, shocked. 'Jesus, Palmer. You're always telling me how great Joanne is. What's the matter?'

He ran his hand over the top of his head. His prematurely grey hair had been clipped short, ready for the wedding. 'I'm not sure I go can through with it.'

'You're joking. I've bought my dress!'

'Yes, go on, laugh. I'm the one being led down the altar with my hands tied behind my back.'

'You're mixing your metaphors there, Palmer. Go and get your coat.'

*

They walked out of the back entrance of the police station, through the car park and stopped as a hubcap from one of the patrol cars freewheeled past them.

'If it's not the snow it's the bloody wind,' said Palmer. 'Maybe we should go after it in case it causes any damage.'

But Connie was transfixed by the movement of the police transportation carriers being buffeted by the large gusts of wind. Their high sides were rocking in a syncopated rhythm of their own.

'I think we need to get out of here.'

Hustle is an old-fashioned word but it best described the action with which Connie virtually shoved Palmer into the Bakers Arms pub at five thirty in the afternoon. He was compliant enough, far too docile in Connie's eyes. She'd never seen him like this. She wasn't sure she liked this new Damian Palmer as much, fearful of his coming nuptials. As a colleague, she'd come to rely on his competence and resolve in dealing with investigations. Palmer's new uncertainty was stirring up that most unwelcome of feelings: pity. But mingled in with the pity was also a sense of protective concern. Something which, given that he was about to get married, wasn't her place to feel. He had his fiancée for that. But now she wondered if there weren't more ill tidings in the distant future. Joanne had him at her beck and call. Connie had seen him scurry off home on nights out after his mobile phone rang. But there was a difference between being under the thumb and sick to the pit of your stomach at the thought of getting married.

He asked for a beer, which went to show how stupid men were. She ordered two double shots of brandy with ice and took them over to the corner table where he was sitting looking at his phone. He showed it to her.

'Look. Ten missed calls, and I spoke to her at lunchtime. Does she think I have nothing better to do all day than take her phone calls?'

'Maybe she's stressed too,' said Connie, taking a sip of her drink and allowing the warmth to trickle down her throat and settle in her stomach.

'We're both stressed, I appreciate that. But what does it say about what the rest of our marriage will be like, if she's like this now?'

Connie shrugged and crunched an ice cube. Palmer's fiancée was behaving in exactly the same way she'd always done. What was different was Palmer's response to it. It was a typical male reaction to blame the woman. He could do worse than look at his own behaviour. But Connie instinctively liked Palmer, mainly because on a professional level she enjoyed his competitive banter, and his uncertainty was revealing an unexpected side to his nature. But if he confided in her, how would he feel about her as a colleague when it had all settled down? Perhaps he would regret his confidences to her.

'It's not too late to call it off . . .' She left the sentence hanging between them.

He was shaking his head. 'You wouldn't believe how many people we've got coming to the wedding. My cousin's even come over from Australia. He's here already. Calling it off is not an option.'

Connie grimaced into her empty glass. 'Then you'd better make the best of it and hope it's just nerves.'

*

Sadler looked at his watch and wondered whether to go back into the office but decided against it. He was nearer his Pedlar Street house and he could work from there. The sun was attempting to break through the February day and Bampton suddenly looked cheerier than it had that morning. As he passed the Bakers Arms the swing doors closed behind someone who reminded him of Connie. He looked at his watch again. Just gone half five. It surely couldn't have been her – hadn't she told him she was off the booze? He considered ringing her mobile but there was something prurient about his interest in her. Even if she had decided to go to the pub after work it was hardly his business.

He parked his car in the small parking area shared by the row of four cottages. He really should call Christina and try and make it up to her, but perhaps now was the time to make a clean break of it. Unbidden, his thoughts turned to Justine Lander and her solid beauty, so different from Christina's glamour. And different again from Rachel Jones's dark attractiveness.

He opened the door and picked up the post while his neighbour's cat made a half-hearted attempt to sneak into the house. He could hear it meowing outside the door as he shut it behind him. Rachel Jones had been genuinely shocked by the discovery of her mother's duplicity and he believed her when she said she knew nothing about the deception. If he was right, and she had inherited her mother's strength, she would start to do some digging herself. The key was for him to get to the solution before Rachel did. Because at the heart of the case was a murderer.

*

'Can I stay at yours tonight?'

Connie stared open mouthed at Palmer. Whatever she had been expecting it wasn't this. 'You're kidding, right?'

'Come on, Con. It's just for one night, so I can get my head straight.'

'You live with your fiancée. She's going to love the fact that you don't come home a week before the wedding.'

'We're not staying together this week. I'm sleeping at my mum's until the wedding. Her mum and dad have moved in with her and her sister's arriving this evening. It's part of the problem. I've got too much time to myself to think about all this.'

'And what good will sleeping at mine do? It sounds like you've a perfectly fine bed at your mum's.'

'She's out tonight at her singing class. Don't laugh, she has group singing lessons every Friday.'

'I'm not laughing. I'm just shocked you think that kipping at mine will help things. What if Joanne found out? And what would your mum say? I'm going to the wedding next Saturday and I would like to be able to look people in the eye.'

'So it's a no?'

'It's a definite no.'

Palmer looked at his watch and then downed his brandy in one go. 'I'd better be off, then. I'll see you at the wedding.' Without looking at her he left the pub. Connie looked at her own watch. Only six – could she clock off for the night?

She was back at her flat by quarter past and, without taking her coat off, flopped down on the sofa. Her bladder was full and she really needed the toilet but the conversation with Palmer had drained her of all energy. What had he been thinking of? She didn't think the request had been about sex. He genuinely seemed not to want to go home. But he was a colleague, and the repercussions if either his family or her workmates found out would be disastrous.

Her phone was vibrating in her bag. She hoped to God it wasn't Palmer. The number was a landline she didn't recognise.

'Connie. It's Sadler. Where are you?'

'I'm at home. We decided there was no point staying late. Nothing new came in this evening.'

'Palmer's gone off on leave now, hasn't he?'

'Yes.' It sounded a little abrupt but she couldn't think of anything else to say.

'I'm just calling to let you know I had a chat with Rachel about her father. I think she took it OK, but she's going to do some digging herself, I can guarantee it. We need to get there before she does.'

'Do you think we'll be able to find someone who was around in 1970? Did she say which of her mother's friends or relatives were still alive?'

'She couldn't think of any. She seemed to be in shock. Will you get onto it, Connie? The strands of this case aren't coming together yet and I need something a bit more concrete. I need to feel that we're making progress. Get onto it in the morning.'

*

Sadler needed to hear some music and he scrolled through his iPhone playlist, looking for inspiration. The jazz records that he had bought as a teenager with his pocket money had sat gathering dust in his sister's garage and it was only recently he'd rifled through them and memories of his teenage years had seeped back to him. But he'd also become acclimatised to the purity of the digital sound, first on CD and then on his iPhone, so he'd packed up the records and sold them on eBay. They'd fetched a decent sum, proof that there was still a market for the old vinyl, but he didn't miss them. He liked the accessibility of his iTunes list and the possibility of change. There was no emotional attachment to that digital list and songs came and went as he wanted. He selected Miles Davis's *Sketches of Spain* and let the sounds drift around the house.

He had some of the files from the office with him but felt reluctant to open them and instead sat back on the sofa and forced his body to relax. His conversation with Connie had, as usual, unsettled him, although it was equilibrium that was usually most damaging to his thought processes. He allowed himself to wonder about Connie's personal life. He knew virtually nothing about her, although he had heard a rumour at the station that she had recently moved to a new flat.

Next Saturday they would both be going to Damian Palmer's wedding. He'd been given an invitation for himself 'plus one' but he had accepted on his behalf only. He'd never felt comfortable in these situations. While he could appreciate that it was a happy occasion for those closely involved, for colleagues, who were generally invited to these things more to satisfy form than from any close acquaintance, it would be a day of small talk and superficial chatter. He wondered if Connie was also dreading the event. He doubted she would be bringing anyone either but he hadn't liked to ask. And she certainly hadn't mentioned it to him.

He heard footsteps on the flagstones outside his cottage, a tip-tapping sound that suggested high heels. Sadler frowned; only two of his neighbours were female and he couldn't remember either of them ever in heels. It must be Christina, although God knows how she had found her way here in the dark, as he'd never invited her to his house. He heard a knock next door and for a moment thought he had been mistaken. But he could hear his neighbour Clive redirecting someone to his house and the determined steps he now recognised as his former girlfriend's.

He opened the door before she could knock and she came into the house without speaking. 'You should have called first. That path is lethal at this time of night.'

She was looking around her, eyes curious as she took in his furnishings and the work spread out over the table. 'I always wondered how you lived. All the time that we were together. And now I'm getting to see it just as we split up.'

Sadler suppressed a sigh. 'I'm sorry. I just don't feel that we're going anywhere. I thought you must feel this same. You have a family, after all.'

'Must I?' She walked through his living room and poked her head through into the kitchen. 'Is there anyone else here?'

'Anyone else? For God's sake, Christina, it's not about anyone else. It's—'

'Is it Connie?'

'Connie?' Sadler was furious. 'Of course it's not Connie. Please.'

She looked at him with huge dark eyes and shook her head. 'I never even knew what music you liked listening to.'

She started to walk out of the door and Sadler put the outside lights on so she could follow the path safely to wherever she had parked her car. He had no inclination to follow her. Christina had always filled a place and after she had left he could smell her perfume and her presence still lingered. Perhaps that was why he'd always been reluctant to bring her to his house. She left her mark on everything she came into contact with.

At the start of their relationship he'd merely taken her word about the state of her home life. Both she and her husband were unfaithful and, as she'd frequently assured him, both were happy with the status quo. It wouldn't have satisfied him, not in a marriage at least, although he had enough insight to appreciate the double standards he was willing to apply to someone else's union. He'd been reassured by Christina's casual approach to their relationship. No commitment expected and he was free to continue the self-sufficient life that he'd made for himself. But now, as he had felt her anger at the end of the affair, he wondered what undercurrents there had been beneath the apparently facile relationship. On her side at least. Crossing the room to the speakers, he turned up the volume.

Chapter 36

Rachel looked at her notebook and resisted the temptation to light the fire and burn it. If Sadler was right, then half of her genealogy was a complete lie and her mother had colluded in the deception. She'd nurtured Rachel's interest in her family while knowing that the foundations on which her entire professional life was based were lies.

She walked over to the mirror at the bottom of the stairs and stared at her reflection. She looked like her mother, although about two stone heavier. Mary Jones had spent most of her life on a diet to keep herself trim, and Rachel's small act of rebellion had been to eat what she wanted when she was growing up. And her solid body had been one of the reasons she had avoided mirrors. But today she forced herself to look at her face with fresh eyes. What was there in her of this other man?

'And does it have anything to do with my kidnapping?'

She spoke the words out loud and her breath misted the glass, blurring the familiar features.

If her natural father was behind the abduction, it wouldn't make any sense to kidnap Sophie too. There had been plenty of opportunity to take Rachel alone in the 1970s, when children had seemingly unlimited freedom. Those days almost certainly came to an end with the kidnapping of Sophie and herself. Bampton's attitude towards its children had taken a radical rethink, playgrounds had been reconfigured, after-school clubs had sprung up and the suburban roads had gradually cleared of playing children. When Rachel saw a child on its bike now it was kitted out as if it was about to enter combat, so ensconced was it in the padding and plastic. She could remember the feel of her hair flying back from her as she careered one-handed down the hill towards her house. A different world.

She walked up to her bedroom and switched on the overhead light. Her mother had lied to her for a reason. And Sadler believed that she had also suspected that her real father was involved in the kidnapping. And they were going to find him first, were they? Well, not if she had anything to do with it.

She crossed to her pine chest of drawers and pulled open her sock drawer. Her socks were short and in muted shades of black, brown or grey. She lifted a pair up and untangled the knot. She felt nothing. She hurried down the stairs and opened her front door. There was no one outside her house. She turned left and walked slightly uphill to the house three doors away. The front door was identical to hers except painted a cheery red rather than her respectable grey. She rapped on the door and Jenny opened it, her large tortoiseshell glasses hiked up on top of her head.

'Rachel! You OK? I've been meaning to come round all this week to see if there was anything I could do. But you know what it's like with kids. I'm lucky if I get an hour to myself before I go to bed.'

Rachel shook her head. 'It's all right, look—'

Jenny shot out her arm. 'Don't stand there on the doorstep. Come in.'

The house was configured as hers was and she stepped

straight into the living room. It was a mess of plastic toys, half-filled coffee cups and strewn gossip magazines.

'I won't keep you long; I do know how it is.' Rachel looked round the living room. 'Look, I was wondering if I could borrow a pair of your daughter's school socks. You know, the long white ones she wears.'

Whatever Jenny had been expecting it wasn't this. Rachel had an excuse ready. 'I have to do a report for a client interested in schoolchildren down the ages. I'm doing something on uniforms and I'm stuck for inspiration. I'm trying to gather a few items together.'

Jenny's doubtful face cleared. 'How interesting. I tell you, when I worked for the local authority nothing like this ever happened to me. It was all procedures and compliance. Hang on.'

Only a person as mild mannered as Jenny would have accepted Rachel's bizarre suggestion so easily. Rachel looked round the living room again, wondering how a family of four could crowd into such a space. But at least it looked like a family lived there, unlike her tidy but sterile house. Jenny came down with a pair of long white socks which Rachel stuffed into her pocket. Whatever effect they would have on her, she didn't want an audience, even one as kind as Jenny.

Her phone was ringing as she re-entered her house.

'It's Richard. What are you up to later?'

The sound of his voice brought a warmth to her stomach that made her want to forget about the past and flee from her obsession with the current investigation. He offered her a refuge, his comfortable home a sanctuary from everything that had come before, but, for the moment, she must resist the pull of safety.

'Are you there, Rachel? How are you?' he repeated and she forced herself to concentrate.

'It's so nice to hear from you. I wanted to call, but . . .'

'Look. It's OK. I just wanted to check you were all right.'

Rachel hadn't realised that she had been holding her breath until she exhaled, her spine bending to accommodate the space left behind.

'I'm fine. You?'

The tone of the voice changed from anxiety into warmth. 'I'm fine too. Are we OK after last time? We left the pub in a hurry and . . .'

Rachel looked up at the clock. Five minutes to seven. She fingered the rough ball of material in her pocket. 'Everything's fine. But I can't chat. I have to go and see Nancy this evening.'

'Is everything OK? I thought Monday was your day for visits.'

'Don't worry, I just need to drop something off.' She clicked off the phone and searched for the charging cradle, gently laying the handset in the holder.

She immediately felt guilty. There were enough stresses in her past to jeopardise a potential future together. Did she need to magnify them by adding secrets to their present? But, then, he hadn't been upfront with her about his visit to the woods. And, deep down, she wasn't yet able to make that final leap of trust.

She then pulled out the white sock ball from her pocket and unravelled the two pieces. Almost immediately she felt a searing pain under her ribs accompanied by a sense of longing as sharp as the physical sensation. Her legs wobbled slightly and she moved herself to the sofa. On its arm, she laid both socks next to each other so that they formed a parallel. They were slightly ribbed with an entwining of flowers running down each leg. They were similar to ones worn by her as a child.

On impulse, Rachel picked up one of the socks and threw it on the floor under the table. The image of the one sock, sitting atop the sofa's arm brought back the longing. She tentatively reached out and touched the material and at the back of her mind images began to flicker like a dream barely remembered. She grasped at the pictures but as soon as she had them in her reach they disintegrated. *Come back*, she silently pleaded. *Come back*.

Then suddenly she had a strong image of a man. Tall with large hands and smelling of tobacco leaning over her. He was reaching out to touch her hair and smiling down at her. And behind him a woman. That woman: frowning.

*

Nancy was having the curlers removed from her hair when Rachel arrived in her room. A mobile hairdresser came and did the patients every Thursday, which was usually a good time for Rachel to telephone Nancy as she was usually in a good mood after having her hair done. Terry Cooper, who'd been coming to the nursing home for years, turned around with a hairgrip sticking out of the corner of his mouth when he heard Rachel enter the room.

'Here she is. Give me another five minutes and I'll be finished,' he said through clenched lips.

Rachel sat in the wing-back chair and watched Terry tease out the curls as he carefully removed each roller.

'You got a boyfriend yet, me duck?'

Rachel saw Nancy smirk at Terry's direct question. 'Maybe.'

Nancy's eyes widened and Rachel had to stifle the urge to quickly retract the confession. Was Richard Weiss really her boyfriend?

'Who is he?' Nancy's voice quivered, and Rachel, for the first time, realised how important it was to her grandmother that she had someone.

'Richard Weiss, the solicitor. And it's only recent, we're taking it easy.' It was a lie. There had been no discussion whatsoever about how they were taking things. But the less Nancy was told the better.

'Richard Weiss? The solicitor's son?'

'He's a solicitor now himself, Nan. He's older than me. Just.'

Nancy snorted. 'Well, bring him in to see me. I get sick of living with all these old people. I could do with some young company sometimes.'

It was a good an opening as she was likely to get. And Rachel took it.

'Did Mum bring my dad home to see you much before they got engaged?'

Nancy looked uninterested. 'Not really. It was too quick, if you ask me. She met him and was engaged and married before you could bat an eye.' She saw Rachel's face. 'Not that it mattered or anything. Lots of people get married quickly. No shame in it.'

Terry Cooper was looking from one to the other. 'Don't stop because I'm here. I've heard it all, believe me.'

'I don't have a problem with Mum being pregnant when she got married, Nan. Honestly. I just wondered if you had seen much of him before. You know, before the wedding.'

'There was none of that. I think that other man put her off. That's what happens sometimes, isn't it? You bring golden boy home and then it goes sour and you're a damn sight more careful next time around. I . . .'

Rachel's heart was beating hard inside her chest and she could feel her innards twist into a hard knot. As casually as she could, she asked, 'A boyfriend? Who was that?'

Nancy looked hard at her. 'I can't remember who it was. But I can remember Mair showing herself up again the one and only time he came around. She was as rude as anything to him. We'd made a special effort too. Hughie put on a suit and I'd bought myself a new dress that morning. Pale lemon, it was.'

Typical of Nancy to concentrate on what she was wearing, thought Rachel.

'And there sat Mum in the corner, knitting with her elbows out like a turkey and needles clacking like a hen. And the radio blasting out hymns. I told her that it'd have to go off when Mary's man arrived. And to be fair, as she always had a soft spot for Mary, she did sit up straight when they arrived.'

'So what happened? How did she act up?' Rachel was impatient for the whole story and Nancy was typically stringing it along.

'She was rude to him. Mary brought him over to Mair's chair and she never even got up. She just looked and looked at him, and then finally snapped, "What did you say your name was again?" like he was some kind of child. And he blushed beetroot red and stammered—'

'What? What name did he stammer?' Rachel practically shouted and Terry was looking at her in alarm.

'Take it easy, Rachel. Your nan is only telling you an old story.'

Rachel took a deep breath and willed her voice to calm. 'Can you remember what he was called?'

'Of course I can't remember his name. This was years ago. My point was after, when the man was gone, your mother turned on Mair and said that she had ruined it all. By being so rude to him. And my mum looked so shocked, which was unusual for her. Normally she couldn't care less about what anyone thought of her. But, as I said, she always had a soft spot for Mary.'

Rachel felt like weeping. She didn't want reminiscences. She wanted hard facts. Which didn't look like they would be forthcoming.

'Mair went up to apologise to her afterwards. I saw her come down with a grim look on her face and when I asked her what she'd said, she told me to mind my own business. But Mary came down later with a face on her too. Couldn't look at any of us. But that was the last we saw of the man.'

Rachel held her head in her hands. 'Can't you remember anything else about him? Anything at all?'

Nancy's face cleared and brightened. 'I remember he was tall.'

Chapter 37

Connie rolled over in her bed and fumbled for her mobile. She'd slept badly and wondered if she'd done the right thing in talking to that journalist. The thought of the possible ramifications kept her awake for half the night. But then it didn't take much. She punched in the number of Rachel Jones's mobile.

'Hello?'

The man's voice threw her. 'Er, hi. It's DC Connie Childs. Is Rachel there?'

'Damn. Have I answered the wrong phone? Rachel . . .'

Connie could hear rustling and a whispered exchange. About thirty seconds later Rachel's voice came on, irritated.

'Sorry about that. Richard and I've both got the same type of mobile. He's mortified that he answered mine.'

'It's not a problem. I just wanted to pick your brains about something.'

'Go on.' The muffled voice suggested Rachel was eating her breakfast.

'I was wondering about your mum's friends. Who she was close to and so on. Maybe someone who had been in her life for a while. Someone who was still a friend around the time you were kidnapped?'

'My mum? I don't know. DI Sadler asked me that yesterday. After the kidnapping we moved to Clowton and our whole lives changed – friends, colleagues and so on. The only constant was my nan, who I saw all through my childhood.'

'And your nan's in a nursing home?'

'That's right. She's completely doolally. I don't think you'll get any information from her at all.'

There was a long pause. *She's lying*, thought Connie.

'Is there no one at all?'

'Well, there was a next-door neighbour that I used to go into if my mum was late home from work and I remember her babysitting a couple of times. This was before the kidnapping. Maybe she will be able to help.'

'What was her name?'

'Audrey. I remember she worked as a nurse and so her shift patterns were really strange, which suited us. I would often drop in and see her. It was in the old Bampton hospital.'

Connie got up and lit a cigarette, the one that she'd promised herself that she wouldn't have, and jotted into her notebook the name of the hospital that Penny Lander had also been interested in.

'And do you think your mum might have confided in her, this Audrey.'

'To be honest, no. My mum was a private person. But they lived next door to each other for a quite a few years, so if anyone knows anything it will be her. But I don't know if she is even in Bampton now. It's been over thirty years. And when the hospital closed she could easily have moved jobs.'

'Last name?' Connie asked and the silence down the phone indicated that she'd been too abrupt. 'Sorry. Early mornings aren't my thing and I've already broken my daily resolution by having my first fag.'

Surprisingly, Rachel laughed down the phone. 'I know what you mean. I've just eaten a croissant and that's before breakfast.'

Connie sniggered.

'I'm pretty sure her name was Audrey Frost. Her last name was easy to remember as a child and I'm pretty sure that was it. Will you let me know if you find her?'

Connie agreed and ended the call. The phone rang immediately. Looking at the screen she could see it was Sadler.

'Connie. Sorry to call again so early but in case I don't see you today we need to have a chat about something outside the office.'

Connie's stomach lurched. Had he found out about her meeting with Nick Oates?

'It's about the wedding tomorrow. We need to think about a present.'

Connie stopped herself from smiling in case he heard it in the tone of her voice. 'A present? I hadn't given it any thought to be honest.'

'Well, we can hardly go empty handed, can we?' He sounded irritated, thought Connie, as she stubbed out her cigarette.

'I suppose not. Do you want me to get something?'

'Could you? Thanks, Con.' There was a brief silence. 'Are you bringing a partner?'

'No one to bring, to be honest. You?'

'Um no. Perhaps they'll sit us together.' He sounded hopeful, but not in a romantic way. It didn't sound like he was looking forward to it. Well, that made two of them.

'Maybe. On the same table as Llewellyn and his wife. They're going, apparently.'

Sadler let it pass. 'Fine. Well, give me a call later with an update how you're getting on. And thanks for getting the present. Let me know how much I owe you.'

*

Sadler sat in his office looking out into the incident room that gave off an air of muted concentration. The tasks had all been successfully allotted and each of the team was working steadily through their jobs. Palmer's temporary replacement, who'd been brought in for two weeks to cover tasks while his sergeant was on leave, was clearly competent. He had his head bent over a laptop and was tapping away. Sadler ran his hands through his hair and let out a deep breath. The confrontation with Christina yesterday had left him drained and to be back at work was a relief.

Penny Lander's murder was connected to the seismic event that took place in 1978, but now it looked like the kidnapping had its roots in events years earlier. So, what had they discovered? Well, for a start, focus had now decisively shifted from Sophie to Rachel. The likely scenario was that Sophie had unfortunately been with Rachel when the kidnapper had struck. And if that was the case, and Sadler was sure it was, then Sophie was almost certainly lying somewhere in Truscott Woods.

The suicide of Yvonne Jenkins, he was now willing to concede, was merely that. The final act of a woman who had finished with life. Why she'd waited so long was a mystery. Connie's description of the house had sounded depressing, but clearly she'd made something of a life for herself. Perhaps it was simply that, on this particular anniversary, the realisation

264

finally struck that, no matter how long she waited, Sophie wasn't coming home. But Sadler wasn't a man who believed in 'simply's. Something had tipped her over the edge. And then Yvonne Jenkins's suicide had unleashed a chain of events that had culminated in the death of Penny Lander. It wasn't the first time that Sadler had seen this. Suicide could break up families, awaken illnesses dormant within unsuspecting relatives, cause fissures in lives. But it was the first time in his career that he would be linking suicide to a murder.

His mobile rang, an unknown number, and he answered it. There was a short silence at the other end of the phone.

'It's Justine Lander here.'

Sadler felt his heart thump in his chest and inwardly cursed. He was now not only technically but actually single, so why the teenage embarrassment?

'Is it a difficult time?'

There it was again. The tang of bitterness that he'd heard in her voice before. 'No, of course it isn't. Are you still at the house, or at your aunt's?'

'I'm still at the house. I've been tidying up and going briefly through Mum's things. Just to see if there's anything urgent that needs doing.'

'Did you find anything? I hope everything was left in good order after our lot had been through it.'

'It was fine. It was pretty tidy, to be honest. Although I could tell someone had been here, if you know what I mean; But I wondered if they had gone through the garden shed.'

Sadler wondered if he had heard her properly. 'The shed?'

'It's where my mum used to keep all the junk she couldn't fit in the house. Old stuff which didn't matter if it went mouldy;

in fact, if it did all the better as she could just throw it out then.'

'Well, they certainly should have done. Why? Have you found anything?'

There was a silence again. 'You might want to come down and take a look.'

*

Audrey Frost was a large-hipped woman with a smallish waist and an enormous cleavage that stretched the nylon blouse that she was wearing so that it gaped in three places. Connie could see the glimpse of a grey-white bra and made an effort not to stare at the enormous bosom. She had been easy to find. The electoral roll showed her living at Arkwright Lane in 1978 and then in 1980 moving to Hugh Street in the north of Bampton. She was still there, in a semi-detached house, slightly untidy but not in the dirty way of those who failed to care for either themselves or their properties. Audrey seemed merely to take a lackadaisical approach to housework rather than making a deliberate attempt to live in squalor.

Connie had briefly explained her interest over the phone and Audrey was clearly curious. She sat Connie down and bustled off to make some tea, her nylon blouse sending off darts of static as she left the room. Connie looked around her, and once more was struck by another room without any photographs. She shouted her questions to Audrey, who was taking her time in the kitchen.

'As I mentioned over the phone, your name was given to us by Rachel Jones. I think you'd remember her as a little girl.'

Audrey came back into the room. 'I remember her very well,

scruffy little urchin that she was. Hair all scraggy like a scare-crow and her school uniform always creased. Some children can look neat and tidy no matter what and others, like Rachel, manage to look like little tinkers.'

'Did her mother look after her properly?'

A flash of annoyance crossed the woman's face. 'Of course she looked after her. It wasn't easy in the seventies to bring up a child by yourself. You couldn't sit back and let the state look after you for nothing. If you were single back then, you had to work to support yourself and no harm it did anyone, in my opinion. For a woman, it at least got you out of the house.'

Connie recalled the interview with Peter Jenkins and thought Audrey Frost had a point. But the woman hadn't fin-ished.

'And don't go blaming Mary for what happened with Rachel and Sophie. Children used to walk themselves to school back then. It wasn't a choice – most people expected it and you kept an eye out for the kids when they were passing your house.'

'What do you think happened, then?'

'I've no idea, and one thing is for sure, neither did Mary. I remember going round to the house the night of the kid-napping. Only the local press had arrived; the nationals were struggling to get up here because of a train strike. I remember Mary was white with shock. She kept asking herself who could have done such a thing.'

'She had no idea at all?'

'I'm positive she hadn't a clue.'

A slight hesitation in Audrey's voice made Connie look up sharply. 'But you're thinking of something?'

'It's nothing, really; I just remember she nipped across to

mine to make a call just after I arrived, asked if I would keep an eye on Rachel. There was a policewoman there who had come home with them but she wanted me to be there too, as I knew Rachel, while she used my phone.'

'She wanted to use the phone in your house?'

'Not everyone had phones in those days. I thought nothing of it. Said go ahead, and I'll keep an eye on Rachel.'

'But you think it was suspicious?'

'Then I remembered that Mary had installed a phone in the house only a couple of months earlier. I had a quick look around downstairs and I found it in the dining room.'

'So why do you think she wanted to make a phone call at your house?'

Audrey's mouth settled into a thin line. 'She must have wanted to speak to someone without me overhearing.'

She turned to stare out of the living room window, her broad back turned to the room. Connie let the silence settle while she digested the information. Mary Jones had installed a phone in her dining room but hadn't wanted to use it in front of either the policewoman or Audrey. Had she suspected who the attacker was? Connie's thoughts went to the father of Rachel Jones.

'Did Mary ever talk about her husband, Paul Saxton?'

Audrey didn't turn but spoke to the window. 'Not much. She never really spoke about her husband at all. He died. That's all that I knew.'

Connie was missing something and she tried to formulate the words properly. 'Did she talk about anyone else?'

This time Audrey did turn round. 'There was someone else.'

'Before her husband?'

'Certainly before and maybe during. I'm not sure.'

'Did she mention his name?'

Audrey shook her head and sat down heavily on her sofa. 'No, never a name. But there was someone. She used to talk about a man who'd let her down. I got the impression that he must have been something of a rogue. She certainly didn't want to talk about him in any detail.'

'But she mentioned the fact that there was someone. How did she seem when she talked about him?'

Audrey looked down at her knees and rubbed her hands over them as if to warm herself up. 'She seemed ashamed.'

Chapter 38

Rachel was feeling guilty about her conversation with Connie. Doolally indeed. Nancy's faculties were all there, despite her great age. There was nothing wrong with either Nancy's mind or her memory, but that policewoman wasn't going to be the one who unpicked it. Nancy could hold her secrets too, though, and Rachel would need to approach her with caution. Nancy's carefree manner was, in its own way, as protective a cloak as her own prickly exterior. She pushed open the doors of Bampton library and Sydney Markham looked up from behind the desk, her expression changing from mild interest to excitement.

'Any news?' Sydney's eyes brimmed with barely suppressed curiosity.

Rachel was too tired to engage. 'What about?'

Sydney picked up on her mood. 'You should take some time out instead of staring at a screen all day. Go and read a book.' She pointed at a sign that was encouraging people to do the same.

Sydney's smile was infectious and Rachel found herself smiling back. 'Got any recommendations?'

'A bit of fiction perhaps, help you escape from wintry Bampton. What about a crime novel?'

Rachel shook her head. 'I've got to work. Got anything on the history of the old Bampton hospital that I might not have seen yet?'

Sydney looked concerned. 'You're not doing some investigating yourself are you, Rachel? You need to leave that to the police.'

Rachel looked at the floor, unwilling to catch Sydney's eye. The librarian relented. 'I'm pretty sure we've got nothing new. You know more about that place's history than anyone else. Why don't you look at the archives in the town hall?'

A recent conversation flashed into Rachel's mind. 'The ones Penny Lander was interested in? Did you send her there too?'

'Penny?' shrieked Sydney. 'Of course not. Why should she want to go there? It's not a place she would have visited.'

'I think she did, you know.' A tall middle-aged man had stopped serving a patron and called over to them. 'It was one of the days you weren't here. I was rushed off my feet and a woman was asking me about the location of the old records for Bampton hospital. She looked like the woman they found in the woods. I saw her picture on TV.'

'And you told her that they were in the town hall archives?'

'It was fresh in my mind as we'd had a memo saying that all the files were being transferred to the County Records Office next year but in the meantime they would be remaining in Bampton.'

'And you told Penny Lander that they were there?'

'If that was the woman's name. It's not secret, is it?' The man was on his defensive now. As Sydney turned to reassure him, Rachel slipped away.

*

The town hall had been built at the height of Bampton's Victorian prosperity. Once, it must have been a gleaming white edifice with its graceful porticos and imposing front lobby. Most of the stone had turned to a dull grey colour but it was still an impressive building, reminiscent of Bampton's merchant past. The archives, naturally, were where archives often could be found: in the very pit of the building. This wasn't a problem. Rachel liked archives, where the smell of long-forgotten records was combined with the archivists' natural sense of order and precision.

Rachel had once been friends with the head archivist at the town hall but the woman had married and moved on. Now a serious young man, the badge pinned to his shirt naming him as Tim Dowling, with piercings down one ear, was in charge of the records. He listened to her request with the gravity of a patient receiving bad news from his doctor, which was probably about right, given what she was asking for. Her first surprise was the amount of files that were available.

'We've got patient records going up to 1993 when the hospital shut down.'

'And up to what year can I get access to?'

'Up to 1993 if you like. But between 1968 and 1993 the only information we have are the death registers. Which are effectively in the public domain anyway.'

'And before 1968?'

'We've computerised some of the patients' records. The bare bones, of course. We have to follow data protection rules. But what we can record is interesting enough. We'd like to do it all if possible but we have time and budget restraints. But for researchers into medical history, we've got a good cross-section of patient details from 1912 when the hospital opened until 1968.'

'And after 1968?'

'They're not here.'

'Did they go to the new hospital when it opened?'

'I doubt it. That's a hell of a lot of material. And anyway, as I said, all records are confidential post-1968.

'Why 1968?'

'Sorry, I've no idea. Is it important?'

Rachel shrugged. Only if it was important to Penny Lander, she wanted to say. 'Do you remember a lady coming in and asking similar questions to me? She would have been in her early sixties and tall and thin.'

'I remember someone like that. It might have been her. She said she was a teacher and needed access to the records. For a school project, I think.'

'Did she ask the same questions as me?'

'Almost identical and I sent her to where I'm about to send you.'

'Do you know exactly what she was looking for?'

He looked at her and silently shook his head.

'Do you think she found what she wanted?'

The archivist, with his cool eyes and shorn head, nodded.

*

Someone at the archives had made an impressive job of putting the records onto the system. The first thing Rachel did when she started looking through the files was to familiarise herself with what the records contained. It was fairly unusual for recent records to be in the public domain, and although Rachel was itching to start looking through the files, her professional instinct warned her to check out the entire catalogue first.

Idly flicking through budget and staffing records, statistics on admissions and discharges from the wards, Rachel was surprised how much work this little hospital had done in the community. With the exception of mental health and isolation wards that had come under the auspices of the local authority, the hospital had over the years, courtesy of benefactors and other local worthies, cared for the people of the community. When the National Health Service was created in 1948, the cottage hospital had attached itself to the new system and, instead of relying on charitable donations, had received money from central government.

Finally happy that she had an overview of what the records contained, Rachel opened up the search page. There were various criteria and she hesitated over date and surname. Penny Lander was originally from Somerset and there should be no reason for her to be looking in Bampton cottage hospital's records. In any case, she didn't know Mrs Lander's maiden name, so there was no useful search she could do for her. She had a try at just putting the name 'Penelope' in the search box, but the system insisted on a last name too. She typed in 'Lander'. Nothing came up so she removed the name of Penelope and waited. Nothing. Either there were no records for any of the Lander family before 1968, or they had been lost or mistranscribed. To be sure, Rachel tried a number of variations of Lander but nothing came up. Rachel hesitated over the keys and then typed in Jenkins. There were over four hundred results. She added Yvonne into the filter and again, nothing. Before 1968, Mrs Jenkins didn't seem to have used the hospital either.

Rachel was frustrated and her throat raspy. She craved a can of Diet Coke. She had seen people smuggle all sorts of things into records offices – food, drink, banned cameras – but her diligence and respect for the records had never allowed her to contemplate doing such a thing herself. The two obvious surnames connected to the case – Jenkins and Lander – had been entered to no effect, and she'd gone even further and tried Weiss and Needham. There was something for Daniel, Richard's father. But it was a minor abdominal operation according to the notes. Surely Penny Lander hadn't come away triumphant from that.

She would have given up if the man at the desk hadn't been so positive that Penny Lander had gone home having discovered something. So she typed in her own surname and was unsurprised to find over 12,000 results. The name Jones – the genealogist's curse. She typed her mother's first name into the filter and managed to narrow down the search to 232 entries but this was still too many. Massaging her temples, Rachel began to click on the results. Her own birth in 1970 wouldn't be there and as she opened up the images, she began to see the futility of what she was trying to do. Her mother had been born in 1946 and a Mary Jones, aged seven, had had her appendix removed in 1954. Was this her mother? It was in the days before unique patient numbers and all Rachel had to go on was the name and the date on the records. It was possible that her mother had had her appendix out in 1954 and it was entirely feasible that another Mary Jones had had the operation on that summer's day.

She knew that her mother had been born in Bampton hospital. So she typed in her grandmother's name. Hannah Jones, the official name never used by the family, who had always referred to her by the diminutive Nancy. And sure enough she was there. Hannah Jones who, on 29 December 1946, gave birth to a daughter. Weight, nine pounds and nine ounces. A whopper of a baby and foretelling the child's robust attitude in later life.

But now, when she thought of her mother, the image that came to mind was not of that vigorous woman, but as she had been in 1978 after the misery of those first few days. Her mother had appeared so strong and yet about a week after the kidnapping, Rachel had chanced upon her looking miserable on the sofa of their small living room. Her red eyes looked like she had been crying. Rachel, not knowing what to do and not used to seeing her mother like that, had simply sat next to her and held her hand. This had seemed to give her mother strength and when she spoke, the question was the last thing Rachel had been expecting.

'Was the man who took you tall?'

Rachel had sharply withdrawn her hand. 'Mum, I remember nothing.'

It had been the last conversation that they had ever had about the event. Her mother had either accepted the truth of Rachel's words or she had simply decided to move on anyway. And here, on the screen in front of her, were the details of Mary Jones's birth. Daughter of Hannah, known as Nancy. The patient information was scant. It had her grandmother's date of birth, 1925, which made her twenty-one at her daughter's birth. Young but nothing unusual in those days. On the top right-hand corner, there was a number 2. Presumably that was an internal reference number, and Rachel was inclined to ignore it, but she should at least find out what it meant.

She came out of the records and looked at the accompanying overview. Flicking back and forth between screens, she finally came to the explanation of patient records. But something must be wrong. Because according to the overview, the digit in the top right-hand corner identified the total number of children that the patient had borne. According to Nancy's records, Mary was birth number two. Rachel knew from her own research that Nancy had married in 1945, at the end of the war. Could there be another child before her mother who hadn't survived? A quick search said no. Hannah Jones had given birth to no other children at Bampton hospital. Rachel sucked her pen in concentration. Perhaps there had been a stillbirth at home. She had seen that before. One lost baby quickly replaced by another, often given the same Christian name too. That would explain why no one had ever mentioned it in their family. There was one thing she needed to check. She typed in her grandmother's maiden name, Price. There was one record for Hannah Price, a baby born in 1942. She checked the woman's date of birth and felt her temperature cool, the ice tingling its way through her body. Hannah Price, born in 1925, had had a baby boy on the 12 June 1942.

Chapter 39

The garden outbuilding was a large, solid stone construction that reminded Sadler of the sheds of his childhood. Warm dried grass competing with darker peaty aromas. Every time he opened a Sunday supplement, he could see a range of outhouses that owed more to extended living spaces than somewhere to keep your garden implements. Penny Lander's shed wasn't one of these. It had presumably been built at the same time as the house, with a tiny window near the top to let in some meagre light.

The forensic team had, in fact, examined the shed. Sadler could see the whitish traces of fingerprint powder on the runner of pine shelves hanging on one wall. But the rest of the structure seemed to have been given only a cursory glance. Decaying garden implements, old flowerpots, some still containing matted earth but no plants and an assortment of bric-a-brac.

'I'm surprised you were looking in here. It's a big job to clear it out.' It sounded like an accusation, and by the tone of her response it was clear that Justine Lander had taken it as such.

'I didn't know where to start so I decided to make a list of everything that needed doing.' There was a large lined notebook resting on one of the shed's shelves. 'When I got here, I started to make a list of what I needed to do and I remembered that old safe in the corner. It's years since I saw it and I wondered if it was still there.'

'So you went to have a look?'

'Exactly. I had to move a load of stuff to find it but most of it had only been superficially laid in its way. Do you see what I mean?'

She was looking at him. Appealing for him to understand rather than explain. He helped her out. 'You mean that you think someone had been accessing it recently.'

'Yes.' She sounded relieved. 'It's been there for years, that safe. Certainly when I was growing up here. I used to play with it as a kid.'

'Was it used?' asked Sadler crouching down to get a better look.

'God knows. My father was paranoid about security. He would never have left anything valuable in an outhouse. But the key did used to turn in the lock. I used to shut the safe like that when I was a kid. It's rusted stiff now.'

Sadler tried to turn the big metal key in the lock and it was stuck rigid. Instead he pulled on it and the safe opened easily. Inside was a plastic file containing what looked like a sheaf of papers. He looked up at Justine, who stared down at him with impassive blue eyes.

'Open it, you'll see what I mean.'

Sadler straightened and looked up at the dim light. 'It would be easier inside with a cup of tea.'

He followed her into the house and, instead of opening the folder, watched as she made the brew. She seemed unperturbed by his presence and, once more, he was struck by how different she was from Christina. Where Christina was glamorous and vibrant with nervous tension, Justine was solid and calm. He forced his eyes away from her movements and opened the folder. There was very little dust covering the plastic cover and it had clearly been placed in the outhouse safe only recently. Inside the packet there was a sheaf of papers, as he had expected. He pulled them out and spread them on the kitchen table. Sadler saw Justine look over at him.

'You've seen them already?' he asked.

'I looked at them in the shed but they make very little sense to me. Mum seems to have been doing some kind of research into the old hospital. I wondered if it was to do with medical negligence.'

Sadler glanced up at her. 'Negligence? Why would you say that?'

Justine came over and stood next to him, her body giving off a floral scent. 'Well, why else would she be prying into the work of a hospital that had shut down? It must have been to do with something that happened there.'

Sadler shuffled through the sheets of paper. There was a yellowing newspaper cutting with the familiar photo of Rachel from around the time of the kidnapping. Sadler put it to one side and instead focused on the notes. Penny Lander's handwriting had been small and neat. It looked like she had meticulously researched the history of the hospital and the procedures that it had used to record its patients. But which patient had she been most interested in? Not herself, as her daughter clearly thought. Sadler skim read the notes and one name, a name that Penny Lander had been interested in, jumped out at him. Nancy Price.

*

Connie met Nick Oates again for an update in the cinema. He was waiting with a large carton of popcorn which he offered to Connie but she refused. It was tasteless whether you added salt or sugar to the mix and it always left her with the need to belch violently. The film this time was another children's story and Connie didn't even bother to find out the title. They sat together at the end of a row near the door at the back of the theatre, making it easier to leave once they had finished, Connie presumed. He was clearly pleased with himself.

'Your first task was the hardest. Find out if there were any men in Rachel's mother's life. I can tell you I've had a nightmare trying to find that out. She seems to have kept herself to herself and all the old neighbours I've spoken to – the ones I've been able to find, that is – tell me that they never saw her with anyone.'

Connie looked at the large cinema screen. 'There was someone. Audrey Frost, an old neighbour, thinks there was a man in her life, long gone by 1978. Or so we think.'

Nick Oates shifted in his seat, clearly irritated. 'I'm just telling you I couldn't find anything.'

She felt him glance at her in the gloom but he carried on in his mild, cultured voice. 'You asked me about the records of Bampton cottage hospital. Well, that was easy enough. They're kept in the basement of the town hall in Bampton. I spoke to the guy there on the phone this morning. And guess what he told me.'

'Penny Lander visited there.'

He let out a sigh. 'Certainly a woman fitting her description. But not only that. While I was telephoning, I managed to get out of the guy that Rachel Jones was there at that very moment, nosing about the records.'

Connie wasn't surprised. Sadler had been correct in his prediction that Rachel would be doing a bit of research herself. 'What do you think she was after?'

'She's a researcher, for God's sake. Why do you think she was there? Looking at the records.'

Connie sat with her arms folded. They'd never catch up with her. Rachel was a professional. Whatever Penny Lander had found, Rachel was certainly likely to discover it too. The question was to what extent would it be putting her in danger?

'And any luck with where the girls might have been stashed for a couple of hours before ending up in Truscott Woods?'

The children's film had reached a frightening part, at least if you were eight years old, and a collective hush had gathered over the cinema. Nick and Connie dropped their voices, although strangely Nick found it easier to do so than Connie. A woman sitting in front of them kept looking round, clearly suspicious of a professional-looking couple watching a children's film.

'You're right about the time gap,' whispered Nick, moving closer to her. 'The children were kidnapped around quarter to nine on the morning of January the twentieth and Rachel was found on the Bampton Road around midday. It's unlikely that they were at Truscott Fields all that time.'

'According to the weather reports, after a clear start it was drizzling from about eleven a.m. onwards. There wouldn't have been many people in the fields or the woods.'

'It's got to have been a residential address. The whole area is full of houses. The driver wouldn't have been able to go far without attracting attention. In my opinion, she must have driven them into a driveway and bundled them into a house.

Most likely a detached house with a driveway or garage, where the girls could be removed from the car without anyone noticing.'

'That narrows it down a bit, I suppose. The posher houses are mainly around the High Oaks area of the town. OK, so we're agreed that the girls were taken to a holding address, probably a house. What about after that?'

He looked at her in the flickering gloom of the cinema.

'It's where Sophie must have been killed.'

They sat saying nothing for a moment, watching the screen in silence. The young mother in front of them clearly found their silence more suspicious and once more turned to look at them.

'But we still don't have a motive for why the girls were kidnapped in the first place. We're agreed that it was Rachel who was the target, not Sophie,' said Connie.

'I think so. Sophie Jenkins has been missing since 1978, and although her mother killed herself only recently, there's no evidence she was looking into anything to do with the girls' disappearance.' Nick was trying to peer at his notebook in the gloom. 'Her death seems to have brought to a head Penny Lander's investigations. Up until last year, she was a busy schoolteacher with a husband and grown-up child. Within the space of a year she lost her husband and retired from her job.'

'And she started to look into something around the old hospitals. In all likelihood something had been bubbling away in her mind for a while and she decided to act on it.'

'Oh no. I've found something much more concrete than that.' He was struggling to keep the satisfaction out of his voice.

'Go on.'

'Penny Lander and Yvonne Jenkins met three days before Yvonne Jenkins committed suicide.'

She turned towards him. 'You're kidding.'

'I'm not. They met in the foyer of the Wilton Hotel and had coffee. The waiter remembered her, Penny Lander, I mean, because he was another one of her ex-pupils. Or something like that. He certainly went to St Paul's school. So I showed him a photograph of Yvonne Jenkins – which, incidentally, was bloody hard to get hold of.'

'I'm surprised you found anything.'

'Well, it was an old passport photo and, as I say, don't ask me how I got hold of it.'

'And the waiter recognised her from it?'

'He recognised her as the woman Penny Lander had had coffee with a few days before she died.'

'So the two of them met.'

'Yes, and what's more, something was handed over.'

'What? What was handed over?'

'Well, I don't know that. The guy couldn't see that much. But it fitted inside an envelope and it was handed over to Yvonne Jenkins.'

'And you think that act might have tipped Yvonne Jenkins into killing herself?'

'Well, it's possible, don't you think?'

Connie shuffled in her seat, the soft velveteen uncomfortable against her black trousers. 'And then what do you think happened? That after Yvonne Jenkins killed herself, Penny Lander decided to confront the person who figured in her suspicions.'

Nick shut his notebook with a slap. 'That's my best guess.'

Connie paused for a second. 'Any idea on identities?'

She felt Nick shrug beside her. 'The girls were kidnapped by a woman but in her early statements Rachel also said she remembered a man. The people who were part of Penny's life then, and that are still potential suspects, are her husband, his sister and her fellow schoolteachers.'

'But James Lander is dead.'

'So it's not him then, is it?'

*

Sadler looked at the name, Nancy Price, written in capitals on Penny Lander's notebook and surrounded by a circle made with a firm stroke of a pen. Sadler thought back to his conversation with Rachel. She had mentioned her mother, Mary Jones, and her grandmother Nancy, née Price. There had been mention of a great-grandmother too. But Nancy Price was the name written here. It would explain the continual clicking on the page on Rachel Jones's website that contained her family tree. Penny Lander had been familiarising herself with the names in that family before her trip to the records office. And it was the name of Nancy Price, Rachel's grandmother, that was the link Penny had been looking for.

'Is it significant?'

Sadler turned to look at the woman standing at his side with a concerned look on her face. This was a bereaved daughter, he had to tell himself, and yet her expression conveyed sympathy to him. He moved his eyes back to the page.

'Does it mean anything to you?'

She looked surprised at this. 'Not at all. Should it? Who's Nancy Price?'

Sadler was flicking through the remaining leaves of paper. It looked like background jottings, the notes that Penny had made leading up to his discovery of Nancy Price's name.

'She's a connection,' said Sadler, putting the notes down on the kitchen table.

'To Mum's murder?'

Sadler turned to look at her now. 'Yes'. He could see her mouth trembling as she tried to contain the emotion.

'Will you find her? This Nancy Price?'

Sadler wanted to reach out and touch her but instead put his hand in his pocket and pulled out his phone. 'I already know where she is.'

He dialled Connie's number and waited. There was no answer and the rings eventually switched onto voicemail. Damn. He scrolled down to Palmer's number, then remembered that he was getting married that weekend. Tomorrow, in fact. Sadler had lost track of which day of the week it was. There was nothing for it. He would have to interview Rachel Jones himself. He looked up at the kitchen clock. It was half-past five on a Friday. A time when people were winding down in readiness for the weekend, although still early enough to conduct a friendly interview. But Rachel Jones wasn't answering her mobile either.

In frustration he put his phone back in his pocket. His eyes fell on the newspaper cutting. He picked it up and looked at the photograph. It was a picture of both Rachel and her mother smiling at the camera. The caption at the bottom proclaimed, 'Mary and Rachel Jones celebrating their tombola win.' Mary

Jones was holding in her arms a large doll that surely would have been too childish for the eight-year-old Rachel. Sadler frowned at the date on the clipping. August 1977. The picture had been reproduced by countless other newspapers reporting on the subsequent kidnapping. But this clipping was from the original event, a school fete in 1977. And it wasn't a modern-day reproduction either. Its yellow crinkled texture gave away its thirty-seven years.

'Have you seen this before?' His tone was too abrupt, breaking the sense of closeness that had been present earlier.

Justine's face fell, but she moved closer and took the clipping from his hands. She shook her head. 'I've never seen it before. Why?'

Why indeed, thought Sadler. *Why does Penny have the original newspaper clipping of an event that took place five months before the two girls were kidnapped?*

'I have to go.' Sadler pulled out his car keys from his pocket and turned towards the front door. He could feel Justine Lander's eyes on him as he let himself out of the front door.

Chapter 40

Rachel stared at the screen, her brain attempting to assimilate the information. She was heart-stoppingly astounded that her mother had a brother. No one had said a word to her. Who else had colluded in this deception? Rachel leaned back in her seat and rubbed her face. *Concentrate*, she thought, her professional training kicking in. If the records were simply those of a client, what would she have thought?

One possibility was that the baby had died at birth and the incident was never mentioned. She came across cases like this all the time in her research. In the days before antibiotics, babies had been stillborn or had died a few days after birth. Even as recently as 1942, the death of a child would have been a sad but not astonishing event. To check this, she would need to look for a death certificate, which would be time consuming with a surname like Price.

Was her grandfather Hughie the father of the child? He and Nancy got married in September 1945, at the very end of the war, but somehow Rachel doubted that they were together a full three years before then. Her grandfather hadn't been called up. His asthma meant he had been given exemption from military service and he spent the war working his trade as a mechanic. There had been ample opportunity for them to get married if they'd wanted to before 1945.

Rachel searched the recesses of her brain. Her mother

had never mentioned a brother. She was absolutely sure of it. The female line had been all-important in the family, that was true. But not to the detriment of all the other men. Hughie had held his own place within the family, first as a breadwinner and then, after he'd retired in the mid-1980s, as a reassuring male presence in her life. Both he and Nancy were bewildered by her kidnapping and Rachel's mother seemed to shrink away from their offered comfort. At the time, Rachel barely noticed this withdrawal by her mother from her family. If it registered at all, she simply assumed that it was part of her mother's retreat from the world, her wrapping of a protective cloak around herself and her daughter. But sitting in the gloomy light of the archive office, she could see that it wasn't normal behaviour. Surely her mother should have turned to her family, not away from them.

Rachel glanced at the flickering screen. Something wasn't making sense. Assuming she had an uncle, or half-uncle, why would he want to kidnap her? There was a connection she wasn't making. Yet Penny Lander was here before her, she was absolutely sure. Penny Lander had discovered this anomaly. Rachel massaged her head and thought. What had Sydney at the library said? That Mrs Lander had been making enquiries about illegitimacy and cottage hospitals. The only male in Mrs Lander's life was her husband, James. Could he have been the illegitimate child? Was James Lander the baby that Nancy had given up?

She picked up her bag and left the basement, her footsteps echoing around the cavernous room as she climbed up the stone steps. Tim Dowling was still sitting behind the reception desk, his body hunched over some document he was reading.

He must have heard her approach but didn't look up.

'Find what you wanted?'

She ignored him and opened the door onto the street.

Chapter 41

The large reception room of the Wilton Hotel was bedecked in white and silver balloons that bobbed up and down as the chill wind percolated through the cracks in the windows. Connie pulled the collar of her black velvet jacket up around her neck and shivered. Sadler, standing to her left, held in his hand an undrunk glass of champagne and was talking to a woman she didn't recognise. Connie was on her second glass, although she didn't really like the stuff. It had a thin sweetness to it that left a metallic taste in the back of her throat. But it was their day off and she was in the mood to let her hair down. She looked around for someone to talk to but, like most weddings, the party was made up of groups of family and friends who had clearly known each other for years. Only she and Sadler were here from the station, which wasn't surprising, given that she had heard Palmer moaning about having to pay for the reception themselves, as Joanne's parents were retired. Llewellyn and his wife were nowhere to be seen.

The woman Sadler was talking to moved off and he was now staring into his champagne glass. What a misery he was, thought Connie. No wonder he'd never married. She wondered if he was still with his glamorous girlfriend. They had been spotted together once in a local pub by an eagle-eyed girl in the forensic ops team and the news had spread like wildfire around the office. But that had been a while back and it looked like it had finished, given the fact she wasn't accompanying him. He caught her eye and smiled and she thought again how attractive and yet remote she found him. Still, he was at least moving towards her to provide some backup in this awkward social situation.

'That was Palmer's sister. She was telling me how much he loves his job.'

Connie rolled her eyes and she heard Sadler laugh beside her. 'So you think he paid her to say that?'

Connie's gaze followed the woman moving away from her. 'I think, given the amount she's drunk already, she didn't need much persuasion.'

Sadler put down his champagne glass. 'That's the problem with weddings. Always too much to drink.'

'You've not touched yours,' she pointed out.

He slid his eyes sideways. 'Are you keeping track, DC Childs?'

She willed herself not to flush but looked up at him and was surprised to see him smiling. They both looked over to where Palmer was standing with his new bride. Joanne had sensibly chosen a long-sleeved dress with a little fur jacket, hopefully fake. She looked beautiful, thought Connie. Beautiful and slightly frightening. There was something about brides that always sent a chill through her. Palmer looked pleased and slightly scared. She guessed he would start to feel better once his speech was out of the way. At least he hadn't tried to practise that on her in the pub, although she was still confused about his plea to stay the night. What had that been all about? Thank God she had sent him on his way. She'd caught sight of the bride's mother, a large buxom woman in a bright red jacket. Not someone she'd want to get on the wrong side of.

'Do you want to go for a walk? It's at least another half an hour before we eat. I've just checked.'

Connie looked at Sadler in surprise. 'It's freezing outside. I've only got this dress and my coat. Where did you have in mind?'

Sadler for the first time seemed to take in what Connie was wearing. She had a wraparound dress that fell to her knees. She had thought about putting heels on but one look at the weather had changed her mind and she had put on her suede boots with the wedges. They would be ruined if it was raining.

'Is this the first time I've seen you in a dress?'

A retort rose to her lips but again she could see that Sadler was smiling at her. 'It doesn't matter. I thought outside because we could get some peace to talk though ...'

A shudder shot through Connie's thin frame. *I'm freezing already.* 'Fine,' she said.

They both retrieved their coats from the bored-looking girl behind the counter and walked out into Bampton's main square. The squall of the wind shot needles of ice at them, pinning the skirt of Connie's dress to her legs. *That's my boots gone,* she thought.

Sadler seemed oblivious to his surroundings. 'I tried to call yesterday evening.'

Connie shoved her hands in her coat pockets and started walking. 'I was at the cinema.'

She felt him looking at her.

'I suppose this could have waited until Monday. Whoever killed Penny Lander isn't rampaging Bampton's streets looking for their next victim. But we finally seem to be making some headway this week. The pieces are starting to come together, even if we're not completely there yet.'

Connie decided to come clean.

'My cinema date wasn't for pleasure. It was with a journalist.'

She could feel disapproval radiating off him. 'You could get sacked for that, Con.'

She looked at the floor and noted his use of her shortened first name. 'He'd been doing some digging himself and thought he might have some information that would help us.' She didn't mention that it was she who had asked him to do the digging in the first place.

'Did he come up with anything?'

'Yes, actually. But I seem to have a jigsaw puzzle of images and nothing is making sense.'

'Why don't you go first, Connie? Let's go back to 1978. What do you think happened then?'

'I think it starts earlier than that.'

He turned to her and smiled. 'Yes, it does, doesn't it? But let's start at the first crime. Start with 1978.'

Connie shrugged, humouring him. 'OK. Rachel and Sophie were walking to the school and were picked up by a woman acting on behalf of someone else.'

'Why don't you think it was the woman who wanted either of the girls?'

'I think we can definitely say that it was Rachel, not Sophie, who was the kidnapper's target. We've looked into Sophie's background. It's tragic but there's nothing to suggest any hidden secrets that we need to continue looking for.'

'We're absolutely sure that it wasn't a random attack? That neither girl was the intended target and it was just an opportunist kidnapping.'

'Not now we know that Rachel's mother had a big secret that

she had kept hidden from everyone, including her daughter.'

'The identity of Rachel's real father.'

'Exactly. But Mary Jones is now dead so she isn't going to be able to give us any information about him.'

'And we're working on the assumption that Rachel doesn't know who NN, the missing person, is either.'

'No, but as you pointed out, I think Rachel is well on the way to finding out who the man is.'

Sadler pulled the collar of his coat up around his neck. Although she was freezing, Connie could feel adrenaline coursing through her.

'And he decided to kidnap his natural daughter because . . . ?'

Connie lifted her arms in a gesture of defeat. 'I don't know. This is where my theory starts to loosen. Why would a father kidnap his own child? Mary Jones sounds a reasonable person; why should she deny Rachel's father access to her? Unless he was some kind of paedophile or mentally unbalanced. That would explain what happened to the missing Sophie.'

'Rachel was unharmed physically.'

'But this has been the problem since the original investigation. We've been lumping them together. Rachel wasn't assaulted so we've automatically assumed that Sophie wouldn't have been either. We have no proof of that.'

'But isn't that likely to have made Sophie the intended victim? If he was willing to abuse a child who wasn't his own daughter. Although that would explain why the two of them were kidnapped together.'

The wind had died down a notch. Connie searched in her handbag for a cigarette and lit it, ignoring Sadler's look of distaste. 'Something's not right. This theory doesn't follow through. Who are the possible men in the case who could be Rachel's natural father?'

Sadler stopped. 'One: James Lander – he's the husband of Penny who was murdered although we're yet to establish a connection.'

'And I suppose we ought to include Sophie's father, Peter Jenkins. There's nothing to link him with Mary Jones but he will have known the family. Although I'm not sure why he would kill his own daughter.'

'You said earlier that you thought the origins of the case went back before 1978. When were you thinking of?'

Connie looked up at him. 'To 1970 and the deception by Rachel's mother.'

'Only 1970? I think we need to go back much, much further than that. I want to add another name to the mix,' said Sadler. 'Nancy Price.'

'Nancy Price?' asked Connie. 'Who's she? Oh, hang on, don't tell me. Price is in the Jones family tree somewhere. She's . . .'

'Rachel's maternal grandmother.'

'Was she alive in 1978?'

'She's still alive now.'

'Alive now – ahh. According to Rachel she's completely nutty and living in a nursing home.'

'I'm not so sure about that. I think Rachel's protecting her grandmother.'

Connie stared at him. 'You don't think she was the woman involved in the kidnapping?'

'I think we can assume Rachel would have recognised her own grandmother. And anyway her description states the woman was youngish. Even allowing for the fact that children aren't brilliant at guessing ages, we can rule her out.'

'But Penny Lander found something out about her?'

Sadler told her about the notepad hidden in the shed. 'It's definitely Nancy Price that was the answer to what she was looking for. That name was the answer. Our problem is . . .'

'What was the question?'

'Precisely.'

'Then Nancy Price clearly holds some of the answers that we need. Do you know where the nursing home is?'

'I made a few calls last night when I couldn't get hold of you. I spoke to one of the supervisors in the home. She's quite frail, Rachel was right about that, but her mind is fine. Apparently she's a bit of a character. The woman seemed genuinely fond of her.'

'We need to go and see her.' Connie could feel the hairs on the back of her neck begin to prickle. This woman was the key. Nancy Price, who had stayed in the shadows up to now. 'It's not Rachel's father who's our NN, it's Nancy Price.'

Sadler turned and looked back towards the lights emanating from the hotel. Connie got the feeling that he felt the same way about the jollity taking place inside the building.

'We can't miss the wedding breakfast. I'm Palmer's boss. I need to be there.'

'But we don't have to stay for the dancing. We could go then.'

Sadler looked down at her, his pale opaque eyes half shadowed in the afternoon gloom. Connie saw him smile.

Chapter 42

Rachel woke up and, for a few seconds, didn't know where she was. This had happened to her before and she'd learned not to panic. She lay still and, as she looked around the room, the objects made themselves known to her and her brain slowly identified them. At last able to recognise her surroundings, she turned and looked at the back of Richard Weiss's head. His pale blond hair was flattened after a night's sleep and she could see the imprint of the pillow on one of his cheeks. She lightly touched his head and he stirred slightly but didn't wake. She leaned forward and kissed him gently on his temple, eased herself out of bed and made her way towards the toilet. As she passed the bathroom mirror she took a look at herself. She hadn't washed her face before going to bed and her mascara lay in a sooty smudge under her eyes. That apart, she didn't look too bad for a woman past forty.

She sat on the toilet and wondered how much caffeine she would need before her brain started working again. When she arrived at Richard's last night she'd said nothing about her discoveries in the records archives. Something had made her reticent about this anomaly in her family. She was willing to accept her mother's lie about the identity of her real father, but the duplicity of her grandmother Nancy left her breathless with shock. Nancy, her gay, carefree grandmother, devoted to her mild-mannered husband, Hughie, had given birth four years before having her mother, Mary, in 1946.

According to the records, the baby born to Nancy had been a boy, which assuming he was still living meant that she had a half-uncle somewhere. But why would that bring about Mrs Lander's death and what role had it played in her own kidnapping? As she flushed the toilet, she heard Richard next door stir and rather than speak to him straight away, she stripped off her T-shirt and stepped into the shower. It was a mistake. She had forgotten the ancient plumbing needed at least five minutes to warm up and she was left gasping as the sheet of cold water hit her body. But it had the effect of bringing her to her senses, which allowed her tired brain to assess the evidence. There was clearly a link to the kidnapping and it was hers to discover.

When she stepped out of the shower, she peeked into the bedroom and saw that Richard had got out of bed and was standing in his pyjama bottoms looking out of the large bay windows.

'The neighbours will see,' she shouted through the door as she dried herself. As she walked back into the bedroom he turned round, smiling at her.

'Nothing much here to excite the ladies of the neighbourhood.' He looked her up and down. 'Are you feeling OK?'

She sat down on the edge of the bed. 'Can I ask you something?'

He nodded and opened a drawer, grabbed a T-shirt and pulled it on over his head. He sat down beside her. It was a strange tableau. She with a towel that was slightly too small for her thick body. He in a T-shirt and striped pyjama bottoms. Hardly the time for confidences.

'Your father wasn't adopted, was he?'

He turned to her and stared with astonished eyes. 'My father? Why are you asking?'

'It's just when I saw you at the woods. I thought maybe your father could have been involved . . .'

She was trembling and he reached out to her. He pulled her towards him and she felt the warmth of his body as he wrapped his arms around her.

'We need to sort this out. Let me have a shower and then we can have breakfast. We'll talk about it then.'

In other men, Rachel would have taken this as prevarication, but in Richard it was oddly comforting. She sat watching the local news while he had a shower, then cooked breakfast and brewed the coffee. It was a heady mix and by the time she sat down she realised that she was nearly faint with hunger. Richard watched her start eating and then began his own breakfast.

'We're not related, Rachel. Whatever is going on in your head, you can discount that. And my family wasn't involved in your kidnapping.'

She was surprised by his lack of anger. 'Nancy had a child. Before my mother. I'm not sure if Mum knew or not. But she definitely had a child. It's in the hospital records.'

'And you thought the baby might be my father. What do you think that would make us, first cousins?' He seemed amused now and Rachel felt anger surge through her.

'It's not funny. I nearly passed out when I thought of it. What makes you so sure?'

'Rachel. Think about it. My family's Jewish. All right we're not very devout and we don't make a fuss of it. But that's what we are. Jews. Family is important to us and so is our heritage. I can categorically say that my father was the natural son of my grandparents.'

'But I suppose maybe the father of the child might be important. Do you think your grandfather . . .'

Richard burst out laughing. 'You never knew my grandfather. There's no way he's involved. He was five foot tall, quiet. He loved books, the solicitor's practice and ornithology. You've told me about Nancy, remember. No way. She'd have eaten him alive.'

Rachel smirked and looked down at the empty plate. Like most times she ate a cooked breakfast, she felt guilty straight away.

'There is something that I need to tell you, though,' said Richard.

'What?'

'Rachel, you need to take it easy. I know it's difficult, but I'm telling you this because I don't want there to be any secrets between us.'

'Go on. Tell me.'

'This case has been preying on my mind too. I'm sorry that I laughed when you asked if my father was adopted. It's just not the question I expected. But you remember when you met me that day in the woods? And I mentioned that I'd gone there after meeting my father in the office.'

'Of course I remember. What are you trying to say?'

'I didn't tell you the whole truth. The reason that I went there was that when I spoke to Dad about you, he mentioned your mother. He remembered the case, of course. But he also told me that he had met her grandmother too. She came to the office.'

'*Her* grandmother? Not mine? Mum's.'

'He definitely said *her* grandmother. So after he'd gone, I went to have a look through the old files just to see if we had had any interaction with your family.'

'And had you?'

Richard sighed. 'It seems that Mair Price, your great-grandmother, came in for a one-off consultation in September 1974. It was fairly easy to find the file.'

'And what did the file say?'

'This is where it's really strange. My father was a very methodical man too. There were no problems when I took over the business from him. I could go to a file and everything about a particular case would be there.'

'But not this one.'

He was avoiding her eye. 'No. It's pretty unprofessional, actually. There's the date of the meeting. The phrase "advice given" and the fee.'

'And that's it.'

'Yes.'

She stared at him. 'Mair went to see him? And you've no idea what it was about?'

'It *is* strange. And I needed to think that day, which is why I went to the woods. Everything was happening so quickly. You and I getting together, then I find out about the odd record.'

'And didn't you ask him about it?'

Richard stared unhappily at her. 'I did. But he wouldn't tell me. Said it was a professional consultation and it was best to leave it. He got angry when I tried to press it. He won't tell me, Rachel. I know my father. The harder you push the more intransigent he becomes.'

Rachel folded her arms. 'This is my past that you're talking about.'

'He did say one thing.'

Rachel could see that he was embarrassed. 'What?'

'He said that the advice given was the best he was able to give at the time. And sometimes you don't realise the ramifications until much later.'

'Ramifications? Like my kidnapping? He does know something.' She was shouting at Richard and she saw a look of pity flash in his eyes.

'Rachel. Whatever happened, it wasn't my dad's fault. He's right. You give advice to the best of your knowledge at the time and sometimes you don't get to see the whole picture. I'm not saying it's to do with your abduction. But something happened in September 1974 for Mair to go and see him.'

Something clicked in Rachel's head. 'She died in the November. Of cancer of the spleen. She must have known she didn't have long.'

Richard held out a hand and touched her hair. Rachel tried not to pull her head away. 'You need to speak to Nancy. Talk to your grandmother. She's the only one alive who might be willing to say something. Please talk to her, Rachel. I think she might have some of the answers that you need.'

Chapter 43

Connie and Sadler left the wedding in full swing. The obligatory photographs had been taken, the meal eaten and guests were now turning their attention to drinking and dancing for the rest of the evening. The sign outside the Maytree care home declared it to be a 'skilled nursing facility', which, in Connie's opinion, could have meant anything. The reception was empty when they walked in, although from a distance they could hear sounds of muted conversation.

'Can I help you?' A small woman emerged from a side office and briefly flicked her eyes over their formal clothes. Sadler looked at Connie and she took her ID from her handbag.

'We're DI Sadler and DC Childs from Bampton CID. We've come to visit Nancy Jones, if she's up to seeing us.'

The woman took the ID off Connie and looked concerned. 'Everything's all right, isn't it? It's not Rachel?'

'Not at all.' Connie wondered if this was a good idea, after all, turning up on a Saturday evening to interview a woman well into her eighties. 'We just need to ask her a few questions.'

The woman didn't look reassured but nevertheless led them down a long corridor and knocked on one of the doors.

Nancy Jones was sitting in a chair beside a single bed. She was dressed in a pale mauve cardigan over a light grey dress from Marks and Spencer that Connie had tried on earlier that week and had decided was too young for her. The woman's hair was styled into rigid curls that licked around her face, suggesting a recent perm. She had no make-up on as far as Connie could see, except perhaps some powder on her cheeks. Even with the wrinkles and the helmet-style hair Connie could see she had once been beautiful.

'Two police detectives are here to see you, Nancy. Are you feeling up to visitors?'

'Police?' Nancy brightened at the thought of visitors, even official ones. She looked Connie up and down and smiled. But the warmth she reserved for Sadler. She pointed to the chair at the end of the bed.

'Take a seat, won't you? No need to stand on ceremony.'

I'll just stay on my feet, thought Connie. The woman didn't seem to notice that they were both dressed for a wedding, Sadler in a blue suit that must have cost him a packet. She in the wraparound dress from Marks and Spencer's, thankful she was not wearing the same one as the octogenarian Nancy Jones.

Sadler, ignoring Connie, went and sat in the wing-backed chair.

'Has Rachel been to see you recently?'

Nancy looked at him in surprise. 'She comes every week. Without fail. Why did you want to know?'

Sadler was choosing his words carefully. 'Has she mentioned anything about a crime committed recently?'

'You mean the murder?' Nancy was clearly enjoying herself. 'I know all about that. She used to be a teacher in Rachel's school. It was in all the papers and, anyway, the nurses here can't keep any local gossip to themselves.'

'So you knew who Penny Lander was?'

'Only that she had worked in St Paul's. I'd never met her and I don't think she ever taught Rachel.'

'Did Rachel say anything about her?'

Nancy's mouth pursed in a thin line. 'Say what? What's all this about? Rachel's suffered enough from that kidnapping. What's this got to do with her?'

'What I suppose I want to know is whether Rachel has asked you anything about the murder.'

Nancy started laughing, and once more Connie could again see the vestiges of the beauty she must once have been.

'Me? Have you seen the state of me? I can hardly stand. It wasn't me, I can assure you. You're barking up the wrong tree, I'm afraid.'

'The reason we're asking is that your name is in a notebook that we found at Mrs Lander's property. It has your name with a circle around it.'

'Mine? What she doing with my name in her notebook?'

'It was actually your maiden name. Nancy Price.'

Nancy looked confused. 'I haven't been called that for years. Nancy Price. That takes me back. I married Hughie in 1945. That's over sixty years ago. She wouldn't have known me then. I doubt she was even born.'

'We know that she had been undertaking research into the old Bampton cottage hospital. We were wondering if there was a connection there.'

'The hospital? What's that got to do with anything? I had Mary, my daughter, there after the end of the war. Not that I stayed there long. I couldn't wait to get out of the place.'

Sadler was regarding Nancy with an amused expression. 'Why? Why couldn't you wait to leave?'

Nancy turned to him. 'It was just like this place. Too warm. They think because we're old we need to be roasted in our rooms. What's the temperature outside?'

Connie shrugged. 'I'm not sure. Zero degrees, I guess. It feels like it.'

'Exactly. And I'm here in my short-sleeved dress and I'm still hot. It was the same with that hospital when I went in to have Mary. And it wasn't even cold out. A nice warm day and they had the heating on. I remember sitting there thinking it was a waste of the fuel rationing.'

Sadler was regarding Nancy and Connie could see the amused look had disappeared from his face. 'A warm day? But Mary was born in December, wasn't she? We don't get many warm days around here in the winter.'

Something flickered in the woman's eyes. It was gone in a moment but Connie wasn't deceived. She had seen it and so had Sadler. A silence settled between the three of them opening out while the sounds of the nursing home continued unseen outside the door.

'I'm tired. You're going to have to leave me alone.'

Connie leaned forward. 'I need to ask you again, Mrs Jones, if you can think of any reason why Penny Lander might have had your name in a notebook. Anything in your past that might have a bearing on the case.'

Nancy Jones refolded her hands in her lap and said firmly, 'I can't think of anything.' Connie looked to Sadler. He was assessing Nancy with calm eyes which the elderly woman was resolutely refusing to meet.

'I think you need to leave now. I don't have anything else to say to you.'

Back at the wedding, Sadler watched Connie making a good attempt at dancing with Palmer and his new wife. Nobody was bothering him, which was just as well as he'd never been much of a dancer, even in his student days. The DJ clearly knew his audience and the floor was packed when Connie and he returned from the nursing home. The music was now a medley from the 1980s. Connie would have been a child then, as would Justine Lander. Rachel Jones would have been a teenager. Sadler felt a shift inside him when he considered those three names: Connie, Rachel and Justine. What was the connection?

He looked at Connie on the dance floor. She wasn't the link. Connie was brought up in Matlock, not far from Bampton, but hadn't been born in 1978. He thought of Rachel Jones, slightly overweight but with an attractive face and an appealing offhand manner. According to Connie, it looked like she was in a relationship with Richard Weiss, which, although not earth shattering, was possibly of interest to them.

He saw Connie realise that he was looking at her and become self-conscious. He turned his back on her and glanced around the rest of the room with unseeing eyes. His thoughts turned to Justine Lander. She was taller than Rachel Jones and differently built with long solid limbs and an ordinary freckled face which made his heart jump. Sadler suddenly had an urge to see what her mother had looked like in her prime. He swung round and Connie stopped dancing and stared across the room at him. He made towards her, squeezing past Palmer's friends and relatives as she too came to him.

'Do you have a photo of Penny Lander?'

Connie didn't bother to ask him why. She led him over to a chair where her handbag lay and started to flick through her iPhone.

'I took some photos in the house the day Penny was killed. Here we go.'

She waved the phone at him and he took it out of her hands. Penny Lander, as a young woman, had the same heart-stopping fair looks that her daughter had inherited. Down to the freckles on her nose and the Germanic blonde hair tied back in a clip. From what Sadler could remember of the post-mortem, she was shorter than Justine, though. Around five foot six to her daughter's extra three inches. Justine must have inherited her height from her father.

Connie was looking at him curiously. 'I took a photo of all the family snaps. You can have a look through them.'

Sadler used his finger to slide the photos across the screen. Most of them were of Justine growing up over the years. There were two photos of the three of them. The first had been taken at a distance on what looked like a Mediterranean holiday. All three were squinting at the camera. They had probably grabbed a passer-by and got them to take the photo. They looked happy. The second one was a more formal setting, taken before or during a wedding perhaps. Justine looked about seven years old in a satin turquoise dress and was giving a gap-toothed smile to the camera. Penny Lander looked unchanged from an earlier photo. And James? Well, James Lander looked unsmiling at the camera. Now it was Sadler's turn to squint at the image on the phone.

'What are you doing?'

Without looking up he moved nearer to a wall light. 'I'm trying to get a clearer look at his face.'

Connie reached over. 'You enlarge the image like this.' She slid her thumb and finger over the phone and sure enough the image got larger but more blurred. And then in an instance the pixels settled into their pattern and cleared. Sadler looked at the face in the picture on the phone and felt his heart, for a moment, stop beating.

Chapter 44

Rachel leaned forward in her chair and Nancy, imperceptibly, shrank back. When she'd arrived, she got them both a cup of tea from the woman doing her rounds with the trolley, hoping to catch Nancy in a relaxed state before she started her questions. But already something was up. Nancy had a heightened colour in her cheeks and her eyes looked watery, although Rachel could swear it wasn't with tears. Rachel added a dash of cold water to Nancy's hot tea and she listened to her slurp it while holding the saucer in her quavering hands.

'Nan, I need to ask you something.'

Nancy looked around the room and finally settled on a spot above Rachel's right shoulder. 'What is it, love? Man trouble?'

Rachel snorted, which brought a smile to her grandmother's face. 'Not me. I don't expect trouble and I don't get trouble.'

It was the wrong thing to say. Nancy bent back down over her tea and concentrated on taking another slurp.

'Nan. I went to the records office last week. I needed to do some research for my job.'

Her grandmother looked relieved. 'Burying yourself in those files. Look what they do to your nails.'

Rachel ploughed on. 'I found the record of you giving birth to Mum, in 1946. In Bampton cottage hospital. It's on file there.'

The relieved look had gone from her grandmother's face.

'But that's private,' she said, outraged. 'That's confidential information. How come you were allowed to see it?'

'Nan, it's not private. Some things are allowed in the public domain after a period of time. Most of it is the same information that can be seen on a birth certificate, it's just a different way of accessing the information.'

Nancy folded her arms across her chest. 'So what was it you wanted to talk to me about?'

Rachel took a deep breath. 'It said on the record that you had another child.'

There. It was out. And Nancy was struggling between outrage and guilt, if her expression was anything to go by. The silence stretched out. Rachel could hear a trolley being wheeled down the corridor outside as the tea woman moved on.

'So what?'

'You mean it's true?'

Nancy clanked her cup down onto the saucer angrily. 'That's the trouble with everyone today. They want to find out your business. Nothing's private any more. So I had a baby before I was married. I made a mistake, that's for sure. But between me and my mum we got it sorted. We made a new life and forgot the old one. And now you're bringing it up for no reason.'

'But Nan, it's important,' wailed Rachel.

'Important to who? You? It's got nothing to do with you. I got pregnant and then I did the decent thing and had him. Not that I didn't try the other.'

'But what happened to the baby?'

'Him. It was a him.' Nancy was shouting now. 'It was a baby boy. And he was adopted. And just as well that it was a boy, as my mother wouldn't have minded getting rid of that. She never had any time for men.' Now Nancy did look near to tears.

'But Nan, who adopted him?'

'I don't know. Mum sorted it out. There was a couple in Bampton who couldn't have any kids and she gave him to them.'

'Is everything all right?' A care worker had put her head through the doorway, clearly concerned with the sounds of arguing coming out of the room. Nancy and Rachel ignored her and she withdrew.

'The police were here earlier.'

'Here? What did they say?' hissed Rachel.

'Apparently my name appears in a notebook of that dead woman.'

'Mrs Lander,' said Rachel. So she hadn't needed to keep Penny Lander's name from her nan. She already knew there was a connection to her. 'What did you tell them?'

'I told them nothing.'

'Oh, Nan, this is serious.' Rachel was near desperation. 'They must think there's a connection.'

'Connection to what? If the child I gave birth to has killed a woman then it's nothing to do with me.'

'But what about me?'

'You? What do you mean?' For the first time the fright was apparent in her eyes. 'What do you mean?'

'They think the case is connected to my kidnapping.'

'But why would your uncle, who you've never seen, want to kidnap you? It doesn't make sense.'

'Nothing in this case makes sense.' Rachel stood up and walked over to the window.

Nancy was back in the past. It must have felt safer there. 'I tried it all. Sunday night it was the gin bottle. I went into the Red Cow in Llandaff North, even though I'd never been in a pub before, and asked the woman behind the bar for a bottle. I might as well have advertised to the whole pub that I was pregnant. The barmaid looked daggers but handed over the gin. One pound, five shillings and thrupence it cost me, I can remember the price now. I had to borrow the money from my friend Phyllis, with no hope of paying her back.'

Rachel could feel her mouth open. Was her nan talking about trying to have an abortion?

'On Monday evening, we had a bad bombing over Cardiff docks. Mum had gone to a shelter near work and I should have been in the one in the garden. But instead, I took the tin bath from the peg behind the kitchen door and filled it with water so hot that my skin was scalded red. Nothing. The next night I tried the gin and bath together and nearly passed out with the heat and the pain.'

'Oh, Nan.'

'Come Wednesday, I remember standing at the top of her stairs and looking down wondering how best to kill myself. And that's how Mum found me. Ready to throw myself down the stairs. And she was more annoyed with herself for not noticing. She wasn't normally one to miss something like that.'

'Who was he? The father of the baby, I mean.'

'Tom Watkins was his name. So persistent, he was, and off to North Africa with the South Wales Borderers that I thought a bit of comfort and warmth would do us both some good.'

'Is that why you came to Derbyshire? To start over again?'

'Mum had been working in the armaments factory in

Cardiff docks. A girl from Derbyshire, who worked next to her on the production line, had told her Litton Mill was now a parachute factory and was looking for women. And they weren't asking too many questions either. So we got on the train and waved Wales goodbye.'

Nancy looked down at the handkerchief clenched in her hands. 'And I didn't miss it either. None of that "How green was my valley" for Mair and me. It had been bloody hard work and I know Mum hated the German planes that used to fly over us on their way to the docks. Derbyshire was colder. But people minded their own business and it was just as well, considering.'

'And did my mum know about the baby? About the fact she had a half-brother?'

'No one knew, just me and Mum. She told me never to tell anyone. And I didn't. Not even my lovely Hughie had an idea I'd had a baby before I met him. We kept it well hidden and now it's all going to come out. And what for? What's it got to do with anything?'

*

Back in her house, Rachel's mobile and landline phones rang continuously. First Richard, who tried her mobile throughout the evening, but she also had a missed call from her neighbour Jenny. She'd left a message on her mobile, and had sounded worried. She hadn't mentioned her daughter's socks that Rachel was now holding once more in her hand.

This wasn't going to hold the key to the mystery. Looking at it she felt the shock of recognition, of something pulling at her. Muddied waters clearing. But not providing the clarity that she needed. *Think,* she willed herself. *Think.* Rachel had, most of her life, believed that her mother knew nothing about the kidnapping. But the last couple of weeks had changed that. She now believed her mother had known something, even if she hadn't made the whole connection.

For the death of Penny Lander to make sense, then her kidnapper must have been James Lander. Her uncle and the same boy child Nancy had given away all those years ago. She had a cousin too, called Justine according to her client Cathy Franklin, although she wasn't yet clear what she felt about her. And James Lander also had a sister living in Baslow Crescent in Bampton, although she would be no relative of hers. A whole family for Rachel to digest. But if he was her uncle, what had been his motive for kidnapping her and Sophie all those years ago. To blackmail her mother?

Rachel put down the sock and leaned back against the sofa. Conversations with recent clients passed through her mind. Eileen Clarke and the woman who had changed her name, but not to deceive. Pam Millett and her wayward son. Cathy Franklin, so fascinated by the idea of blue-blood illegitimacy. She had unwittingly chosen a profession that also held the key to the events of 1978. Had it been something deep in her subconscious that had steered her towards her unusual career? The long hours that she had put in over the years had been moving her towards the solution to her own mystery.

She began to think about what some of those families must have gone through. The ones she'd been interviewing over the years. Behind her closed eyelids, strange patterns were beginning to form and she saw Richard's face in front of her. What had he said to her that weekend? *We're not related, Rachel – I promise you that.* But now something more horrific was beginning to shape in her mind.

She grabbed a piece of paper and began to sketch once more her family tree. The design had become so familiar to her over the years, and yet now it was pruned. With a question mark above her father's name. From her grandmother's name, she drew a dotted line, indicating illegitimacy, and added in James Lander and his wife and daughter. Then with trembling hands she forced herself to face what her mind was telling her. Something so terrible that, as she was weighing up the possibility, her subconscious was also rejecting it. She struggled to hold on to what was solidifying in her mind. She drew a shaky dotted line between two boxes and the whole was there.

Chapter 45

Rachel rang the doorbell of the house. For the first time she knew the meaning of the phrase about scales falling from your eyes. She felt that a physical barrier that she'd been refusing to acknowledge had blinkered her. And now at last it was removed. And the person who had done the removing was herself. She, Rachel, had solved the mystery of 1978 where all others had failed. Well, all except perhaps one. Mrs Lander, that aloof teacher whom she'd seen only from a distance in the school, had worked it out too. And now Rachel knew why. She knew the reason for Penny Lander's sudden obsession with the kidnapping and what had been the result. The police were nearly there too, she was sure of it. They'd interviewed Nancy and it wouldn't take them long to piece everything together either. But these were her demons and ones that she intended to face alone.

Rachel's sense of triumph was also mingled with fear of what she was about to do. She'd made up her face before coming here, her hands trembling over the unfamiliar bottles and tubes. She'd taken time over her mascara, making sure that each lower eyelash was coated evenly. It was nonsense, of course, but with each dab of the brush Rachel had felt control return to her and her fear give way to fury that made her hand shake slightly. And of course the mask gave her the confidence she so badly needed. She had to distance herself as far as possible from her

1978 self and that black-and-white photograph that linked her inexorably to the past.

Outside the house, Rachel paused for a second and looked up at the door. A light had come on as she'd approached the house, illuminating the front door. It was a greyish white and made of what looked like uPVC. It was probably replaced in the last ten years or so, judging from its condition. The thick green hedge was still there – glossy green against the shiny white that had replaced the glossy black that she remembered.

Rachel pressed the doorbell again and waited, unsure if it had rung inside the house. A light was switched on in the hall and a woman opened the door. She was a shock. Tall with long blonde hair, she had a wide-hipped grace that made Rachel feel gauche. She hadn't been expecting anyone else here and this woman was a distraction. Rachel suspected she was now only just ahead of the police and she needed to get a move on.

'Is Bridget Lander here?'

The woman frowned. 'She is. I'll get her for you, hold on.'

Rachel stepped over the threshold. 'No need. I'll wait inside.'

The woman looked aghast. 'What are you doing? What do you want with Auntie Bridget?'

Rachel nearly faltered as she assimilated the information. This was Justine. She cast a quick glance at the woman who was trying to shut the door on her.

'I want to talk to her.' With that Rachel took the step into the small hall and looked around her.

A shadow moved into view from the room on the right. From behind her, Rachel could make out the signs of a clean but old fashioned kitchen. She refocused her gaze from the room and onto the woman. Also tall, but thin. But not the thinness that comes from weakness. This woman had a wiry strength, like an aging athlete. She was at once unrecognisable from 1978 and yet it was still her. Rachel was positive. She swallowed the bile rising up her throat.

'Remember me?'

Bridget Lander stood calmly in the hall, her hands at her side. Justine was looking between Rachel and her aunt with growing unease. The three of them seemed stuck in a triangle, each waiting for the other to break the spell. Finally, it was Justine who spoke.

'Auntie Bridget, what's going on?'

The woman stirred. 'This is nothing to do with you, Justine; you need to go back to the house and let me sort this out.'

'But I can stay and help if there's a problem.'

Rachel watched the exchange, fingering her pocket to check the item she had placed in it earlier was still there. 'Why don't you tell her, Bridget? Tell her why I'm here.'

Justine looked angry, two red spots appearing in her cheeks. 'Look, you have no right to—'

'You need to go, Justine'. Her aunt's voice was harsh. It was a tone that clearly Justine wasn't used to. She spun round and stared at her in astonishment. But she also had a determination inherited from her mother.

'I don't understand who this person is or why she's here.'

Still Bridget and Rachel looked at each other.

'I'd never have recognised you from 1978; you don't look the same at all.'

Either could have spoken but it was Rachel who had broken the spell. Now Justine looked scared.

'From 1978? You're Rachel Jones, aren't you? You don't mean to tell me that you think Auntie Bridget was involved in your kidnapping? It's ridiculous. You can't come to people's houses spreading accusations.'

'Can't I?' said Rachel. 'Perhaps your aunt would like to say something first.'

Bridget Lander calmly undid her apron from around her waist and folded it up neatly into a tiny square. She looked at her niece. 'You really need to go, Justine.'

'Auntie Br—'

'I said go.'

Something in the finality of Bridget's tone seemed to defeat Justine. Her shoulders slumped and she walked wordlessly into a room and came out with a camel-coloured coat. She wouldn't look at either of them but said to her aunt, eyes averted, 'You know where to find me. I'll be at Mum's.'

As the door shut behind her, Bridget Lander walked into a room off the left of the hall and Rachel followed. It was a large living room, sparsely furnished, with two long uncomfortable-looking sofas with wooden frames facing each other across the room. Rachel walked over to the large picture window and stared out into the neat garden. The style of the house reminded her of Yvonne Jenkins's bungalow.

'This is where you brought us, isn't it? Sophie and I were brought here after you kidnapped us.'

'Yes,' the woman replied simply.

'Over the years I've had this image in my head of glossy green and glossy black. Flashes of colour that didn't make sense. The green was from that tree out there.'

Bridget walked over to join Rachel by the window.

'It's a yew. They're often found in churchyards.'

'And the black?'

Bridget turned to look down at her. 'The front door. I got rid of it years ago. I'm surprised you remember. I had to chloroform you both in the car. The other girl was shrieking so much.'

'What about me?'

'I can't remember, it was all so long ago. But that other girl, I couldn't get her to be quiet.'

'Sophie. Her name was Sophie.'

Bridget stared out of the window. 'It was a stupid idea to kidnap you in the first place. But your mother wouldn't let James see you. And he was desperate. Hell-bent on seeing what you looked like properly and desperate to have a conversation with you.'

'When did he find out about me? Did he always know I existed?'

Bridget's eyes were like hard pebbles of granite. 'After your mother dumped him, he heard that she was pregnant but never thought anything of it. Just assumed that she'd moved on quickly. But then Justine was born and it must have got him thinking. Men can be incredibly dense sometimes. It takes nine months to make a baby.'

'So Justine helped precipitate everything.'

'You leave Justine out of this. It's got nothing to do with her. All I'm saying is that it suddenly made him think through the dates. And then he saw that picture of you at the school fete. You and your mother standing side by side. And it was obvious. You look like him. You were standing there and suddenly everything clicked.'

The photo, thought Rachel. That photo, frozen in time, of

her and Mary determinedly enjoying themselves on a blustery summer's afternoon had started all this. How utterly random and depressing.

'And after everything had happened, I just couldn't get over the sheer stupidity of it all. Everything ruined because of a compulsion to see you.'

'So you kidnapped us both just so he could have a conversation with me?' Rachel suddenly felt sick to the teeth of everything. 'You kidnapped me and killed Sophie so your brother could see me.'

'No!' Bridget Lander held up a hand. 'Sophie died accidentally. It was my fault. I got some chloroform from the hospital where I worked and used too much on Sophie. Either that or I held the pad over her nose too long. She struggled. Unlike you, who passed out straight away.'

The memory of the sickly smell assailed Rachel's nostrils again. Nauseated, she forced herself to concentrate.

'Where did she die? Sophie, I mean. Was it in here?'

Bridget shrugged. 'It was here that we found out she wasn't breathing. I tried to resuscitate her but it was no use. She'd gone. It's harder with children – resuscitation, I mean. I learned that over the years in the hospital. Often when they've gone, they really have. Miracles rarely happen.'

Rachel sank to the sofa, oblivious of her surroundings. 'But you're a nurse . . .'

'We didn't mean to kill her, I told you. It was an accident.'

'Where was my father during this?'

'He was waiting here to see you. I was bringing you to him. But, in the end, he spent no time with you at all, as soon as we realised the other girl had died.'

'So you decided to bury her in Truscott Woods.'

Bridget looked angry now; red blotches had appeared on her neck. 'We weren't animals, you know. We panicked. James wanted a look at you and a chance to get to know you. We thought if we picked you up with a friend, it would be easier.'

'You mean you were planning to return us back to our mothers after the kidnapping? How would have that worked? Were you expecting us not to say anything?'

'Of course not. But you were old enough to be talked to and James wanted to explain the situation to you. Say that he was your real father and that he loved you even though he wasn't allowed to see you. So we chose a time when you'd both be together so that you could reassure each other. But the minute I started driving with you both, I knew we'd made a mistake.'

'She started screaming.'

'Well, it was you who noticed I'd made a wrong turn at the top of the road. You whispered something to her and she started wailing like a banshee.'

'But why the sunglasses? Was it supposed to be a disguise?'

Bridget could only stare at Rachel. 'I didn't want to be recognised by either of you afterwards. It was James who wanted to see you. I was only helping him out. I was going to help him pick you up and then I wanted nothing more to do with you.'

'What about the chloroform?'

'The chloroform was only supposed to be in case of any problems. Instead, it sealed our fate.'

'Sealed your fate?' Rachel spat the words out. '*Your* fate? What about *my* fate? What do you think my life was like after the kidnapping? I was treated like some kind of freak. And what about Sophie? Her fate is to be buried in some grave with no proper funeral. And Mrs Jenkins and my mother. What about their fates?'

Bridget Lander was looking at her with cold eyes. 'I'll take on board everything you say about everyone except your mother. It was she who started this. She denied James access to you for no reason so he had no option but to try and see you in secret. James was your father. He started seeing your mother and the minute she got pregnant she dumped him. What woman in her right mind would do that? He was only a father wanting to see his child.'

'I knew my mother. There's no way she would have kept a father from his child without good reason. And there was one.'

'What?'

Rachel reached into her pocket and pulled out an A3 piece of paper folded in half. She handed it over to Bridget. 'You don't think she might have had a reason for stopping me seeing my uncle?'

Chapter 46

Sadler stared into the flickering fire as the wood creaked and sparks spat angrily up the chimney. James Lander had without a doubt been involved in the kidnapping of Rachel and Sophie. The reasons for the abduction could only be half-guessed but, given the physical resemblance between James and Rachel, he must be the man who had made Mary so keen to hide their very existence from the world. Rachel's father. And yet, it was Nancy Price, he was sure, who was the key to the whole case. Strands were coming together but he was failing to see the whole.

So, if James Lander was the man, who was the woman? Not Penny, his wife; she'd been teaching the day that the girls were abducted. No, if James Lander was the man, then Bridget Lander must be the woman. But could they arrest her on this supposition? She was curiously protective of her brother. In this investigation the old adage, that blood was thicker than water, was taking on strange resonances. Blood secrets and family ties were intermingling to produce a kaleidoscope of possibilities.

He heard a noise. A soft knock on his door. He prayed it wasn't Christina. Then it came again. A loud thump. He smiled. Connie. With her tiny frame and loud movements. He moved to open the door, but, just in case, picked up the poker by the fireside on his way.

As she walked in, Connie didn't remark on the poker, although he saw her glance at it. 'I've parked the car out front.

I hope I'm not taking up anybody's space. I did think about walking here; I only live round the corner, it turns out.'

'What made you change your mind?'

'I'm not brave enough to take the canal path in the dark. If there's a problem I don't fancy being stuck with a wall on one side of me and a stretch of water on the other.'

'Very wise. Do you want a drink?'

'Why not? One will be fine, won't it?'

As he walked through to the kitchen she shouted after him. 'We're nearly there, aren't we? On the case, I mean. We've nearly cracked it.' He could hear the excitement in her voice.

'We've cracked part of it.' He came through to the living room and tried to swallow the annoyance he felt as she sprawled across his sofa. 'I'm pretty sure I know what happened in 1978 and why.'

Impatience was rising off her like steam. He needed to slow her down. There had been too many hasty assumptions in the early days. Suppositions that had been allowed to go un checked.

'I can't believe you made the connection between the photograph of James Lander and Rachel. I saw her at Richard Weiss's house that time and I never spotted a thing.'

'You weren't looking, Connic. We were focusing on Penny. But Rachel has the same facial features as James Lander. A family likeness.'

Connie heard the hesitation in his voice. 'What? What is it?'

His brain was beginning to make a connection that seemed both fantastic and logical. 'It's a very strong likeness,' he said to himself.

Connie looked annoyed and responded by sinking further into the sofa. 'Our problem is that we don't know what precipitated the more recent deaths.'

'Yvonne Jenkins's suicide?'

'Yes, for a start. Why did she commit suicide in the Wilton Hotel?'

Sadler sat down in the chair opposite. 'The package that was handed over by Penny Lander appears to be the catalyst to the more recent deaths. For a start it was given to Yvonne Jenkins in the Wilton Hotel. The location must have had a profound effect on Yvonne. She went back there to kill herself.'

'Yes, but why? What was in the package?'

Sadler thought back to the yellowing newspaper cutting that he had found amongst Penny's notes and jottings.

'A connection was made by Penny Lander that may or may not have been correct but, in any case, proved to be the final straw for Yvonne Jenkins.'

Connie grimaced.

'We're both childless, Con. Can you imagine what it's like to lose your daughter? I can't, and I doubt . . .'

Connie's phone was ringing in her pocket. He watched as she fished it out and answered it. She listened without speaking, all the time looking at him.

'Hold on, will you?' She covered the phone with her hand.

'It's Richard Weiss. He's concerned about Rachel. She was due to be at his house about an hour ago. She's not answering her phone so he called a neighbour of hers – a woman called Jenny. She left in her car about ten minutes ago. He wants to know if we have any ideas where she might be headed.'

Chapter 47

Rachel spent her professional life roughly sketching out family trees on scraps of paper: backs of envelopes, pieces of wallpaper, once even on the back of her hand. The diagram on the sheet of paper she handed to Bridget Lander looked no different from those others hastily put together. She could draw the trees free-hand and this one, sketched in anger and passion, held the key to much more than family secrets. Bridget opened the paper and scanned the contents, a red flush spreading from her neck up into her cheeks. And still it continued, onto her forehead and into her hairline. For the first time, Rachel saw the suppressed emotion and wondered if, finally, she would come to harm from this woman. Bridget Lander seemed unable to believe what she was reading.

'Is this some kind of sick joke?'

'It's the reason that my mother was preventing your brother, or should I say adopted brother, from having contact with me.'

Bridget Lander stared at the paper, clearly horrified.

'Did he know he was adopted?' asked Rachel watching the angry flush fade.

The woman's head shot up and she looked at Rachel, her eyes two pins of hatred.

'Of course he did. We were both adopted. So what? We were both babies and we never knew anything other than the family our parents made for us, for better or worse.'

'And he never expressed any interest in who his natural parents were?'

'What for? It's not like today where everyone wants to know the ins and outs of everything. Employing people like you. We didn't care then. James and I were like any other brother or sister. It didn't make any difference at all.'

'And he never thought to find out his true origins?'

'There was no need. Our parents brought us up as true siblings and neither of us were interested in finding out where we came from.'

We. Whenever Rachel asked about James, Bridget responded as 'we'. Rachel wondered how truly united they had been as siblings, and what her father must have thought about the events that had occurred. And what had she meant by her comment that they were a family, for better or worse?

She walked over to Bridget Lander and jabbed at the A3 paper that the woman was still puzzling over.

'Those are his origins. He was the son of Nancy Price and a soldier she had a one-night fling with. The date of birth of your brother tallies with the date that Nancy had her baby in hospital. I think he was given away to your parents by Mair, his grandmother and my great-grandmother.'

Bridget was shaking her head.

'And that should have been the end of it. Bampton's a small town but there was no reason why he should come into contact with his real family. Nancy was working class and your parents lived much more affluent lives. But that isn't what happened.'

'He met your mother.' Bridget's voice was calm now. Too calm. 'He met that woman who decided that he would never see his daughter.'

'She must have found out,' said Rachel, almost to herself. 'It's the only thing that makes sense. Why else would she break it off like that?'

Nancy, today, was convinced that Rachel's mother hadn't known that she had a half-brother and, yet, what other reason could there have been for the break? If Mair was the only family member who had known what had happened to the child, then it was Mair who must have told her granddaughter Mary that she'd been sleeping with her half-brother.

Rachel, who days earlier had panicked at the thought of a close family relationship with Richard Weiss, could well imagine the dread her mother would have felt. Had she also known she was carrying his child? Perhaps. But she'd gone on to have the baby anyway and had set off a train of events that would result in the death of little Sophie Jenkins eight years later. And then the death of Yvonne Jenkins over thirty years after that. But perhaps this was where it would all end. Could there possibly be more reverberations?

'The question I want to know is – why kill Mrs Lander?'

'Penny? She found out. Threatened to go to the police with what she'd found.'

'But how? How did she find out?'

For a moment, Bridget looked stricken. 'James died suddenly. It was a shock to us all but Penny started to clear out his things straight away. She discovered a package that James had kept. The photo, the one of you at the fete. He kept it for some reason. And your sock, the one you left behind in the car. He put the two together in a package and hid it.'

Bridget was looking directly at her and Rachel held on to the curtain as the room began to spin. 'My sock. The one I lost that day. It was you, wasn't it? In the bungalow. I climbed out of the window but you'd come to get the sock back.'

'Penny told me she'd met Yvonne and handed over the sock to her, thinking it was Sophie's. I didn't want the police to find it.'

'It'd link you to the kidnapping.'

Bridget took a step closer to Rachel. 'It was never about me. Don't you see? I'm trying to protect your father's reputation. It wasn't his fault. I suggested to him that we take you for a day so you could get to know him.'

Rachel felt the cool fingers at her throat. It would be a funny way to die, with these strong hands around her neck. Rachel had always seen herself as a survivor and, during the unravelling of the case, she realised that her mother Mary, grandmother Nancy and great-grandmother Mair had passed on the survivor gene to her. But all the genes in the world couldn't negate the twin forces of desperation and opportunity. She'd arrived at this house in her usual blasé way and she would now face the consequences.

She wanted to live very much, she realised, and the reason for that was Richard Weiss, the casual friend she'd grown to love. Someone who was prepared to accept the person she'd become, even if it had been moulded by her history. Because, as she'd gradually realised over the last few weeks, there was nothing she could change about what had been done to her then. But by trying to take ownership of the past she had jeopardised her future.

There was a new generation inside her, and when she'd guessed and then checked, with that thin blue line which confirmed everything, she'd been glad. And she didn't care if it was a boy or a girl. Because, unlike her mother and great-grandmother, she liked men. Nancy's influence had given her that legacy. Nancy, the flirt who even after years of marriage to Hughie had been able to turn men's heads. Well, she hadn't inherited Nancy's beauty, but the child inside her would be loved whatever its gender.

The fog in Rachel's head cleared. The baby. Of course, the baby. Wasn't it time that a child had a chance to live?

The power of Bridget Lander surrounded her. Her resolution to do Rachel harm and her experience of violence felt too much to overcome. With all the strength she could manage, Rachel struck out at the woman and twisted her head so that her neck felt less exposed. For a moment, Bridget faltered. Rachel grabbed hold of Bridget's head and pushed her body against her. Together they toppled over and hit the floor hard.

The impact stunned Rachel and her arm wrapped protectively around her stomach. What had the jolt done to the baby? It was a moment of weakness that Bridget Lander had been looking for. Once more, two hands grasped at her neck and slowly Rachel's eyes began to dim.

Chapter 48

Connie jammed the accelerator to the floor of her small car, which was struggling to keep up with Sadler's. He'd insisted on separate cars in case Rachel wasn't at Bridget Lander's house and they needed to split up to look for her. Procedurally it made sense of course, but she was wasting precious time when they both knew full well where Rachel would be. She was following his grey Audi, although she didn't recognise the route that they were taking to Bridget's house. For someone who had been brought up in Bampton he was literally going around the houses. He decelerated suddenly and, sick of following him, Connie swung her car left and sped through the back streets.

They'd suspected that Rachel might reach the same conclusions as them but hadn't anticipated that she'd strike out and act on her own. The problem was that Connie wasn't sure which one of those women would be doing harm to the other. She scrolled down her contacts list and tried Rachel's mobile, which still went on to voicemail.

She threw the phone onto the passenger seat and it squawked alarmingly. Frowning she picked it up and saw an incoming call again from Richard Weiss.

'Yes, Mr Weiss?'

'Where are you? Do you know where Rachel is?'

'We're heading towards an address in Baslow Crescent. Stay

where you are and I'll call you when we have more information.' The line went silent. Connie looked in alarm at her phone. They were still connected. 'Hello?'

'Baslow Crescent? I can get there before you.'

The phone slipped from Connie's hand and she made a grab for it. 'I need you to stay where you are. Rachel might still be making her way towards you. Leave this to us.'

'You're kidding! I think Rachel has discovered something. And you're asking me to just sit here?'

Another silence. But this time the connection had been cut. Connie squinted at her phone. There was still reception; it had been Richard who'd ended the call. This spelt trouble: a civilian was making his way towards the house, and she'd told him the street, if not the exact address.

Negotiating a left turn with just one hand on the wheel, she dialled Sadler's number.

'We've got another problem.'

*

She was the first to arrive at the house, screeching up to the front gate so fast that for a moment she thought she would career into the low garden wall. The lights were on in the living room but a dark tree was shadowing most of the window. As she shot out of the car door, she saw Richard Weiss arrive and park, leaving the engine running as he dashed across the road. Where the hell was Sadler?

'Stay there,' she shouted, but he ignored her and for a big man reached the front door with a surprising speed. It was shut and in desperation he started to heave his shoulder against the hard plastic, which failed to give.

'I need to look through the windows.'

The garden was well kept and Connie stepped over a low hedge, cursing as the spiky branches snagged at her new trousers, catching a small thread which she tore at with her fingernails. The house had a large picture window, presumably the living room as the kitchen, where Connie had last seen Bridget Lander, was at the back of the house. The large tree blocking her route presented a problem, but her small frame was able to squeeze behind it to give her access to the window where the curtains were undrawn. Balancing on one foot, she held on to a branch and peered in through the glass.

*

Sadler arrived in time to see Connie's bottom half go through the front window. For one moment he thought he was watching a break-in until he realised that it was his detective constable, who'd managed to reach the house before him, squeezing herself through the window. He ran towards her and, seeing large shards of glass poking alarmingly towards her legs, he used his tie to pull them towards him. They splintered as they hit the concrete path in front of the window. But Connie was in and he watched as she hurled her small frame at the pair on the floor.

She went first for Bridget Lander, seizing the woman's grey hair in her hands and yanking back her head with such force that Sadler thought her neck had snapped. He had created enough gap in the window to heave his tall frame through, although he felt a sharp pain in his thigh and blood begin to trickle down his leg. He ran over to the group and seized Bridget Lander's hands, still clenched around Rachel's neck, despite Connie's efforts. As he pulled the fingers from Rachel's throat, he saw suddenly that she wasn't breathing.

'Call an ambulance.' Sadler heard the sound of the front door giving way and Richard Weiss came into the room. He knelt down in front of Rachel and gently lifted her head in his hands.

Chapter 49

Rachel woke in the building that had been built as a replacement for the old cottage hospital. Her first thought was total blankness. The antiseptic room could have been anywhere and she was alone. She could hear noises coming from outside the room, the sound of clanking, metal hitting metal perhaps, and talking. A man's voice too low to hear. The door opened and a doctor entered, too hearty for her ears, which had developed a fragility she didn't recognise.

'Ah, you're awake. That's good. Can you hear me OK?'

'Too well,' she said. Her throat felt sore and she reached up to touch it.

'Sorry. Don't worry about your throat. There'll have been some vocal damage but we're going to run some tests on you later. But you can hear me OK, yes?'

'Aren't you going to ask me how many prime ministers you're holding up?'

He understood that and smiled, his cocky manner slipping into the boyish student he had once been. 'You probably don't remember, but you came round in the ambulance. Spoke about the baby you were expecting. The paramedics got enough out of you to let us know there wasn't any brain damage. We'll still need to run the tests though?'

'Baby?'

She had forgotten about her baby. It had been her last

conscious thought but not her first waking one. Was it still there?

The doctor looked troubled. 'The baby's fine, as far as we know. It'll be part of the tests. Assuming you were only deprived of oxygen for long enough to pass out, I'm fairly confident the baby will be OK, although it is early days in your pregnancy.'

Rachel laid a hand on her stomach and thought of the life beneath her. Not another victim, surely? Not now. The doctor left and a nurse came in, all busy efficiency. Then a knock and Richard appeared at the door, smiling uncertainly at her.

'You're awake again. Do you remember the first time?'

She shook her head.

'You gave us all a shock. We thought we'd lost you and then you came round and announced you were pregnant.'

'Sorry.' Rachel reached for a sip of water and relished its icy coldness against her throat. 'Only just found out. Well, a few days ago.'

'I forgive you.' He smiled at her and reached for her hand. 'If it's any consolation, my family are reassuringly normal.'

Rachel started to laugh, silently, so not to hurt her red-raw throat.

'I'm so sorry, Rachel. My family had a role in all this. I stormed round to see my father last night. I've never spoken to him like that before. It shocked us both. But I did get the truth out of him. That Mair had gone to see him after she discovered she had a terminal illness to get advice about your legal position, given that your father was also your half-uncle.'

Rachel made an effort to swallow. 'And what did he tell Mair to do?'

'He said to do nothing. It's always been his default position. If in doubt, maintain the status quo. And to be honest, I would probably have advised the same. None of us could have foreseen the later events. But, without a doubt, your mother knew the whole story.'

He didn't need to say any more. They were both thinking the same thing. Rachel's mother had known something that could have helped solve the case in 1978. But she had chosen to remain silent. Secrets and more lies.

'There's someone who wants to see you, though.' Richard disappeared and came back moments later guiding Nancy through the door. He deposited her in the chair beside the bed.

'I've got a bone to pick with you.'

'Oh, Nan, not now. I'm not up to this.'

'Telling that handsome policeman that I'm doolally. Are you trying to ruin my chances?'

Rachel's eyes filled with tears and her throat constricted. 'I was trying to protect you.'

'Everyone's always tried to protect me. How do you think I feel, finding out that all this mess came about because of me? And you nearly died because no one told me the truth.'

Rachel moved her head on her pillow and held out her arm. 'They were wrong about you. You were always tougher than you looked. Perhaps you need to forgive your mother like I need to forgive mine.'

Chapter 50

The woman sat in the hard chair in the interview room staring at her knuckles. Sadler was opposite her, studying her broad, flat features. Next to him, Connie was shifting in her seat, probably uncomfortable from the stitches that she'd been forced to have in hospital. He hadn't shown them the puncture mark on his thigh. He'd covered it up with a bandage when he got home, although the red heat of the wound suggested he might end up regretting it.

The woman, Bridget Lander, was feeling the oppression of silence. As Sadler expected, she sought to fill the void and began to speak. 'When James died, Penny was clearing out some stuff and came across a sock from one of the children that we took in 1978. It must have been Rachel's, because James had kept it all these years. Something as innocuous as a child's sock. But he placed it with the newspaper cutting. The one where he first spotted Rachel and her mother at a school fete.'

'The photograph that first made him want to contact Rachel?' asked Connie.

The clarification was unwelcome. Bridget stared at her hands and clenched her teeth.

'He shouldn't have kept either. But he must have hidden them all these years.'

'Did Penny say where she'd found them?' Sadler was curious

how something so damning could have been kept hidden all these years.

'She said she found it taped to the underside of a wardrobe drawer. It may have been there since they moved into the house in the mid-eighties. She turned the drawer upside down to tip the contents into a bin bag after his heart attack. And there it was. An envelope containing the photograph and a sock.'

And Penny realised the significance of the two items, even if the conclusion was wrong.

'She thought the sock belonged to Sophie Jenkins,' said Sadler.

Bridget nodded without looking up. 'Because it was Sophie that was still missing, she assumed that the sock belonged to her.'

'But first she wanted to find out why her husband would have an item of clothing from a missing girl.'

For a moment, Bridget faltered. 'She wasn't stupid, Penny. She knew that James was no paedophile, certainly no killer, but she remembered that neither girl had a father. So she assumed that James must have been involved in one of their lives in some way.'

'So she went to look at the records of Bampton cottage hospital, but they only go up to 1968,' said Connie. 'Instead, she came away with something else. In the records she discovered that James, who had never made a secret of being adopted, was the son of Nancy Price.'

'Because she assumed the sock must have been from Sophie,' continued Sadler, 'she arranged a meeting with Yvonne Jenkins to give it her. That's what the waiter saw being passed between the two women at the meeting.'

'And it was the act that brought it all back and precipitated Yvonne Jenkins's suicide,' finished Connie.

She looked up at them now. 'That's not my fault. Penny should have left well alone. Not least for the memory of her husband.'

'She was trying to make amends,' said Connie, shifting in her seat. 'Penny Lander would have been devastated by the thought that her husband had been involved in the kidnapping of two children from the school where she was a teacher. Was it Yvonne who told Penny who Nancy Price was?'

Bridget looked down at the table. 'I don't think so. Penny had been looking at the family tree on Rachel Jones's website and I think she made the connection that it was Rachel who was the relation of Nancy Price, not Sophie.'

'By which time it was too late for Yvonne Jenkins.'

Sadler shot Connie a look. 'But Penny still needed to talk to you. Because she knew that whatever James Lander had done, there must have been another woman involved. And she immediately thought of you.'

'I went round to see her. On foot. I told her to calm down but she was threatening to go to the police with what she knew. Said it was my fault that woman had killed herself.'

'So you decided to kill her,' said Sadler. 'Why?'

Now it was Connie who was looking at him. It was a question that needed to be out in the open. Because, if he was right, this woman hadn't killed to protect her own reputation.

And she was desperate to tell them. 'We didn't have a great childhood, James and I. Nowadays I've heard it's actually quite difficult to adopt children. It wasn't like that when we were younger. Childless parents had the pick of babies. And they weren't always great parents. In our case, it was our father. He was violent. Not towards us, but to our mother. And we stood together, James and me. We looked out for each other.'

'I can see that.' Sadler's voice was calm. 'But why kill Penny?'

'Because our family survived all that. And James made a success of his life and so did I. And Penny wanted to blow everything apart. What about Justine? Wasn't she entitled to remember the wonderful father James was?'

'Penny wouldn't have forgotten about her daughter. She must have thought it was more important that the truth came out,' said Sadler. More than anyone in this case, it was Penny who Sadler felt the most empathy for. Penny who had weighed the cost to herself and decided to reveal a long-buried secret.

Connie stirred beside him. 'How did you manage to get her to Truscott Fields? Wasn't she scared of you at all?'

Bridget Lander refused to meet their gaze. 'I offered to show her where we'd buried Sophie.'

'And she went? Just like that?' Connie was disbelieving and rightly so, thought Sadler. Penny Lander had confided to a neighbour that she was scared of someone. Almost certainly Bridget Lander. And yet she had gone to a wood in the evening with a woman whom she knew was capable of kidnapping two girls and then hiding the proof of her involvement.

Bridget Lander looked sadly at the floor. 'We went in her car. I was sorry to have to kill her. I always admired Penny. But sometimes you don't get to choose.'

'Choose? You don't get to choose what?' Sadler leaned forward.

She looked up at him. 'The end.'

His men arrived just after dawn, shuffling their heavy boot-clad feet against the cold with polystyrene cups of tea warming their hands. Desultory chat, muted laughter and a few asthmatic coughs against the cold morning. Then the work started. First the long traipse into the woods, the route already marked out with yellow flags taped to trees to mark the way. Silence then, until they reached a spot. A space where the trees refused to grow or perhaps had once and could no longer. He stood to one side, his presence making a few of the men anxious. Procedure not being followed.

The first clink of a spade hitting rock amongst the compacted ground. Sometimes they spun a coin for the first turn of the sod. An old tradition started amongst gravediggers, and why not? Ritual aligning with nature. But perhaps, here, they found the practice too flippant and had decided against it. They carried on in silence. No chance of getting a mechanical digger in through the dense trees.

They stopped and Llewellyn moved forward to assess their work. Not strictly his job. No deeper, he decided. Wider only. They spread out and carried on. He once more stood to one side. He should have been in his office. There was a personnel meeting taking place without him, to talk about cuts to the policing service. He should have been there. Arguing for the constables he still needed to solve the mundane cases that make up policing in Derbyshire in the twenty-first century. Cycle thefts, burglary, minor drug use, too much drink. But life wasn't made up of the mundane, was it? It comprised the things that go deep under the skin and which won't go away.

'Sir?' He looked at the white-clad man who was beckoning him forward like a wraith. Llewellyn suddenly felt old. Too much had happened over the intervening years for him to confront what he was about to see. He walked forward and looked down. A long fawn-coloured bone lay on top of the dark soil.

'Femur,' said the man next to him. 'There are others there too. It'll take some time.' The unspoken question lay in the air between them.

'I'll stay.'

*

Back in his office, Sadler heard Connie's mobile ring. She took the call and then walked in to see him. 'They've found her. Where we marked, more or less. We were slightly out but, anyway, they found her.'

'Did you speak to Llewellyn?'

'He made the call. He sounded fine.' Connie answered the unasked question. 'The bones are going to Doctor Shields now. He's going to look at them today. His choice. He wanted to do it. Shall I join him?'

'Good idea. He misses you, I think. He didn't look happy last time when I said that you wouldn't be attending the PM.'

Connie looked pleased. But there was clearly something on her mind. 'It feels like an ending. Finding the bones, I mean. I feel like we've brought about a resolution of sorts.'

Sadler stood up and walked across to the window. It had started sleeting again. Spring was just round the corner but the weather hadn't eased up yet. The diggers had got to the woods in time. Even if the snow hadn't penetrated the forest, the returning ice would have made their job harder.

'I think we've done everything we could have. As for a resolution, I'm not so sure about that.'

'But we found out what happened, didn't we?'

Sadler thought about Justine Lander. Whose mother had been murdered by her aunt. And whose father had been partly responsible for the death of a young girl. As usual, Connie had that uncanny knack of reading his thoughts.

'You think Justine Lander would have preferred to leave things alone? Well, it sounds like her mother was prepared to lay open all the family secrets in the pursuit of the truth.'

Sadler felt exhausted. 'I think teachers, when they're good ones, are a little like us, Connie. We feel protective towards those we're supposed to look after. Penny had taught children all her life. Her outrage at events would have overridden any sense of family.'

'As opposed to Bridget Lander.'

'Bridget has a distorted view of family, which I can't even bring myself to fathom. I wouldn't try to do so, either. Go along to the PM and let me know how you get on.'

'Of course. But we know what we need to know, don't we?'

Sadler turned and stared out of the window. 'I think we do.'

*

As she was walking out of Sadler's office, Connie's phone rang and without looking she answered it.

'Connie, it's Nick.'

She felt herself flushing. 'Look, I can't answer any questions about the case, there's a press conference scheduled for—'

'I know. I'd be a pretty crap journalist if I didn't know the time of the press conference.'

Connie walked over to her car and slid into the driver's seat. 'You did me a massive favour, digging out the details of Yvonne's meeting with Penny. But I gave you enough for a better story than your competitors, didn't I?'

'Can you hear me whingeing? I'm happy; the news editor is happy. Look, I wasn't calling about that. I was just wondering if you fancied going for a drink, you know, after the conference. I won't ask you about the case, I promise.'

Thank God he couldn't see her face, thought Connie. *It must resemble a boiled beetroot at the moment.*

'I'm not sure. I mean, we've managed to keep our collaboration quiet so far. What will the other reporters think if they see us having a drink together tonight?'

'Don't worry about them. They've seen it all before. It's your colleagues I'm more worried about. The tall one, Sadler. I don't want to get on the wrong side of him.'

'As long as it's somewhere away from the station, I should be fine. I don't want to be the star of the latest gossip.'

'What about the bar of my hotel?' he suggested. 'I'm staying in the Wilton tonight but most of the other journos will be heading back to London after the press conference.'

The Wilton Hotel, where it had all started. There was a kind of symmetry to the venue.

'Sure. Why not.'

Chapter 51

Rachel heard on the radio that they were digging in Truscott Woods and, for a while, time stood still. She switched off the radio and, in silence, continued to work on the family tree of Cathy Franklin. The silence in the house wasn't oppressive but it was all encompassing.

She'd managed to find evidence of Cathy's great-grandmother's stay at Needham Hall and details of her marriage to one of the grooms, three months before the birth of her first child. Did Cathy have aristocratic connections? Rachel thought it likely, but it would be impossible to prove except by DNA sampling. And Rachel doubted that Charles Needham would be willing to undergo that. Why had he been so angry when she had asked him where he was born? A family secret she was unlikely to get to the bottom of. And now she had come to accept that some things would remain that way. And perhaps Cathy Franklin would have to accept secrets as well, with her complicated family tree that was nowhere near as catastrophic as Rachel's ancestry had turned out to be, but complex enough to demand Rachel's attention while the radio sat reproachfully silent in the kitchen.

There was a knock on the door and Rachel jumped up from the table, ready to do battle with one of the posse of journalists once again encamped outside her house. She flung open the door and came face-to-face with a tall woman, clutching her handbag across her chest.

'You probably don't want to see me.'

This wasn't the usual approach of journalists and Rachel, with a lurch in her chest, realised who the figure was. 'You're . . .'

'Justine. I know you won't want to see me, but I wanted to say I'm sorry about everything.'

'I'm not sure that you've got anything to be sorry for.' Rachel stepped back and let Justine into the room. A flash from a camera outside caused white orbs to float around her vision. Her half-sister walked into the room and stared around in frank curiosity, her eyes briefly resting on an old photograph of Rachel's mother.

Justine dropped her bag to the floor as if the weight of it was sapping her strength. 'I still can't believe it about Auntie Bridget. She was always so kind to me when I was little. She was always marvelling how like Dad I was. I never thought she could do something like that.'

Rachel sat down on the sofa, a different type of nausea now assailing her, from the baby growing within. 'Nothing was ever hinted at within your family?'

She saw Justine hesitate. 'I have these half-memories that keep rising to the surface. Do you know what I mean?' She looked to Rachel for reassurance and seemed happy with what she saw in her face.

'I know Dad and Aunt Bridget were close, but I *think* I remember Mum once saying that she was scared of Auntie. It was years ago, though, when I was an adult. Dad was sick with the flu and Auntie Bridget wouldn't stay away. There was something almost fevered in the way she fussed around

Dad. And I think Mum said that it wasn't natural.'

'Not natural?'

'I just remember this throwaway comment, but it's coming back to haunt me. You can understand that, can't you?'

The past haunting the present. Well, yes, she did know about that. But she was also learning that some things were also just too difficult to solve. And there could be too much reality to face. Justine would need to come to the same conclusion in her own time.

Justine looked out of the window. 'Do you know they're searching Truscott Woods?'

'I'd heard on the radio.' Rachel felt a deep weariness come over her.

'There's a police car just drawn up.'

Rachel joined Justine at the window. Together they watched as Llewellyn climbed out of the car.

'It's unlocked,' Rachel shouted as he reached the front door and together they watched him enter the room, his tall frame filling the space.

'You've found her?' Rachel knew the answer before he could reply. Why else would he be here?

He nodded at them both and didn't comment on Justine's presence. 'We've found bones. The size is about right for Sophie but we're waiting for the post-mortem to see if the dental records match.'

Rachel looked at him. 'But you think it's her.'

'I'm almost sure of it. We just need official confirmation.'

'And what now?'

'In terms of the kidnapping? Well, James Lander is dead. Your father.' He included them both in the look. 'But we'll be pushing for kidnapping and possibly manslaughter charges against Bridget Lander to be brought in relation to your case.'

'But she killed Mrs Lander too, I mean Penny. I mean your mum.' Rachel looked at her half-sister.

Llewellyn was rubbing his face. 'The CPS will almost certainly try that as a separate case. There's more chance of a conviction given forensic and other evidence. She'll face a murder charge.'

'But my, I mean our case – mine and Sophie's – will be heard? Will it come to trial?'

Llewellyn looked grim. 'It will if I've got anything to do with it.'

His eyes fell to the stack of papers that she'd been working on. 'She's your aunt, Rachel; don't underestimate the power of family ties, even non-blood ones. Don't be surprised if you start to feel mixed emotions during any future trial. I've seen it happen before.'

Rachel shook her head. 'I feel nothing. When I look at my matrilineal line I do feel something. I always have done. It's sustained me over the years and it continues to do so now. There's a resonance that slowly takes shape down the ages.'

Llewellyn's eyes were on her.

'With my father's side, or rather the father that I thought I had, I never felt anything. I thought it was due to the fact I'd never known him. Then when things became clearer, I expected to feel something. About James Lander. After all, he is part of my maternal line too.'

'But you feel nothing.'

Rachel swept her hand over her stomach. Not flat, it never was. But the curve already felt different.

'There are some things that are impossible to articulate. I think of my natural father and I feel nothing. Mair was dead right. You take what life throws at you and you carry on the best you can. She was right to do what she did. And so was my mother. They did what they thought was for the best. And I would have done the same.' She was out of breath.

'Have you thought about your heritage though, Rachel? You are the child of incest, even if it was unwitting.'

Rachel grimaced. 'I've come across it a few times in my research. Another secret that never fails to shock my clients when I tell them. I never thought it would be my lot too. But I remember what one woman said to me when I told her that her great-grandmother had, almost certainly, been the result of a father–daughter union.'

'What did she say?' Justine moved forward, towards her.

'She said that it was women's lot in life to get on with it and make the best of things. And I think that could apply to my mother, Nancy and Mair too.'

Llewellyn smiled. 'I always admired your mother. If it's any consolation, you remind me of her. I've also known Daniel Weiss and his son Richard for years. Your baby has some fine genes.'

Epilogue

The pale watery sun attempted to sneak through the branches and infiltrate the gloom of the cold wood. The nocturnal inhabitants stirred as the chill seeped into their pelts and disturbed their dreams. It would be hours before they awoke in the familiar environment that allowed them to forage in peace every evening.

A lonely badger stirred early, his dreams punctured by an unfamiliar sound that permeated his sleep. Now wide awake, he sensed that something had changed around him, a foreign scent betraying the shift that had fractured his familiar world. In the distance he could hear noise. Too far away to cause alarm but an unwelcome trespass onto his territory. Human voices briefly came towards him. Perhaps he needed to flee deeper into the wood. But suddenly they changed direction and once more the landscape was engulfed in silence.

The new inhabitant of the wood lay at peace in her unfamiliar bed.

Acknowledgements

Thanks to my agent, Kirsty McLachlan, who loved *In Bitter Chill* at first sight and helped tease out its title.

To my editors Katherine Armstrong at Faber & Faber in the UK and Anne Brewer at Thomas Dunne Books in the US. The novel is better for your comments.

To early readers of the book: Tana, Alison, Sylvia, Clare, Ed. And Eve Seymour.

To the Petrona Award judges: Karen Meek, Kat Hall and Barry Forshaw for their continued encouragement.

To the Iceland Noir gang, especially Quentin Bates. Great curries beckon in the future, I'm sure.

To Chris, Jill, Carol and Socrates for the long-distance cheering from Greece.

To Brian for advice about policing and Edith for insights into buried memories.

To my family – Dad, Adrian, Ed and Katie – for the support. Especially during 2013.

Finally, love and thanks to the crime fiction community. Bloggers, reviewers, writers and readers – you really are the friendliest and most supportive bunch of people.